Praise for *My Name Is Not Friday*

A *Shelf Awareness* Best Teen Book of the Year

A *Bustle* "12 YA Novels That Will Make You See the World Differently" pick

★ "Samuel's endearing, immersive narration makes the novel a fascinating and unforgettable account of a brutal and shameful chapter in America's history. A heartbreaking story about family, justice, and the resilience of the human spirit."
—*Kirkus Reviews*, starred review

★ "Walter masterfully constructs the world of the plantation and presents a large population of complex and distinctive characters, resulting in a rich, thought-provoking, and deeply satisfying book."
—*Publishers Weekly*, starred review

★ "Walter skillfully tells a thoroughly riveting, elegantly nuanced story of an orphan sold into slavery in the Civil War South. . . . Teen readers will be cheering for Samuel in this insightful, hopeful, gut-wrenching and truly fine novel." —*Shelf Awareness*, starred review

★ "Remarkable. . . . A multilayered epic that weaves together history and humanity while confronting the elusive grays between right and wrong, this work proves to be a significant, resonating addition to the Civil War canon."
—*School Library Journal*, starred review of audio edition

★ "Compelling. . . . Lyrically written."
—*School Library Journal*, starred review

"[Walter's] first foray into young adult literature knocks it out of the park. Samuel's journey is nuanced and engrossing, told in beautiful language and embellished with well-researched details. . . . Samuel's own story retains primary focus, and he is fantastically understandable and relatable." —*VOYA*

"Vivid. . . . The historical details in terms of setting and objects are accurately portrayed. This young adult novel is abundant with interdisciplinary subject areas, such as medicine, science, agriculture, American literature, military history, and geography."
—*School Library Connection*

"This coming-of-age narrative introduces to readers, with great emotion, a character who, though a slave, remains forever freeborn in his mind. Historical notes include a helpful primer on the economics of American slavery." —*Booklist*

"This is an epic, vivid, emotionally involving, thought-provoking novel from a writer of distinction."
—*Sunday Times* (UK), Children's Book of the Week

"It isn't often I'm left lost for words, but that's the way I felt when I finished reading this superb YA novel. . . . It will keep you utterly gripped." —*Guardian* (UK)

Praise for *Close to the Wind*

A Summer 2015 Kids' Indie Next List pick

"Walter's debut novel is a profile of innocence maintained in the face of war. . . . The roller-coaster ride of experiences and emotions, taking Malik and readers from fear, despair, loss, and grief to love and hope, is accurately drawn."
—*Kirkus Reviews*

"Walter does not name the country that Malik is escaping from or the details of the source of the conflict, allowing readers to concentrate on Malik's tender-hearted character and his responses with the attention and respect that he and others like him deserve."
—*Shelf Awareness*

"Richly developed and empathetic characters."
—*School Library Journal*

"Crisply plotted, somber, and suspenseful. . . . The moving denouement is fully earned." —*Horn Book*

"Walter turns the heart-rending emotional toll of war on the civilian population into a very personal, poignant story that the reader will remember." —*VOYA*

"Malik's story is simultaneously worldly and gentle, reminding readers that though life is sometimes breathtakingly disappointing and war can certainly bring out the worst in people, bad guys don't always win in the end." —*BCCB*

"His prose is almost invisible: nothing comes between the reader and the book's action and emotion." —*Guardian* (UK)

"[An] original and cleverly plotted tale of betrayal, sacrifice and ingenuity." —*Sunday Times* (UK)

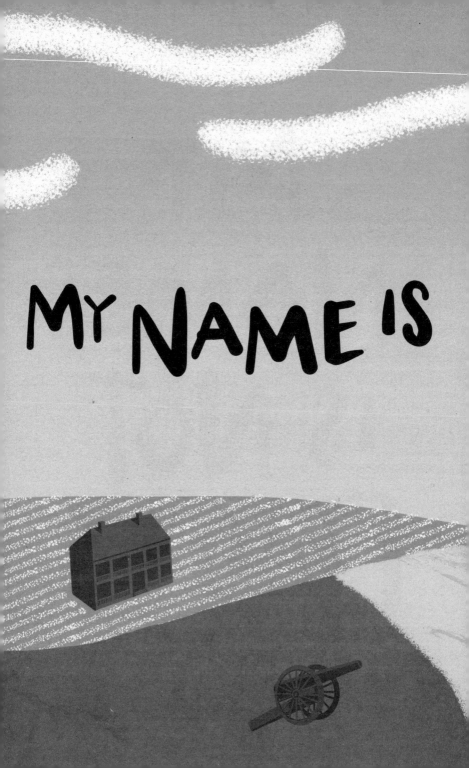

NOT FRIDAY

Jon Walter

David Fickling Books

SCHOLASTIC INC.

To my lovely boys, Jonah and Nathaniel

This book was originally published in hardcover in 2016 by Scholastic Inc., by arrangement with David Fickling Books. First published in the United Kingdom in 2015 as *My Name's Not Friday* by David Fickling Books, 31 Beaumont Street, Oxford OX1 2NP.
www.davidficklingbooks.com

ISBN 978-1-338-16064-2

10 9 8 7 6 5 4 3 2 1   17 18 19 20 21

Printed in the U.S.A.   40
First printing 2017
Book design by Ellen Duda

CIVIL WAR

MISSISSIPPI

PART 1

HEAVEN

CHAPTER 1

I know that I'm with God.

He's with me in the darkness. He's close to me.

Not real close.

But close enough I know He's there.

Somewhere.

I can feel Him—so I know He must be.

—

It was Him that brought me here.

At least, I think He did. Only it ain't what I was expecting.

I never thought it'd be dark here—but it is. It's real dark. Pitch-dark. And it can't be nighttime 'cause there's birds singing. There's a blackbird and a sparrow. There's all sorts. And them birds don't sing at night.

'Cept maybe they do in heaven. Maybe they sing here all the time.

—

If I shift my head, it hurts me inside and out. So I don't try to move. I stay as still as I can.

—

It's kinda damp here in the darkness. I got it up inside my nose. A musky smell. Like fur. Like rabbit. Yeah, maybe it's like a rabbit.

And there's another smell, a whiff of old shoes, like when you wear 'em for too long after they get wet. But I ain't wearing shoes. I left 'em in the Sunday box and they ain't no good to me there. Not anymore.

I can feel the dust beneath my toes.

And there's a bag on my head. The cloth's against my cheek. That's the reason I can't see my feet. I got a bag on my head that's been used to carry rabbits.

——

I still don't move a muscle. But in my skin, in my head and my heart, I panic. I feel like a cornered rat, scrambling up against the wall of a deep, dark cellar, breathing fast enough I could've run a mile.

So I say to slow down, Samuel.

Slow down now and calm yourself. Take one step at a time. Give yourself the time to think this thing through.

——

I know I'm lying down. I got a sense of me stretched out upon the ground and it feels like I'm lying on twigs and stuff. Yeah, I'm sure I am. I got one sticking in my side and my hands are forced around behind my back and my wrists are sore 'cause of the rope that's tying 'em close together. My arms ache too, all up around the shoulders.

I try to move an arm—start to wriggle and twist.

And that's when I hear the footsteps, coming over to me on the hard ground, making me freeze like a rabbit in a trap, 'cause all I can think is that God's coming, that it's the foot of God upon the ground and He's coming for me. He's coming. And He's wearing big boots.

Well, He lifts me up. My Lord, He lifts me up. He's got big hands. He's got strong arms. He flips me on my back and then flips me again, laying me over a mule like I'm some big ol' bag of potatoes. I know it's a mule 'cause it snorts when He lays me upon its back, like it's tired of me already. That's mules for you. Always complaining. Even in heaven.

When He walks away, He don't go far. I hear Him moseying about in the bushes, shuffling around like He's collecting things together, putting pots inside of other pots, that sort of thing. There's the creak of a leather strap being tightened on a saddlebag.

I'm finding it difficult to breathe now I'm slung over a mule with my hands behind my back. My chest begins to hurt and I have to take tiny little breaths that don't fill me up with enough good air.

Why's God want to put me on a mule? And why'd He need to tie me up? We made a deal, Him and me, but this ain't what I expected.

I can't ask Him. That's the last thing I can do. It'd show a lack of faith, and I can't show any weakness. Not now. I won't show any doubt in my darkest hour. And so I don't say a thing. I just lie where I am, listening to Him walk around in the bushes, the twigs all snapping under His big clomping boots. One time He stops, stands still a while, and relieves Himself upon the ground.

I try to wriggle a bit, try to slide down one side of the mule to get myself more comfortable, and I hope God's not watching me 'cause I must look like a worm that's just been unearthed, what with my backside in the air and wriggling for all I'm worth. He sees me, though. Comes and stands nearby. And I stop wriggling.

God sucks His teeth. He slaps the saddlebag over the back of the mule, close enough that the thick leather edge pushes up into the top of my arm, and then He leads the mule on, and the bones in its back begin to shift as it walks and that makes me even more uncomfortable. In fact, it's just about the most uncomfortable thing I can remember—that mule's bones on my bones, the both of us grinding each other up the wrong way and getting on each other's nerves. If the mules here in heaven are as stubborn as the mules back at home, then this one'll spit in my eye if he ever gets a chance. My Lord, he will. He'll try and kick me to kingdom come.

We walk like that for a long time. I don't know where we're going.

I'd always assumed that when you got to heaven, you'd turn up right where you're supposed to be. I hadn't figured on having to travel nowhere and I'm wondering how long it'll be before we stop. But we don't ever stop. We just keep on walking till I'm hurting so much that I lift myself up to ease the aching in my bones.

And that's when I fall off the back of the mule.

I hit the ground hard and that mule sees his chance and he kicks out, catching me in the stomach so that all the air rushes out of me.

"Damn you, mule," I curse him. "Damn you to kingdom come."

Straight away, I hear them boots. They walk right up to me and I sit up quickly, turning my head first one way, then the other, trying to get a sense of where God is, 'cause I'm afraid of Him more than ever on account of me just cussing His mule.

God sucks at His teeth again. I can sense He's real close, probably crouching right down beside me with His face up close to mine. And He lays His hands upon my head and takes hold of the sack, intending to lift it up, I'm sure, and I quickly shut my eyes because I'm afraid to look upon the face of God, and we're about to be right up close, my eyes looking into His eyes, and that don't seem right to me. That don't seem right at all.

I hold my breath. I squeeze my face so tight it's as small as I can get it.

Two pink discs appear on the lids of my eyes. I feel the warmth of the sun on my face and I have the breath of the Lord in my nostrils, all smelling of bacon like he's just had breakfast.

"Open your eyes," He tells me.

He ain't got the kind of voice you might imagine. He's all high-pitched and squeaky. A bit like a girl, only not a girl.

I shake my head.

I know it doesn't do to disagree with the Lord, but I'm full of the fear of Him, full of the fear it's not Him, and I try to look away.

He don't sound pleased. "I said, open your eyes."

My eyelids are like two heavy doors that I pull up on a chain, all creaking and stubborn. I lift my head to look at Him.

God is smiling at me.

Only not in a loving way.

He has a tooth missing. A half-chewed stick of licorice sits in the gap between His teeth, and His mouth has got a wicked smile, kinda lopsided, like He's gonna laugh in my face at any moment.

Truth be told, He looks more like the Devil himself.

And I'm asking myself, how could this be? How could it have come to this?

But I know it only too well.

And it wasn't my fault. Not none of it.

CHAPTER 2

When I was first delivered into the hands of God, I brought my brother with me. I was just seven years old, and when Mama died giving birth to him, there weren't anyone left to look out for either of us. Not knowing she was dead, I'd wrapped him in our blanket, folded Mama's arms against her chest, and rested him there, thinking he'd be the first thing she'd see when she opened her eyes.

Once Old Betty arrived like she said she would—bustling in with a bag under her arm and the linen in her other hand—she took one look at Mama, put down her things, and crossed herself before the Lord. She said she wished she'd got there sooner, but then forgave herself immediately, confessing that in all probability, there was nothing she could have done that might have saved our mama's life. "When God decides it's time to go," she told me, "there ain't nothing to be done about it."

I learned the truth in that—felt it shake its way right through me till the snot ran from my nose.

"Come on, now." Old Betty put a hand upon my head to ease my pain. "Least the baby's good." She took him out of Mama's arms and lifted him high in the air, so his little legs were waving around like he just couldn't get away from her fast enough. "Did you smack him?"

I shook my head.

"You shoulda smacked him. Always smack a baby soon as it's born. Gets it out the way." She hit him harder than she needed, just once on his behind, to see if he would cry. He didn't let her down. "You got a fine baby brother, Samuel. You see how strong he is? This one's a fighter for sure."

She gave him to me, saying he was mine to look after, but I held him at arm's length like she'd just given me a lizard or some such thing hatched straight from its egg.

Yes. From the very beginning, my brother was both strange and wonderful and I didn't know what to make of him.

"What you gonna call him, Samuel?" Old Betty had put some water on a cloth and she wiped away the smears that had dried on his screwed-up little face. "You're the only one left who's got the right to name him."

"Joshua!" I said immediately. "His name'll be Joshua. The same as my daddy."

I couldn't remember any more of my daddy than his name—it had been that long since I saw him—but it still felt right to me.

At the time, we lived in a little shack of a house on the edge of a town called Haven. It weren't so big and had only recently got itself a railway. There was a man there who gave me a fair price for everything we owned. That's what Betty told me. She arranged everything. She took us on the steam train to meet a priest by the name of Father Mosely at another little town called Middle Creek, where he was starting up an orphanage for colored boys in similar circumstances to our own.

Old Betty took safekeeping of our money, giving what remained of it to the Father by way of a fee for our upkeep, though I doubted it could ever be enough, 'cause in the six years that I lived at that orphanage, Father Mosely never missed an opportunity to tell us boys about the cost of us living there.

We were given food twice a day—once in the morning before lessons and once in the evening after we'd been to the chapel. We had a new set of clothes if we needed 'em, given to us at Christmas, with a spare shirt for Sunday. We had shoes too—a pair of hand-me-downs that we were allowed to wear across the yard when we walked to Mass—though we had to put 'em back in the box by the door once we came back in. I marked the inside of mine both times I got a new pair. That way Joshua could tell which ones to take by the time they came his way, and he walked in my shoes for a full six years.

By then, I was the oldest and the best of the boys who lived under Father Mosely's roof. He told me so himself while he was busy punishing Joshua with the end of his cane. Sister Miriam had caught my brother and Abel Whitley stealing apples from the kitchen, and Joshua had called her a sour old maid.

Father Mosely shook his head while he delivered the punishment. "Samuel, why did the good Lord have your mother deliver two boys so very different?" He took a good strong swing, and I saw my brother wince. "One of you is a thief who won't even learn to spell his own name." Thwack. "And the other one's a saint, the very brightest and the best I've ever had the pleasure to teach." Thwack.

It was one of the Father's favorite speeches, how the both of us were two sides of the same coin—one good, one bad, but always inseparable.

Father Mosely had his hand on Joshua's neck as he pressed him down into the table to deliver his fifth and final blow.

"Sir?"

"Don't interrupt me, Samuel. I will not spare the rod. In case you hadn't noticed, there's a war on and I won't tolerate the stealing of food. Not ever." I held my tongue while he struck the last blow, then set my brother free. "Teach him, Samuel." He pointed us toward the door. "Teach him to work hard and obey the rules, I beg you, 'cause he'll be the death of me if he can't find it in himself to behave and get on with his work."

Joshua was crying so hard with the rage and hurt of being hit that he couldn't keep his mouth shut. "It was only an apple!" he shouted, and I quickly took hold of his ear and turned him around before the priest got hold of him again. "I'm sorry, sir," I called out as I led him away. "I'll try and teach him, sir, I will. Only he ain't a bad boy. Really he ain't. You know he's got a good heart. He surely has, sir."

But we both knew that weren't true. Joshua had been bad since the day he was born, and I think Old Betty must have known it when she slapped him.

I did the best I could with him. I'd take him aside and read to him from books, sometimes getting him to copy down the words, though he never had the willingness to learn. He was always looking out the window, always had something else on his mind, and besides, it weren't only Joshua that I had to look after. Being the oldest meant I had to look out for all the kids 'cause Sister Miriam used to blame me when they did wrong. She'd tell me I shoulda stopped 'em, though I never knew how. Sometimes, I didn't even know right from wrong myself.

Anyway, everything changed when we got a new teacher at the school. Miss Priestly was her name and she was different from the others we'd had before. She told me I might become a teacher, the same as her, on account of how I was good with words and how I liked to help the others in the class. She didn't use those exact words to me, preferring to put it in the form of a question.

"Samuel," she asked me one morning when we were all in class, "are you supposed to be the teacher here?"

"No, ma'am," I answered her correctly.

"Then why are you helping your brother with the work I set?"

I thought that would have been obvious, but I didn't say it—not wanting to make her look a fool—but the fact was that Joshua couldn't do this particular task. He don't have a love of words the way I do. He don't see the shape of 'em, and anyway, being that much younger than me, he's got less of 'em to choose from.

She had read out the following example: "'The old man had never been known to change his mind. No. Not ever. The whole town knew him to be as stubborn as a mule.'"

She asked us to think of something that was more stubborn than a mule and we were all having difficulty. I was sitting next to Joshua. "This is stupid," he whispered. "Everyone knows there ain't nothing more stubborn than a mule."

"You don't have to tell me," I whispered back, but Miss Priestly heard me. That's when she asked me about whether I was the teacher or not and I said that I thought it was good to help others less

13

fortunate than yourself. To my surprise, she smiled at me, all gracious and golden, and she agreed. "Yes, it is." Then she asked, "What word would *you* use instead of a mule, Samuel? I mean, if you wanted to illustrate stubbornness."

I had to think fast, but I got one and I told it to her in the full sentence, as it would be used if I were writing it down. "The whole town knew him to be as stubborn as a screw that weren't for turning."

"That's perfect, Samuel," she said. "I think it does the job very well, but next time, please wait until you're a teacher yourself before you interrupt my lessons."

I knew she meant that one day I might be good enough to teach the class myself, though it wasn't long before any hope I had of teaching at the orphanage disappeared for good.

—

Sister Miriam had asked that I sweep out the floors and polish 'em to a shine so good she could see her face in it. That's why I was late for class. I had finished up and was walking across the dry, red clay between the old school building and the main house. It was a Wednesday. That meant mathematics all morning and I could hear the children singing their nine-times table out loud, their little voices drifting out across the air in the old yard. We were good at our tables and there weren't a child in that room who didn't know 'em, 'cept maybe little Jessie, on account of him only being five years old and never gone to school till he came to us only a few weeks before.

I was walking across to the classroom, when I heard the chapel door fly open with a bang and I turned to see Father Mosely come running outside, his hands in the air and his cheeks all red with the rage that was in his heart.

He comes out howling. He's taking big staggering strides toward the center of the dusty yard, and his black gown is open at the front and billowing in the breeze, so he looks twice the size he really is.

When he drops his gaze from the heavens, I must be the first thing he sees, because he points his finger at me, a finger so straight and deadly it could have been a gun, and he shouts out to me, "Samuel Jenkins, you come here to me now."

His finger turns a full circle in the air till it points straight down at his black polished shoes, and he reels me in so tight I might as well be a fish on the end of his line, 'cause before I know it, I'm standing there toe-to-toe, the top of my head nearly touching the bottom of his chin, close enough that I have to put my head back to get a look at his face.

He takes a deep breath. I can see the sweat glistening in the lines across his forehead as he takes hold of my ear and twists it tight till I'm up on my tiptoes. He walks me swiftly into the chapel and I'm taking quick little steps like a pigeon, maybe five of mine to every one of his, and I'm doing my best not to squeal out loud because my ear is sharp with the pain of being turned right around and inside out, though to be honest, it hurts me more to be treated like my brother.

The air is cooler indoors than out. The chapel is dark and there's the usual smell of polished wood coming from the pews that we pass on our way to the altar. Father Mosely lets go of my ear and points his finger at the table. "Look!"

And I do look. I don't have no choice.

"There is a turd upon the table of the Lord!" he tells me, and I can see it clearly in the light from the candles, a solid log, all big and brown. I find myself sniffing the air, but there's no smell to it, at least not that I can tell. But still, there's no mistaking what it is, and the fear grips my heart because there'll be hell to pay for this. I know there will. I've seen it before. There'll be someone made to sit in the chair of judgment, same as there was when the golden cup of Christ was stolen and they found it in Billy Fielding's box of things and he was taken down by the Devil himself.

There's one of us here will pay the price.

Father Mosely squints up his eyes, and his mouth goes all small and puckered. "Do you know anything of this?"

I shake my head.

He walks behind my back and stands on the other side of me. "Is this some sort of joke?"

"Who would do such a thing?" I ask him.

"Who indeed?" Father Mosely speaks with some satisfaction, like at last we're getting somewhere. His voice is hard and unafraid. He's gonna find the boy who did this—I know he will 'cause he has before. "Is there anything you want to tell me, Samuel? I mean, before we ask the others. Now that it's just you and me alone."

I shake my head again. "I don't know why these things keep happening, Father. Honest. I don't know why people have to do bad things."

Father Mosely walks behind the table and stands leaning over the turd. He's looking down on it with his hands clasped together in front of him. "Another good question, Samuel. Why do people do bad things?" He nods his head as though he has the answer. "It seems to me that we only have to be weak. Weak enough that when the Devil comes calling, we let him in. We let him put ideas into our heads. We let him put his poison in our hearts." He fixes me with one of his looks, the one he does where his eyes get bigger and he can see right through you. "Do you let the Devil in, Samuel? Do you? Is the Devil in your head?"

I immediately shake my head.

"Are you sure, Samuel? Are you sure you don't let the Devil in? Because I know you hear him—I know he calls to you to do bad things, same as he calls to all of us."

I close my eyes, just in case Father Mosely can see the Devil in me, 'cause I know he's in there somewhere. I can hear him whisper to me: *You do let me in, Samuel. I come in with your dirty thoughts.*

Father Mosely puts a hand on my head. "Pray to the Lord, Samuel. Pray that He protects you from the words of Satan."

And I pray to Him. I pray to Him. I pray to Him.

When I next look up, the bright blue eyes of Jesus Christ are staring down at me from the crucifix above the altar. Father Mosely is holding a white handkerchief and a cardboard box, a little smaller than a shoe box. It's got the words MRS. HARBURY'S DELICIOUS CANDY on the side and there's a drawing of a pink rosebud. He scoops up the turd with a handkerchiefed hand and places it inside the box. He puts the lid in place and then sweeps past me, making for the open doors, the cardboard box held up in front of him as he calls for me to follow. "Come, Samuel. Let us find out who is weak before the Lord."

We go out into the yard, and the classroom is quiet as we climb the steps of the school porch. I run ahead and open the door for Father Mosely so that he don't even have to break his stride before going through into the classroom.

Miss Priestly is sitting at her desk with an open book. There's an easy equation on the blackboard behind her and the children are sitting in silence, their chalkboards all in front of 'em. The classroom stirs to life as Father Mosely walks up the aisle and I see Joshua sit up straighter in his chair. I sit down too, 'cause it don't do to stand out in a room where people are going to start pointing fingers.

"How nice," Miss Priestly says as the Father places the box, very deliberately, on her desk.

But the Father shakes his head. "No, Miss Priestly. There is nothing *nice* about this box." He taps a finger on the lid. "Despite what it says on the side, there is nothing *pleasant* in the contents of this box." He scans the room, from the back row to the front, where the little ones sit. "Who would like to tell me what is in the box?"

Little Jessie's hand shoots up in the air. "Is it insects?"

Father Mosely takes two steps to Jessie's desk and slams his hand down so hard it frightens the child. "This is not a game of guesses, Jessie! If you do not know, then you would do well to keep your opinions to yourself."

Even from behind, I can see that Jessie looks scared—I can see it in the way he hangs his shoulders. And he ain't the only one. All of us are scared.

Father Mosely pauses for effect. "One of you doesn't need to guess. One of you knows what I have in the box because you left it in the chapel as a present for the Lord." He straightens a finger and stabs the air. "A foul and stinking gift that reeks of the Devil himself!"

I take a look at Abel Whitley. He's always saying smutty things, so he's the face I go to first, but Abel looks as shocked as the rest of us.

Father Mosely walks slowly across the front of the classroom. "Perhaps whoever left this thinks it's funny. You might be laughing because you think you'll get away with it, or you might be quaking in your boots with the fear of what you have done." His eyes are all wide in his face. "Either way, I say to whoever has done this—own up. Confess your sin so that the Lord may be merciful upon your soul, although why He should want to be, I do not know."

When he walks between the rows of desks, every boy in that classroom lowers his eyes and looks away for fear of being blamed. I keep my eyes on Miss Priestly. She's sitting still as can be, looking about as scared as everyone else. The Father walks in a slow circle, going all around the room, and when he comes back to her desk, he stops and takes a look at the watch that he carries in the front pocket of his waistcoat. "Will no one tell us what I have in the box?"

Nobody says a thing.

His manner changes. He puts his hands together, becomes all bright and brisk, trying a different kind of game to trap us. "Very well, then. I shall show you. Miss Priestly, would you find me a sharp pair of scissors, please?"

Miss Priestly nods quickly, stands up from her chair, and goes into the supply cabinet next to the blackboard. She brings back a pair of scissors, then watches as the Father removes the lid of the box and cuts the cardboard down each end until the edge makes a flap, which he folds out, turning the box into a stage. When he stands aside, we all gasp at the sight of the turd, even me, and I already know it's there.

Father Mosely smiles with satisfaction at our shock. "It's hard to believe, isn't it? Hard to believe that a boy from this class would go into the chapel and climb upon the table of the Lord to leave Him such a gift. But I will give that boy one last chance to confess his sin and ask for mercy." He gestures to the open box. "Will the boy responsible now put up his hand?"

No one moves. We sit and wait. I don't know for how long, but it seems like a lifetime. At one point, a pigeon lands on the roof. He sits there cooing and tiptoeing about. You can hear his claws scratching on the old tin, but still not one of us moves a muscle. We hang our heads and close our eyes, each one of us praying to the Lord that it won't be us that gets the blame, all of us doubting our own minds because although we know one way or the other whether we're guilty, it feels like whatever we know could just as easily be wrong. That's how I feel anyway. At any moment, the finger might point in my direction and I'll believe it must have been me. It's all I can do not to admit it right away, and it would be easier for all of us if I did, 'cause it'd put an end to this awful silence that's gonna last until Father Mosely points at one of us and asks for him to stand.

Because he *will* point at one of us.

Like he has before.

We all of us realize—'cept maybe little Jessie—that Father Mosely knows who has done the deed. He always does. He knew that it was Billy Fielding stole the cup. He knew that Doddie drew the rude picture on the privy door and wrote underneath that it was Joseph and the Virgin Mary. He knew because God had told him, and I have a pretty good idea that right now, God has stopped doing all the other things He has to do and is looking down at our little school-room, concentrating just on us and telling Father Mosely who it was that shat upon His table.

"So be it." He breaks the silence with three quiet words, unfolds his hands, and lifts his head. "Close your eyes," he tells us. "Close your eyes and let us wait for the judgment of our Lord."

I'm already there, I'm already praying, muttering, "Let it not be me, let it not be me," as we close our eyes, but I open 'em quickly to see which desk Father Mosely goes to, and I'm only just in time as I watch him stop right in front of Joshua's desk—he really does—and my heart drops to my feet and I can't even breathe.

I watch the Father's hands come apart. I see his finger with the gold ring lift high into the air above Joshua's head and it twitches into life. He's about to point the finger at my brother.

I stand up, my chair legs scraping on the wooden floor. "It was me!"

All the boys open up their eyes as Father Mosely looks across at me. I can see he wasn't expecting it and he's in a dilemma now, because God's told him one thing and I'm telling him another, so I have to be convincing and I have to be quick.

"It was me who shat upon the table. I did it this morning when I should have been cleaning floors. I went into the chapel and climbed upon the table of the Lord. Then I dropped my pants and did it. I did. I did it right there on the white cloth before the holy eyes of Jesus Christ upon the cross, so help me Lord."

Father Mosely becomes impatient and annoyed. I think he's going to tell me to sit down and be quiet, to stop being so stupid, only he hasn't moved from in front of Joshua's desk and I know I've got to do more, I've got to get him to walk away from my brother.

I start shaking from the fear of what I've done, so I exaggerate it, biting my lip till I can taste the blood and rolling my eyes back into my head, the way I do when we speak in tongues. I stagger to the desk in front of mine and lie on it, scattering the boys like a flock of birds. I screw up my face and stick my tongue out at 'em, all red with blood, as I roll my head from side to side, saying, "I got the Devil in me. I got the Devil in me and he made me empty my bowels upon the table of the Lord. It was the Devil made me do it."

I can feel Father Mosely step away from Joshua. I see him pass back through the middle of the class, coming toward me, half-crouched and moving slow, like I'm some animal he's afraid of.

Then he tries to trick me. "What does the Devil look like, Samuel?" He stands over me as I twist upon the desk, rolling from my front to my back, making spit rise up around my lips. "How did the Devil appear to you, Samuel? Tell me exactly what you saw."

"I saw . . . I saw . . ." Suddenly, I rise up on the desk and come right up close, to his face. "Why, he looks just like you, Father."

He takes a step back.

"At first I thought it was you, come to visit me in the night, come to lean across me and whisper in my ear, but when you opened your mouth, I could see the snake inside and I could smell the licorice on your breath, and when I looked down, I could see you had nin-nies, just like Miss Priestly, and they were bare underneath your gown and you said to me, 'Samuel, you shall defile the table of the Lord and bring all manner of wickedness upon this place,' and so I did it. I did it like you told me to. I did it just like you said."

And suddenly it's like the Devil's really there inside me, like I ain't myself anymore, and I climb up on my desk, making the room of boys all gasp, and I turn my back on Joshua, 'cause I don't want to see his face as I drop my trousers and squat, straining for all I'm worth.

Father Mosely must have found his strength from somewhere. Suddenly, he grabs my arm and pulls me off the desk in one quick movement, throwing me to the floor with my trousers still around my knees, all bruised and with my elbow hurting.

He puts his hand between my eyes and pins me down. I could struggle, I could make more of a show of it, but I know that it's over. Father Mosely's got no choice.

"Pray for the soul of the sinner here before us," he calls out loudly, beginning the intonation of the words we know so well. And the boys begin to chant with him, surrounding the two of us as we crouch together on the floor.

"Let us pray that God has mercy on his soul."

CHAPTER 3

Father Mosely's got me groveling in the dirt of the privy, my head and feet against the wooden walls with the chair of judgment hard up against my back. It ain't much to look at—just a small wooden chair, same as the ones we sit at for supper—but I knew that already, 'cause the day Billy got taken by the Devil, we sneaked around the back and looked through a hole in the wood, expecting to see a burnished throne and a hot pit of ashes.

Father Mosely brought me out here. He put me inside and locked the door. He's taken the other boys back to the house, where they will go without supper as they pray for my soul, and in the morning, he'll bring 'em back so they can see what judgment has befallen me.

I been here a long time now, long enough for the last rays of the sun to squeeze through the gaps of the wall in thin, bright golden lines. A short while ago I heard the footsteps of Father Mosely trudging through the gloom. I know the noise of his walk—the long stride and the heavy step, firm upon the ground like there ain't no uncertainty in him at all. He must have gone over to the chapel and he must still be there, 'cause he ain't come back this way.

He'll be praying. I expect he will. Probably discussing with the good Lord what to do with me.

Perhaps God'll be angry with him. He'll say, *Look what you did! You chose the wrong boy!*

Father Mosely will have to apologize: *I'm sorry. He confused me. But we can't let the Devil take him. We can't let an innocent boy burn in the fire pits of hell for the rest of eternity.*

God'll shake his head. *I don't see how I've got much choice.*

Well, there's some truth in that. We ain't never opened the door on the chair of judgment the next morning and found a boy still sitting there. He's always been judged good and proper and there ain't nothing left of him to see.

I know Father Mosely will stick up for me. *But we can't let the Devil take him.*

He lied, didn't he? He spoke with the tongue of the serpent?

And I did lie. I did. I got the tongue of the serpent in my mouth and I got wicked thoughts in my head about Miss Priestly.

I slap my face. Slap it hard and put dirt in my mouth, 'cause I am undone. The Devil's coming for me with red-hot pincers. He'll pick me up and drop me in a pot of boiling oil. Maybe he'll string me up by my wrists and never let me go. Maybe he'll whip me till I'm red raw.

Father Mosely will plead for me. I know he will: *But, Lord, Samuel done a noble thing. He sacrificed himself to save another. Surely he shouldn't be damned for that?*

He'll argue it well. 'Cause he likes me.

But God will look down on him with those big blue eyes. *Well, someone has to pay, and I told you who it was. It was Joshua that did it. I made that very clear.*

Yes. It was Joshua. Same as it always is. He's been getting into trouble since he learned to crawl. Never stays in one place. Doesn't matter whether I hit him or speak to him nicely, he won't take any notice of me. Never has. When he was a baby, I had to stop him crawling through the legs of horses. I had to stop him pulling the plates off shelves. If it weren't one thing, it was another. One time he tried to pick up a glowing coal and throw it on the rug, nearly set the whole place on fire, and he couldn't have been more than two years old. I got the blame for that too.

No. There's no escaping it. Joshua's got the Devil in him for sure. I reckon that's why Mama died giving birth to him. But he's done it for us this time. He really has.

Outside the privy, the light has faded. I hear footsteps in the darkness, some quick little steps that patter across the dirt in the yard, and when I put my eye to the hole in the wood, he's suddenly there—my brother, Joshua—but I don't want to see him and I shuffle away from the door, putting my spine against the far wall.

"Samuel," he whispers loudly, his mouth up close to the privy wall. "Samuel, you in there?"

When I don't answer, he says it again louder and I have to stop him or we'll both be caught. "Quiet yourself!" I whisper sharply. "You'll have the Father or Sister Miriam out here. My Lord, you will."

"I can't find the key to get you out."

"Go back inside, Joshua. Go back inside and pray to the Lord. You ask Him for forgiveness. Do you hear me?"

"I been praying for hours, Samuel. We all been praying for the Lord to let you out, but I don't think it's gonna work, so I'm looking for the key, only it ain't in Father's jacket pocket like it usually is. Do you know where he coulda hid it?"

"What you doing going through Father Mosely's pockets? And

how do you know that's where his keys are? Have you been thieving as well, Joshua? Have you been stealing from a priest?" I hear his little body slump against the door of the privy and he won't answer me, so I know it must be true. "Go back to the house, Joshua, before you get caught."

"Why'd you do it, Samuel?"

I ain't exactly sure how he means, but he asks me in such a way that it melts the very heart of me. He's only a little fella, and that's easy to forget when I get angry with him.

"I did it 'cause someone has to pay for what you did wrong. The good Lord holds us to account, Joshua, and someone always has to pay. That's the way it works. You gotta remember that while I'm gone. You gotta try to be good, 'cause every time you do something bad, there's someone has to pay the reparations on your soul. Can you remember that? Can you try a little harder to be good?" He puts a finger through the notch in the door and I touch the tip of it where he still has the scar from that burning coal. "It's gonna be all right, Joshua. Everything's gonna be all right. Now go on back to the house."

I got a fistful of dread lodged in my throat at the thought of losing him, and he must know, 'cause he won't leave me, even though I told him to. "I don't want to be left here on my own."

"I know, Joshua. But you gotta be good. You gotta stay out of trouble and you gotta wait for me. Do you understand? 'Cause I'm coming back for you. Wherever it is I go—I don't care whether it's heaven or hell—I'm coming back. Do you hear me?"

I swallow hard, pushing his finger back out through the hole. Joshua puts his lips to the gap. "You're the best brother a boy could have, Samuel. I ain't gonna forget you and I'll try to be good, I will, 'cause you're the best. Always will be."

There! He breaks the very heart of me, same as always.

"Stay away from that Abel Whitley," I tell him as he makes his way back to the house, but my voice cracks and he don't hear me before he disappears into the dark.

Just then, the chapel door opens and the Father's footsteps come past. He don't stop to talk to me. He just goes on into the house.

So it has been decided. Whatever God wants to do with me, there's no way I can change it. All I can do is wait. I get myself up off the ground and sit in the chair 'cause I reckon if I'm sitting straight, it'll make a better impression on whoever it is comes to take me away.

Perhaps God and Father Mosely have made a compromise. Maybe they struck a deal. Yes. That'll be it. I know they have.

From somewhere high above me, God is laughing gently. I can hear Him. He's saying it's all gonna be all right. He's saying He was never gonna leave me for the Devil. He was only kidding, and He's gonna come for me Himself. He's gonna have me sitting up in heaven on His right-hand side.

But later, when the night is fully dark, I'm still there waiting.

I need some sleep, so I push the chair of judgment to the edge of the privy and curl up on the floor. I close my eyes. Try to clear my mind and calm my beating heart.

God ain't gonna hurt me, I can be sure of that, 'cause I've always been a good boy.

But it still ain't easy to sleep. If I can remember something happy, then that might help. So I think of the trips we make into the village, on the first Saturday of every month, when Father Mosely gives us a nickel each for sweets from the store and we get to see the girls in their pretty dresses. Those Saturdays sure are nice. Those days are lovely and warm.

And I fall asleep with the smell of the marzipan all up inside my nostrils.

CHAPTER 4

On no account will I speak to this man first.

If it's the Devil himself kneeling before me, then I have nothing to say to him. And if he is God? Well, there's more chance of me being Moses than there is of this fella being God. That much is for certain. He don't have the stature. Not by a long way.

Oh, he looks smart enough. I get a good look at him as he kneels over a tiny silver pot, pouring water from a kettle that he takes from the fire to make tea. He dresses like a gentleman, but his eyes are far too busy in his head. And they're little. He keeps 'em wide open and they dart around like he can't decide on any one thing to look at. Makes me think he's the kind of man who ain't got full control of his nerves.

He wears a brown suit that would fit a slimmer man, and though he has no waistcoat, he wears a plain shirt with an old silk necktie. The lining of his brown bowler hat has come away at the back and hangs a full inch below the rim.

And then there is his smell. He smells of . . . well . . . he smells of many things and none of 'em are fresh, 'cept maybe the sweetness of the licorice stick he has in his mouth. It's a relief when he straightens up and walks back over to the mule that still stands a few steps to the side of us, giving me the evil eye.

I lower my head, not wanting to appear confrontational to either of 'em.

"Go on over to the shade of that tree."

There's that voice again. High-pitched. Like a girl, only not a girl. Not ladylike in any way. I see an arc of four trees, only littl'uns, hunched up against the wind that must blow through here most times. They've got enough leaves to give me some shelter from the sun, but it ain't easy to stand with my hands tied behind my back, so I scramble across on my knees till I'm sitting at the foot of a trunk. I can see we are somewhere on a plain, in the lee of a low hill. A brook trickles through the ground behind us, so it's not exactly desert, though it sure ain't no hospitable place.

He takes a good long look at me. "You ain't the fella I was expecting. I was told you'd be younger."

"That'd be my brother."

The man crouches down. "That's right, that's right. That's what the priest said."

He puts his face up close to mine and sniffs. He takes hold of the lid under my eye and pulls it down so I can feel the air on my eyeball where it shouldn't be. I'm holding my breath, but he opens my mouth to look at my teeth, and when I breathe in his face, he grimaces. He runs a finger along my gums, then stands, leaving me openmouthed. "How old are you, boy?" He chews on the licorice stick and it moves from one side of his mouth to the other. When I hesitate, he slaps my face. "I asked you a question."

"I'm twelve, sir," I say quickly. "Close to turning thirteen, I think."

"Don't look it." He sniffs. "Expect you haven't been fed much. Expect you haven't been made to work too hard neither."

He walks back to his teapot and produces a china cup and saucer from a hinged wooden box that he has on the ground. He pours himself a cup, then sits down in the dirt, lifts the cup to his lips, and drinks, his little finger all cock-a-hoop and dainty. He don't sip quietly.

I watch him, wondering whether he really could be the Devil. I got a bump on the back of my head, all bruised and tender, which tells me that whatever my fate is, it ain't gonna be good. But maybe there's still hope. Maybe this place is some sort of purgatory, the sort of place where I might still be able to influence how things turn out, and if it is, I gotta have faith.

I start to pray, out loud, speaking the words of the 27th Psalm, which I know by heart. "The Lord is my light and my salvation; whom shall I fear? The Lord is the strength of my life; of whom shall I be afraid?"

The man looks up at me, but I ignore him.

"When the wicked, even mine enemies and my foes, came upon me to eat up my flesh, they stumbled and fell."

He puts his saucer down in the dirt and I bow my head so as not to meet his eye, but I carry on paying testament to the Lord in my darkest hour. "One thing I have desired of the Lord, that I will seek after"—I hear them big boots again—" that I may dwell in the House of the Lord . . . and to inquire in His temple."

A hand yanks my collar hard, pulling me upright to my knees before the sack comes back over my head. He ties it around my neck with a piece of cord and everything is dark and muffled like it was before and I'm on my knees when he kicks me in the stomach, just like the mule did, kicks me hard when I don't see it coming. And it hurts like hell.

He jerks the sack close to his mouth. "I won't have your kind preaching at me. Do you hear me, boy? Did you hear what I said?"

But I ain't saying nothing at all. Not anymore. I ain't saying nothing to no one.

———

In the evening, when he takes me from the mule, he lays me down in the dirt and lifts the sacking from my head. I don't take much interest in where we are. It seems much like it was before, though there ain't no trees for shelter.

He doesn't speak to me but crouches close and stares, pleased that I'm miserable, like he's satisfied if he don't see the life in my eyes. He gives me water from a tin can. Unscrews the lid and tips it up so that I have to move my mouth to the side to stop the steady stream from falling and being wasted in the dirt. It tastes dirty, like he's got it from a stream and not from a well. I notice he drinks from a different can from me.

I watch him eat his supper. Mostly, I try not to look, but I think he wants me to, 'cause he makes noises when he eats and if I lift my head, he's always watching me, waiting for me, like he knows what I'm thinking.

"Expect you're hungry," he says eventually. He comes across and crouches down, lifting the last chunk of bread to my mouth, feeding me as though I'm a horse and he's scared I'll nip his fingers. I have to hold the bread in my teeth and chew it at the same time, knowing if I drop it, he won't pick it up.

He stays crouching close. The sun is setting and behind his head the light is fading fast, all tinged at the edges with blues and reds. "Where'd you learn your scriptures? Is that from the priest back there?" I nod. "You know a lot of that stuff?" I nod again. "Well, I suggest you forget it. Where you're going, if you want to pray, you better do it in your head."

He smiles coldly. "You learn to read?" I nod. "Bet you can write too." He's smiling like he knows everything about me. "Well, you better forget that too. When we get to town tomorrow, if I hear a word out of you about knowing how to read, I'll whip you till you're dead and then I'll get back on my mule and have Father Mosely give me your brother by way of a refund."

He walks to the mule and returns with a long length of rope and a blanket, ties my feet together, and then fastens the loose end of the rope around his own ankle so the two of us are twinned, one to the other. "That's so you don't get any ideas about running away." He walks a few yards away from me, unfolds the blanket, lies down upon the ground, and pulls it across him, keeping his hat on to sleep.

If he means for me to sleep as well, then he's mistaken, 'cause I want to kill him for what he just said about Joshua. I want to find a rock and smash his skull in. I want to hold a gun to his head till he cries like a baby, and I never had such wicked thoughts before.

I'm so angry I start slinging questions like they're stones. "Who are you anyway?" I don't even care when he lifts his head. "Are you meant to be some sort of devil? Is that it? Well, are you?"

Oh, how he laughs at me. That man damn near splits his sides, rolling onto his back and kicking his legs so the rope that joins us tugs at my ankles. "Oh, my Lord! You as well! I thought you were too clever to believe it, but it seems like I was wrong." He sits up in the dust. "That other one, the last boy I took, do you know, he thought I was going to eat him for breakfast? He really did." He puts a finger to the rim of his bowler. "He actually asked if I had horns under this here hat. Can you believe that? Ha!" He shakes his head in disbelief.

"Do you mean Billy Fielding? Did you take Billy Fielding, same as you took me?"

He lowers his voice as though the place is full of listening ears. "Now, it don't do to name names. That would be unprofessional." He points a finger toward my eyes to threaten me, but then he smiles sweet as you like. "I'm no devil, Samuel. You can rest assured of that. I'm an honest-to-God businessman, a man of some means, and you . . ." He takes off his bowler, placing it on the ground beside him, and I spot a folded ten-dollar bill tucked up inside the lining. He slaps a hand across the top of his head to smooth his hair. Finally, he points a finger at me. "You're gonna be my payday."

He lies back down and gathers the blanket across his shoulders, but then he sits up again and leans in my direction. "I nearly forgot to tell you. Tomorrow is Friday. Now, you better remember that day real good 'cause from now on, that's gonna be your name." He smiles, expecting me to be pleased. "Friday. I like the sound of that." Then he calls out to me, like we're standing across from each other in a busy street. "I say there, what's your name, boy?"

I won't say it. I won't even open my mouth.

"I said, what's your name, boy?" He cocks his head to one side, waiting to hear me speak. "If I have to untie this rope and come to you, you will be sorely sorry. Now you tell me your name."

It don't do to pick fights you can't win. I learned that at the orphanage. So I lower my eyes and say it. "Friday."

"What did you say? I couldn't hear you. I said, 'What did you say?'"

A little piece of me dies right then. I can feel it leave me as I raise my voice. "Friday. That's my name."

There, I said it for him, clear as day—and I ain't never felt so ashamed.

—

In the morning, the man gives me different clothes. He says, "Here's your linsey-woolseys. Put 'em on now."

The trousers and shirt are loose-fitting, neither of 'em new except to me. They're made from a cream-colored cloth that is rougher than I'm used to.

He hitches my rope to the saddle and lets me walk behind the mule, my hands tied out in front of me. People pass us on the road in wagons, and the drivers take a look at us as the town comes into view. I don't know what it's called and I don't ask. It wouldn't mean much to me anyway. But this town's bigger than any I've been in, and it's busy. I can feel the life and soul of it as we reach the main thoroughfare, where the shopkeepers sweep out the front of their shops and pull awnings over their windows with a rattle of the ironwork.

There are groups of ladies wearing hooped skirts, who stand and chat on the sidewalk with little drawstring purses hanging from their arms and fancy hats pinned to their heads. I catch snatches of their talk as we walk past, but they don't notice me at all. They don't even see me.

We walk on along the main street. A marching band strikes up a tune and processes out from a side road to fall in behind us. We go past a building that has a banner up saying: ENLIST HERE TODAY. My man pulls the mule to the side of the road to let the band pass, and I go where the mule goes, I ain't got a choice, and we stand by the sidewalk, watching the spectacle.

The parade has old men in uniform, blowing on trombones. They've got boys on tin drums with gray caps on their heads, some with muskets pushed into their belts, and all the boys have wooden toy rifles slung over their shoulders.

In the next few moments, it seems like the whole town empties out onto the sidewalk to watch. People come out of the buildings and stand in the doorways or they open up their windows and lean across the sill to get a better look at what is going on. Some of 'em know the tune the band's playing and they sing along and clap their hands, shouting out the words about a bonnie blue flag with a single star. I don't know that tune. Anyway, this ain't got nothing to do with me. I'm only standing here watching it 'cause I have to.

The band is followed by a regiment of soldiers, about thirty or so, marching in ranks of three, and they're young men, proper soldiers, I'd guess, though they sure look untidy, with their uniforms all different. They each got a rifle, though. And there's a cannon that they pull on ropes. The metal rims of the wheels make a scrunching sound as they roll across the dirt, and everyone seems mighty proud of that cannon, and I think they must've polished it up.

A posse of women with bright blue sashes runs right past us, shouting at the men who are watching from the sidewalk, telling 'em to join up, saying all the ladies love a man in uniform. They're giving out leaflets to anyone who'll take one and they're shouting to the fine-looking women on the sidewalk, telling 'em to come and join 'em, saying there's a cartload of scraps just been delivered that needs stitching into uniforms.

The whole parade goes on up the street, and after they've passed, the man moves the mule forward and we walk out into the empty road, him in front of us, the mule in the middle, and me trailing along behind as before. We turn into a quieter street, away from the main drag, where the sides of the buildings don't have too many windows. About halfway down, we stop at a wooden door and he knocks loudly, giving it two raps with his knuckle. The door opens quickly.

"Tell Mr. Wickham that Gloucester is here. Go on, boy. Go get him. Tell him it's a matter of some urgency."

The door closes and a bolt slides back into place. So now I know. My devil has a name and he calls himself Gloucester.

Gloucester turns me around by the wrists and begins to pull and tease the rope, then, once I'm loose, he takes hold of the collar of my shirt in a clenched fist, walks me a few steps to the door, and tells me not to move.

By and by, a man comes to the door—a gentleman of forty years or so and dressed very smart, his top hat in his hand. He steps outside and takes a good look at both of us, but his eyes stay longer on me.

"Mr. Wickham!" I can tell from Gloucester's voice that he doesn't consider himself the equal of this man. He sounds like he'd be happier on his knees. "Good day to you, Mr. Wickham. I have someone here for your catalogue, an unexpected arrival on my books. Now, I know that it's late . . ."

The man frowns. "You've missed the viewing." He sounds bullish in comparison to Gloucester. "Most of the stock has been here for the past two days and the buyers have already assessed their options." He looks at me again, shrinking me by a couple of inches. "You know I don't like to sell off the catalogue."

"I know that, sir. I do know that. I realize my situation ain't ideal, but if you could put him on the list, I'd be ever so grateful. It would be a favor that I owed you—I understand that—only I do need to realize my assets and there ain't another sale around here for a while now."

Mr. Wickham takes hold of my upper arm and squeezes hard on the muscle till I tense. "He from out east?"

"That's right, sir. His name is Friday. I got papers for him."

Mr. Wickham don't look impressed. "He's not a good age for a nigger."

"No, sir. He isn't. But he'll grow up fine. He's from good stock and he's been well looked after. I can vouch for that. He ain't no trouble, I can assure you. I got his papers right here." Gloucester shakes 'em out so Wickham can see the details.

The marching band passes by the end of the street, and the sudden music makes me glance behind.

"Is he educated?"

"Not so you'd know it, sir, no, although he speaks well enough and he's bright. I'd say he has a noble temperament. He won't be no embarrassment to a lady or a gentleman if they decide to keep him in the house."

"You'll have to be satisfied with what you get for him." Wickham waves me inside without taking his eyes from Gloucester. "You're familiar with my terms?"

Gloucester touches the rim of his hat. "You're very kind, sir."

I take a step inside the door, then stop. Ahead of me is a long shed with wooden boxes for cattle, and bales of hay that have been lined up along the edges of the open walkway. It's gloomy, the only light coming from beams of sunlight that make their way down through the roof. By the door, there's a single dusty window with bars across it. Wickham steps inside and sweeps past me with my papers in his hand. "I'll be in my office," he announces to the doorman, who slides the bolt back into place. And then he is gone and I'm left where I stand, unsure of where I am or what I should do.

I take a few more steps inside the shed. I can't see anyone else hereabouts and yet the place don't feel empty. I sense a movement, maybe hear a breath, and I figure I must be in with livestock, maybe cows or something, but there's a voice, a low murmur, and it's answered by a whisper. I take another step into the gloom, my hand out ahead of me, ready to take hold of the first stall I come to, and it's their eyes that I see first, the eyes of men and women, sitting on bales of hay with their children lying on the floor at their feet. There's eight of 'em. A family, I reckon. And in the next stall, there's another six, and after that, there's more, a whole lot more, all of 'em sitting quietly.

I can't find a place to sit down at first, and no one wants to talk with me as I creep by them in the half-light. None of 'em is here alone. Not that I can see. Everyone but me has got someone—there's whole families together, or men who might be friends leaning toward each other and talking quietly. They keep themselves to themselves and I don't bother 'em. At last, I find a free bale and sit down, tucking my legs under me, making sure I won't be in the way if someone were to walk past, making myself so small they could probably tread on me and not notice.

I got a hollow feeling in my chest. I'm all empty. And I know for sure this ain't no limbo like I thought it might be. No. This is hell right here on earth.

———

I am not alone when they bring me to the auction—there's a girl a few years older than me and a man in his twenties. They lead us out into the bright light of a real big hall made with proper brick walls and pillars of stone set every ten paces around its edge. It has tall windows with bright, clear glass that let in a fair bit of sunlight, and it's full to bursting with people, both men and women, all standing and chatting.

The three of us are stood at the edge of the hall, close to some stairs that lead up to a platform. I watch the crowd. The air in the hall smells of tobacco from all the pipes and cigars. These people look rich to me. They keep their hats on their heads and there's some fine-looking jackets hanging from their shoulders.

And they're all white folks. There's only one black man here who don't look like a slave, and he's stood at the back by the door, dressed neatly in a brown jacket and a matching bowler hat. I can't take my eyes off him 'cause he's a proud-looking man, tall and strong with a short beard that don't disguise the fact that he's got a good chin.

Wickham catches my attention as he mounts the steps of the auction block and calls for some hush. The hall quiets down. "Lot thirty-eight is a young man of twenty-three by the name of Cedric." Wickham flicks his head, his eyes darting in our direction. "Come on up here, Cedric, and let the folks see what's for sale."

The man beside me walks out across the floor. He don't hurry himself and he don't lift his head any more than he needs to keep himself from stumbling. He drags a leg as he walks and looks to be in some discomfort as he mounts the steps to stand beside Wickham. "As you can see, the man claims to be lame, but my understanding is that this is a recent injury."

"He ain't lame!" A man with a pointed gray beard waves a hand in the air when he shouts out. He stands at the front of a group of men who have drawn close to the platform, intending to bid. "He only started limping when I said I was going to sell him. He's fit and young. He's a good worker. Pick you two fifty pounds a day and he's handy as a carpenter too."

A man from the back shouts out, "Why you tryin' to sell him, then?"

The owner shakes his head. "Why I'm selling him is my own business, but I tell you he ain't lame. He's putting it on. I tell you that for nothing. Trying to keep his price low. That's what it is.

Probably reckons he's got a chance of buying his freedom with a lower price."

The man at the back shouts out again. "Either way, I don't want no uppity nigger."

"Gentlemen, please." Wickham holds up his hands. "This ain't a debating society." He turns to the man beside him. "Take off your trousers, Cedric."

The slave don't even seem surprised to be asked and he unbuckles his black leather belt, lets his trousers fall to the platform, and steps out of 'em, his hand cupped in front of him to cover his shame. "Now walk the length of the block and back." Cedric steps along the platform in front of the men, his left foot dragging out to the side of him.

His owner prods his cane at the man as he passes. "See? Look at his leg. Everything looks just fine. He ain't lame. There's no injury there that I can see."

A murmur of voices rises up around the hall, but Wickham calls 'em to order. "Gentlemen, please. You've seen the man and you have formed your own opinion. Can we get this started? Do I hear five hundred dollars? Can I start the bidding at five hundred?"

It sure goes quickly. They bid with a nod, sometimes with a raised finger, and the price goes up twenty dollars at a time, sometimes fifty. It's Wickham's voice that calls the shots, keeping a finger pointed at the highest bidder till another man comes in. Cedric follows the bids, flicking his eyes from one man to the next until Wickham finally calls out, "Going . . . going . . . gone!" and Cedric is sold for eight hundred and fifty dollars. I don't know whether that's a good price or not. It's just what it is. Cedric buckles up his belt. I can't tell whether he's pleased with who he got, because his face shows no expression as he limps from the platform and walks away with the man who bought him.

Wickham looks our way again and shuffles a sheet of paper to the top of his hand. He calls the girl up next, and it's only when she's stood on the stage that I take a good long look at her. She's pretty. She sure is pretty indeed. I ain't seen many girls who are around my own age, but I know that she's the prettiest I've ever laid my eyes on. That's a fact. She don't have the same cream-colored linsey-woolsey as the rest of us either but wears a clean white pinafore dress, made of cotton, with a little blue bow on the front at the neck.

The crowd of men draws closer to the auction platform. It seems like everybody wants a good look at this girl, whether they get to buy her or not. They're doing more looking than talking and there's an anticipation hanging in the air as Wickham takes his top hat off and holds it in his hand. "Gentleman, this next lot is a rare opportunity to make a fine addition to your stock of slaves, but I have to remind you there is a condition of sale upon her that means she must be sold to a purchaser who resides outside of this state." A murmur of disapproval rises up around the hall. "I know, gentlemen. You're bound to be disappointed, but there are plenty of you here that can still retain an interest. She's a fine young woman, fifteen years of age, with experience working in the house as well as in the fields. I know her owner personally and I can testify that she has a personality as sweet as her looks."

A commotion starts up from somewhere in the middle of the crowd. I can hear a woman's voice rise up above the noise: "I got a right to be there at the front. Come on and let me through. Make way. I'll answer any questions you may have directly."

The tall black man I saw earlier is moving from the back of the hall to the front, his fine hat a good head and shoulders above the other heads in the crowd, but it ain't his voice I'm hearing, that's for sure. The people part to let him through and I look to the front in time to see a little lady with bright golden hair bunched up at the back. She's about half the size of the black man who follows her, and she's one of the women from the procession, wearing one of them blue sashes. She pushes on to the front of the platform and brings a boy with her, holding him by the hand, a little boy soldier with a gray cap and a wooden rifle slung over his shoulder. The black man comes through last, and the lady turns back to him. "Help Gerald onto the stage would you, Hubbard?"

The black man moves toward the boy, who turns away, saying he can do it himself, and reaches up and pulls himself onto the platform. Once he's standing there, I can see he's not as young as he looks and he's got the confidence of a boy about my age or older.

Cedric's previous owner, the man with the gray beard, is still there at the front. He shouts out, "You gonna sell us your stepson, Mrs. Allen?" There's some laughter in the hall. Someone else calls out, "This ain't no place for a boy or a lady. I don't know what the world is coming to."

There are a few guffaws of agreement, but the lady turns quickly to face her accusers. "The girl for sale is the property of my stepson. He's got a right to be where he can see what's happening, and he'll do well to learn the business, seeing as his father won't be back any time soon."

"Damn right too." Wickham walks across and slaps the boy's shoulder with a big hand. "Make a real man of him."

Mrs. Allen shakes her head of yellow hair. "Oh, there's not a real man left in this town. I can assure you of that, Mr. Wickham." She stares directly at the man who had the nerve to make a joke of her. "Any man worth his weight in salt has already gone to war."

"And the sooner your husband whips those Yankees and gets back home, the better." The man turns and pushes his way out through the crowd, shouting over his shoulder as he goes, "I remember a time when the women of this town knew their place."

But Mrs. Allen won't let him have the last word and she takes two steps up the stairs of the platform, pointing a finger at his back as he departs. "You can pick up a form to enlist at the door, Mr. Peighton." She sweeps the room with a frosty glare. "That goes for any man here who still possesses the wits to fire straight."

Mr. Wickham holds his hands up for peace. "Please, please, Mrs. Allen. This here's an auction room. Can we continue with the business at hand?" He pauses till the hall becomes quiet and all our eyes return to the girl. "What say we begin the bidding at one thousand dollars?"

Mrs. Allen nods her approval.

Someone calls out from the middle of the crowd. "Mrs. Allen? Say, Mrs. Allen? Can you please tell your nigger to move to the side? I can't see over him and I can't see around him."

Mrs. Allen looks over to the big black man who still stands at the very front of the stage. "Go on, Hubbard. Wait for me over there." He leaves the front of the platform and comes to stand next to me.

"Thank you, thank you." Mr. Wickham raises his voice again. "I believe we were about to start at a thousand dollars."

Now, that sure seems like a lot of money to me, but a man puts his hand in the air straight away and the price goes up fifty dollars. Another man bids against him. There are only a few men bidding, but they don't give up and the pace of the auction is fast and furious, though the girl herself won't even look at who is bidding for her. She stands with her chin bowed so low she won't see no one, 'cept maybe Mrs. Allen's stepson, stood there at the edge of the stage. He keeps his eyes firmly on the girl and it seems to me he looks sad.

At the final bid, her price is just under two thousand dollars. Wickham appears to be pleased with the result. I don't understand how a young girl could be worth so much more than a full-grown man, even if his foot ain't so good, but there it is, that's the price she sells for, and she's been bought by a man in a green waistcoat whose accent ain't the same as the rest of 'em here. He leads her away to the back of the hall, where there is a desk with an open ledger and a man who will make out her new papers.

I'm watching how they do things, when Wickham calls the hall to order again. "The next lot is off catalogue, but don't let that dissuade you, because he's a fine young man." Wickham looks my way and suddenly all thoughts of the girl leave my head. "Come up here, Friday. Come on and let everyone have a good look at you."

The people in the hall turn their heads toward me and I feel as though a hand has wrapped around my heart and started to squeeze. I've got to go up there on my own and no one's gonna help me.

Wickham holds his hand out, expecting me to join him, and for a moment I think that I could run for it. Maybe I could make it out the door and away before they grab me. But my legs don't dare to run. Instead, they take me up the steps of the auction platform and stand me next to Wickham and I don't know why they did that. It's like they belong to someone else already.

Wickham sees me shaking and he places a hand upon my shoulder. "This boy's been brought from Tennessee, where he's worked in a house, and he's twelve now, so I reckon he could work the field if you had some lighter duties to mix into his day." He takes my chin and lifts up my head. "Keep your head high, boy. Let 'em see your face. He does have a pleasant face, don't you think, ladies and gentlemen? He's got a gentle nature in those pretty eyes. I can see why the lady of his former house didn't want to give him up."

I can see Gloucester here inside the hall. He's come up close to the stage and is watching me like a bird of prey might watch a mouse from the air. I clench my hands together and remind myself to trust in the Lord and the goodness of His ways. I even say a prayer for my deliverance, and that's when I hear His voice: I hear the voice of God telling me to look at the boy who's still there on the stage, look him straight in the eye. *Do it, Samuel.* That's what the good Lord tells me. *Do it now.*

I raise my eyes and the boy holds my gaze. He's got white knuckles where he holds the strap on his wooden rifle.

"Shall I start at three hundred dollars?" Wickham calls out over the crowd. "That seems to be a fair price. Anyone want to start us off at three hundred?"

The boy puts his hand in the air immediately and it seems like everyone pauses. Wickham looks over at Mrs. Allen. "Did you intend him to bid, madam?"

"I did," she says, and there's some shuffling of feet before Wickham points to a gentleman who's raising a finger. "Three twenty." And another bidder. "Three sixty," then "four hundred."

And then we're away, but I can't take my eyes from the boy as he bids for me, can't help but notice how his tongue touches his top lip and moistens his mouth into a smile as the price goes up and the other bidders fall away till there's only him and one other man left, but that boy keeps sticking his finger in the air. He's determined he's gonna get me, and he only looks into the crowd once, to see who's still bidding against him.

Five sixty. Five seventy. He thinks he's going to win. I can see it in his face, a kind of tension at the corners of his mouth. I've got a lump in my throat that's so large I don't think I'll ever get it out.

And suddenly, Wickham stops shouting and everything goes quiet. I don't know what happened, and I look from Wickham to the boy and I see his mouth turn up into a smile so big I know he must have won. Yes, I'm sure of it. This boy has bought me. This white boy who don't even look as old as I am. He owns me body and soul, and my worth has been set at six hundred dollars.

CHAPTER 5

Gerald's got golden hair and I see it sparkle in the sun when he pushes his cap to the back of his head. It's clean and bright, cut short at the back and sides, though longer at the front where a wedge flicks across his forehead as the wagon rolls us on along the dirt track. It's just the two of us in the back of the wagon, settled down against the rolls of cloth that Mrs. Allen had us load before we left town.

Gerald's looking at me. I can feel it. But I ain't looking at him. No. My guts are made of rope, all twisted up and tight, so I'm looking anywhere else but at him and I ain't said a word since he bought me. Not to him, nor anyone else. I don't think my mouth works anyhow.

He reaches out a foot. He's wearing black leather shoes that are polished to a shine and he prods my shin with his toe. "You play baseball?"

Now, I don't know the rules of this. I don't know how I should be speaking to a boy that just paid six hundred dollars for my company. I don't know what I should be saying or what I should be thinking. All I know is, he should leave me alone. He ain't got the right to make me speak. It don't matter how much money he has—it don't make it right. So I don't say a word, I just stare at my toes, pretending I ain't heard him, though both of us know I heard him well enough.

Next time he pokes a little harder. "How old d'you think I am?"

I put a finger to my shin and shrug my shoulders. Just a little. Barely enough to be seen.

"Take a look and make a guess. Go on. You won't be right. Hardly anyone ever is, not if they're being honest." He leans over, puts a hand upon my knee, and shakes it like he's waking me up. "Hey, Friday! You're a shy one, aren't ya? Look at me. Come on, now. I ain't gonna bite."

"Gerald?" Mrs. Allen shouts back to him from the front of the wagon. "You leave that boy alone!"

I raise my eyes and Gerald's smile ain't unfriendly. I size him up and he's just a little pipsqueak of a boy to look at, a little older than Joshua but not as old as me.

"Fourteen?" I reckon on exaggerating so as not to cause offense.

Gerald looks disgusted with me. "Now, you ain't being honest." He shakes his head. "I wanted you to be honest and that's a ridiculous answer. We both know it. Try again and this time be honest 'cause you won't hurt my feelings, I can promise you that. You won't tell me nothing I ain't heard before."

"Nine." I guess again quickly.

That makes him happier. "See! I knew it!" He laughs out loud. "You don't have any idea, do you? Well, I'll tell you. I'm twelve. Same age as you, only I'm small for my age, that's what the doctor says. Won't be forever, though. He says I should be having a spurt come along any time now. I bet you already had yours, haven't ya?"

I don't know 'bout no spurts and I look at him, confused.

He tilts his head. "You are twelve, aren't you? That's what Mr. Wickham said. I remember it clearly."

"I suppose so."

"You suppose so?"

"I don't exactly know. Not for sure." I struggle for the right words, not knowing what I can or can't say. "Well, I expect it were different from yourself . . ."

A faint blush comes to his cheeks, then disappears. Did I just embarrass him? Maybe I did. He says, "I understand. Well, the thing is, you look twelve. That's what matters the most, and I'd say you look about that age."

"Yes, sir."

I don't know why I called him sir. I look away, taking a sudden interest in the landscape, which is greener now that we've left the town. We're passing fields that are dotted white with cotton buds, and sometimes there are lines of people, women and men, with sacks strung from their shoulders, their backs bent double and their heads close to the bushes. They must be slaves. I know they are—though there ain't no chains or manacles. I rub an idle finger around the top of my foot. I could jump over the side of this wagon if I wanted and I reckon they'd be hard pushed to catch me 'cause I was always the fastest runner at the orphanage.

Better not. Better to stay put a while and think things out.

Up in the front of the wagon, Mrs. Allen raises her voice and it catches my attention. "Why did you allow the men to leave early yesterday?" she demands. "I saw Connie and Isaac outside their cabin at seven thirty, and I couldn't find Levi for love nor money. He wasn't in the barn with the gin and he wasn't anywhere near the house."

Hubbard answers her with a calm and steady voice. "I sent Levi into town, miss."

"Well, you should have asked me before he went. I want Levi out in the fields. I want him working all the hours God gives us. We picked less yesterday than we have for the previous three days and yet I told you to keep everyone out in the fields till sunset. How is it possible they pick less cotton when they have more time? Can you tell me the logic of that?"

"I said they wouldn't like the change, miss. They're not used to working a gang. They're used to tasks. That's how Mr. Allen always ordered it. If I give 'em tasks, they do the work double-quick so they can have some time of their own, but if I take that away from 'em, then they ain't got no reason to work fast. Now we changed, they don't have no incentive."

Mrs. Allen curls her little hands into fists. "But they don't need no incentive! Good God, man, there's a war on! Ain't that incentive enough?"

"Yes, ma'am. You'd think it would be, but—"

"I don't want to hear no *if*s and *but*s, Hubbard. When people are taking liberties, it's your job to stop it."

"Yes, ma'am. I understand that. But if you want my advice, ma'am . . ."

Mrs. Allen shakes her head quickly and the sunlight makes it golden, just the same as it does for Gerald. "Now, you listen to me, Hubbard. You can advise me all you like, and I'm glad that you do, but the fact remains that the yield should be greater. It's simple mathematics, Hubbard. That's all it is. If you can't see it, then I will find a man who can and I'll answer to Mr. Allen for my decision. Do you understand me?"

"Yes, ma'am. I understand you perfectly."

"I want every person picking two hundred pounds of cotton tomorrow. I want it put through the gin and bundled."

"Yes, ma'am."

She rests her hands back in her lap. "I hold you responsible to do your own job, Hubbard, so please don't let me have to speak to you of this again."

Hubbard don't shift his eyes from the road and he don't raise his voice. "I hear you, Mrs. Allen," he says calmly. "Two hundred pounds, miss. I heard that, right enough.'

I turn back to see Gerald staring at me all over again. It makes me uncomfortable and I don't know where to look 'cause it feels like he's staring right through to my soul, and it ain't right. He takes a baseball from the pocket of his gray tunic and holds it up for me to see. "You look like a handy pitcher to me. You got good long arms. I bet you can pitch as fast as the best of 'em if you wanted."

This time, Mrs. Allen turns right around in her seat to scold him. "Will you leave that boy alone, Gerald! I've told you already! Don't you go getting ideas about him being your new plaything, because he ain't. He's here to work, same as all our Negroes. That's why I allowed you to buy him—just you remember that. It's about time you took on some responsibility around the place, and you can't do that if you're off playing with the slaves."

Gerald puts the ball back in his pocket, all indignant and surly. Now I'm the only one in the wagon she ain't turned on, and I won't

57

give her cause, not if I can help it. We cross a wooden bridge and it goes over a lazy ol' river, where the weeping willows dip down into the water. A half mile farther on, Hubbard turns the wagon onto a long dirt driveway, all lined with sapling trees, and the sight of the big white house makes my heart skip a beat.

That house is made of painted white boards with doors and shutters the color of ripened corn. It has a tall and striking roof, and although it's not grand, it's bigger than most of the houses in Middle Creek and set nicely in its own space. A red maple tree grows on the green lawn out in front, and that big ol' tree must give plenty of shade from the sun on a hot day.

This ain't what I expected. I thought I'd end up somewhere that looked like a prison, but this is, well . . . it's heavenly. It really is. I didn't ever think I'd live in a place as pretty as this one.

An old lady is out front, sweeping leaves from the veranda, and she lays aside her broom as the wagon approaches, then reappears at the back door just as Hubbard brings the wagon to a stop beside a little black buggy with a tall white mare standing upright in the harness.

Mrs. Allen is all vigor and push and she jumps down from the wagon without help. "Winnie?" She addresses the old woman. "Will you call out Harriet to occupy Gerald before he finds a bat and ball from somewhere? Take him into the house, will you? Sicely can unload the cloth. No, better let Hubbard do it. Would you do that, Hubbard? Deliver it to the parlor table and we can move it to the hallway once we have set up one of the rooms for sewing."

"Yes, ma'am," says Hubbard as he secures the horse.

Winnie says, "The preacher's here to see you, ma'am."

"Thank you, Winnie. I recognize his carriage. Have you prepared lunch for us?"

"It's all ready, ma'am. We were just waiting on you."

The old lady waits for us two boys to step down into the yard and she shepherds Gerald away into the house without another word. Hubbard walks across the yard to an outhouse and returns with a man in a leather apron. The man wipes his hands down the front of it, then helps Hubbard lift the cloth from the wagon and they walk it into the house, one of 'em at each end to carry the heavy load.

I'm still standing at the back of the wagon like a spare piece, not knowing where to go or what to do.

"Friday."

I hear the name, but I don't pay no heed to it.

Mrs. Allen shakes me by the shoulder. "I said, Friday? Come along with me, if you please."

She walks me to the cookhouse, which is situated next to the back door of the main building, and the smells that reach me through the open doorway are delicious. I can make out bread and some sort of broth and all of it makes my stomach churn like it's the Devil's own pot.

Inside the building, there's a large kitchen. A long table runs right down the middle of the room. Its top is laid with open pots and large brown jars and there are platters of food all ready and waiting to be eaten. A big plate of breaded ham has sliced pickled cucumbers that smile up at me from around its rim and there's a board with thick hunks of bread. A woman stands at a range and stirs a pot in the dim light, the steam rising up around her, all full of flavor and good things. Mrs. Allen calls out to her. "Hey, Sicely. This here's Friday. He's new from the auction. Have him help you with the lunch, will you?"

Sicely turns and looks me up and down like she don't approve of me one little bit. And I can see she ain't a woman either, not full-grown at least. She's only a year or two older than me. My stomach suddenly makes the noise of a train pulling up at a platform and I smile weakly, knowing everyone heard it. The girl makes a face like I'm some bullfrog brought in from a pond, but Mrs. Allen puts a kind hand on my shoulder. "When did you last eat?"

"I had a bit of bread for yesterday's breakfast, ma'am."

I swallow hard and her fingers squeeze my shoulder softly. "Good Lord! Give this boy some bread and soup, then have him help you serve at lunch. I'll get Winnie to come down." She walks back outside, calling for Winnie before she reaches the back door. "Winnie!" She's got a voice as loud as a man's when she shouts. "Winnie, where are you? I want you back down here!"

Sicely turns back to the pot, saying, "Get yourself some bread," as she ladles a hot spoonful of the soup into a bowl she has at hand. I reach out and take a hunk and I have it heading toward my mouth when she shrieks at me. "Not that bread! What you doing eating the bread laid out for lunch?"

I put it back from where I took it.

"Don't put it back! What you doing putting it back? Who's going to want a piece of bread that you already touched? You should have cut yourself a piece of your own from the loaf out back. Anyone would know that."

I pick up the bread again, not knowing if I should eat it or not, so I just keep ahold of it, all the while pretending it ain't even there in my hand. *Now* I see the loaf she meant. It's right there on the wide windowsill, sitting on its own board with a sharp knife lying next to it.

"This the new boy?" Winnie comes through the door at my back. She's got the kind of face it takes a whole lot of years to make, like the bark of an old oak tree. She's as wide as an oak at the waist as well. She views me with deep-set eyes that shine brightly between the creases of her skin. "Let the boy eat, Sicely, and hurry up about it." She lifts my hand till my lips touch the crust. Then she goes and gets that bowl of soup and puts it on the table in front of me.

Well, that food is just about the nicest thing I've had in a long time. I hurry through it, slurping down quick spoonfuls and wiping my bread around the bowl once it's gone.

Winnie clears up after me. She tells me to help with lunch and I follow Sicely into the house and through to the dining room, her carrying the platter of ham, and myself with a tureen of soup so big it makes me nervous to carry it in case I trip and drop it, only I don't trip. I get it safely onto the middle of the table in one piece. Sicely scolds me anyway. "It don't go there. If you'd come from a decent house, you'd know that I serve it from the side and bring the plates to table."

She sure can be severe. I pick up the tureen and take it over to where she points, and when I've set it down again, she says, "No point in sending you back for the bread and butter 'cause you'll probably come back with eggs and jam. You better stay right where you are while I go back for it."

So I do. I stand in the big room on my own, my hands folded behind my back for somewhere to put 'em, my bare feet flat upon the polished floorboards. The room is pretty, with pale blue walls and lots of light from the four tall windows that look out across the lawn at the front. It's more homely than grand, I suppose. There are pictures on the walls and shelves full of knickknacks. I notice little statues of animals. They got a glazed china horse and a rabbit sitting up on its hind legs, its ears bent forward, pretending to listen. At the orphanage, we didn't have no clutter.

The table here is long enough for eight places, each of 'em laid with a full set of cutlery and a tall cane-back chair standing behind. Above the table hangs a large wooden fan. The room is divided into two by a closed set of sliding doors and there are voices from the other side, the preacher with Mrs. Allen, and I can't help hearing what they say.

"Unlike some of our community, Mrs. Allen, I am of the opinion that our Negroes should be delivered the word of God, particularly now that we are at war. The Yankees will have filled their heads with ideas of freedom, you can be sure of that, so we should be making sure they understand the dignity bestowed by the Lord on those that serve."

"Yes, indeed," replies Mrs. Allen.

"Did I tell you that the number of slaves running away has doubled since the war began? There isn't a day goes by that our patrols don't find some runaway darkie skulking in a barn, trying to make his way north of the lines. I have found 'em myself, and I can tell you, there won't be jails that are large enough, Mrs. Allen, you mark my words."

Outside the window, the leaves of that maple ripple like a wave, all restless in the breeze.

"I can assure you they won't be my slaves," Mrs. Allen exclaims. "As you will know, my husband has always run this plantation upon progressive ideas. We treat 'em with a firm hand and a fair measure of respect, so they've got no reason to run away. And yet it's true that with Mr. Allen gone, they have had little instruction in the Bible of late. I suppose I could make a point of reading to 'em. Do you think that might help? We could set aside time after the evening meal. What do you think, Mr. Chepstow? Does that strike you as a good idea?"

The footsteps of the preacher pace just the other side of the partition door. "Well, that's right and proper, Mrs. Allen, but the word of God can only be delivered of its true force through a direct link, a preacher like myself, whom He has entrusted with His wisdom and knowledge. Take, for example, the choosing of texts . . ."

Sicely enters the dining room again, this time carrying a platter of sliced bread and a porcelain butter dish. "What you doing, standing there listening?" she hisses like a snake. She puts down the bread and butter and moves toward the double doors, pushing me to one side as she knocks and then slides 'em open. "S'cuse me, ma'am, but lunch is ready."

When they come on through to the table, I see Gerald is there with 'em. He's changed into a clean shirt, and his black leather shoes squeak when he walks. He looks bored as he takes a seat beside his stepmother, who places her hand upon his, seeming to indicate that he should remain silent until she has finished what she is saying.

"Of course, you are absolutely right, Mr. Chepstow. Abolition would be a disaster. If they were left to fend for themselves, they would die of starvation. I'm sure of it. The best place for them is here, working beside us in our homes and in our fields as God intended, the two races working together for the good of both." She lifts a forkful of ham to her mouth, but leaves it poised. "They must surely understand that the Yankees will not win this war. They cannot. God will not allow it. And the Negroes must be made to see it is in their own interests to work hard alongside us and hope for a swift conclusion."

Sicely meets my eye and looks down at her feet, meaning for me to come and stand beside her, which I do. She leans across and whispers in my ear, "You oughta be fanning."

I don't know what she means. I think I must be standing wrong and I move my feet apart so my toes point outward. Sicely leans across and unties a rope from where it is fastened to the wall, and I look up and see that the rope goes through a pulley and over to a big old wooden fan that hangs above the table. She puts the rope in my hand. "Pull it," she tells me quietly, and then she stands on my toe for good measure, though it could have been an accident. I tug the rope, not too hard, and that big wooden fan begins to swing in its metal frame above the table.

Mr. Chepstow has a finger to his preacher's collar as he leans closer to Mrs. Allen. They're still talking 'bout the war as Master Gerald helps himself to ham. He takes a slice of the cucumber and a piece of the bread. Across from him, the preacher half turns in his chair and flicks a finger at Sicely. "Would you find me some mustard?"

Sicely goes to fetch it, leaving me alone by the wall, still pulling on that rope to make a breeze.

Mr. Chepstow continues where he left off. "You are so right, Mrs. Allen, so right indeed. And that is why a regular prayer meeting is the only thing to do. These Negroes must know whom God favors in this war, and to that end I have made it my mission to go to the plantations hereabout and preach the good word to 'em all. I would like to come here too if you would be so kind as to allow it."

I watch as Gerald cuts a square of the juicy ham and sneaks it from his fork to his fingers, holding it under the table so only I can see it. I don't know why he's doing that. He looks again at Mrs. Allen and the preacher, making sure they haven't noticed, before tossing the ham onto the floor at my feet.

I try to ignore it but I can't. I keep pulling that rope, behaving as though there's nothing there, but there is. That ham's right there at my toes, all glistening and pink.

I start to sweat. I begin to pull the rope a little faster and when Mrs. Allen claps her hands in excitement, I nearly jump out of my skin. "Oh, yes! Then we shall do it," she says loudly. "Of course we shall! A meeting to be held here on the second Sunday of each month, to hear the word of God spoken clearly in these troubled times. We shall all attend, Mr. Chepstow. We shall pray for deliverance through hard work and for the victory that our men deserve!"

She's got her back to me, same as Gerald has, but that preacher has a view straight across the table to my feet, and if he weren't so concentrated on Mrs. Allen's speech, he'd be sure to notice that piece of ham right in front of me, so I kneel quickly, pick the ham up off the floor and pop it in my mouth. I daren't swallow it, though, and the ham seems to expand in size, getting trapped between the back of my tongue and the roof of my mouth.

Sicely comes back into the room. She takes the mustard to the preacher, puts it down in front of him, and comes to stand beside me while we wait for them to finish their lunch. They're still planning and talking about the state of the world as I chew slowly, but I manage to swallow without being seen, and when they stand to leave the room, Gerald looks to see if the meat is still on the floor, and he smiles when he sees it gone.

Once the sliding doors shut, Sicely tugs at my earlobe. "Don't just stand there. Help me get these plates downstairs. And don't go pinching any of that ham either, 'cause I know how much there is of it left."

She gives me a look like I'm the Devil himself.

Now, I don't know much about girls—I haven't had the opportunity of finding out. But I sure hope they ain't all like Sicely.

CHAPTER 6

Once the meal is over and the preacher has left, I'm stood outside the cookhouse, looking like a little lost boy. Mrs. Allen thinks for a moment, putting a hand to her forehead. "Have him go in with Lizzie, will you, Winnie? It'll help make up for her loss. And have Nancy put the kettle on too. I'll take tea upstairs. If Harriet is in the kitchen, have her bring Virginia to me in the nursery. Would you do that?"

"I'll deal with the boy first," says Winnie, and she leads me out across the yard. She's got one of those walks where she don't hardly seem to move her legs and yet she scoots along pretty quickly for an old lady. I can tell she knows what's what around here and I got a whole lot of questions as I chase after her skirts. "Where we going, Winnie? And who's Lizzie? Won't I be sleeping in the big house with everyone else?"

Winnie comes to a stop and she's got puzzled eyes. "You're one strange child. Don't you know anything? And where'd you learn to speak that way? That ain't Tennessee drawl, least as far as I can tell."

I nearly tell her I ain't from Tennessee, but I don't. I've been thinking I'll trust in Hubbard, tell him Mrs. Allen has got it all wrong, tell him I'm a free black and I shouldn't ever have been sold at auction. Hubbard strikes me as someone I can trust. I reckon he'll be the one to advise me how best to leave.

Winnie walks on. "Well, wherever you come from, don't go getting ideas you're something special, 'cause you're not. You be starting at the bottom, same as the rest of us, and there ain't no way up from there, so you better get used to it if you ain't already."

On each side of the path where we walk, there are rolling lawns of green turf. A line of tall trees shelters the back of the house from the weather, and as we pass them, a view opens out onto the cotton fields that lie out back of the estate. But before the fields, only a couple of hundred yards from us, I see a large fenced-off area where the green turf is all scuffed out to mud. Two rows of wooden cabins stand opposite each other with a fire pit between 'em in the middle of that mud. They're the only thing in the whole place that ain't nice to look at and Winnie nods in their direction. "Lizzie's place is the second one along, over on the left there. You go on and wait for her. She won't be so long."

I must be stupid to have thought I was ever going to live up in the pretty house.

I go on toward the huts. There's no one about that I can see, save a couple of children skipping with a rope, but they catch my eye—I don't know why. There's something 'bout the way one of 'em moves, a little boy who has his back to me. When he jumps over the rope, he leaves a foot dangling, lifts it just high enough to clear the rope by an inch or two. Joshua used to do that. I squint into the sun, suddenly excited, and put a hand over my eyes. Could it actually be Joshua? Could he already be here, playing over by the tree?

I race toward the tree, shouting, "Joshua, Joshua!" and those boys stop playing and they turn to watch me come, but even before I reach 'em, I know I have made a mistake and it ain't Joshua at all.

I arrive all out of breath and panting. "Is this one Lizzie's place?" I point over at a cabin.

"Next one along," says the boy I mistook for Joshua, and he looks at me strange, a mix of wariness and wanting to please. "She ain't there, though. She's still in the field." He sizes me up just like my brother would.

"What's your name?" I ask him.

"Gil."

"You skip pretty good, Gil. You ever get caught by the rope?"

He shakes his head. "Never."

"No, I didn't reckon you did."

I wander across to the cabins, which are lifted up on brick blocks to keep 'em from the mud. Two wooden steps lead up to each door, and every cabin has a mud-brick chimney that leans away from the outer wall and is propped at the top by two tall poles. They look all old and broken, those chimneys, like they could collapse from only a little gust of wind. These cabins ain't much to look at and they're probably worse to live in than they look, all drafty and cold, I'll bet.

Two cabins stand out from the crowd. The first only because it's a few feet longer than the others and has a porch. I don't know why that is. But the second is the one I'm looking for. Lizzie's cabin has a little vegetable garden out back that she's made look nice. I can tell she cares for it from the way she's pushed all those sticks into the earth to make the fence. I practice my smile before I knock on her door. No one answers, but I suppose they warned me.

A dirt track leads down toward the woods on the eastern side of the plantation, so I decide to take a look around and see how far I can go. I carry right on into the woods and out the other side, where the land is just scrub. I know I must have left the plantation grounds by now, but I ain't heard a by-your-leave from anyone and so I make for the river and follow it along the nearest bank where the last of the cotton fields comes right down to its edge. The only folk I see are a single line of cotton pickers way off in a field, and it seems to me I could walk out of here whenever I want.

I'm passing a cornfield on the way back to the cabins when I see Hubbard walking up ahead of me, his green shirt tucked in tidy at the back of his trousers and a whip pointing up from the line of his belt. If I'm quick, I can get to talk to him alone and I run to catch up with him, my quick feet making no more sound than a rabbit in full flight. When I get close, I call out his name. "Mr. Hubbard! Say, Mr. Hubbard!"

The big man turns and sees me. He waits for me to reach him. "What do you need, Friday? You found Lizzie yet? I heard Mrs. Allen's put you in with her."

I shake my head. "I ain't seen her yet, Mr. Hubbard, but I'm going there directly."

Hubbard nods. "That's good. The day's almost done. She'll be back soon. You go wait for her there and tell her that the mistress has said you're to come in with her."

"I will, sir. I'll do that. Only there was something else, Mr. Hubbard. Something I wanted to say to you. You see, sir, I think you should know . . ." I stumble on my words, too anxious to get 'em out quickly. "My name ain't Friday," I tell him. "My name is Samuel, sir, and I was taken from my home in the orphanage and sold at the auction by a man named Gloucester. He's a rogue trader, sir. I'm certain of it. He never had the right to sell me and he forged my papers, but the thing is this, you see, sir, I have a brother by the name of Joshua and he's only very little." I take a quick breath, not wanting to stop till I've told him everything. "I've got to look after him 'cause he's got no one else to do it. Do you see, Mr. Hubbard? What I'm saying is that there's only him and me. There ain't no one else can help him."

The big man has been listening closely, I can tell. He has bowed his head, his eyes staring to the edge of the field as he concentrates on what I'm telling him. He puts a calm hand on my shoulder. "Who've you told 'bout this?"

I take a deep breath. "Only you."

He bends closer, so we're face-to-face. "You ever been whipped, Friday?"

"No, sir, I never have."

He slaps my face hard enough that I go spinning to the ground, then he takes the whip from his belt and the end of it falls to the ground as he stands over me. "I ain't never been whipped either," he tells me grimly. "Never once. And that's the way it's gonna stay, Friday."

I ain't cried for a long time, but a tear escapes me now. "Don't you believe me?" I plead with his boots. "I thought you'd believe me!"

"Don't matter if I believe you or I don't. It won't change a thing for either of us. Do you understand that? I advised Mrs. Allen to buy you, even though you was off the catalogue and had no references. Now if you tell her you ain't no slave, do you know what will happen?"

I made a mistake telling Hubbard and nothing I can say will put it right. I want to hurt him. I want to get up and punch him.

He flicks the edge of his boot into my face so it cuffs the side of my eye. "Well, do you?"

"What'll happen?" I spit out.

"She'll ask me to whip you till you stop telling lies and then she'll most likely have me whipped as well. Do you understand me? It'll hurt the both of us and it won't change a thing, though like I said, I ain't never been lashed. I'm just taking other people's word for it." He leans right over me. "Around here, it's me that does the whipping when it's needed."

And then he offers me his hand to help me back on my feet.

Well, I refuse to take it. I get up on my own two feet, my eyes all narrow with staring so hard at him, trying to see the man I thought he was. He still looks proud, but there ain't no kindness there like I had assumed. No kindness and no sense of justice. That much is obvious, and I tell him so. "I ain't never been so disappointed in a man before!"

He might flinch at that, I can't be sure, but I flinch myself when he flicks out the whip, coils it up, and stores it back in his belt.

"That's something we'll both have to live with, Friday. Now get yourself over to Lizzie's cabin. I want you out in the fields when the horn sounds first thing tomorrow morning."

I don't want to be near this man a moment longer than I have to, and I walk away with the mark of his big hand on my cheek, still sore to the touch and burning.

When I get back to the cabins, there are more people around than there were before. A bunch of kids are skipping over at the tree, all talking at once like little birds. A woman squats on her doorstep, scrubbing something in a pail of water, and three young men have brought wooden chairs outside their cabin door and are sitting smoking. They watch me pass the fire pit and stop at Lizzie's cabin.

To my surprise, it's Sicely who opens when I knock, and she leans on the doorframe, blocking my view inside. "What do *you* want?"

A voice calls out from behind her back. "Who's that, Sicely? What they want?"

"It's the new boy, Mama," Sicely shouts back inside. "The one the missus brought back 'stead of Milly."

A hand grasps the door above Sicely's head. "Come on, now, Sicely. Open it up and let me see."

Sicely slides back inside the cabin and a woman appears at the door in her place. She's about the same age as my mama would have been. She's got a similar line in her nose and cheeks as well—at least as far as I remember. Her head is bound up in old rags and she has a shawl across her shoulders that looks like it's seen more years in this world than she has.

"Are you Lizzie?" I ask. "Mrs. Allen said I was to stay with you."

The woman stands there looking at me. It's like she ain't seeing me at all, like she's seeing someone else entirely. Behind her back, I see Sicely move across to the fire and she kneels, blowing a tiny flame that lights her face. The young boy I saw at the tree squeezes out from behind Lizzie's skirt to take a look at me, but Lizzie puts a finger to his head. "Go on back inside, Gil." She folds her arms when she speaks to me. "You come from the auction?" I nod. "Then you musta seen my Milly."

"I don't know, ma'am. I didn't talk to no one there. I don't know who anyone is." I'm awkward, standing here on the step without being invited inside, but I want to make an effort to please this woman if I can. "What did she look like?"

Lizzie's lip twitches. "Oh, Milly's pretty. You'd remember her if you saw her."

"Oh, yes! You mean the pretty girl? I do remember. Yes, I do. The girl with the blue bow at the front of her dress?"

"That's her!" Lizzie's face lights up. "She had her best dress on, the one I made for her last birthday. Did you see her sold? Do you know who bought her and where she went?"

"I saw the man who bought her. Yes, I did. He was wearing a green jacket as I remember."

"He was? And where'd he take her? Did they say where he was from?"

"I don't know." Lizzie's eyes drop like a stone in water and I know I haven't helped at all. "Won't Mrs. Allen be able to tell you?"

Lizzie looks like I made her eat a gooseberry and she don't answer, just stands at the door, staring at her feet, but I still try to make it better. "She sure is beautiful, just like you said. And she got a good high price. Two thousand dollars, I think it was. She was worth more than anyone else there. I know she was. So that man must have thought she was special. He must've wanted her real bad to pay—"

Lizzie slaps my face.

I stagger back from the cabin, but this time I stay standing 'cause her arm don't possess the power of Hubbard's. Now I've had about as much as I can take of people slapping me. I don't know who they think they are, these no-good slaves, slapping around a boy who's done no harm to no one, who always says his prayers and tries to do right by the Lord. I take a step toward her, pulling myself up as tall as I can get, but then Sicely bursts out through the door, brushing her mother aside in her rush to get at me. She pushes me in the chest, making me stagger backward with little flicks of her hands at my face. "Don't you dare hit my mother!"

I run away. I just get out of there, like a scared, angry rabbit, and I don't see a thing 'cept the dirt beneath my feet as I run back toward the fields and the river.

I run pretty fast. I've got my arms bent and pumping like a steam engine. I got nothing on my mind but moving forward 'cause I'm going home and there's no one gonna stop me. I'm going back to find my brother and I don't care if the Lord don't like it or if Hubbard whips me. If they don't agree, they can burn in the Devil's fire for all I care, because I have had just about enough of this place and I'm going home. I'm going back to Middle Creek.

"Hey, boy! You got a pass?"

I don't see the person who calls to me from beneath the weeping willow on the riverbank—but I stop running. I clutch my stomach and I'm taking in big gulps of air as I watch the tree. A man walks out from under the branches. He ain't old but he ain't young either. He wears woolseys, though, and I'm relieved to see that.

"What's it to you?" I make as though I'm gonna walk on.

"Oh, it ain't nothing to me, but it's a question the men up yonder'll ask if they see you. They out on patrol, you see. They looking for strays who don't have passes."

"I ain't afraid of 'em."

"No? That's right, boy. You shouldn't be afraid of no one. But they got dogs. That's the thing. They got dogs that'll sniff out a black man from the thickest of bushes. Not that there are no bushes. I been a long way up this river and there's only these here willows to weep under. I can assure you of that."

He comes closer. I'd reckon he's about thirty. He's got honey-toned skin, lighter than my own, and his short curls are looser and flecked with hints of red. He's wearing a porkpie hat with a rabbit's foot stuck in the brown band around its edge, and his nose is spread out so wide it's almost flat across his left cheek, like someone has taken a real dislike to it being straight. It makes him sort of snort when he breathes. "Where you from anyways?" he asks me. "You been sneaking into the Allen place?"

I take offense at that. "I ain't sneaking anywhere. I'm going home." I hesitate, not knowing whether I still have a home or not. "Well, leastways I'm going back to Middle Creek. Do you know where that is?"

The man shakes his head, wide-eyed. "I can't say I've heard of it. Don't you know where it is?" I shake my head. "Well, that's a problem." He pauses and takes a deep breath through his mouth. He's wearing shoes that are busted up around the edges and tied to his feet with string, though I suppose they're a step up from my own bare feet. A dog barks from somewhere up ahead and the man twitches. "I got to go." He looks behind him quickly. "If you ain't got a pass, I suggest you come with me."

He walks away along the riverbank and I let him go. I don't want to go with him. But then that dog barks again, so I catch up with him and follow in silence. After a little while, I start to notice the countryside around me, the fish jumping up for flies, the cattle feeding on the far bank. Somewhere on the air, there's a humming-bird, but I couldn't say where it was 'cause I'm too busy asking myself what I'll do when darkness falls, whether I'll keep on walking or find a place to sleep.

"So have you got a pass?" I ask him.

"Why'd you ask?"

"Just wondering. How'd you get 'em?"

"Hubbard's got a few he gives out."

"Oh."

"But you gotta have a good reason. He won't give you one just 'cause you fancy it. He's got a wife and child on another plantation, so of course he gets one for himself before anyone else." He looks over his shoulder again, just to make sure we ain't being followed. "I don't have one, since you asked, so if you don't mind quickening your step, seeing as how you've held me up and all."

We pick up our pace and the soles of his shoes flap against his feet as we trot ahead. The man offers me his hand. "The name's Connie."

I shake on it. "They call me Friday."

That makes him laugh at me. "It ain't every day of the week I meet someone with that name."

"That ain't funny."

"No, I guess not. Guess you heard 'em all before."

We turn away from the river and start back beside the cotton fields and I stay with him, thinking it'd be better for me to go back to the cabins till I can find a good way to leave.

"You're new here, ain't you? Did Mrs. Allen buy you at this morning's auction?"

"She did."

"So how come you're running off as soon as you got here? This ain't such a bad place to be."

"Yes, it is."

He raises his eyebrows about as high as they will go. "I don't know where you come from, boy, but I reckon this is about as good as it gets around here. I been worse places, I can tell you. I been to a lot worse. What was your last place like?"

"I ain't going in with Lizzie," I tell him quickly. "Hubbard can whip me all he likes, but I ain't going in with her."

Connie takes another deep breath. He lifts his hat up, then puts it back on his head, exactly as it was. "Lizzie ain't so bad. You'll see she's all right once you meet her."

"She slapped my face."

"OK. So you already met. What did you do to make her slap you?"

"I didn't do anything 'cept try to be nice."

"Well, Lizzie don't suffer fools. Was it something you said?"

It ain't often that I'm likened to a fool and I don't appreciate it. "She asked me 'bout Milly. She wanted to know who had bought her and I said how she fetched a higher price than anyone else at the auction, and then she just went and slapped me."

"And you don't know why?"

"I meant it as a compliment."

Connie shakes his head like I'm some fool. In the setting sunlight, I can clearly see the red in his hair. "No mother wants to have a beautiful daughter. Not when you're a slave."

But I still don't understand. Connie thinks about the best way to explain. "Have you met Harriet? Harriet's the nursemaid to Mrs. Allen's baby. When you see her, take a good look, 'cause Harriet's black as coal, same as her husband, Levi. They're both Africa black. I mean they're real dark. Well, now, Harriet's got a baby of her own by the name of Richard. He's coming up two years old and I believe it was Mr. Allen himself who named him. But baby Richard, you see, he ain't black. Not Africa black. Do you hear what I'm saying? Baby Richard ain't the color of coal." Connie tuts when he shakes his head. "I reckon Mrs. Allen's getting rid of any more temptation before the master gets back from the war. That's what I think. And if Milly fetched a good price, it weren't 'cause she's good in the cookhouse."

I'm shocked at what Connie says. Just hearing it makes my ears burn. And it makes me think about the boys back at the orphanage, how some of us were darker than others, and I remember Joshua lying naked in the sun one Saturday morning, hoping to make himself the same shade of black as me. I hadn't seen my daddy for four years before Joshua was born, but I hadn't ever thought of it that way. It makes me ashamed to be so stupid.

"Lizzie's a good woman," Connie tells me when we're in sight of the cabins. "She'll look after you. But she just lost her daughter and she don't know if she'll ever set eyes on her again, so you've got to meet her more than halfway."

Once I'm there, I stand a little while before her door. Ain't no point knocking if I don't apologize. I say a little prayer, asking for the strength to be better than I am. I reckon she'll be sorry for slapping me if I make the first move.

So I'm glad when Lizzie opens the door herself. "I'm sorry 'bout earlier. I didn't mean to be rude about Milly. And I'm sorry for your loss. I truly am."

Lizzie stands aside and lets her door swing wide and I step past her into the cabin.

It's a small room, with bare wooden floors and a single window in the wall opposite the fire. Sicely and Gil are sitting at a low table with bowls of food in front of 'em and they're watching me closely. Lizzie follows me in and closes the door. She takes a grease lamp from the shelf above the fire and lights the wick. "You can sleep there in the corner. Use Milly's mattress. It's over by the wall. See? Now come and get some food."

"Thank you, but I ain't hungry."

I take the mattress and lay it out on the bare floor. All I want is to be still and quiet and I curl up with my face to the wall. In the darkness, they won't see me cry and I try not to, I try to keep it all inside, but my eyes won't obey me and my nose runs away from me like a river.

I pray for Joshua. I don't want to—after all, this is all his fault—but I do, and I try to think of all the good things I've done since

Gloucester took me from the privy. There ain't much to be proud of—all I can remember is murderous thoughts and cursing every little thing I could think of.

But I forgive Lizzie for slapping me.

I'm glad to do that.

It's something good I get to add to my account.

CHAPTER 7

I wake to the sound of a horn.

Up at the window, the light that creeps past the rag of a curtain is dawn light, all blue and somber. On the floor beside me, Gil turns on his mattress, moaning softly, struggling to wake. I roll over. Lizzie's already up. She puts a jar of molasses onto the table, then kneels, rattles the grate, and pats ashcakes onto the hearth, nice and close to the embers, where she prods and scrapes at 'em with a wooden spatula.

Joshua will be waking up about now. He'll be putting on his clothes and making his way to the washroom with the other boys, all under Sister Miriam's stern eye. I wonder if he feels the same way I do—kinda empty and small.

Lizzie's got a stern eye of her own and she casts it over the mattresses on the floor. Sicely stands up, wiping the sleep from her eyes. She stashes her mattress against the cabin wall, then takes a cup and fills it from the bucket of water on the floor.

"Come and get it," Lizzie says to none of us in particular.

From outside our door, the horn calls us again.

I've been sleeping in my clothes 'cause I didn't want to get undressed with everyone looking. I get to my feet and put my mattress away, the same as Sicely did. Over at the bucket, I take a drink of water as she watches me crossly. "By rights I oughta be sleeping in the big house," she tells me, though I didn't ask her nothing. "That's where I'm living now, but I asked Mrs. Allen if I can sleep here so as to be a help to my mother now that Milly's gone. Winnie's still got Mary to help at the house if things need doing in the night, so the missus said she don't mind."

I don't know who Mary is. I didn't see her yesterday.

"Hush now, Sicely," Lizzie tells her bluntly. "Give the boy some peace first thing in the morning."

Sicely takes an ashcake from the hearth and goes out the door without saying good-bye.

"Get up, Gil," Lizzie says, then raises her voice. "Get up before I come over there and get you up myself."

I feel awkward sitting at the table, not knowing what to do.

"Take a cake," Lizzie tells me, and I do. It's warm in my fingers. "Now go on out to the fire pit and wait with the others." She points me to the door.

There are men waiting in front of the cabins, shadowy figures standing out against the half-light dawn, their faces outlined by the small glow from the rekindled fire. Some of 'em hold steaming cups. I recognize Connie and he nods to me, so I go and stand with him. He's with two other men, Antoinne and Isaac. He says all of 'em share a cabin.

The fella called Antoinne puts a hand around my shoulder. "Hey, Connie, this the boy you told me 'bout? You shoulda let him run away. There ain't nothing for him here." He winks at me. "Did you want to join up, boy? Is that what it is? Do you want to fight the good fight for freedom?"

Connie shoves Antoinne away from me. "Don't put fool ideas in the boy's head." He puts his own arm around my shoulder. "Don't listen to him, Friday. Everyone knows that the clever man is staying put right now. He's waiting for freedom to come to him. You know what I'm saying?"

I shake my head 'cause I don't know what he's talking about, and he leans in closer and lowers his voice. "I'm saying that the Yankees are sailing up the big ol' river as we speak, and it won't be long now before those soldiers are here."

"How do you know?"

"I go to market. I talk to people." He taps the side of his nose. "There ain't no reason to go nowhere right now. Do you hear me? You stay right here and things'll work out just fine."

"But I don't have a choice."

"Everyone's got a choice, and I'm telling you that you won't get away. You'll just run into a whole load of trouble and you won't be no good to anyone after that."

I think about that for a moment. I can't bear the thought of Joshua being on his own, but like Connie says, I ain't no good to him dead.

"How many boats they got coming?"

Connie wipes a hand across his face to clear his nose. "Oh, they got lots of boats. Big ones, little ones. They got 'em full of guns and full of men and they're coming up the river. Just you wait and see."

I don't know what to do or who to trust, and that makes the world feel heavy on my shoulders. "Connie, will you tell me when it's time to go?"

"Sure," he says. "I'll tell you."

"You won't forget, will you?"

He swigs the last of his coffee. "I doubt it. It's not like I've got anything better to think about."

We move off as a group, heading toward the shimmering fields that stretch away to our left, all lit up by the first rays of the sun. Ahead of me, there's nothing but cotton, and I tap Connie's arm and nod at the fields. "It looks pretty, don't you think? Looks like the world's all full of rabbits."

But Connie shakes his head. "I don't see nothing but another day of work."

Soon as he says that, I can't see the rabbits either.

We ain't the first to arrive in the field but we ain't the last. I reckon there's about twenty of us in total. Connie takes me over to where Hubbard sits on a piebald mare, waiting for us to begin. There's a wagon beside him with three empty baskets and they're 'bout as tall as I am and twice as wide.

"You want the boy to work with me?" asks Connie.

Hubbard looks us over. "He might as well. Show him how he should weed the ground as well as pick the cotton. Mrs. Allen says she's gonna mix his duties. She wants him here in the mornings and helping around the house in the afternoons, so be sure to send him along there for lunch."

Connie says he'll show me what to do. He leads me back to the line that has formed at the edge of the field, where everyone has a white cotton sack slung over their shoulders and hanging down their backs. Connie finds one of 'em for me. "You ever done this before?" I shake my head. "Well, don't worry. It ain't difficult."

At the first row of bushes, he holds up a rabbit's tail. "See this here? It's called the boll." His fingers pinch at the fluffy white ball and he puts it in my hand so I can get a feel for the thing. "You see what's left behind when I pick it? That's called the burr and you got to leave that where it is. You start picking the both of 'em together and Hubbard'll be picking on you."

Connie's fingers are already working like a busy spider, picking the bolls and holding 'em in his palm till he's got a fistful that he throws over his shoulder into the sack. "Go on now. Give it a go yourself." I start to pick at the cotton and Connie nods in encouragement. "That's right. That's good. Now try to speed up a little. You gotta keep up with the line."

There sure seems a lot to do, 'cause the field is fit to bursting with bushes. They're planted so close together that if you're not careful, the one behind will scratch the skin from your back when you bend down low to pick the one in front. I move with the line across the field and can barely keep up. It ain't long before my back aches, but I get to do some talking while I work and that makes it easier. I learn that Antoinne, Connie, and Isaac are the men Mr. Allen hired in from another plantation owner before he left for the war. They're young and fit and they tell me they can pick twice as much as the rest of us put together. Only they don't. They just talk about it. I reckon they pick about the same as everyone else, and no one picks more than a boy called George. He's about a year older than me and this is his first harvest. He's so desperate to prove himself that he works like some sort of lunatic and the men keep telling him, "Slow down, son, slow down," only he don't, not until his dad, Albert, clips his ear and tells him how he's making everyone else look bad, and that if Hubbard ain't telling him to work harder, then he shouldn't be doing it of his own accord. "That's the way to an early grave, son." That's what Albert says. "There's plenty more years for picking. You don't want to use yourself up before your time, boy."

I ain't got the problem of going too fast. Connie tells me to go the whole way down the bush, leaving the ones that are still closed. If I do it properly, I can just keep up, so sometimes I skimp on it, always looking to make sure Hubbard ain't close enough to see what I'm doing. When my bag's full, I drag it back to the edge of the field and tip the cotton into the tall wicker baskets right next to Hubbard. He sits on his horse with his whip in his belt, watching us work and making sure it all runs smoothly.

The early shift goes quickly, but once those first baskets are full, we lose Henry, Levi, and Antoinne. They go with Hubbard to the barn to put the cotton through the gin. That next shift feels a lot slower without 'em, and I swear those new baskets are bigger than the ones before.

I work next to Lizzie for a little while. She don't say nothing to me 'cept when I prick my finger on a bush. Then she stops me from picking the bolls, tells me to put my finger in my mouth and suck it till the blood stops. "If Hubbard finds blood on the cotton," she tells me, "there'll be hell to pay." I can't decide whether she's helping me or scolding me and I still ain't sure she's forgiven me like I have her.

When we break for lunch, I get sent off to the house and I get to eat.

I leave the field hungry and arrive at the kitchen even hungrier and yet all I get is a single bowl of soup. That's all. And Winnie won't let me eat it till I've cleared the table upstairs and laid it out ready for their lunch. It don't matter that I tell her I've been working in the field and that I'm ready to drop if I don't get some food in me. She just looks at me with those deep-set eyes, like she heard it all before.

—

Days go by where I don't do nothing but work and sleep. There ain't much time here to call my own, 'cept after sundown. Most evenings I sit out by the fire or go and call on Connie for the hour I get to myself before sleep. They don't seem to mind, and it means I don't have to sit with Lizzie's unhappiness and the hostility I get from Sicely.

I thought she might improve with time, but a week after my arrival, the two of us are in the dining room preparing lunch and she tuts when she sees how I laid out the table, then makes a point of showing me what I did wrong.

Mrs. Allen comes into the room. She asks me to fetch Gerald from the nursery and I take to the staircase, my bare feet padding up the carpet runner till I reach the top and follow the cries of baby Virginia along the landing. At the nursery door, I knock and go in. Gerald is standing by the window with a book in his hand, staring out across the front lawn.

"Excuse me, Master Gerald, but Mrs. Allen has asked for you to come for lunch."

From the corner of my eye, I see the bare breast of Harriet as she feeds Mrs. Allen's baby and it makes me all confused, and my heart jumps into my mouth at the sight of Harriet naked and I know that I couldn't speak, not if someone were to ask me something. Harriet sure is black, just like Connie said. She's holding baby Virginia in her arms, already moving her into position to suckle at the breast and adjusting the cloth that covers her modesty, though not from me, 'cause I see her big black nipple as she brings the screaming child to her chest and I hear the baby stop its noise and drink her in, all greedy, its small, fair cheek pressed up against the mound of Harriet's blackness.

"Come on," says Gerald, tugging at the sleeve of my shirt.

I follow him from the room, swallowing hard and closing the door behind us. He waits for me to walk beside him. "That's my little sister with Harriet. She ain't much fun to have around. She's too small. I was hoping for a brother instead of a sister. You got a brother back where you come from?"

I shake my head.

"That's too bad." We reach the foot of the stairs, and the double doors of the dining room are right ahead of us. "Perhaps we'll have ham again today," he says, and smiles at me before we go inside.

He takes a seat at the long table while I stand to the side with Sicely, hoping no one looks at me closely, 'cause I'm burning up. I never felt so ashamed—denying my own brother like that. Surely everyone'll see it on my face and know me for the coward that I am, but I pull on the rope to fan the room, and when I look around, no one seems to have noticed.

On the table, there is soup and bread and a big piece of cheese, but no ham, and I thank the Lord for small mercies. Gerald helps himself to the food. "Mother, can I take Friday with me to the woods after lunch? I want to finish the logs and bring 'em up to the barn."

Mrs. Allen shakes her head. "I know you," she tells him. "You want someone to play with, same as always. You got to learn to grow up, Gerald. You got to put away childish things, like I've been telling you."

"But I am, Mother. Those logs need doing sometime soon and it'd be good for me to learn how to manage my own slaves. Don't you agree?"

Mrs. Allen thinks for a second. "I suppose I don't mind so long as you get the work done."

So after I've cleared away the lunch, Gerald arrives at the cookhouse and takes me to a clearing in the woods, where there are tree trunks cut into lengths and sawn up ready for splitting.

I take an axe from the barrow full of tools. "Tell me what you want me to do."

He sits himself down on the stump of a tree. "That's the beauty of it. We don't have to do a thing. I just said it so we could come out here, but we can do whatever we want." Gerald flicks his eyes to the woods behind me. "We could go and check the traps. There's rabbits and all sorts in there. George and me once caught a pig."

"What would Mrs. Allen say when there weren't no logs?" I mumble.

"She won't say nothing 'cause she won't look."

"I think she will. I'd rather you told me what to do, sir."

"You don't have to call me sir."

"I thought I should."

"Well, you don't. I don't like it and neither does my daddy." Gerald lifts his face and takes a deep breath of air. "I expect people have told you about my daddy."

"How do you mean?"

"I mean 'bout the way he runs this place. I bet it was different where you come from. Ain't I right?"

"I don't know. I suppose so." I stare at the ground again. "Please, would you show me what you want me to do?"

"Well, you split the logs, stupid! There ain't nothing to it. You just split 'em."

It seems like whatever I do, I'm heading for trouble. I feel trapped.

Gerald watches me lean down, take a log, and put it on the stump. I lift the head of the axe to get a feel of the weight of it, then notch the log, lift the axe up above my shoulder, and slam it down, splitting the wood clean down the middle so the quick crack of it comes back at us off the trees still standing. I do it with one eye on Gerald, wondering if he'll come and grab me, if he'll make me stop. But he don't. I take another log, put it on the stump, and split it the same way while Gerald sits there festering. I can feel his displeasure. He has his head in his hands, his elbows on his knees, and his jaw cupped in each palm. "This is gonna be really boring," he says after a little while, and then he stands and starts kicking his feet into the ground, leaving scuff marks on the polished toes of his black leather shoes. "What'd you do if I ordered you to come with me to the traps? You'd have to do it, then, wouldn't you? You wouldn't have no choice."

He's got that look in his eye that I saw at the auction, a little bit mischievous, a little bit cruel, and I can see he's on the edge, not knowing whether to be nice to me or not. He could be a bully if he chose to, and I ain't never liked bullies, but I know how to handle them. I learned it at the orphanage, and right now it's probably the only choice I've got. So I give him a straight look. "You're saying I'd have to stop work and go with you to the traps?"

"That's right. You'd have to come with me if I told you to."

"And will you have me whipped if I don't?" I put the head of the axe on the ground and lean against the handle. "'Cause your mother will have me whipped if I do."

I try to look like a teacher, try to stay calm and composed, but inside of me, everything is churning.

"I won't whip you," Gerald says quickly. "I didn't mean it like that."

"I heard she gets Hubbard to do her whipping, and he's a big man. I sure don't intend to be whipped by him. Not if I can help it."

"Hubbard don't like to whip anyone and neither does my daddy. They try to do without it if they can." I'm thrilled at my daring as Gerald backs down. "Look, I don't mean no harm. All I'm saying is, we could be having fun. Splitting logs is hard work. Everyone knows that. Going to the traps'd be a treat for you."

"Like the ham was?"

"I s'pose so. It was good ham, wasn't it? Better than you get in your rations."

I turn away from him, notch another log, and split it. But he comes and stands at my shoulder. "I figured you must be hungry. Weren't you hungry?"

"I don't eat from the floor," I tell him bluntly. "I ain't never eaten from the floor."

Gerald hadn't thought of that. I can see it in his face. "All I want is for us to be friends."

"Friends don't get each other in trouble. That's a first rule, the way I see it."

And suddenly, Gerald looks like a little boy, like Joshua used to look when Father Mosely had caught him out again. He says, "Yes. You're right. I'm sorry. I didn't mean no harm by it."

I put the head of the axe on the ground and relax against it. "You told your mother we'd do the logs—so we got to do the logs. There's no two ways 'bout that, but I reckon if we work fast enough, then we might have time to get to the woods as well. Why don't you show me how things work? Then we can get it done."

Gerald fetches the other axe and now he's eager to show me how much he knows, pointing out this and that and telling me things I don't need to know to do the job at hand. "All the trees around about us have been girdled," he tells me. "That means we cut through the bark around the trunk and then wait for 'em to die before we bring 'em down. Look!" He points at one of the standing trees. "Do you see there? About a foot from the ground, there's a circular cut."

"Sure. I see that."

"I know pretty much how everything should be done around here, so you can always ask me." He nods at the pile of sawed-up wood. "We need to do about half of 'em. These are for the stove. We just split 'em and lay 'em up to rest. That's how it works."

So we work hard, the two of us splitting logs and taking 'em away to the barn in the barrow, and once we're done, it feels like a bond of sorts, the both of us all hot and sweaty. Gerald takes a canteen of water from his bag and offers it to me before he drinks himself. "You don't talk much, do you? Mother always says I talk too much. Are you always this quiet?"

"Not always. It depends what I got to say."

When Gerald smiles, there ain't no trace of the bully in him this time. "The way I see it, we're gonna be working together for a long while to come, so I'd like us to be friends as best we can."

I take a drink of water and wipe the top of it with the palm of my hand. I hesitate again, not sure what I should say. Living here's like walking through a swamp and not knowing where it's safe to tread.

Gerald can see I'm struggling. "I'm just saying it'd make sense."

"It might be difficult."

"Do you mean 'cause you're a darkie?"

"Because I'm a slave, yes. Anyway, your mother don't like it."

Gerald takes a deep gulp of water. He wipes a hand across his mouth. "Listen, I've grown up playing at the cabins. George was my best friend till he went into the fields, and the way I always seen it, we're the same. Black or white—it makes no difference. I know that might surprise you, but I mean it. It's what my daddy taught me, see, 'cause he's got a lot of new ideas about the way things should be done. So, for instance, he don't like to call you boys slaves. He calls you workers instead. Do you see the difference? He says there'll come a day when you get paid to work, so we'd all better get used to it. He said there's people done the math of it and that planters like us will make more money working with free men. Can you believe that? Well, it's true. It's got to do with the rise in production that happens when people work for themselves and have a vested interest. That's what he told me anyway. It's all about the vested interest."

I tell him I don't know nothing about that and I glance down at my bare feet, my big toe pointing at his black leather shoes. I know we ain't the same. I don't say it, but I know it.

"So how come your daddy's gone to war? I mean, if he believes the things you say he does."

"Why's he gone to war? Because he don't like being pushed around by Yankee politicians who don't know our business. This war's about freedom, Friday, and we got to stand up for ourselves. My daddy's as patriotic as the next man, and so am I, come to that."

"But if he says he wants to set us free, then why don't he just do it?"

"He can't."

"Why not?"

"'Cause *he* don't own you. *I* do." He gives me a little bow and he's smiling so wide, I can see his teeth. "After my mother died, I inherited all of our slaves direct from my grandmother, but I don't come into my inheritance till I'm twenty-one, so my daddy manages the estate for me."

I don't know what to say about that.

"Come on," he says, taking my arm and making for the path that winds deeper into the woods. "Let's go check on some traps."

We find a snare with a rabbit in it. The poor thing's all tangled up in the wire, and when it sees us, it goes tense with the fear and its eyes are wide and bright as we edge closer. Gerald kneels beside it. "You can have it if you want it," he whispers in my ear, "but you'd have to kill it yourself. I don't like to do it." He strokes the rabbit, untangling its legs from the wire, and he's ever so gentle with it.

I kneel beside him, putting my hands in its fur. "I don't know how."

"You hold it either side of its neck." He shows me where he means. "And then you pull till it snaps. I've seen it done, but I ain't never done it myself."

Both of us look at the poor thing too scared to even move. "Do you want to do it?" Gerald asks me again. "Lizzie would know how to skin and cook it. I'm sure she would."

But even though I'd like to make a present of it to Lizzie, I don't have the nerve to do it either and I take my hands away from its throat. "I don't think it's big enough. Be better to let it go and wait till it's full size."

Gerald nods solemnly.

He puts the rabbit on the ground and lets it go, but the animal can't walk straight—it can barely walk at all—and we watch it crawl away under a bush. I can't see how the little thing will survive, not if it can't run away. It'll get caught by a fox. Perhaps something worse.

Over supper, I tell Lizzie what Gerald said about Mr. Allen and how he wants to set all the slaves free. "Do you think he will, Lizzie? Do you think he'd actually do it?"

"Talking don't cost nothing," she says.

"It don't do to gossip about who says what in the house," Sicely warns us with her nose in the air.

"Ain't that the truth," Lizzie says, giving her daughter a very straight look.

Later that night, when I'm settled on my mattress, I pray for the Lord to look after that rabbit and I pray for Joshua too, listing all the good things that I've done to keep him safe and out of trouble.

Today I worked hard for Mrs. Allen.

Today I was nice to Gerald and I helped keep him on the straight and narrow.

Yes. Those are the good things I have done today to keep my brother safe.

CHAPTER 8

On the second Sunday of the next month, when Mr. Chepstow arrives to preach the word of the Lord, he does not come alone. He brings three men with him, all of 'em on horseback, and he leads 'em down the driveway at a steady pace, with him in his little black buggy being pulled by the white mare.

Winnie sees 'em first and she comes bowling out the back door and down the steps into the yard. "There's men coming, missus. Looks like the preacher's with 'em."

Most of us are in the yard, waiting for Mrs. Allen to dish out our rations for the coming week. The supplies have already been brought out in sacks and laid up by the cookhouse door, with Sicely on hand to help Mrs. Allen if she needs it, though she prefers to do the giving-out herself.

I watch as the men ride into the yard and tie their horses to the side of the barn. Mrs. Allen comes across to meet 'em. "You're early for the service, Mr. Chepstow. We weren't expecting you till after lunch."

The preacher takes off his wide-brimmed black hat and shakes her hand weakly. "A little early, ma'am, yes, I am. We had some business in the area, taking stock for the government. Do you know Mr. Peighton?"

The man behind Chepstow lifts his yellow-brimmed hat by way of a greeting and I recognize him as the man who sold the limping slave at auction. Mrs. Allen acknowledges him with a curt nod. "Mr. Peighton." She turns back toward the cookhouse. "Sicely, would you bring these men some refreshment? Perhaps some tea. How can I help you, gentlemen?"

Mr. Peighton steps up and offers Mrs. Allen a letter, held at arm's length. "As Chepstow says, we're here taking stock for the government. We wanted to take a look around, assess the plantation for ourselves, see if we can make some notes on its size and your workers." He gives her half a smile. "We need to look at any equipment you might not need."

Mrs. Allen makes a point of looking around her yard. "You can see we don't have much."

"No, I'm sure you don't. None of us do, ma'am. But it's all part of the war effort. I know you understand. You've put a lot of those soldiers into the war yourself."

"That's right, I did." Mrs. Allen folds her arms, perhaps expecting an argument. "If a man can shoot, he can go to war."

"That's very patriotic of you to say so, ma'am. Now, tell me, how many horses do you have?"

"We have three horses and a mule," Mrs. Allen tells him straight. "Though one of those horses is nothing but a nag."

Peighton looks over his shoulder. "They in the barn? All right if we take a look?" He offers the letter again, but Mrs. Allen ignores it. "I don't need reminding of my duties, Mr. Peighton."

"I'm sure you don't, Mrs. Allen."

Peighton orders the two waiting men into the barn and they swing open the tall door and go inside. After a moment, they shout out that we have two decent horses as well as a nag and a mule, just like the lady said, and my heart feels a little lighter for the thought of 'em taking the mule.

Peighton asks the men to bring out the two fit horses. He stands 'em side by side in the yard and walks around each of 'em, feeling the strength in their legs and lifting their lips to check on their teeth. He points to the piebald mare. "We'll take this one for now, but I can't guarantee we won't be back for the other one. Men gotta have horses. Ain't that right, Mrs. Allen? No use having soldiers on foot when they can ride a horse." He leads the mare across the yard till it stands next to his own horse, which he mounts.

Sicely emerges with a tray full of tea. She has already poured it into cups from the pot in the kitchen, and Mrs. Allen says to the men, "Would you gentlemen like some tea?" She picks a cup and saucer from the tray and takes it over to Peighton, handing him the tea as he sits on his horse. He drinks it all in one go and Mrs. Allen takes back the cup. "Do you have a bill of receipt for my horse?"

Peighton nods at the preacher. "Chepstow does the paperwork. He'll write you one up and he'll take a proper look around for us, make a list of everything that might be useful in the future. You can expect to see us back here, ma'am, unless we go and win the war by Christmas, but I can't see that happening."

He touches his hat and leads his horse from the yard with Mrs. Allen's horse following riderless behind. Those other two men gulp their own tea, saddle up quickly, and ride out after him.

Mrs. Allen calls me over and gives me food from the sacks to take back to Lizzie. I thought it weren't as much as we usually had, but I can't be sure that the sack feels lighter. "See if you can find Hubbard for me," she tells me. "I need to talk with him about that horse."

Once I'm on the path to the cabins, I hear steps behind me and Gerald runs up to my side. "You wanna come with me to the river?"

I swing the sack of food to my other shoulder. "I got things to do."

"But it's Sunday! You can do as you please, can't you? So long as we're back for the preacher, then no one'll know, and I got a great place where we can play some ball."

Hubbard comes out of his cabin as we reach the fire pit. "'Scuse me, sir," I call over to him, "but the missus asked for you up at the house. They took your horse and she wants to speak to you about it."

Hubbard is dressed all in his Sunday best with a clean white shirt and his boots newly polished. He eyes the two of us suspiciously. "How do you mean? Who took the horse?"

"I don't know. Some men, sir. From the army, I think."

Hubbard dismisses us with a frown and goes on up to the house without another word.

"Meet me in half an hour by the picket gate," Gerald says, then skips away to catch up with Hubbard.

Connie comes across to me and he leans into our sack of supplies, putting his fingers through the corn and feeling the weight of the pork that's in there. He smiles with satisfaction. "I told you they're losing the war. It's beginning to bite." He moves his tongue around the front of his teeth. "Price of food's going up every day and the rations are down." He winks at me. "It won't be too long now."

I don't think I can survive on any less food than I been getting to eat right now, 'cause every day my stomach moans more than it did the one before, and when I give the sack to Lizzie, she rolls her eyes and tuts at me. "Just corn and bacon," she complains. "No peas or carrots. No jars of molasses." She sucks at her teeth, maybe hoping to find some last bit of goodness stuck somewhere in the gaps between 'em.

"Did I do something wrong, Lizzie?"

"Not that I know of. You got something I should know 'bout?"

I shake my head. I can't think of anything. Then again, there's always something you got to feel bad about.

———

First time I remember Joshua being caned was after a trip to the Middle Creek store. Mr. Randolph was the owner and it paid to be on his good side 'cause if he liked you, he could be a generous man, but if he didn't, he could be mean as hell.

We all went into town with a coin in our pocket, and his wife had made a pretty display of candied fruits along the front of the counter. There were cherries and orange peel and there was ginger. There was toffee and peanut brittle too, both of 'em a deep orangey brown, looking like a piece of melted sunset, and we stood there wishing we could have 'em all.

Joshua pressed his nose up against one of the glass jars. "Mister," he asked Mr. Randolph, "can I have a taste?"

"They're five cents a quarter." The shopkeeper eyed my brother suspiciously. "You can taste 'em once you've paid for 'em."

I loved the look of those sweets just as much as anyone, but I had my eye on other things and I was saving my coin to buy a metal toy soldier. I was a week away from being able to afford it and I asked Mr. Randolph if I might take a closer look at his collection and he obliged me, coming around from behind the counter and taking me across to the window display, where he brought some of the little metal figures out so that I could hold 'em for myself. There was a redcoat with a musket held to his face and a little drummer boy with a flag. I was about to engage Mr. Randolph in conversation, when we were startled by a scream from Mrs. Randolph, who had arrived from the storeroom out back.

She looked like she'd seen a rat, but it was my brother that she pointed at. "He licked it! I saw him lick it and he put it back!"

Mr. Randolph hurried back and saw that all the jars were open, with their lids all on the counter. He put his hand inside the first and brought out a piece of toffee that was glistening and wet. "You did this to all of 'em?"

"It wasn't me!" Joshua protested brazenly, but Mr. Randolph already had ahold of him by the scruff of the neck. "So you're a liar as well as a little thief."

"It wasn't me! Honest it wasn't! It was Johnny Bradshaw and the little bastard's run off out the door!"

Mrs. Randolph slapped the back of his head for his bad language, and her husband marched the both of us outside in search of Father Mosely. Joshua got a dozen strokes of the cane on a bare backside, and since Mr. Randolph suspected I was his accomplice, we both lost our money for a month. It didn't matter that it wasn't me who did it, and I never did get my toy soldier.

———

Gerald flips the ball up for me to catch and I drop it. He sidles away from me, his back to the river and his bat held up to his shoulder. "Pitch the ball for me, Friday. Go on, pitch it hard as you like. I bet you can't beat me."

I throw the ball, but it falls short of him. "That's no good," he tells me. "Try again." He scurries forward, picks it up, and throws it back, but then I throw the ball so high and wide he ain't got a hope of hitting it. It's closer to going in the river than it is to him and he shakes his head as he runs to pick it up. "You sure ain't no pitcher like I thought." He throws the ball for himself, straight up in the air, hitting it hard and high so it flies over my head and out across the field behind.

"Well, go on, then. Go and get it."

I run and fetch the ball, then I pitch again and Gerald hits it again and off I go, backward and forward, like a dog after a stick. I don't know why someone would want to spend their day doing this, but it makes Gerald as happy as it makes me miserable. Each time I return with the ball, he's ready and waiting, the bat already slung across his shoulder. He's good at sport and he knows it. He's got a kind of confidence in the way he stands and pushes the cap back on his head, so it's clear of his face. "You want a go with the bat?"

"No. I'm fine." I wipe an arm across my forehead to take away the sweat. "I could do with some water, though." I come across to him and we stand by the river as I swig from the canteen. Gerald looks up into the bright blue sky. "There's only one way to cool off properly on a day like today." He takes off his cap and shirt, steps out of his shoes, and drops his trousers too. He really does—stands there without a stitch on him, all lily-white clean and bright, like a scrubbed potato. Then he runs and jumps, hitting the water with a splash. He screams so loud I think he's been bitten by a big fish. "It's so cold!" he says, ducking his head under the surface and popping up like he's about to feed on a fly. "Come on in! Come on!"

But I won't do it. I ain't even tempted. It's just another thing he can do that I can't. I roll up the legs of my trousers and sit on the edge of the bank till Gerald stops his nonsense and comes across to me. "Why won't you come in?" He splashes water at me. "You ain't scared, are you?"

"Sure I'm scared."

"What of? The fish ain't gonna hurt you."

"It ain't the fish. I'm scared of drowning."

Gerald looks like he don't believe his own ears. "You telling me you can't swim?"

"Nope. Never had the opportunity. Where I lived before, there weren't no rivers, at least not close by."

Gerald suddenly becomes all serious. "Come on in and I'll teach you."

"No. Thank you."

"You can trust me. I'll look after you."

"I'm sure you will, but I'm happiest with my feet on dry land."

Gerald shakes his head solemnly. "Everyone should know how to swim, Friday. What'll you do if you fall in a river?"

"I wouldn't be that stupid."

"You might. Accidents happen. People make mistakes. It happens all the time." Gerald becomes the grown-up and he does it well. He's all earnest and calm. "See where I'm standing now? That'll still be in your depth. So long as you stand here, you can't drown and I won't make you go any deeper, I promise you. Not till you're ready."

"You ever taught anyone before?"

"Never. But my daddy taught me and I can still remember how he did it. First thing you got to do is float. You got to get used to the water so you ain't scared and then you won't panic. That's half the problem. If you panic, you start to sink." He opens his arms out to me. "C'mon, Friday. You can do it. I know you can."

I put my foot in the water and it feels cool on my skin when I move it in a circle, stirring up the mud below the surface. "OK. I'll do it!" I jump up, taking off my trousers and shirt so I'm naked on the riverbank. Gerald takes hold of my hand to steady me as I step down into the river. "There's a branch there," he points out. "Do you feel it with your foot? That's right, step on that and you're halfway in."

Another step and the wet mud squelches up between my toes as Gerald walks in front of me, showing me the depth before I take my next step. I go in up to my waist.

"Now watch what I do." He lets go of my fingers and falls slowly back till he's floating on the surface, his arms and legs stretched out at his sides, with the water calm around him and his golden hair fanned out around his head like a halo. He stays like that for a little while before kicking out and coming to stand upright again. He wipes the water from his eyes. "That's what I want you to do."

"I can't do that!"

"Yes, you can, 'cause I'm gonna help you." He comes behind me and takes hold of my shoulders. "Put your weight back on me and bend your knees. Go on, do it."

I want to do it, I really do, and I feel like I can trust him. So I lean back slowly and the water creeps up my chest till it's over my nipples and all up in my armpits.

"Can you feel the river take your weight?" Gerald holds me ever so carefully and I can feel myself rise. I can feel my legs wanting to join in with the rest of me. So I let 'em go.

"Put your head back," he tells me. "I dare you to put your head right back."

I do as he says till the river fills my ears and I lie like a water boatman or a dragonfly, all light and sleek on the glittering river. When Gerald speaks, I can see his mouth move but I can't hear a thing. Only my breathing and my pounding heart.

Gerald moves me slowly around in a circle and I ain't never been so peaceful. Not ever.

When we're done, we dry ourselves on the riverbank and then we get dressed, both of us lazy in the afternoon sun like a couple of big ol' cows that's had a good day's eating and ain't got nothing to do but rest. When we get up to leave, I see Hubbard coming into view and I panic, knowing he's already seen us. "Quickly. It's Hubbard. Let's go the other way before he gets here."

"Hubbard's all right." Gerald walks casually out to meet him, but I follow two steps behind. "I've known Hubbard since the day I was born," he tells me. "He's always looked out for me."

But Hubbard ain't smiling when we meet him. "Mrs. Allen was asking after you up at the house," he tells Gerald. "And don't let your mother see you with a bat and ball or she'll know what you're up to."

Hubbard's eyes go right through me, like he's inside my head, like he knows everything about me. I think he's going to punish me, but he don't. Not exactly. "The preacher's getting ready to do his sermon," he tells me. "I want you to bring all the chairs up to the barn."

So I scamper on ahead of 'em as we go back to the cabins.

—

When Chepstow gets to sermonizing, he holds his Bible like an axe above his head. "'Slaves,'" he tells us, "'be submissive to your masters and give them satisfaction in every respect.'"

You can tell he knows that particular verse off by heart. He looks around the gin barn and his eyes take in each of us, sat in three neat rows beneath the tall roof, all hung with spiders' webs and the white wisps of stray cotton. Every one of us is there 'cause Mrs. Allen has made it clear that none should be missing, even if it is a Sunday and supposed to be our free day to do with as we wish.

Chepstow repeats those words again, 'cause he wants to make sure we heard 'em good and proper. "'Slaves, be submissive to your masters.' Those ain't my words. No, sir. Those are the words of

God that are written for all of us to read. It tells us this in the book of Titus, chapter two, verse nine, and again in Paul's letter to the Ephesians, chapter six, verse five. Let me see now." He brings the Good Book down and flicks through the pages, finding where he's put his markers. "Yes, here it is. Slaves, it says, obey your earthly masters with fear and trembling." Chepstow turns the book outward and points to the passage so we all can see. He lifts it up for the people at the back and walks along the front row, holding the book open under the noses of those sitting closest so it makes 'em uncomfortable.

"Are you the kind of servant that steals from your master? And do you think that gives him satisfaction? I don't think so."

Lizzie fidgets in her chair beside me.

"It may be that all you do is help yourself to a mouthful of brandy from the cask out in the shed. It may only be a slice of food from the dining table, and you will probably say to yourselves, Well, it doesn't matter, Mrs. Allen's got enough, and anyway who's to know? Who's gonna find out? There's no one here to see me. Well, let me tell you that God sees you. He sees you every time you steal and He will know whether you have indeed given your master satisfaction in every respect."

Chepstow snaps shut his big old Bible and steps back to look at us. "Well, you might say to me, 'I don't like my master whipping me, I don't like my mistress being unfair.' Let me tell you that God sees your master same as He sees you, and He knows when your master might treat you unfairly. Your master answers to God, and He has told us that we should look after those that cannot look after themselves." Chepstow walks with open hands held out to us. "Slavery does that for the black folk. Do you see? Slavery is God's way of keeping you safe, of keeping you warm in bed, of making sure everyone can feed themselves. He's saying we should work toward a common good and remember this: We are all slaves before God, we are all obedient to His will, and we will pay for our sins on the Day of Judgment, both the master and the slave, and there ain't no whip like the Devil's own whip, no, sir, 'cause if you're burning in the fires of hell, that pain don't ever go away."

I know all about them hellfires. I've seen the pictures. But what Chepstow is saying ain't true, at least not if Father Mosely was right. And yet they can't both be right, even though they're both preachers and both of 'em privileged to have the ear of the Lord.

Chepstow smiles at us all. "So you see, slavery has been given us by God for the good of us all. He has ordained it." He holds the book back in the air above his head and he shakes it as he speaks. "These are but a few verses and there are many more, both from the New and Old Testament, beginning with the curse of Ham and ending in the book of Revelation, where we are told of slavery still in existence on the final day of this blessed earth. Yes, that's right. Even Jefferson Davis himself has said that slavery has been found among the people of the highest civilization and in nations of the highest proficiency in the arts. There are those in America who would have you believe us to be uncivilized, and yet the fact remains that our brightest civilizations, the very best that mankind has achieved, have been built upon the institution of slavery."

Mr. Chepstow points a finger toward the heavens, and his eyes are glistening with the zeal of everything he says. He's standing close enough that I can see inside his mouth when he speaks and I can smell his rotten teeth.

He points his finger in my direction. "I say to you people, follow the Ten Commandments and serve your masters well. That's the only way you'll get to heaven. I'm here to tell you that. And once you get to heaven, the good Lord will give you your reward, as He Himself has promised it."

His eyes suddenly fall on Levi. "Young man, do you want to go to heaven?" Levi nods. Chepstow turns to Harriet. "Do you want to sit at the feet of the Lord? Do you want to eat at His table?" Harriet nods as well.

It's Connie who coughs and says, "Excuse me, sir," and when he stands up, those of us in the front row turn in our seats to look back at him. "Mr. Chepstow, sir, I'm sorry to butt in and everything, but I have a question I was hoping you could help me to understand."

Chepstow don't seem to mind the interruption. He's all sweetness and light now he's delivered his sermon, and he opens his arms in welcome. "Go ahead, young man. Ask me what you need to know."

Connie pauses. He's taken the rabbit's foot from his hat and turns it in his fingers. "Well, I was thinking about heaven and how it works up there, I mean, in respect of us slaves because . . . well . . . there'll be white folks there. Won't there? Surely they get to go to heaven too?"

Chepstow laughs at him. "I've got a congregation back at the church who certainly hope so. What's your point, young man?"

"Well, my question is this. Are we gonna still be slaves when we get to heaven? Only, if all our masters are going to be up there with us like you say, will I be a free man when I get there or am I going to have to slave away the same as I do down here? It's a question that's been on my mind, sir, 'cause if God likes slavery as much as you say He does, then I can't see how I'll ever be free."

Mr. Chepstow can't help but smile. He even allows himself a chuckle. "Well, you don't have to worry about that. The direct answer to your question must be yes—I expect your master will still own you. After all, it's a point in law. Ain't no getting around that even in heaven. But just stop and ask yourself this, my man—What's he going to get you to do?" He spreads his hands apart, giving us time to think it through. "Ain't no work to be done in heaven. Do you see my point? Morally, he will still be your master, just as God will still be master over him. But I don't think you've got a whole lot to worry about on that score. And remember, if you've done your duty here on earth, God has promised to reward you in heaven. You have His word on that."

Connie don't make no argument about it and he says, "Thank you, sir," and he sits back down, but I can tell that there's a whole lot of dissatisfaction in the barn. People are shuffling their feet or staring up at the strands of cotton hanging high in the rafters, and I'm troubled too, because Father Mosely always said the orphanage saved us from a fate worse than death. But then again, given my own predicament, that doesn't make a whole lot of sense to me either, 'cause if God hates slavery, then why did He deliver me into the arms of Gloucester, knowing all along that he would sell me at auction? Unless, that is, God hates me too.

I go and see Connie that very evening to tell him I've been thinking 'bout what he said. "I don't think the preacher's right," I say to him as he smokes his pipe by the hearth. "I can't be certain, but I don't believe you'll still be a slave in heaven."

"I ain't interested."

"I thought you were?"

Connie suddenly looks at me like he hates me. "You like to hear the priest preaching, don't you, Friday? I've seen you praying and I've heard you too."

"Doesn't everybody?"

Connie shakes his head. "Do you know who it *is* you're praying to? Are you sure it's *your* God, Friday?"

"I don't know what you mean."

"What I mean is this—is your God a black man? Or is He white?"

"I don't know."

"I think you do."

And Connie's right. I do know.

I want to tell him that when God speaks to me, He speaks the same way I do, that He has the same voice as me—a black voice. But I remember the picture in Father Mosely's office and I remember the face on the wooden crucifix in the chapel, those bright blue eyes staring down at me since I been seven years old.

I know the answer to Connie's question. I've always known it and I tell him so. "He's white, Connie. The good Lord's a white man, sure as eggs is eggs."

"That's what I thought." He runs a hand across his tired-looking face. His teeth are clenched hard, but I don't know why he looks so angry. It's just the way it is. It's the way it's always been.

"Go on now," he tells me. "Time to get some sleep."

He stands and prods at the fire one last time, making a flame leap up around the last remaining log as I leave him. But at the door, I stop and look back, intending to say good night one last time. Connie is already pulling his shirt up over his head, and his back is a mess of scars, all standing out in the firelight like the furrows of a fresh-plowed field.

"Holy Moses! Connie? What happened to your back?"

That man turns on me like a dog. "I thought I told you to leave! Why can't you leave me alone in peace, huh? Go on and get out!"

He grabs at a grease lamp, maybe meaning to throw it at me, but I'm gone before he gets the chance, and I resolve not to speak of God to him again. Not unless I got good reason.

CHAPTER 9

Hallelujah for small mercies.

My heart skips a beat when Sicely announces she's moving back to live in the house. She gives us the news one evening when we're sat at the table about to eat corn pancakes.

"Mrs. Allen has said it makes more sense if I go back to live with her."

"That's fine," says Lizzie.

"Mrs. Allen needs my help if she's gonna get those uniforms finished. She's taken on more than she can chew, if you ask me."

"You should do as you see fit," Lizzie tells her.

Sicely casts a glance my way. "Do you think you can manage here without me?"

"Yes, thank you, Sicely. I can manage just fine."

I offer to look after Gil. "I'll make sure he's keeping out of trouble."

Lizzie don't thank me for that. "Gil's a good boy," she tells me curtly. "He don't need no looking after."

And so we finished our meal with little else said. That was typical of how things were between us. Lizzie didn't make things difficult for me, but she didn't go out of her way to make 'em easy either. I was a cuckoo in their nest and I knew it.

Sicely leaves us that very night, and the next day is a Sunday, our day of rest, just as the good Lord intended it to be. I have learned to count the weeks in Sundays, looking forward to 'em like they're Christmas Day. The only thing missing from 'em is a good church service, since Chepstow only preaches to us once a month and his meetings don't exactly bring us together in worship.

Mrs. Allen has begun to give us religious instruction in the evenings, but it ain't the same thing. She gathers us around the fire pit at the end of each day. Sometimes, she gives a reading from the Bible or recites a prayer to us, but I can't find no religious fervor in any of the other slaves, and when we pray, the loudest "amen" always comes from me or Mrs. Allen herself.

That's why I'm surprised when I wake on Sunday to the sound of Lizzie's voice coming from outside the cabin. She's singing songs about Jesus, the same that I learned at the orphanage, and I lie on my mattress, wondering where she might have learned 'em and what it means for her to be singing 'em out loud the way she is.

Cracks of light come past the rags that are stuffed in the holes of the wall and Gil is beside me on the floor, his breath all heavy as he sleeps. He won't wake up for a while yet. If he could stay in bed all day, that boy surely would.

I fetch a cup of water from the bucket before I go outside. Lizzie's digging her garden at the back of our cabin and I watch her while she sings her songs. *"Soon to glory we will go, down by the riverside."* I know that tune and I start to sing it too—not loud or anything—but joining in so she knows I'm here. Lizzie stops singing and looks up at me. "Where d'you learn that song? They let you go to church back in Tennessee?"

I shrug my shoulders. "Guess I've always known it. Where'd you learn it?"

Lizzie straightens up and puts her hands on her hips, smiling as she remembers. "A few summers ago, we went to the Baptist camp. Me and the kids. Mr. Allen took all of us who wanted to hear the words of the Lord spoken by a proper preacher, on account of there being no chapel within easy reach of here."

"Didn't Mr. Chepstow have a chapel then?"

"Chepstow? Sure he did. But it's too far to walk there and back on a day pass." She comes closer, treading carefully along the single line of carrot tops till she's only a few feet away from the little wooden fence that divides us. "Henry went there once," she confides in me. "He's always had a hunger for the Lord, has Henry, but he got caught on his way back by a patrol, led by the very same preacher who'd blessed him in church only an hour before. That preacher stood by and saw Henry whipped to the bone, even though he knew where he'd been and what he'd been doing."

"You mean Chepstow did that?"

Lizzie raises her eyebrows nearly halfway up her head and I know that's who she means without her having to say, and it makes my mind up once and for all about that priest. "Does Henry still believe in Jesus?"

Lizzie looks at me like I'm stupid. "Sure he does. He just don't go to Chepstow's church. But he came to the Baptist camp with Nancy and the kids. Yes, he did. Got 'em all baptized so they know the ways of the Lord in case anything was to happen to 'em. Harriet and Levi were there too, though it was before they jumped the broomstick. Before they'd had baby Richard too." Lizzie looks at me square on, like she's had an idea. "So you like to sing to the Lord too? Hmm . . . Well, I never." She sees a weed near her feet, bends down, and pulls it up. Then she changes the subject. "You want to fetch me some eggs?"

Now, I know that her asking me to fetch eggs is a mark of trust, 'cause Lizzie owns all the chickens that scurry out back of the cabins. She bought 'em with her own money and no one else goes near 'em without her say-so. Everyone knows that. She takes their eggs in on market day and sells 'em to the man from the store, along with the vegetables that she grows.

So anyway, she hands me a basket and tells me to look over in the bushes on the far side, but I do better than that. I do a real good job for her, looking under the floors of the huts and in among the trees where those chicks like to scratch around in the evenings, and I don't mind doing it, even though I could still be in bed.

The chickens sure make me laugh when they come clucking and clicking around my feet, and I remember how Joshua loved 'em to bits when I was back at the orphanage. He'd play with 'em all the time. He thought they were the funniest things, the way they couldn't keep their feet or their heads still. He used to act like 'em— he could do the walk and everything—used to stick his arms out like they were chicken wings and he did that thing with his chin, pointing it in and out while he strutted around. Sometimes he would catch one and we'd see that chicken's eyes get bigger an' bigger, all puzzled and nervous, with its little chicken brain wondering why its feet weren't taking it nowhere. It used to make us laugh, though I'd always tell him to let it go if he held it for too long. They don't like it, see. It ain't in their nature to be standing still like that.

Anyway, I don't try to catch Lizzie's chickens. All I do is collect the eggs, and once I've got six of 'em, I take the basket back to her. She's still in her garden, bending down and digging at the earth, but she straightens up and takes the basket. "You did well, Friday. Thank you."

"You saving 'em up?" I ask her.

"Sure. I always got something to save for."

"Are you hoping to buy back Sicely?"

I said that without thinking, and for a moment my heart is in my mouth 'cause she's in swinging distance if she wanted to slap me. She don't, though. She just looks thoughtful.

"I doubt I can afford Sicely." She puts her hands on her hips while she thinks it through. "Sure, she ain't pretty like Milly, but even so, it would take more eggs than I could sell and more time than I got to stitch. Sicely can look after herself," she decides. "She's independent-minded."

I can't argue with her there. Sicely's just about the most independent-minded girl I've ever met.

"Maybe I could afford Gil, though," she continues. "I got a bit more time on my side for him, and he may not cost so much while he's still young."

I feel uneasy 'bout listening to her weigh up the odds of buying her own kids with eggs and needlework. "Connie told me the Yankees gonna set us free. He said they're sailing up the Mississippi as we speak and they'll be here soon."

"Is that what he says?"

"Yes, it is, and I believe him too." I feel bold enough to pull her leg a little. "So maybe you don't need to sell your eggs after all.

Maybe we could have 'em for lunch." I lick my lips and make her smile. "Well, we could, couldn't we? Maybe fry 'em up with a little milk?"

"You keep your ideas about my eggs to yourself, young man." She makes as though to hit me, but she's only kidding. "And I wouldn't pay no heed to Connie neither. I heard them Yankees don't like to sit down with a Negro any more than they do down here in the South."

"Yeah, but, Lizzie, people are saying Lincoln's already set us free."

She dismissed the idea with a quick shake of her head. "The only way we're gonna get set free is by doing it ourselves. Just like Moses. You ever hear 'bout Moses?"

"Sure I heard about Moses."

Her face softens and her eyebrows lift themselves a little higher up her brow. She comes out of her garden and walks back around the cabin, putting the basket of eggs down by the door. "There ain't no white man gonna free us, Friday. We need God to give us a Moses, a big ol' black Moses who'll lead us to the promised land. That's the only way it's ever gonna happen."

Those are Lizzie's last words on the matter. She sends me up to the big house for rations and I bring back cornmeal, molasses, and bacon in a sack. But she's waiting for me when I get back and she strides out to meet me as I bring the sack back down the path. She takes hold of my arm and puts her head close to mine. She's so serious I wonder if I got the wrong food. "I'm gonna tell you something, Friday, but you need to know it's a secret. You got to keep it to yourself. Do you hear me? You let on about this and you'll answer to God Himself."

I say I heard her and I cross myself before the Lord so she can see I mean it.

And then she tells me.

———

They take me to the river in the dead of night—these night-owl Baptists—they take me down into the woods.

There's ten of us when we go, following one after another in the dark, a pine torch held in front of us to light the way, and no one makes a sound—not a whisper or a word—until we know we can't be heard.

It don't take long before we stop in an open space, a circle of grass on the riverbank where the trees don't reach the edge and the mud slopes gently to the water. On sunny days, it's just the kind of place that'd invite you in for a swim, but tonight it looks haunted, with moonlight shining on the surface, and the trees seeming to move when you don't keep your eye on 'em.

Henry takes charge. He tells us to gather ourselves together and I'm expecting us to sit in rows, crouched down on the grass with our hands clasped together in our laps. That's the way we did it at the orphanage, because Father Mosely always taught us it weren't no good to stand before the Lord. No. You were better off on your knees. But these here Baptists show no sign of sitting down.

They start to shuffle on their feet and I get taken by the arm and we start moving in a wide circle, like a lazy old current in a slow stream, with Nancy humming a tune, not singing any words that I can tell but moaning away from deep inside herself until we're all humming along, like some great old religious swarm of bees, all of us content to work our way to God.

An owl hoots from a tree across the river. I close my eyes and we're moving and moaning. We're whispering, "Take me, Jesus! Take me to your loving heart!" And it feels good to be praising Him again, so good I even forget I'm in the woods at midnight and the air becomes a little warmer. Everything's gentle. Everything's so gentle it seems we're in a bright bed of summer flowers, all full of reds and yellows, with the honeysuckle smelling sweet.

I ain't much of a mover, but I shuffle around a bit, and I'm warming up to it 'cause it's easier letting go when you've got your eyes closed. One moment I think I'm next to Lizzie and then maybe I'm with Mary—I feel her thighs brush up against me. Then Levi shouts out, "Save me, sweet Jesus, save me," and the others tell him, "Shushhhh!" and he puts his hand upon my head and I feel the power of the Lord, right here in this woods like I used to at the orphanage, and I know He's here for me, I know He's here for all of us, like He never went away. And I'm crying for the love of God, crying like I ain't cried for a long, long time, letting it all out, all the hurting and the worry and all the woes of the world—they all lift from my shoulders. "Save me, Jesus," I pray to the Lord. "Save me."

Henry drags a cross out from under a bush and hammers it into the ground so it stands upright, about three feet high in the middle of our circle, and the sight of it shining in the moonlight gives us a whole new energy. We start clapping our hands softly and we whisper louder than ever. "Oh, Jesus!" We got our fingers in the air. "Oh,

Jesus!" We're pointing the way up to heaven, and the moonlight don't seem creepy anymore, but it seems like it's the light of God shining down upon us and I know the only spirit in these woods is the Holy Spirit and His hand protects us from the wolves as though we were a flock of sheep and He were our shepherd, though of course we left little Gil and Benjamin to keep a watch out—but even so, that's how it feels.

Henry places his hand on the top of the cross. "Jesus, hear my prayer," he calls out boldly, and the circle answers him, "Oh, sweet Jesus, hear our prayers."

"I got to thinking the other day about them Israelites and how they had to wait so long till Moses delivered 'em from slavery."

"Tell us about Moses, Henry, tell us about that blessed journey."

"Well, those Israelites were the slaves to the Egyptians and they had suffered for so long, they couldn't remember what it was like not to suffer. But when the time was right, God gave 'em Moses and he rose up among 'em and he led 'em through the wilderness . . ."

Lizzie takes hold of my hand. "Hallelujah!" she shouts out, not caring whether it's too loud, and we all shout out together, saying things like "Take us through the wilderness! Take us to freedom, heavenly Lord Jesus! Take us to the promised land!"

Lizzie steps up into the circle and she calms us down to keep us quiet. "Show us the Good Book, Henry. Show us where Moses led his people 'cross the great sea, where the waves parted some to the left and the rest to the right."

And Henry picks up his bag from the ground and he reaches inside and brings out a book, a great thick Bible with a cover of tanned leather, which he holds in the air. "I have marked the place where it is." He crouches beside the cross, rests the book on his knee, and opens it up at a page where the corner is as floppy as a rabbit's ear and looks almost as soft.

Nancy holds the flickering pine torch as everyone gathers around to listen. I'm at the back, but I don't mind, I don't need to see the Bible, and I wait to hear the words of Exodus, which I know so well, how Moses lifted his arm across the sea and brought the waters crashing down upon the Pharaoh and how the Israelites were delivered safely to the farther shore.

No one says a word.

I move closer, thinking Henry must be speaking quietly, and I lean across the backs of Lizzie and Harriet, hoping to hear. But then I realize Henry ain't reading to 'em at all. No. He's pointing at a picture.

Lizzie sees me looking and she shifts, letting me in closer, and Henry lifts the book from his knees and puts a finger to the page of the illustrated family Bible. "Here you go, Friday. Look. That's Moses right there, I'm sure it is. See how he holds that staff up to keep the sea from closing in? I'm sure that's him."

And I know it then for the first time, though I should have guessed before. There ain't a man or a woman here who can read. Not one of 'em.

I reach for the book and Henry lets me take it. "You can touch the Good Book, Friday. Sure you can. You can put your finger on the face of ol' Moses."

But I begin to read out loud, using the light of the moon to guide my eyes. "'And it came to pass, when Pharaoh had let the people go, that God led them not through the way of the land of the Philistines . . .'" I read it clearly, loud enough that everyone can hear me, and at first those slaves don't seem sure how I'm doing it. Maybe they think I'm good at remembering or that I'm telling 'em a story. But they see my eyes move along the written lines, sometimes squinting to make 'em out, and soon they realize I must be reading, though it's little Gil who says out loud what they're thinking. "Mama," he asks Lizzie, "is Friday reading?"

"I doubt it, Gil." Lizzie looks at me with fear and respect when she answers him. "We ain't allowed to read. You got to remember that."

——

Later in the cabin, Lizzie uses her don't-disagree-with-me voice when she talks to me. "How come you can read?"

We're sitting at the table and Henry's there too, pacing in the darkness at the back of the cabin. So far, I ain't said a word, 'cause I can't decide whether to trust 'em.

"I guess I picked it up here and there."

Lizzie shakes her head. "Reading ain't something you pick up here and there. It's gotta be taught."

I take a sudden interest in the top of the table, see a mark, and run my finger over it. Lizzie draws a deep breath like she's losing her patience and she leans in close to me. "You're putting us all in danger," she hisses. "Do you know that? Now, we don't mind so long as we know the truth. We'll take that risk. We'll cover for you. We'll even lie for you. But you got to be straight with us."

I stretch a finger to the grease lamp, seeing how close I can go before it gets too hot. "Is that true of Sicely? Are you saying she'd lie for me too?"

Lizzie looks embarrassed. "You don't need to worry about her. She likes to do right by Mrs. Allen, but she knows who she is underneath that apron."

"That go for Hubbard as well?"

"Why? What's he said to you?"

"He said he'd whip me if I told anyone 'bout where I come from. I went to him for help, soon as I got here."

Lizzie and Henry exchange looks. "And you told him what?"

I'm thinking that I have to trust her. Henry too. After all, they've trusted me. They took me to the woods.

I take one last look at Lizzie before I jump in for good 'cause there ain't no going back from here, I know that, so I say it slowly, hoping I won't have to repeat a thing. "I told him I'm a free black, that I been taken away by force and sold. I reckon he's already guessed I can read."

Once I start, I can't stop. I tell her 'bout the orphanage, 'bout Father Mosely and my brother, Joshua. I tell her 'bout how I need to get back to him but Connie said to wait. I tell her everything and she listens to me, hardly says a word herself, just listens to me, nodding and waiting till I come to a stop.

She takes hold of my hand and holds it tight. "They must have changed your name before they sold you. Did he do that?" I nod and she pats the top of my hand as though she knew it all along. "So what's your real name?"

"Samuel." There. I said it out loud. It's been a while since I've heard my own name, but it feels good, so I say it again. "My mother named me Samuel."

Lizzie repeats it like she knew it already. "Samuel. Course it is. From the Good Book." She takes her hand away. "Well, we all still gotta call you Friday. You know that, don't you? I won't use Samuel again, even when we're on our own, but I won't forget it neither."

"Why won't they let us read, Lizzie?"

She gives me a straight look in the dim light, but it's Henry who tells me, putting a hand on my shoulder before pulling up a chair and sitting down heavily. "They couldn't treat us the way they do if they thought we was their equals," he tells me. "It don't work. They'd be ashamed if they knew the things we could do. I mean, what with 'em being Christian people. They'd be too ashamed."

Lizzie nods in agreement. "And I guess they don't want another Nat Turner."

"Who's Nat Turner?"

Her eyes go all huge in her face. "You never heard of Nat Turner? Boy, you do amaze me. One minute you know it all, and the next you don't have a clue." She hesitates. "Well . . . Nat Turner . . . he weren't no Moses, that's for sure."

Henry taps his finger on the table. "Nat Turner was a man who could read. He was a preacher too. The long and the short of it was that he got himself a posse of slaves and talked 'em around to going on the rampage. They spent two days riding through the country-side killing white folk. The whole thing was a bad deal from start to finish and it scared the living daylights out of everyone. When they caught him, they said he was too clever for his own good, blamed it on him being able to read, reckoned he was half-taught and only understood what he wanted to. They said a black man lacks the wisdom and insight to go alongside the knowledge you can get from books."

"And they been saying it ever since," adds Lizzie. "They saying we're not up to the responsibility of reading for ourselves."

"But that ain't true." I think of our classroom at the orphanage, brimming with black boys and all of 'em reading.

"No." Henry lowers his voice. "I don't see how it could be. But that don't matter. What matters is that just the mention of his name would be enough for 'em to string you up. They'd hang you from a tree. I'm telling you, Friday, they wouldn't think twice."

"Do you mean Hubbard?"

Lizzie shrugs. "Maybe. You better not let him find you with a book in your hand, that's for sure. Not him, nor Mrs. Allen. It wouldn't be good for any of us."

And suddenly, I know why God has brought me here. It's as if He's right there in my head, telling me Himself, explaining why He has piled misfortune and misery upon my head. I understand that He got Father Mosely to lie and do terrible things so He could bring me here to live among slaves. It was all part of His plan. He didn't mean for me to become one of 'em. No. He wants me to lead 'em. He wants me to show 'em the way out of their wilderness. He surely does. I can hear His voice. I can hear Him telling me, I'm sure I can, and I take hold of Lizzie's arm. "I can teach you to read," I tell her. "I know how. I could teach all of you to read if I only had the right books."

Lizzie nods like she's thought of it already, but Henry looks more worried than pleased. "That's kind of you, Friday, it really is. But we couldn't take the risk if we knew that we'd be caught."

Lizzie shakes her head in wonder. "I can't decide whether you been sent to us from heaven or from hell. Guess only time will tell."

I leave the two of 'em sitting at the table, talking quietly and staring into the grease lamp as I lay myself down upon the mattress in the corner of our cabin.

God is so close tonight, it makes me tremble. I can hear His gentle heart beating a rhythm in time with my own. "If I stay here . . ." I tell Him, "if I do your bidding and I don't run away . . . you got to look after Joshua . . . You got to look after him real good and keep him safe till I get back to him . . ."

God lets out a deep breath and it's like a breeze across my face, touching my lips lightly and reaching up into my nostrils. And I know it means He will.

CHAPTER 10

These hands ain't my hands. Not anymore. They're changing. I got patches of dead skin on the inside of my thumb and the tips of all my fingers. They're growing larger too—growing stronger—turning from the hands of a boy into the hands of a man.

Not long ago, they spent their days holding a book to my face. These days they pick and pluck till I'm good for nothing but sleep.

And I'm beginning to feel something different, a kind of strength creeping into me, so that if someone were to hit me hard, I think I could take it. I don't think anyone wants to. I'm just saying that if they did, it might not hurt as much as it would've before. At least that's what I think until I meet with the mule. Once the mule kicks me, I know all about it, 'cause this ain't just any old beast of burden, this mule's on a mission from God.

I don't hear the voice of God for a little while after the night with Lizzie in the woods. That's the way it works sometimes 'cause He's a busy man. He's got a lot of people He needs to talk to, and that means you have to figure things out for yourself.

God has a way of revealing Himself slowly, bit by bit, and you got to look out for the signs if you're gonna know what He wants you to do. Often there'll be a series of strange coincidences, all of 'em arranged by His guiding hand into a pattern. Once you spot the pattern, everything becomes obvious. Take, for instance, that meeting in the woods. Well, that didn't happen by chance. God led me there. He gave me Lizzie and took me to the woods so I'd see for myself that they couldn't read. He knew Lizzie and Henry would come to trust me and I would trust them too. That's why He revealed them to me. It was all part of His plan. It had to be. Same as the mule.

— —

I'm in the field. I'm working alongside Connie and Albert. Hubbard sits on Mrs. Allen's one good horse, watching us work, making sure we do everything right and we aren't slouching. We're still harvesting the cotton, and now I can pick as quickly as anyone. When it's time for lunch, I'm sent to the house, same as usual, and I go by the path, the same way that I always do.

Well, I don't see the mule until I walk right into him. He isn't meant to be there anyway because it ain't his spot. Normally, he's in the barn, skulking about like the no-good animal he is, or else he's in the field, complaining that he has to work. Only he ain't in either of those places. He's right here, standing at the corner of the barn, next to the path that takes you up to the house, but I don't see him till it's too late 'cause he's standing on the blind side. First thing I know is when he kicks me and he gets me high up on the thigh, right on the muscle at the front of the leg, and I'm on the ground before I know what's hit me.

That mule looks down his long nose at me and I swear he snickers.

That's when I hear a woman's voice. It ain't the mule. It's Mrs. Allen hanging out of an upstairs window in the main house and shouting down to me. "Friday. Oh, my Lord, Friday." Her hand holds the edge of the window to steady herself, 'cause she sure is leaning a long way out. "Stay right there," she shouts, and ducks back inside the house.

I lie on the ground like a wet blanket and don't move at all, just like she said. Moments later, the door to the yard is flung open and out comes Mrs. Allen, followed closely by Winnie and Sicely. She runs across to me, then she kneels and lifts my head onto her knees, 'cause she must see that I'm looking faint, and her golden hair falls down across her face so she appears something like an angel to me. "Why, you poor thing. Are you all right?" She puts a hand onto my brow. I don't know why.

"It's my leg that hurts, ma'am."

"I know," she says. "I saw the whole thing from the window. Sicely, take that mule to the barn right now and make sure it's kept well away from everyone."

Sicely looks down at me with the same face as that mule and I know she thinks I'm faking. "It's just a mule, missus. It ain't harmed none of us before."

"Do as I say, Sicely. It was an unprovoked attack. I saw it all."

"There's something about me and mules," I try to explain in a weak voice. "They don't like me. I've had trouble with 'em before."

Mrs. Allen lifts the leg of my trousers. She takes it right up over my shin and she don't ask me or nothing, she just does it, putting her fingers up above my knee and feeling my thigh, finding the place where it hurts when I flinch.

"Ouch!"

"Does it hurt that much?"

I don't know why she needed to ask. "Sure," I tell her. "It hurts a lot."

Winnie leans over the two of us. "If it was broke, he'd be screaming," she offers in her gravelly voice.

"He'd be squealing like a little pig," adds Sicely.

I don't try too hard to be brave. Mrs. Allen's got nice hands. Gentle but firm. She slides the leg of my trousers back down my leg. "Can you walk?" She taps the top of my head, indicating for me to get up, and I raise myself onto my elbows and then my knees. "You look a little shaky." She gives me a hand to steady me.

"I feel shaky, ma'am, but I'll be fine, I'm sure I will. Thank you." I get up onto my feet.

Sicely has her hands on her hips. "See. He'll be fine."

But Mrs. Allen gives her short shrift. "I told you to take that mule away, Sicely. Now you go and do it." She takes me by the waist, helping me make a step or two, but I ain't putting on a limp. Every time I put my foot on the floor, it hurts.

"I think you may have been lucky." She lets me go, then watches me step gingerly and I wonder how much it must hurt when you're not so lucky.

"Winnie, will you get this boy some lunch?" Mrs. Allen walks back to the house. "Send him up to me in the library when he's eaten. He'll need to rest that leg this afternoon."

When Sicely returns, she puts my bowl down sharply on the table. I get soup with chunks of vegetables and I get fresh bread, but it would taste a whole lot better served with some sympathy. "What did you do to that mule that made him wanna kick you?" she asks meanly.

"I didn't do anything. I told you already, they got it in for me. Bit like you have. Always have done and always will. They know it and I know it. It's just how it is with me and mules." I pull up my trouser leg to show her the bruise and I think she softens a tiny bit 'cause you can see it plain as day and it's gonna get worse as time goes by. She shows me up to the library without another word of malice, knocks on the door, and delivers me through into the room.

Gerald and Mrs. Allen are sitting at a desk by the window at the far end of the library, and between them and me, there's nothing but books—shelves and shelves of books, the length and height of that lovely room. I've never seen so many books in one place, not even in Father Mosely's office.

"Are you feeling better, Friday?" Mrs. Allen smiles and beckons me toward them. I'm thinking she's gonna sit me down for an afternoon's rest in one of those empty chairs, but she's got other ideas. "I thought you could clean the books and dust the shelves for me. It should be less stressful on that leg. I'll bring you up some water and a cloth and show you what needs to be done. Dust the shelf. Then the books should be taken out, wiped with a damp cloth, and the shelf cleaned before they are dried and returned. If you work along the bottom shelves, you won't need to stretch and you can rest your injury." She smiles sweetly, and though it ain't how I imagined, I can't complain 'cause compared to working in the field, this is child's play.

It's only when I begin the task that I realize what a gift God has given me.

There are books here that I never dreamed existed. I get to handle big, red leather volumes with descriptions of every bird and animal under the sun, all of 'em with pictures drawn in ink so you can see what they look like. They've got a book with maps of the world and books about people too, all sorts of people—some of 'em I heard of but most of 'em not. I take one out called *A Peep at Our Neighbors*, by a man who calls himself Uncle Frank, and I wipe it down, opening the cover to sneak a look inside when I know that Mrs. Allen won't notice me. I put it back and crawl farther along the bottom shelf, the feather duster in my hand, being careful to not spill the bucket of water as I bring it along on the floor behind me.

I get to the storybooks and there are all sorts. There's a book about a man who goes hunting a great white whale and another one for children, called *A Wonder Book for Girls & Boys*. I have to be careful that she don't see me looking, but she's at the far end of the room, setting Gerald a math problem, though by the sound of it, he ain't interested in learning. She asks him, "If one Confederate soldier can whip seven Yankees, how many soldiers can whip forty-nine Yankees?"

Gerald pleads with his stepmom. "I been working hard for hours, Mother. Can't I stop and have a rest?"

"No, Gerald," Mrs. Allen scolds him. "You've got another thirty minutes of math before I'm gonna let you go, and if you choose not to concentrate, then I'll keep you even longer."

I read the opening line of the book. *Beneath the porch of the country-seat called Tanglewood* . . . Those words take me to a world I can only imagine, but I know I can't go there, not right now, so I close up *A Wonder Book for Girls & Boys*, still scared she'll see me with it open in my hand.

I get to my feet and flick a duster at a book of poetry bound in black leather. My leg doesn't hurt too much. I hardly notice it at all as I take the books from the shelf, wipe 'em down and dry 'em off, before putting 'em back the way they were.

I know God's with me when I crouch back down to begin a new shelf. I know it as sure as if He'd placed the book in my hand Himself, 'cause the first book along is a primer. I recognize it as the very same one I was taught with. I've opened it so many times, I could recite it with my eyes closed. The first pages have got the alphabet written out, all of the letters in both capitals and small. I turn the pages slowly, remembering the feel of the paper. It's got a version of the alphabet in print, and another as though written by hand, so you can see how the shape of the letters might be different, depending on whether you might be reading a letter or something set in type.

I sit down on the floor and turn to the first page proper, but I already know what'll be there and I'm right—there's the drawing of that big ol' dog running full tilt across that field with his tongue hanging out, and underneath, clear as anything, the first words I ever learned to read. *The dog ran.* Surely this is too good to be true?

"What are you doing, Friday?" Her voice shakes me out of my spell and I look up from the book to find Mrs. Allen standing over me. She's got a strange expression, kinda edgy and her eyes are nervous.

I move my finger from the word *dog*, make it look like I don't know a thing. "This one's got pictures, missus. See?" I run my finger across the page, pretending to stroke the dog.

Mrs. Allen reaches down and closes the book. "Put it back, Friday. I asked you to dust the books, but that does not require you to open 'em up. They're not for you. Those books are for those of us been blessed to read."

"Yes, ma'am. Sorry, ma'am." I slide the volume back into its place as Mrs. Allen walks out of the room, but as soon as I know she's gone, I go across to Gerald, who's been sat at the desk watching what went on between the two of us. "Can I meet you by the river?" I ask him.

Now, I ain't been too friendly since Hubbard found us on the riverbank, but a smile still races around his mouth. "Do you wanna go swimming again?"

"Sure. I'm ready for another lesson. Let's say five o'clock? But be sure you bring this book with you." I show him the book in my hand.

"Why?"

"I got something I want to ask you."

—

I wasn't sure that Gerald would do as I asked, and when he arrives, I still ain't certain. He comes to the river with an armful of things—a baseball glove, the bat and ball, a blanket, and a wicker picnic basket.

"Did you bring the book?"

He lets everything fall to his feet except the basket, which he puts carefully on the ground. "I still ain't sure this is a good idea," he tells me, and he opens up the lid. Inside, there are four slices of bread and a little clay pot with a spoonful of butter, all sitting on a cloth. He reaches underneath and pulls out the book. "I had to sneak it out. I told Winnie I was having a picnic."

I take hold of it greedily and open it up. There's my dog. The first words I ever read.

Gerald says to me, "I take it you want me to teach you how to read?"

"What?" I weren't expecting that, but it's better than the reason I was about to give.

Gerald looks doubtfully at me. "I ain't sure it's such a good idea. I've never heard of it before."

"How do you mean? It ain't illegal, is it?"

"I don't think so, no, but I can't see why you'd want to. You're *lucky* you don't have to sit in lessons like I do."

I shake my head solemnly. "It's a matter of principle," I tell him. "You can't find your way in the world if you can't read and write. Didn't your daddy tell you that? There's no point in setting us free if we haven't got the means to be independent."

"I suppose so. I hadn't thought about that."

"It'd be good for you too. Think of all the things we could do better if we could read. Can you imagine how it'd be if you draft the papers for our freedom and we can actually read 'em when you hand 'em to us? That would show your daddy a real mark of intent, wouldn't it? And if I learn to write, I'll be able to sign my name on the contract of work too. Wouldn't that be something? I bet your daddy would be pleased at that. Wouldn't he?"

I can see the idea take hold, 'cause Gerald's eyes start to shine. "You'd be the only slave here who could do it. That's for certain."

"I'd be the first. Yes, I think your daddy would be pleased with that and he'd know for sure you're a boy with progressive ideas just like his own."

"OK. I'll teach you if you like." Gerald takes the book from my hands. "But you can't let anyone know we're doing this. Do you understand?"

I go to take it back. "You don't have to teach me. I think can figure it out on my own if I have the book."

But Gerald shakes his head. "No, Friday. That ain't gonna work." He lays the book on the ground between us. "It takes a lot of effort at first. You got to learn all the letters. There's twenty-six of 'em in total. Then you got to learn how they go together to make sounds. It ain't as easy as it looks, and anyway you may not be able to learn it at all on account of being a Negro." He must see me bristle 'cause he quickly adds, "Leastways, that's what I been told. I've never heard of a Negro who could read before. That's all I meant."

"I knew a Negro who could read. I saw him do it myself. Heard him read from the Bible."

Gerald pulls at the Confederate cap on his head. "Well, that's good, then, isn't it? If he could do it, then so can you." He touches my arm. "I didn't mean no harm, Friday. It's just what people say." He closes the book and thrusts it back at me. "You'll have to work hard, though. It's more difficult than swimming."

"Can you let me borrow the book in between? That way I can practice it in my own time. I'll keep it secret—I won't let nobody know 'bout it."

Gerald bites at his bottom lip. "If my mother finds you with it, she'd have you whipped for stealing. I know she would."

"But I won't let her. I'll hide it so well that no one can find it." I open up the book and point to the picture. "I want to know 'bout that dog. Come on and tell me what it says 'bout the dog."

"Here." Gerald takes hold of my finger and places it on the letter *D*. "That there's a *D*. Sounds like *duh*. And you use it for *dog*. You hear that? *Dog*." He runs my finger along the line of words. "*The dog ran.* That's what it says. That's the words, and there's a picture there to help you. Go on. You say it."

I repeat the words slowly back to him, making 'em sound like they're difficult and new, making me sound like I don't know a thing.

"Now, listen, we're running ahead of ourselves here." Gerald turns to the alphabet page and shows me all the letters, laid out from *A* to *Z*. "This is where it all starts. This is the beginning. See the shape of these? Well, this is the alphabet written out as ordinary letters, but you can have the same letters looking different if they're capitals. Like the *D* for *dog*. Do you see that? That's because it's the start of a sentence, and every new sentence has to begin with a capital letter and end with a full stop."

He makes it sound so hard, I start to doubt that I already know what he's telling me, but that only helps with the pretense. "I ain't sure I understand. A capital letter's taller than the rest. Is that right?"

Gerald breaks into a smile. "You learned something already." He ain't a bad teacher, though not as good as me.

When we're finished with the lesson, we ease ourselves into the river, on account of my bruised leg, and I float on my back, do it all by myself, and I don't need his help when I put my head in the water either.

I wonder if I can hear the engines of the Yankee boats that I know are coming up the river on their way to free me. I can't hear a thing—but now I don't mind so much if they take their time.

———

It ain't easy to look natural when you got a book all up inside your shirt or tucked into the top of your trousers. I got the primer hidden about me like a dirty secret and I ain't used to lying to people, so I go the long way back to the cabins, hoping I won't meet a soul. When I see Albert, I have to head for the latrines and I sit in there a long time, so he'll be gone once I come back outside.

Father Mosely used to always say that if something makes you feel bad, then you're definitely sinning. Well, I feel bad about this. I don't like sneaking around behind Mrs. Allen's back and I don't like lying to Gerald either. I'm getting him to thieve for me and I'm treating him like a fool.

But God wants me to do it. It's all in His name. It's all about doing His good works—though right now, it don't feel so good.

I tell myself that slavery ain't good. Treating people like they're no better than a mule, that's a much bigger wrong than stealing a book, and anyway, Mrs. Allen's got no need for it. She'll have it right back on her shelf once we're finished and she won't even know it was gone. So really it ain't stealing at all—it's only borrowing.

Lizzie's alone in the cabin when I get there and we sit at the table with the book in front of us. We don't open it. We just sit there looking at it. "It's a primer, Lizzie," I say eventually. "It's a book for teaching reading and writing."

That might be what it is for me, but it ain't for Lizzie. For her, that book is a whole new world of opportunity and it could be a whole heap of trouble too. Either way, she's too scared to touch it and she keeps her hands folded on the tabletop in front of her. "Where'd you get a thing like that?"

"It's from the house. Gerald got it for me."

Lizzie stands up from her chair, all alarmed. "Why'd he do that? That's no good, Friday! He'll tell on us! He's bound to!"

"No, he won't, Lizzie. It's all right. C'mon and sit down. Gerald don't know about the rest of you learning. He thinks he's teaching me to read and he's doing it 'cause he wants to be my friend. He won't tell Mrs. Allen."

"What if you both get caught?"

"Then it'll be me who takes the blame. C'mon and sit down. C'mon and let me show you."

Lizzie sits back down, but she's shaking her head. "There's no point showing *me*. It won't mean anything to *me*."

I open the book anyway. I take hold of her finger and put it on the page, but she pulls it back. "No . . . I don't want to touch it." She puts the knuckle to her teeth. "It don't look the same as other books I seen." She points a finger. "What word is that one there?"

"Oh, that ain't a word, Lizzie. I been misleading you. This here's the alphabet page. It's got all the letters you might need to make a word." I flick through a few pages. "See here? These are words. That one there says *pillow*."

"It does?"

"Yes, it does."

"Is that a difficult word?"

"I'd say about average. There's some that are shorter and others that are longer. You see how these words here are grouped together? That's a sentence. And then there are paragraphs. That's where all the sentences fit together, like verses in the Bible, but this book ain't so advanced that it's got paragraphs."

Lizzie shakes her head and closes up the book. "There's too much to learn," she says.

"It gets easier once you got a few things to build on. And you won't need to worry. I'm a good teacher. I can teach you how to do it."

"Uh-uh!" Lizzie's mouth makes the shape of an *O*. "It's not for me! I never meant for it to be for me! I meant it for my kids. I want you to teach Gil. Sicely too, if she'll do it, though she may not."

"Sicely ought to do it."

"She don't like to do things that the missus don't allow."

"I know that. Do you think she'll tell Mrs. Allen?"

Lizzie shakes her head. "Even Sicely ain't so proud she'd see her own brother flogged." I'll have to take her word on that. "Anyway," she continues, "what I'm saying is that this is something for the kids."

She fetches Henry and he sits for a while, turning the pages without saying a word, then all of a sudden, he's got a plan. "We'll do it on a Thursday night and a Sunday after the missus has said our prayers. I'll send Benjamin, Lily, and Charles to join Gil. You should be able to begin as soon as Hubbard leaves."

That reminds me that Hubbard has a wife and daughter over on the Hope plantation and he has a pass to see 'em on those days. He's gone for most of the night, getting back before dawn for the next day's work.

So that's how we begin—with me teaching the kids.

We wait till Hubbard leaves, and when Henry gives the signal, they come around to Lizzie's and I sit 'em on the floor to start the lesson. They all got their own grease lamp, so they can see the words of the book when it's passed to 'em, and all the time Henry keeps a watch outside in case anyone should come by and see the light. One night, when we were finished and he came back inside, he told me that our cabin glowed in the night like a little star of learning. That's what he said—it really was.

After two weeks of lessons, Henry sends along his eldest, Mary, and George comes along too, on account of the two of 'em being inseparable. I put 'em in a row of their own behind the little ones, to show 'em some respect.

I teach the alphabet the way we used to do it at the orphanage, by singing the letters to a tune so it gets inside your brain and stays there. I have 'em humming that tune before they go to sleep and when they get up. I get 'em humming it out on the swing, knowing they got to say the letters in their head so no one can hear 'em. It ain't long before they know the sounds of all the letters and some of the words that you can make with 'em.

"Anyone know a word beginning with *F*?" I ask one night, but all they do is giggle and laugh. I don't know why it's funny.

One time, Joshua said to me, "I know more swearwords than you."

We were sitting in the orphanage yard, our backs to the privy on a hot afternoon, and I swatted away a fly. "That ain't nothing to be proud of."

"You just saying that 'cause you don't know 'em. I can do a whole alphabet of swearing. Billy's been teaching me. Bet you ain't even got one for *A*."

"Don't be an ass." I smiled at him, all sarcastic. "Everyone knows how to cuss, Joshua. It don't mean you're clever."

"Uh-oh! You said *ass*." Joshua put a hand across his mouth. "Now you're gonna have to burn in hell with me."

"I was only saying it to prove you wrong. Everyone knows that word. It's nothing special."

"I got another one for *A*."

"No, you ain't. There ain't another one."

"*Adventuress*. It's another word for prostitute."

Well, I could not believe my ears. "Stop it now! Do you hear me?"

"I got three for *B*."

"No, you haven't. And if you do, I don't want to hear 'em."

"*Boat licker*, *blazes*, and *bastard*. Billy told me I'm a little bastard. He says I got to be."

"If he says it again, you come and tell me and I'll take him to Father Mosely's office. That boy's no good for you, Joshua. You hear me? He ain't no good at all."

"*Crap!*"

"Stop it."

"*Drafted!*"

I walked away from him. I told him I didn't want to hear another word of it or God would surely strike him down.

But all the time, I was trying to think of a word that might begin with an *E*.

—

Gerald lies back on the grassy bank to dry himself off. "You're doing good with your swimming."

I shake the water off my legs and sit beside him. "Now that I'm treading water, I reckon I'll learn real fast."

"Reckon you're right," he tells me. "Your reading's coming on good too. You must be practicing it a lot on your own."

"I do."

"How'd you find the time?"

"You wanna know a secret? I read it on the latrine." Gerald makes a face like that's about the most disgusting thing he's ever heard. "Fifteen minutes in the morning and the same every evening. I'm as regular as clockwork."

"Don't you have people knocking on the door?"

"I might be getting a reputation, that's true enough, but the way I see it, it's worth it."

Gerald shrieks with laughter. "Ooh! They must think your guts are something rotten!"

"Some people've been steering clear of me, that's for sure."

I'm laughing along with him and I don't remember when it got so easy for me to lie. "Say, Gerald?"

"Yeah?"

"What about the writing? You gonna teach me how to write as well? It ain't no good me reading if I don't know how to write."

The next time we meet, he brings a piece of slate and some chalk so I can write the letters out. He tells me I can keep it like I knew he would, and I get my class to pass it around and write out the first letter of their own names.

And then something new happens. I start to hear the grown-ups humming my alphabet tune when we're in the field and I begin to wonder whether they're doing the letters in their heads. I ask Albert straight out. "Hey, Albert, you humming my tune?"

Well, he gives me a little *ABC*, whispers it in my ear when we're bent down sawing at the trunk of a tree. Turns out George has been teaching him and he can go all the way to *J*. He says he'll know the whole thing come Sunday. A few days later, Lizzie and Henry tell me they want to learn too and so I arrange for the parents to sit in the back of the cabin, and soon enough I'm giving 'em their own class for an hour after the littl'uns have finished and gone off to bed.

———

Today I taught Lizzie to read the word *Jesus*.

I taught George how to write in sentences and he even remembered to use a capital letter and a full stop.

See! I'm doing it, God! I'm doing just what You asked me to. And that's all You can ask for any day, to keep my brother safe.

CHAPTER 11

It's Sicely who brings us the bad news, same as it always is, when she comes running to the fire pit, shouting out that Mrs. Allen can't sell our cotton.

Mr. Wickham had turned the missus away from the market only this morning on account of an embargo issued by Jefferson Davis himself. "They won't let us sell our cotton," Sicely tells us, all breathless and wide-eyed. "They reckon it's unpatriotic and we should hold on to it so the English don't have a choice 'cept to join the war and break the Union blockade. Wickham said we ain't gonna give 'em any cotton till they beg for it."

She has other news too. Tells us she saw a train pull into town full of the wounded and dead from the war. She says the hospital is full of broken men looking sorry for themselves, and there weren't enough wagons to carry all the coffins from the train, there were that many. That's what she tells us.

Lizzie shakes her head. "Things'll get a lot worse before they get any better, that's for sure."

In Connie's cabin, they got a different view. "I told you they were losing the war." Connie smiles broadly and leans back in his chair like he's sitting in rays of warm sunshine.

Antoinne lights a grease lamp so we can see ourselves more clearly. "I'll be gone soon. You wait and see if I ain't."

"You'll be dead soon." Connie taps his pipe on the table and takes a pinch of fresh tobacco. "That's what you'll be if you can't wait. I told you before and you oughta have the sense to control yourself. It won't be long now."

Antoinne paces around the room, unable to stay still. "All I got to do is get behind those Yankee lines and there ain't nothing they can do about it. I'll be a free man and I'll have my rights."

"And how you gonna do that? This is the most dangerous time to go. They'll be strung out along the river waiting . . ." Connie looks crossly at me. "You still itching to get away as well?"

"I ain't exactly itching." The truth of it is, I ain't thought of leaving here for quite a while.

"Good. Least someone here has got some sense."

"What happens if the Yankees lose the war?"

Connie clears his nose. "They won't lose no war. I heard they passed Baton Rouge already and they got gunships coming up to Vicksburg. There ain't no way they can lose. Just you wait and see."

"They'll lose if they ain't got the men to fight," Antoinne interrupts us angrily. "We got to fight for the right to be free. We can't sit around, waiting for some white folks from the North to do it all for us. We got to do it for ourselves."

Connie snorts at him. "I heard they won't even let you carry arms. I heard they'll have you digging ditches for 'em, same as if you would if you was still a slave."

"Don't you worry about that." Antoinne sits back down at the table, but he keeps his fists clenched. "I'll be fighting for the right to be free. Don't you worry 'bout that."

The two of 'em take to arguing about how many soldiers each side has and the size of the gunboats. They argue about who's the better general—is it Grant or is it Lee?—and I listen carefully to 'em, all the time wondering which side God's on and why He doesn't hurry up and get it over and done with.

At dusk, Mrs. Allen comes to the cabins with Gerald and she gathers us around the fire pit. She confirms everything Sicely told us but says she has a plan to store the cotton till it can be sold. "Come the spring, we'll only plant half the amount of cotton and turn the rest over to corn or another crop that will feed us till the embargo is lifted. It'll be hard work to make ends meet," she tells us. "You'll have to put wood aside in the fields too, Hubbard, just in case those Yankees come up the river. I'd rather burn the whole crop than see 'em get a cent of my hard work, I swear to God I would."

So there it is. Now we've heard it from the horse's mouth, so to speak, no rudeness to Mrs. Allen intended.

She goes on to read to us from the Bible, reciting the story of how Abraham gave up his own son as a sacrifice to the Lord. She leads us in prayer and we each put our hands together and lower our eyes as she remembers those brave Confederate soldiers who are away from their loved ones, fighting for their right to be free.

When she's finished praying, Mrs. Allen still won't let us go and she turns up the wick on her oil lamp so we can see her face clearly. "I want you to remember that we're likely to have less food than we've enjoyed till now and we're going to have to work twice as hard to see us through the winter. Now, I know you ain't gonna like this, but I've decided there will be no more leave from the plantation until further notice."

A murmur of disbelief rises up around us and when I look to see what Gerald thinks, he won't meet my eye.

"Hubbard, would you fetch the passes that you have in your cabin and bring them here to me?"

Hubbard hesitates, but he does it, coming back outside with the signed passes and handing 'em over to the missus for her to count and make sure she's got all of 'em.

Henry steps out into the circle as our spokesman. "But, ma'am, we can't work every hour God sends. We gotta have some time of our own."

The missus shakes her head. "I hope it won't be for long, but that's exactly what we gotta do, Henry. If we ain't working every hour God sends, then we might not prevail, and I won't let that happen, not with my husband away from home and putting his life on the line for everyone. I hope you'll see the sense of it in time."

"But, miss . . ."

Mrs. Allen puts her hand out to stop him. "This ain't up for discussion, Henry. Now good night to all of you." She takes Gerald by the hand and starts up the path to the house, while Winnie and Sicely follow on behind with the lamps.

Hubbard goes back inside his cabin and shuts the door firmly, but the rest of us stay put at the fireside. "She can't do that," Antoinne complains. "A man's gotta have some freedom. It don't matter if he *is* a slave."

Isaac's angry too and he empties his pipe onto the ground and runs his thumb around the bowl. "How am I going to meet a girl if I'm stuck here the whole time? I tell you, she ain't got the right."

"No. It's us ain't got the rights." Antoinne's got a face like thunder. "This is the last straw."

Connie puts a hand on his shoulder. "Come on inside." He walks Antoinne to the cabin and shuts the door behind 'em and I put my own arm around little Gil's shoulders and follow Lizzie back to ours. I light a grease lamp and fetch the primer from under the floorboard. "Time for ten minutes more before bed."

"I don't want to." Gil lays his mattress down.

"Don't give me any of your cheek," I scold him. "It doesn't matter if you want to or not. You got to do it anyway."

"Let him be." Lizzie looks at me, annoyed. "We got enough to be thinking of without you opening up your books."

So I put it away, replacing the piece of board in the floor so it won't be found.

Come the morning, Antoinne and Isaac are gone. I ask Connie where they are as we walk out to the fields, expecting him to say they're down at the latrine or been sent on an errand. "They've gone," he tells me. "Least I expect so. Their stuff's gone too."

"Have they gone to meet the boats?"

Connie shrugs. "They didn't tell me. I expect they've gone north. Now, don't you go talking about 'em to anyone. Do you hear me? The more time they have to put some distance between us and them, the better. Chances are they'll turn up later, and when they do, they can answer to Hubbard themselves."

I nod in agreement. I tell him I won't say a word. So we don't say no more about it. We go out into the field, same as we always do, and Hubbard is already there, same as he always is. He's pulled the wagon into place and has positioned the tall baskets where we can empty out our sacks. The missus has taken the horse for herself today, but Hubbard's still big on his feet and he stands on the wagon, looking back up the path to see who's coming.

When everyone's out in the field and working the line, our sacks slung over our shoulders, Hubbard comes across to Connie. "Where's Antoinne and Isaac? Why aren't they here?"

Connie straightens himself up, looking over the field toward the cabins. "They were coming this morning. I know they were. Perhaps the missus asked 'em for something."

We go right on back to picking and Hubbard walks along our line, having a quiet word here and there with some of the others if he thinks they aren't doing something right. Everyone relaxes when we see him walk in the direction of the house. Even George stops picking so fast.

"Where are those boys, Connie?" Henry calls out. "I saw 'em sneaking about in the night. Have they run off? They sure looked up to no good. They have, ain't they? They've gone and bolted. That Antoinne was itching to join up. I know he was."

Connie wipes the back of his hand across his face and speaks quietly. "I think they've gone, but I don't know. Not for sure. If they have left, then they don't have much of a head start and they hadn't made a plan, least not one I knew about."

Lizzie straightens up and looks out to where the river runs through the fields. "They shoulda planned it first," she says quietly, before we move away from one another, shuffling back into line to bend low and pick the cotton from the base of the plants so we don't show our troubled faces, though we all fear the worst.

I don't see Hubbard come back into the field. I just hear him call out Connie's name and hear the lash of his whip. The first blow catches Connie across the shoulders as he rises. He puts his arm to his face, and the second lash meets his forearm, and the tip curls around to sting the edge of his eye.

"Don't you lie to me again. Do you hear me?" Hubbard walks away down the line, his whip held high in his hand as a show of force to the rest of us, and we all pick faster than we did before. Everyone 'cept Connie, who stands and watches Hubbard walk away before he bends back over his stem and picks them bolls the way he always picks 'em, all slow and steady. He don't do nothing different.

That evening, we go down to the woods to pray and I read to 'em from the Bible. Afterward, Henry tells me I oughta take more of a role in leading the ceremony 'cause I got more knowledge than anyone else here, and I'm pleased he asked me and I feel all warm inside as we come back toward the cabins.

Connie's the only one at the edge of the fire pit, so I go and sit with him as the others take themselves inside.

"Hey, Connie, guess what. Henry told me I could lead the prayers next time we meet. He said it makes sense for me to do it since I've spent more time in a proper chapel than anyone else here."

Connie takes a long drag of his pipe and blows the smoke up into the night and I can see he's got a face as long as a horse's. He don't even want to look at me. "Do you think God'll save you when they catch you teaching slaves to read? Do you think He's gonna suddenly appear when they discover you been leading slaves in prayer?" He turns to meet my eye. "They'll beat you till you're black and blue. Probably put you in the cotton gin and close the lid on you. I don't imagine you'll feel so good then."

"God won't let that happen." I shake my head. "Not while I'm doing His good works. He'll keep all of us safe from harm."

Connie spits down into the dirt. "God don't help people like us. He never has."

"You don't believe that."

He turns away from me.

"Connie?"

But he won't answer me. Just shuffles his feet with his back to me.

"Why you being like this?" He stands up to leave and I stand up too. "Don't ignore me, Connie! I know you ain't as mean as this. Have you been drinking? I bet you have, 'cause this ain't you."

I'm expecting him to shout at me, to have a go at me like he did in the cabin when I saw his back—but when he turns on me, he's got a blank expression and I don't know how he feels at all. "Everyone's got two faces, Friday." He's breathing heavily through his broken nose. "Sometime you ought to take a proper look at mine."

He walks back to his cabin without even saying good night, and I let him go 'cause I know there'll be no talking sense to him tonight, and anyway he'll feel different in the morning. He'll be the Connie with a big heart that likes to look out for me.

I walk back around the fire pit, intending to relieve myself before I turn in. When it's dark like this, I use the clump of bushes on the far side of the cabins, same as everyone else, and I go there now, creeping past Hubbard's cabin, where light seeps out from under his door. I wonder if he's still awake and then I notice a hole in the wall, 'bout the size of a walnut—a golden nugget of light that winks to me as I pass, sure as if it were sitting on a riverbed, urging me to pick it up.

I ignore it and go behind the bushes, but as I stand there wetting the leaves, I can still see that tiny hole of light and I'm gripped with an urge to put my eye to it and look at what Hubbard's doing. I don't know why. Chances are that whatever I see ain't going to be worth the risk of getting caught, and yet the more I think about it, the more I want to do it, and so I step up to the edge of his cabin, daring myself to take a look.

I can't hear a thing—not from inside the cabin or here outside. Everything is still. Everything is quiet. So I step closer, put my hands on either side of that hole, put my eye to the nugget of light, and I see Hubbard instantly. He's sitting in a chair over by the fire and he has his back to me. He's very still and I think he might be asleep, but then he moves, lifting up the hand that I can't see and transferring a book to the hand I can.

A book! It really is a book. Hubbard has an open book in his hand and I can see it clearly as if it's daylight, a slim volume from which he reads.

I blink and look again. Hubbard's reading. He really is.

I take my eye from the wall and look back over my shoulder, checking that I'm still alone, and then I look again.

Hubbard turns a page. He puts a finger up to the words so he can make 'em out, the way I do when I read the primer to the kids in Lizzie's cabin.

So Hubbard can read.

Well, I weren't expecting that.

CHAPTER 12

Mrs. Allen works us hard in the weeks that follow, but every minute I ain't in the fields, it seems I have my head in a book. Sometimes I'm at the river with Gerald as he teaches me to read and write, amazed at how quickly I'm coming along. The rest of my time's spent smuggling myself from one cabin to another so that I can be the teacher.

Now that Mrs. Allen has taken back the passes, Hubbard can't visit his wife and child and that means changing how I give my lessons. I go from teaching a single big class to teaching in ones or twos. That way it don't seem suspicious, and Lizzie and I put a rota together in our heads to make it work. Sometimes, I arrive at a cabin to sit with Mary or Harriet before I scuttle across to George and then go back over to Lizzie, who now has her lessons with Gil. We snatch at little pieces of time between work or on a Sunday, but mostly we study late into the night, with someone watching out in case Hubbard might show at his door or Mrs. Allen come down from the house.

It ain't unusual for me to be stopped as I go scurrying between the cabins. It might be little Gil or it might be George. "Hey, Friday"—they'll catch my arm and bring me right up close so we ain't overheard—"I been telling Kofi that cotton is spelled with a *K*. I'm right, ain't I?"

"No, George. You're not right on that one. It's spelled with a *C*."

"Well, how's that, then?"

"Ask me again in class." I take my arm back and edge away toward my next appointment. "We'll write it down together so you can see."

Only the little ones still use that first primer with the dog. Everyone else is on the second primer or proper books, all of 'em brought to me by Gerald, who thinks I must be the cleverest Negro he's ever had the fortune of owning, while the truth of it is that Mrs. Allen don't hardly have a slave on the plantation that can't say their alphabet, 'cept Connie, who says he don't want to learn, and Winnie, who says she might have, once upon a time, but you can't teach an old dog new tricks, so she won't be doing it, thank you very much.

And then there's Sicely. That Sicely sure is high-and-mighty. Even her own mother rolls her eyes at the things she says: like how the missus told her she couldn't manage without her, or how the master had promised her a new brooch as a reward for her devotion to his family. Sicely still can't read a word, but only because she's too well behaved to partake in something the missus don't allow.

What's more, she don't approve of our meeting in the woods either. She's a Christian herself—she tells me this often, mostly before she starts preaching at me for not doing something or other the correct way—but unlike the rest of us, she puts great store by the visits of Mr. Chepstow, who still arrives on the second Sunday of the month to preach to us slaves. Sicely keeps faith with him because he's Mrs. Allen's choice and she often tells me, "He's a proper preacher, teaching the word of the Lord the way it was intended to be and not skulking away in the woods like common vagabonds."

One day we are alone in the kitchen preparing food, when Sicely confides in me that this coming Sunday she will be asking Chepstow to baptize her. That surprises me. "I thought you was baptized already."

Sicely looks uncomfortable, but she don't lash out at me the way she usually would. Instead, she goes a little coy. "I didn't want to do it when I was with Mama at the summer camp. I didn't like the thought of going in that river, so I said no, but I was only young."

"Were you scared 'cause you can't swim?"

Sicely looks shocked. "A lady don't have need of swimming! It ain't decent."

I step away, thinking it's better to be at a distance, but she chops at a potato till it lies in little pieces and that calms her down, so when she next speaks to me, she's very civil. "Have you been baptized yourself, Friday?"

That makes me smile, remembering Father Mosely standing over me, pouring water from a silver jug and marking a cross on my forehead with his thumb. There weren't a boy arrived at the orphanage who weren't baptized the same day they walked through those gates. "Sure," I told her. "I been baptized, though it was a long time ago and I didn't have to go in a river. I been nervous of the water myself too. I couldn't swim when I came here, but I've been learning how and I'm getting better since I've been practicing."

Sicely gives me a nervous smile. Not much of a smile, but I see it. "Well, I'm older now." She nods like she's certain of it. "I decided I got to be braver, and the preacher will have a good grip of me. If he agrees to it, I'll be baptized the month after this one. That'll give me time to make my dress and get myself ready."

She takes another potato and chops it up the same as before, and I don't expect her to say any more since this is the first time she's said something pleasant to me and it can't last much longer. I move across to the hearth to check on the fire. I bend down to rake it through, but when I straighten up, there is Sicely hovering close to me. She's pretending to stir the pot in her hands, though I can see she has something on her mind. "I was wondering"—she lowers her voice and I'm all ears, straining to catch every word, wondering what she's got to say that means she has to be this nice to me—"could you teach me my name? I mean to read it and to write it too?"

I hesitate and perhaps she misunderstands, 'cause I see the temper flash behind her eyes and she says by way of justification, "It don't seem right to be baptized without knowing how to write your own name!"

"I'll teach you," I tell her quickly. "Course I will. Only why stop there? I can teach you a lot more besides. I mean, if you want me to." A sudden idea makes my eyes widen. "You could join our class!"

Sicely shakes her head. "I won't be doing that. Mrs. Allen wouldn't like it if she knew. Anyway, I only need to know my name. That will be enough. That's all I need to know."

"OK. That's up to you."

We make a deal to meet in secret, down in a copse of trees that were girdled the spring before last and are standing dead, ready to be felled. Although it is close to the house, there are plenty of bushes to shield us from view and give us the privacy we need.

Sicely and I sit together on a log. As part of my own lessons, Gerald has made me a copy of the alphabet, written out by hand on a loose piece of paper that I have in my pocket, and I unfold the sheet and lay it on my knee so Sicely can see. We're sitting real close, but it don't feel uncomfortable like I thought it would.

I start by getting her to say her name. She says it real fast—"Sicely"—and looks at me like I'm a fool for not knowing. I repeat it back to her. Slowly. Breaking it down into parts and sounds so she can hear how it might be spelled. I hiss the *S* like a snake and point to the letter. "That's the easy one on account of it both sounding and looking like a snake." I take hold of her finger and put it on the page, make her trace the shape of it, slinking to the left and right across the paper.

"Hissss . . ." I say to her.

"Hissss . . . to you too," she says, smiling.

I point to the letter *I*, tell her it looks like a person standing up straight, and she repeats it. She's doing well. I can see she's concentrating, and when she smiles again, it's with her whole face, so I know it's real. She points to the letter *S* again. "That's the next one, the same as last time, that little old snake, coming back for more."

"No. That ain't the one, Sicely." I point at the letter *C*. "That's the next letter in your name."

Sicely never likes to be wrong. "They sound the same," she objects. "Why'd they have a different letter do the same thing?"

"It don't do the same thing. Well, it does here, but there's other places where it does its own thing, like the word *cure*. You hear the sound it makes there? It's all hard. It ain't soft like a snake when you say *cure*."

Sicely ain't happy at all and she stands up off the log. "That don't make any sense. Are you sure you're a teacher? Do you think

I'm some fool that don't know my own name? My name's Sicely."
She says it quickly, hissing like a snake, and this time, there's no
smile at all.

"It don't make any sense—you're right."

She watches me impatiently and I know she might walk away
at any moment. I can't explain why it has to be that way. It's just
the way it is, but she's not gonna like me telling her. "Sometimes,
there are rules that you've just gotta learn and get on with." She
scowls at me, uncertain whether I'm telling her off. "Like . . . like
when you showed me how to lay a table. Do you remember? I
didn't understand why it had to be one way and not the other,
but you told me that was just the way it was. I think it's the same
thing here."

Sicely looks back over to the house. "Well,"—she smooths the
front of her dress and sits back down on the log—"I want to make a
better job of it than you did with the table."

"You're clever, though, so you won't do it wrong again. It'd help
if you could see it written out, but I didn't bring a board."

At our feet, there are twigs that have fallen from the dead trees
and they give me an idea. "Help me gather these up," I tell her, suddenly all excited. "We're gonna write your name, Sicely. We're gonna
spell it out in big letters."

I show her what to do, bending down and picking up sticks,
kicking away leaves with our feet to clear the space, and we make a
letter each, glancing at the paper so she knows the shape of 'em as
we write her name on the ground.

We climb the tree easily. We don't need to go high, just a few feet
from the ground, and I help her up and she don't mind holding my

hand till she's steady on the branch. When we look down, there are the letters of her name, three feet large on the ground beneath us:

S I C E L Y

She smiles. "So you're saying that's me?"

"That's you," I tell her. "That's how you spell your name."

———

Before Sunday arrives, Sicely has learned the letters off by heart. We have spelled her name to each other, whispering it as we work in the house, right under the noses of Winnie and Mrs. Allen without them knowing a thing about it.

Sicely.

It don't matter if I fan too slow or the table ain't been set correctly, 'cause with sweet *Sicely* on my lips, I am safe from harm. I even think she might like me.

But when I find her alone in the cookhouse on Sunday morning, she's got a face like thunder and I know we're back to normal.

"What's up, Sicely?"

"Don't you what's-up me! There's plates on the side need going up for lunch. The preacher's already here, so you better be on your best behavior."

No politeness. No smile. Nothing.

I put a sullen hand out to take hold of the platter, but Sicely's suddenly upon me, seizing my arm and burying her head in my neck. "He said he won't baptize me," she sobs. "Says I have to be in church to have it done and it has to be at a time that's convenient to everyone concerned."

I answer the back of her neck, where the tufts of hair peek out beneath the edge of her white linen cap. "Does he expect the missus to bring you in the cart?"

That makes Sicely howl. "I don't know! I told him it won't be convenient till the war's over, and heaven knows when that'll be, but he said I'd just have to wait. He told me patience was a virtue."

I know to tread carefully, but I ease her off my shoulder. "Baptism is something between yourself and God," I tell her. "It's personal."

"I know that!" She folds her arms and glares at me. "What's your point?"

"My point is . . . well . . . I know it wouldn't be the same, but . . . I been doing a lot of the services down at the river . . . If you want me to do it for you, I think it would still count. I mean between you and God. It would be like it was at the Baptist camp. It wouldn't matter that it wasn't in a church." I hold my breath, not sure what she's thinking or whether I even have the right to offer. "I can remember most of the proper words," I tell her, hoping it might help. "I'm sure I can. If you want me to."

And to my surprise, Sicely says yes.

———

A few days later, Gerald brings a book to the river, called *Robinson Crusoe*. "Hey, Friday!" he shouts to me before he's even close. "You're in a book! Look here!" He arrives at a run and opens it up to show me the bits where the shipwrecked sailor meets a savage on the beach. "You're famous! See here? Crusoe—that's the poor ship-

wrecked sailor—he names him after a day of the week. He calls him
Friday! Exactly the same as you!"

He thinks I should be pleased, but I scowl. I can't tell him why, but
inside my head I'm screaming the same thing, over and over again.

My name is not Friday! My name is not Friday! My name is not Friday!

"Ain't no one ever been called Gerald in a book," he tells me
when he sees I ain't impressed. "Not that I can think of. You should
be happy about it."

He smiles at me, all big and generous, but I can barely bring
myself to look at him.

*Friday's the boy that lies to you. Friday's the boy that makes you steal
your mother's books.*

He holds it out to me. "Don't you wanna read it?"

"I expect it'd be too difficult."

"But you got to try. What if it's all about you?"

*It won't be. My name's Samuel. That's the boy you want to be
friends with.*

"It's just a name," I tell him. "It's nothing special."

We lie back in the grass, both of us silent and resentful, and I
get to thinking 'bout Joshua and how he always loved his name. He
was so proud of it—proud of the stories from the Bible and proud
of how he was named after our daddy when he weren't even the
eldest son.

Once, when he'd been caned unfairly, he got together an army
of his little friends and made 'em march around the schoolhouse
seven times, trying to make it fall to the ground. Sometimes he
got the other boys to fight for him, got 'em to hunt out Johnny

Bradshaw and his gang in town 'cause they were dirty little sneak thieves.

One time he came back with a bloody nose, but I reckon he gave as good as he got and I told him he deserved it. It don't do to fight. I never seen any good come of it.

Gerald's still lying in the grass beside me, looking up at the clouds, when I pick up the book. "I been ungrateful, Gerald, and I apologize. I don't know where I'd be without you bringing me books, and I'd like to read this one if that's still all right with you."

———

We go down through the darkened woods, a long line of us Baptists, with me out in front, holding Sicely's hand as we head to the river-bank. She's in her new white dress and her hair's tied up in pretty new rags. Her fingertips are soft to the touch and I weren't expecting that, but it's nice to hold hands and it's strange being here in the dark with Sicely.

I don't know which of us is more scared—her or me.

I'm trying to think what I'll say when we arrive and how I'm going to lead these people in worship. I don't know why I ever thought this was a good idea, and I'm praying to myself, "Don't drop her. Oh, Lord, whatever you do, please don't let me drop Sicely in the water."

We get to the riverbank, same place we always go, and Henry sets the cross up on the grass and we start singing and dancing, same as we always do. We work ourselves up into a steam and Sicely takes her hand from mine, but she stays close to me in the circle and she's shuffling her feet on the grass and her hips are swaying in her lovely white apron. I can still make out the shape of her beneath the cotton of her dress and she never looked as lovely as she does now. When I close my eyes, the smell of her lingers in the air beside me and I feel like a honeybee, all covered in the goodness of her, feeling like I might drown if I breathe too much of her in, but we're both swaying with the will of the Lord and singing softly of the psalm as it is told. *"By the rivers of Babylon, where we lay down and wept."* We got our hands up in the air. Singing *"Take me to the river, take me down into the water."*

I reach out for Sicely. Everyone parts to let us through when we step from the bank of grass and go down into the water, just the two of us, and then we step again, the water rising to our knees, so cold it takes our breath away, and Sicely comes closer to me, her fingers held tight around mine, and I whisper for her to trust me, tell her it'll be all right, and we step again, we go right up to our waists and her dress rises to the surface like a lily on a duck pond.

I put my arm around her waist to hold her steady. She's got her hands up at her chest. They're clasped together, real tight in prayer, and her eyes are closed and her teeth are chattering away as I raise my voice. "Before God we die and are born again. We take our name before God as a confirmation of our love of Jesus Christ." Sicely smiles and she trembles in my arms. "You already know this young girl's name."

Lizzie calls it out, as loud as she dares. "Sicely!" She looks to the left and right of her. "I named her myself the very day she was born and I called her Sicely!"

So then the rest of us chant her name again, singing it softly like a beautiful song that we all know. *"Sicely! Sicely! Sicely!"*

Well, I ain't so nervous now. I'm full of the power of the Lord and I ask 'em to spell it out, same as they do in class, and they call out the letters like I taught 'em to. Sicely says it too, whispers it softly under her breath, but loud enough that I hear her hiss that *S*.

"Sicely, do you promise to keep the commandments of God?"

"I do."

"I didn't hear you! I said, do you promise to keep the commandments of God?"

Sicely opens her eyes and shouts out, "Yes, I do!"

"And do you reject Satan and his wicked ways?"

"Yes, I do!"

"Well, Sicely gives herself to God." I lift one arm in the air while still holding her sweet waist in the other. "I bathe this girl in the holy waters of God's love, I bathe her in the light of Jesus and let Him cleanse her soul so she might enter into the kingdom of heaven, just as He Himself intended."

I pause, coming closer to her ear. "Get ready," I whisper. "Here's where I'm gonna dunk you."

Her fingers dig into my arm and I clench the back of her dress, praying that I won't let her slip, not for the life of me. "In the name of the Father, of the Son, and the Holy Ghost, I baptize you, sweet Sicely."

I plunge her down into that dark water till she disappears completely. One . . . two . . . I bring her up on the three, all gasping and fresh, like a newborn baby with startled eyes, just how Joshua looked the moment he was born, though she don't start crying like he did and I don't slap her either. I wouldn't dare. Not for the life of me.

Sicely breaks into a smile and everyone on the riverbank starts clapping and shouting out, "Praise the Lord!" without a care of being overheard.

Lizzie wraps us both in blankets as we step from the river and then the two of us sit on the grass, all shivering and smiling in each other's arms, feeling like we're the bravest and most beautiful people in the whole wide world.

I never felt so close to God as I do right now. Every nerve in my body is fizzing and alive. And I could be Moses. I really could.

CHAPTER 13

Connie was returned to his owner the week after I baptized Sicely, and the whole thing was done sneaky, so maybe that's what upset me. One minute he was in my life and the next thing I knew, Connie was gone and I never even had the chance to say good-bye.

The two of us were in the yard when Hubbard told Connie to make the wagon ready instead of going to the field. "You gotta come with me," he tells him. "We gotta fetch a couple of sows from a farm about ten miles down the road."

Connie lifts his hat up and scratches at his head. "Which farm's that?"

"The one up by the crossroads," Hubbard answers him calmly. "Up near Hare's End. We're meeting a farmer there. He's coming to us from over near the border and he'll give us the pigs to bring back."

I should've guessed we didn't have the money to be buying pigs, and even if we did, it wouldn't need two fellas to bring 'em here. Connie mumbles something about seeing me around and turns away. "What'd ya say?" I ask, and catch his arm.

He turns back to face me, though he won't hold my eye. "You take care while I'm gone."

That was the closest I got to a good-bye, and all I got to say in reply was "Sure."

After lunch I'm cleaning the dining room windows, when I see Hubbard come back up the drive and he don't have no pigs and he don't even have Connie sitting next to him on the wagon, so I know immediately that something's wrong and I hurry downstairs.

Hubbard is seeing to the horse when I reach the yard. "Is everything all right?" I ask him, my voice all high and breathless.

That big man barely turns to look at me. "Everything's fine, Friday. Why wouldn't it be?"

"You didn't come back with no pigs, and Connie ain't with you either. Is he hurt?"

Hubbard stands upright and steps closer to me. "He ain't hurt. Why would he be hurt?"

"'Cause he ain't come back." I can feel the panic rising up into my throat. I feel like screaming, feel like crying out in pain, and I need to know why that is, even though my guts already ache with the truth of it, 'cause Connie ain't coming back. I already know it. He's gone. Just like my daddy left. Just like all the men who've ever looked out for me.

Hubbard seems unsure of what to say, but then he shrugs. "I suppose you'll find out sooner or later. Mrs. Allen asked for him to be returned to his master before the end of his contract. I'm sorry, Friday, but he won't be coming back."

"Why'd she want to do that?"

"That's none of your business."

"But it ain't fair!" I shout out, feeling like he's lit my fuse. "You could have told me! You should have said he had to go!"

"The missus decides how things get done," Hubbard tells me matter-of-factly and turns back to the horse like that's the end of it, but I'm full up with a hurt and righteous indignation that won't be ignored.

"I'll ask her myself!" I turn on my heels and head back for the house, where I know Mrs. Allen will be working on them uniforms.

"Now, hold on there!" Hubbard shouts to my back. "Don't you go . . ."

My head's all light and giddy, like I'm walking on clouds that carry me inside the door and on into the hallway, where Mrs. Allen is already there before me, walking down the staircase on her way to the parlor, with her arms full of cloth.

"Excuse me, miss?"

I pretty much run toward her, taking the first few stairs in one long stride so that she looks alarmed. "Friday? Whatever's happened? Is everything all right?"

"No, ma'am. No, I don't think it is."

Hubbard bursts through the door at my back. "Friday!"

"Is someone unwell?" Mrs. Allen asks the both of us.

"No, ma'am," I tell her. "No one's ill. It's not that. But I want to know why Connie left."

Hubbard grabs a fistful of my shirt and pulls me two steps back down the staircase. "That ain't no way to speak to the missus. Now you get back outside and stop your bothering—"

"Hubbard, let him go." Mrs. Allen looks surprised at the sudden fuss. "Whatever the matter is, I'd prefer to hear about it." Hubbard releases his hold of me, but he stays right there, breathing down my neck and ready when he's needed. "Take this into the parlor,

Hubbard." Mrs. Allen offers him the folds of cloth and he takes them reluctantly and carries them down the stairs.

"Mrs. Allen?" Harriet comes to the top of the stairs with the baby. "Do you want me to bring Virginia to you?"

"Not right now, Harriet. Come and find me in another half hour."

When Mrs. Allen eventually turns back to me, she has such concern in her eyes that all my anger disappears. "Are you upset about Connie?" I swallow hard. I got tears welling up and she can see 'em. I know she can. I nod.

"I'm sorry to hear that, Friday, but needs must. I don't have two cents I can rub together at the moment, and once his owner let it be known he'd take him back without my having to pay up the contract—well, I have to say, I jumped at the opportunity, and anyway, it's November tomorrow, so there ain't as much to do as there was."

"But you should have told us, ma'am!" I blurt out. "I'd have liked to say good-bye to him properly."

Mrs. Allen cocks her head to one side like a listening dog. "I hadn't realized the two of you were close."

"Yes, ma'am. He looked out for me when I first came here. He's someone I can go to for advice."

It strikes me then that Connie won't be here to tell me when it's time to leave and I won't know those boats are here till I see 'em with my own eyes. That's just about the last straw, and a tear slides over my cheek toward my mouth. I lick it away just as Hubbard reappears. "Come away, Friday," he says, more softly than before. "You've had your say. Now let the missus get on."

Mrs. Allen puts a hand on my shoulder. "Come with me." She leads me briskly toward the parlor, with a rustle of her petticoats. "Hubbard, you may leave us. Thank you for your help."

She shuts the door behind us and pours me a glass of water from the jug on the side table. "It's never easy losing those we're fond of, Friday, but I always think these things are better done with a minimum of fuss. Sometimes it doesn't do to let things stew."

I hold the glass to my chest, not sure what I should say. The missus takes a sudden interest in her fingernails before she says uncertainly, "I myself left behind a loving family in Alabama when I married Mr. Allen. I still possess both my parents and I have three sisters of whom I am particularly fond." She nods at the glass in my hands, meaning for me to drink, and I take a sip of it, enough to wet my lips. "It's such a long way for them to come and stay," she continues. "I do find that hard."

She collects a small oval frame from the mantelpiece and holds it up for me to see the picture of a young lady who looks a lot like her, although she possesses an easier smile. "This is my younger sister, April. Until two years ago, we did everything together. I must admit, I wondered how we'd cope with being apart, but she writes to me often and I believe she's managing quite well. I have less time to think of her now that I have a whole new life here that needs my attention."

"I have a younger brother, miss."

She looks alarmed. "Do you?"

"Yes, miss."

Her eye twitches as she pours herself a glass of water. "And your mother and father?"

I shake my head. "It's just me and Joshua, ma'am. It's only been the two of us for a while now."

"I see."

I smile weakly, uncertain whether I have said too much and wondering how much more she might ask. She puts the picture back in its place. "Well, I'm sure he's coping well without you—just like April has to do without me. All of us are stronger than we think we are, Friday—I can tell you that." She hesitates, then adds, "It's important that we make the best of the cards life deals us. That way we become stronger."

"Yes, ma'am."

She smiles at me. "I've been watching you work and I have to say I'm very pleased with the way you apply yourself."

"Thank you, ma'am. I try to do my best."

"You're not like the others. You have a quality about you, Friday, a certain something that marks you out. I'd say you have the makings of an excellent foreman if you were to work hard."

"Thank you, ma'am."

"Would you like that?"

"Yes, ma'am. I suppose so. Thank you, ma'am."

She takes my glass and places it back beside the jug. "You need to run along now, but I'm glad we've made time to have a chat, Friday. I really should have done it before, though with the war on, I find there's so much to be done and so little time to do it all."

I leave the room feeling all stirred up, like a glass of muddy water. Something has happened between us, but I don't know what it was, and when I reach the yard, Hubbard is still there waiting for me to come outside, and he watches me walk away toward the fields.

———

That evening, Mrs. Allen comes down to the cabins before prayers. She knocks on Lizzie's door, but opens it herself before we have the chance to answer. Leaning inside the cabin, she sees me. "May I speak with you, Friday?" she asks, and when I get to the door, I see Hubbard standing at her back, looking all uneasy.

"I've decided to move you," Mrs. Allen tells me. "You need to collect your things and go across to stay with Hubbard."

A shudder passes through my chest and runs down to my feet. I don't think there's a piece of me that don't feel a fright. "How do you m-mean?" I even stammer a bit, and that's not like me.

"You need to come along with me," Hubbard says gruffly. "You'll have to bring your mattress with you as I only have the one."

Lizzie must've heard what was being said, 'cause she appears at my back. I can feel her come right up behind me and I want to lean back into her, I want to sink right back into her chest as she puts a hand on my shoulder. "Oh, no, missus, there's no need for that." She takes hold of the door and opens it out wide so we all got a good view of one another. "I've got plenty of room for him here, and he's friends for Gil. He looks after him. Now that Milly's gone and Sicely's sleeping up at the house, it's good for me to have him here to help."

"That's kind of you, Lizzie, but the change will be good for Friday."

Lizzie steps past me and stands just outside the door. "But the boy should be with the other kids, ma'am. He don't wanna be cooped up with a grown man on his own. It won't be good for either of 'em." She turns on Hubbard. "You don't want to be looking after a boy of his age. You don't know what they're like, of course, but I'm telling you. They're messy. They can't cook and they don't clean up. My Sicely don't have a good word to say for him, but I don't mind him, see, and I'm used to having a full house. It keeps me from thinking too much."

Hubbard has got nothing to say on the matter—he simply stands waiting, his head slightly bowed—but Mrs. Allen is resolute as always. "I'm not prepared to argue with you, Lizzie. This boy's never known a father and he's at an age where he needs a strong male figure in his life. I reckon Hubbard fits the bill about right and he's willing to take him on and show him how to behave." Lizzie shakes her head, but so does Mrs. Allen. "He's past the age of mothering, Lizzie. I realized that when we spoke this afternoon."

"But, ma'am—"

"That's enough, Lizzie. It's not as if he's going far, so be done with it."

"You better fetch your mattress," Hubbard says again. "I'll clear a space for you."

Lizzie comes back inside and watches me take the mattress from the wall as Hubbard and Mrs. Allen walk over to his cabin.

"What about our lessons?" I whisper as I walk out past her.

"I don't know," she mutters, and shakes her head as though nothing good can come of this. She follows me outside and watches as I walk across the strip of mud that divides our cabins. Hubbard has left his door open and I take my mattress inside.

He closes it behind me, and when I turn around, he's standing there blocking the way. In the shadow, I can barely make out his face. I nod at the mattress. "Where'd I put this, sir?"

Hubbard steps across to me. He reaches out, takes the mattress from me, and places it on the floor in the opposite corner to his own. At least I'll be a distance from him when I go to sleep.

"I'll cut you some new fir to stuff it with," he tells me. "It'll make it more comfortable."

"Thank you, sir."

"Don't call me sir," he snaps back, making me jump half out of my skin. But when I look again, I can see he looks as nervous about me as I am of him and that's strange. He seems somehow . . . ashamed? Can that be right? He softens his voice. "I ain't the master here, am I?"

"No, sir. I mean—no, Mr. Hubbard, you ain't the master."

Hubbard walks to the small hearth, takes a pot that's hanging there, and fills it with pone. "Have you eaten?"

I take a deep breath. "Lizzie cooked me something already." I think of the half-finished bowl of food still sitting on her table and know it won't do to work in the field tomorrow without first having a decent meal.

Hubbard nods at the only other chair. "You don't have to stand. You can sit down."

He unwraps a side of bacon, takes a knife, and cuts enough for himself, rendering the lard and saving it for shortening the biscuit, the same way Lizzie always did. I know how to do it, but he doesn't ask me to help. I thought he would have wanted me to work for him, but he don't seem to. He just carries on as though I'm not even here and he don't talk to me at all.

This is the first time I have been inside Hubbard's cabin. It's larger than the others—I reckon about three feet longer—and it has two windows, one on either side, so there's a bit more light than in Lizzie's.

Everything is neat and tidy. He has a set of shelves up on the wall above the hearth and he stores his cutlery and plates in wooden boxes. A spare set of clothes hangs from a nail on the wall. He also has a few possessions of his own, the sort of thing Lizzie couldn't afford, such as a proper brass oil lamp, the same type that the missus uses to guide her on the path when she comes to the cabins in the evening.

That night, when Mrs. Allen reads to us from the Good Book, I say a little prayer of my own, asking God to keep me safe, and once we finish, I follow Hubbard back to his cabin and retire straight to bed, where I pray again, making a show of it by kneeling at the side of my mattress so Hubbard can see I'm doing it right, though I don't know if he cares. I whisper the words under my breath, asking God to take as good care of me as he has with Joshua, 'cause the truth of it is, I feel like Daniel in the den of lions.

"Today, I forgive Connie for leaving me, though it wasn't his fault. Today, I was kind to the missus and I forgive her too, for what she did to me. She's only trying to do what she thinks is best, even if it ain't what You intended. I hope those are enough good things today to keep my brother safe. And me too, Lord. Keep me safe too."

I pull the blanket up around my ears as Hubbard turns the lamp down low. He don't say no prayers—not that I can see—just steps out of his boots, folds his clothes onto the back of a chair, and falls asleep before me, his big ol' breath reaching me through the darkness, more like I imagine a bear to breathe than a man.

——

The next day is cold in the way November has of letting you know that winter's on its way.

Hubbard wakes me earlier than Lizzie did, taking hold of my shoulder and shaking me briefly before he walks back to the fire. He has a pot of hot coffee by the hearth, and his lamp is already lit upon the table. He sits down on a chair to lace up his boots.

"Come over by the fire." He stands and walks across to the door, taking up the horn that hangs there. "You know how to make ashcakes?"

"Yes . . . yes, I do."

"Then put some on the hearth. I'll be back presently."

He watches me rise and come to the fire before he goes outside. He must have gone to the latrine, because it's a while before I hear the horn blow and then he returns, putting the horn back on the wall and coming across to the fire, where my cakes are blistering and brown. He picks one up, moving it quickly between his hands as he blows on it, then takes a bite. "Needs a pinch of salt." He pushes a small pot across the table to me. "I keep it here. So you know for next time."

I take off the lid and stare at it. "Lizzie don't have salt to cook with."

He might have taken offense at that, but he don't. He only says, "I see."

Once we're finished, we rinse out our own plates and tin cups without so much as a word to each other. It's still too early for the field and there won't be anyone at the fire pit. I get the feeling he's watching me, waiting for me to do something. He says, "I got to go up to the field and get everything ready." He walks to the door but hesitates there, seeming like he doesn't want to leave me in his cabin on my own.

"I can wait outside for the others."

"There's probably no need. You could stay if you want."

"No. It's all right. I should see Lizzie before we go to the fields." I hurry past him, and Hubbard closes the door behind both of us.

Lizzie brings me into the warmth and sits me down beside Gil. "How was it?" she asks me. "Did he leave you alone?"

"Sure. Why wouldn't he?"

"I don't know. He can be a difficult man when he chooses."

"It weren't his idea. Least I don't think so. Say, Lizzie, do you think he knows about the lessons?"

"It wouldn't surprise me. It's his business to know everything, but I reckoned he was turning a blind eye so long as we didn't rub his nose in it." Her forehead creases up as she thinks it through. "We'll have to stop for the time being. I can't think of anything else we can do."

The day after that is cold and so is the one after that.

There ain't no cotton left to pick and the fields are full of the dry old husks of the plant, looking like twigs sticking up from the ground, just dead wood waiting to rot. We cut back the stems and plow the stubs of 'em back into the ground, making it fit for planting again come the spring.

Now that there's nothing for us to do in the fields, Hubbard gives us new tasks to keep us busy. Some days, I mind the pigs, and on others, I learn to make horse collars from husks of corn or from strips of poplar bark, made soft so they can be braided. I spend a day with Kofi at the smithy. He's supposed to teach me how to make new grubbing hoes and how to hammer rims for the wheels of the wagon, but I only spend a few hours over the heat of the fire before he sends me back to Hubbard, saying I have two left feet and thumbs that can't hold on to anything useful. That's hurtful and he didn't need to say it. I thought Hubbard might be angry, but he doesn't show it. He sends me back to Winnie with a message that she was right all along—I am a house slave and better put to work in the cookhouse when I'm not out picking cotton in the field.

During the working day, Hubbard behaves the same way toward me as he does with everyone else, and when we're together in the evenings, he mostly leaves me alone. We don't sit around the fire chatting, like I used to with Connie or Lizzie. We ain't got much to speak of anyway. When we eat, we make polite conversation. Sometimes he asks me something specific about my day, or he shares a piece of news, but it's always something I have already heard from someone else and I get the sense he don't give much away.

He's been fair with me, though. I'll say that for him. He don't bully me or boss me around, and I'm less fearful of him than I was before. I do my fair share of the chores, deciding myself what I should do, since he rarely tells me to do anything in particular. I can see he's neat and tidy in his ways and I should try to be the same if we're not to fight. Also, I don't want him thinking I'm a good-for-nothing.

Mostly, I spend the evenings outside by the fire pit while Hubbard stays inside the cabin. He never mixes with the rest of us, but, then, he never has. I come and go without him asking where it is I'm going or when I'm coming back, so after a little while, I begin giving lessons again, starting out slowly, just a half hour here or there, with Lizzie keeping watch like an owl. I'm careful never to be too late back and run the risk of questions, but none ever comes my way, so we begin to increase the time I give to everyone, and after a few more weeks we start to breathe a little easier. Sometimes, I wonder whether Hubbard reads his book while I'm out teaching, and it seems to me we're both playing a game of sorts.

"Do you think he knows?" Lizzie asks me one night as we put the books away.

I have to stop and think about it. "I really don't know, Lizzie."

"You make sure it stays that way. You can't ever let him know, Friday. Once it's out in the open, he'll have to act, and if the missus ever finds out about us learning to read, then heaven help us."

I let myself out of Lizzie's cabin and into the night. There's a clear sky and the stars are shining brightly as I step quietly across to our cabin, where the lamplight shows underneath the door, telling me Hubbard's still awake. I go inside and he is sitting at the table with his back to me, so I say, "Good night," then creep across and kneel by the edge of my mattress to say my prayers. Once I'm finished, I lie down and pull the blanket up over my shoulders. I'm falling off to sleep, when I hear Hubbard's chair scrape upon the floor and he walks across the cabin, approaching me as I lie in my bed. I keep my eyes tight shut, but really I'm wide-awake, listening for his every step. Hubbard stops walking. A board creaks with the weight of him, so I know he's close. I can feel him standing over me as I pretend to be asleep, hoping he'll go away. But he doesn't.

"Are you awake?" he whispers.

I'm clenching my eyes too tight. Maybe he can't see 'em, but if he can, then he'll know I'm faking.

"Friday?" He ain't whispering no more. "Friday! Sit up and let me see your face."

I open my eyes and that big man is leaning over me, close enough he scares the living daylights out of me. "Get up," he says. "I want to talk to you."

He goes back to the fire and kindles a flame from the embers, using bits of twig and cones that he blows on. I don't know what he wants of me, but it can't be good, I just know it can't.

I come and stand just a few paces from him, waiting as he turns from the fire and regards me for a moment. "Can you read and write?"

All the blood rushes from my head, along with any idea I might've had to lie. I can't think of anything to say. All I can think of is how he might have found out. Has Sicely told him? Has he spied on me at Lizzie's? Perhaps he looked through a hole in her cabin wall, the same way I looked at him. Perhaps he saw me getting Gil to write on a board with chalk.

Hubbard sits at the table, but his eyes haven't left mine. "I asked you a question."

"I ain't allowed to read."

"That ain't what I asked."

Hubbard waits for me like a lion, knowing he can catch me whichever way I go.

He stands up suddenly and I stagger back a step or two, glancing over at the whip that's all coiled around itself and hanging on the hook by the door. It looks like a snake in the grass. Hubbard reaches for the oil lamp and turns the wick higher, making the light dance up onto the walls. He takes a wooden box from the shelf behind him and places it on the table. It's about the size of his hand, perhaps a little bigger. He slides off the lid and takes out a book—the same one I saw him with?—and holds it out to me. There's a man's name, John Keats, written in gold leaf along the spine. Hubbard flicks it open, then holds it up to my face, right under my chin. "Read it to me."

I shake my head, knowing that taking hold of that book is sure to be the death of me.

Hubbard glares at me. "I know you can read it. Go on and take it. Show me you can do it."

And so I chance my arm. "You can read it for yourself. I know you can."

Hubbard lowers the book a little bit. "You're wrong, Friday. I can't read it myself."

The way he says it makes me believe him, but I know what I saw. "If you can't read it, how come you've got it? You know we ain't allowed books."

Hubbard closes it up, places it on the table, and sits back down in his chair. "This belonged to my mother. It ain't my book." He lays his finger on the cover before flicking his eyes back to mine. "I can't read a word of it."

"But I've seen you read it. I've seen you sitting with it open in your hands."

"When have you seen that?" His temper flares. "Have you been spying on me?" He flicks a finger in my direction, then says more calmly, "Sit down."

I don't. I stay where I am.

"I said, sit down! You're making me nervous." I take a tiny step toward the table. "Don't try my patience," he says harshly, and then softer again, "I'm not gonna hurt you."

I pull out the chair from under the table and sit slowly, watching him closely, knowing I ain't got a chance anymore of getting to the door if he comes for me.

"Listen to me, Friday. I never learned to read or write. My mother would have taught me had she had the opportunity, but that never came. Sometimes, I do get the book out and look at it—it reminds me of her—but I can't read it. I only stare at the writing, wondering what it says." He sounds embarrassed. "Friday, I need your help."

"How do you mean? Do you want me to teach you to read?"

"No, it's not that. It's something else I had in mind. It's not even the reading. It's the writing." He reaches up and brings a second box to the table, larger than the first. He takes out some paper and a pot of ink and I can't believe my own eyes, seeing him with such things. "I want you to write me a pass. You have to make it look as though it's from the missus. Can you do that for me?"

"You want me to forge you a letter?"

Hubbard nods. "I've got a wife and daughter I haven't seen in weeks. Someone came and found me. They told me my wife's ill. But I can't risk going without a pass. Not at the moment. Do you understand me?"

I touch the edge of the inkpot. "And you want me to do it? Now?"

Hubbard nods. He takes a slip of paper from the box and pushes it across the table toward me. I pick up the pen, but I don't write a word—not yet. "How come you think I can help?"

Hubbard meets my eye again. "I know what you do, Friday. I know about the lessons. I know everything about you." He ain't threatening me. In fact, when he says it, he looks smaller than I'd ever have thought possible. "We've all got to do what we must, Friday. We don't have a choice. Not any of us. But now you know about me too. That's all I got to give you if you help me."

I write Hubbard his note and I take my time, trying to think how Mrs. Allen would word it, making my handwriting as neat as I reckon hers would be, and while I'm writing it, Hubbard gets ready to leave. He packs a few things in a canvas bag—a blanket and his pipe and some food from our rations.

"Are you gonna go tonight?"

He nods, taking the slip of paper from me without thanks or ceremony. But I don't mind. It's enough for me to know that now we have an understanding, and I can't wait to tell Lizzie the good news, that we can go full steam ahead with our learning and Hubbard won't bother us at all.

I give my thanks to God that night. I didn't think He knew what He was doing, putting me in with a man like Hubbard, but now I see I was wrong again.

"Today, I helped a man I thought might hurt me. I helped him visit his wife and child. These things I have done today to keep my brother safe."

But then I hesitate, unable to go to sleep but unsure what else it is I have to share with God. And so I confess to my misgivings.

"Today, I cheated on Mrs. Allen. I disobeyed her rules and I know that if she ever finds out, she'll think the less of me, never mind what she'll do to punish me.

"I hope You won't let it count against me. I hope it doesn't cancel out the good things I have done."

I say amen to that.

CHAPTER 14

I pull myself from the river, shivering and flapping my arms together as the gooseflesh raises the tiny hairs. It's too cold for swimming and I tell him so.

"You might be right." Gerald's already dressed and lying in the grass. He has wet patches under the arms of his cotton shirt, but he's warmer than me. I rub my legs dry and dress quickly, all the time jumping up and down to make the blood reach my feet.

"Hey—I brought you another book!" Gerald takes hold of his satchel and brings out a large black volume, holding it up so I can read the title. *A Christmas Carol*. "Can you read that?" He don't wait for me to answer. "I'll tell you what it says." He turns the book around and reads it for me. "*A Christmas Carol*. By Charles Dickens. Maybe it's too difficult, but I brought it anyway 'cause you might manage some of it."

"Let me see." I snatch the book, open it at the first page, and begin to read out loud. "'Marley was dead: to begin with. There is no doubt whatever about that. The register of his burial was signed by the clergyman, the clerk, the undertaker, and the chief mourner.'"

I don't hesitate or stutter. I don't even put a finger to the page to follow the letters. The relief of not having to pretend overwhelms me.

Gerald sits up, suddenly alert. "Hey! Let me see that." He pulls the book closer so he can see it, not believing I could read it without making a mistake. He puts a finger to a new paragraph halfway down the page. "Read that bit there."

I lose my nerve and make a mistake on purpose. "'Mind! I don't mean to say that I know, of my own knowledge, what there is part . . . partic . . .'"

Gerald leans across to look at the word, but he can't say it either. "'Parti . . .' That's a difficult one, Friday. I ain't even sure of it myself."

And I just can't help myself. "'*Particularly*'—least I think it could be."

Gerald's eyes are wide as saucers. "Why, you can read it better than me!" He snaps the book shut. "How'd you manage to get that good?"

"I been practicing with the books you gave me." I can't help but smile, seeing him so impressed. "I've been working real hard at it. I thought you'd be pleased."

"Why, I am pleased. That's great news. Isn't it? It's what we've been working for after all?" He slaps my shoulder harder than he should, but then he says, "I'm really proud of you, Friday. I knew you weren't like the others. I knew you could do it."

He looks at me differently. I don't know how to describe it, but I feel kinda naked, like he's seeing me for the first time and we both know something's changed between us—like we're more equal than we were before—and I'm grateful for Gerald's big heart, 'cause it ain't easy to be generous when you don't seem to be getting nothing back.

"It's 'cause you're a good teacher," I tell him, feeling guilty 'cause I don't really believe it.

I get a sudden urge to confess it all, to tell him that I could read all along, that it ain't what he thinks—not any of it. After all, he thinks he knows me. He thinks we're friends. And we are friends, I suppose. I like him more than I liked anyone before and so I should tell him everything. But just as I'm about to, he stands up and prods me with his toe. "Come on, smart aleck. Let's go check on those lines."

And the moment passes as we walk along the riverbank. There'll be a better time to do it. Sometime later. Once everything changes.

We're looking out for the lines we'd set to catch bass. Some of 'em are for catfish. "I got some news about my daddy," he tells me after a little while. "We got a letter saying he'll be back for Christmas."

I've heard this already, on account of Sicely's gossip, but I still act surprised. "That'll be grand!"

"You've never met him, have you?" I shake my head. "Well, there ain't a better time to make his acquaintance than at Christmas. You'll see him at his very best. He gives the best presents—everyone says so—and he'll always have something for you in his pockets when you ask him for a Christmas gift. I help him wrap 'em up, so I know he does."

"I like the sound of him already."

We come to a stick we'd pushed into the ground as a marker for our line, and Gerald kneels and puts his hand into the water, feeling for a fish. "I don't think they're biting," he tells me as we walk on, stopping at each stick to check for fish, though we haven't caught a thing. We never do. I don't think Gerald chooses the right places.

He don't mind, though. He's so excited about his daddy, he just keeps on talking and I barely get a word in edgewise. "He'll arrive Christmas Eve and he's already told us he wants a side of beef for the fire pit. It's what we always have." I nod as though we wouldn't have anything else. "Do you know how big that beef will be?" I shake my head. "It'll be big enough that we have to start cooking it before the sun's up. That's pretty big. We got a spit that we bring down to the cabins on Christmas Eve so everything's ready for the next morning. That'll probably be the first thing he does when he gets here. You ever had beef?" I shake my head. "Best meat you ever tasted, if it's cooked right. And Winnie knows how to cook it too. My daddy always says so. Says she does the best beef roast this side of town."

We reach the last stick and Gerald kneels again and slips a hand in under the water. "He's got two weeks' leave. Maybe he'll get to stay longer. They've got the Yankees on the run, so they don't need him as badly as they did."

"You reckon the Yankees are on the run?"

"Sure."

"How do you know?"

"It's obvious, ain't it?" He brings his hand up and shakes the water from his fingers and I wonder what stories he must have been hearing about them boats back down the river. He stands up quickly, like he might have actually caught a fish, 'cept he ain't. "What if you read to my father when he's home?" he says excitedly. "He'll be so impressed; I know he will."

Suddenly, I ain't so sure of myself. "I don't know about that, Gerald. I don't think I'm good enough. Not yet."

"Sure you are. I'll tell him I taught you myself. I'll tell him I chose you and bought you at the auction and then taught you how to read. I want him to know we own the best-educated slave in the whole county and that when we give you your freedom, you'll be able to sign the papers with your own name. Oh, he'll be pleased at that; I know he will. And he'll be proud of me too."

I'm finding out what it's like to be on board a train with no brakes, and I want to jump off. "Well, hold on there. Let's think it through. I mean, there's enough things all stirred up around here without having a Negro knowing how to read. Perhaps it'd be better to wait till times ain't so hard."

But Gerald don't give it a thought. "I can't wait. It'll be fine, Friday. My daddy'll make everything work out for the best. He always does. It's going to be some Christmas. You'll see."

That's easy for him to say. But then, it ain't gonna be his head on the line. It's gonna be mine.

——

" 'It was with great astonishment, and with a strange, inexplicable dread, that as he looked, he saw this bell begin to swing. It swung so softly in the outset that it scarcely made a sound; but soon it rang out loudly, and so did every bell in the house.' "

You could have heard a pin drop as I say those words, though there ain't no space to drop a thing. Everyone's crammed into Lizzie's cabin except Hubbard and Lizzie herself, who's outside keeping watch. They're sitting on the floor in front of me, listening to me read, and I can see their faces in the dim light, hanging on my every word. Even Sicely's here, right there by the door, crouched on the floor with the rest of 'em, wanting to hear the tale 'bout a mean old master who learns the error of his ways at Christmas.

I've planned for each of the readings to last an hour and am hoping to finish the book on Christmas Eve, since I already know the story has a happy ending and I reckon it will be a fitting way to begin the festivities. The grease lamp gives the right atmosphere as I read on, making it feel like the story's happening right here in this room.

" 'They were succeeded by a clanking noise, deep down below; as if some person were dragging a heavy chain over the casks in the wine merchant's cellar . . . The cellar door flew open with a booming sound, and then he heard the noise much louder, on the floors below, then coming up the stairs . . .' "

"There's someone outside!" Benjamin shouts, and we all turn to the door, hearing the footsteps on the ground and the creak of a foot on the step. The latch begins to lift and little Gil screams as the door flies open to reveal Lizzie, looking more scared than any of us. "Why you screaming?" she shouts out, her mouth all agape. "What on earth is the matter?"

Well, there was uproar. The room becomes full of hooting and hollering as we all shout at one another, but mostly we shout at Lizzie. "What're you doing creeping around outside? We thought you was the ghost of Jacob Marley!"

"Who?"

Little Gil slaps his mama's leg. "You shouldn't have scared us."

"Who, me? I didn't mean to scare a soul. I just wanted to know what was happening. I didn't know you were hearing about no ghost. Who do you say he was again?"

I know they ain't never gonna let me go till they've found out what happens in this book—no, not for love nor money—and by the end, they all want to take the book away so they can try to read it for themselves. I tell 'em it's too difficult. "By next Christmas, you'll all be good enough." And it's true too.

——

The next day, Mrs. Allen takes Sicely into town to buy supplies for the Christmas dinner, but when they arrive, they find the store is empty. There ain't a hunk of beef to be had. There ain't a turkey nor a piece of venison. Sicely says that Mrs. Allen came out of that shop with little more than a bag of sweet potatoes, so we already know that we'll be having pork or bacon for Christmas dinner—the same as we do every other day of the year—and that's a disappointment.

When Mrs. Allen comes down to the cabins in the evening, she finds us surly and lacking in the Christmas spirit. She reads us the Christmas story of Mary and Joseph going to the stable, 'bout how they didn't have no food and they couldn't find a place to stay, 'cept to sleep in with the cows. Once she's done, she tells us we'll be given three days of free time over Christmas and she'll issue passes to all of us if we want 'em, so we can come and go as we please.

"Three days?" Henry complains. "Master gives us four days minimum, ma'am. Always has."

"I know that, Henry. I was already here last Christmas, if you remember." She lifts her chin to look him in the eye. "But this year we've all got to make sacrifices."

"Even so, ma'am," Henry persists, "it's still a day we lose at Christmas. Is it true there won't be any beef? Perhaps it wouldn't be so bad if we knew we had a bit of beef, ma'am."

"I'm sorry, Henry, but that store ain't hardly worth its name these days. Mr. Williams told me he hadn't seen a side of beef for a couple of months now."

"So we got to have pork on Christmas Day? That's a sad thing to hear, missus. It really is."

All this talk of food makes me realize how hungry I am since I been here and that ain't a good feeling to get used to.

But Mrs. Allen's got other ideas. "No, Henry," she tells him, "you're mistaken. We ain't having pork." She nods at the ground to our left where the chicks have gathered and are pecking at the dirt. "I want these chickens strangled and brought to Winnie in the morning so she can pluck 'em ready for the roast on Christmas Day."

"But, missus . . ." Lizzie steps forward, looking confused. "Those are *my* chickens."

"I know that, Lizzie, and I'll pay you for 'em." Mrs. Allen nods as though it's as good as a handshake. "I'll give you thirty cents apiece, though it'll have to be owed to you and settled the next time we're able to sell our cotton."

"But, missus"—Lizzie seems to swell in size—"they're worth more to me alive than dead. I can sell the eggs, you see. I can sell 'em and save my money. Where am I gonna get myself new chickens with a war on?"

We're all thinking the same thing, but Mrs. Allen stands her ground. "The master is home for Christmas, Lizzie. He's been away at war, getting shot at and risking his life for the rest of us. Most days he'll be lucky if he gets pork to eat, the same as you do, and so help me God, on Christmas Day, if we can't get beef, then he'll taste some chicken." She looks around the circle. "We all will, and we'll thank the Lord for providing it."

Lizzie must know it won't do no good to argue, 'cause she walks over to them birds. "I'd rather you took 'em now, missus. Let me rest up in the morning. If we only got three days off work, then I'd like to make the most of 'em."

Well, those chickens come to meet her, thinking they're gonna get some feed like they usually do, but Lizzie bends over and picks one out and she wrings its neck. My Lord, she did. She don't even hesitate, and I see its eyes bulge and its little legs twitch before it goes all limp. "Go get me a basket, Gil. Help me carry 'em over to Winnie." She drops that dead bird to the ground, right in among its little friends, before she picks out another one and kills it just as quickly. "How many do you want, missus? You want 'em all? Hey, Henry, you got that one over by the tree? You bring it here now. We don't want anyone to go hungry on Christmas Day."

Lizzie won't look at any of us while she does it. She keeps her eyes to the ground and chases the chickens who run away from her, though they don't go far before she breaks their necks, talking to us all the while in a voice as happy as a songbird, like she's out at the river washing clothes with Harriet. The rest of us don't move an inch. We don't know whether to help her or stop her, though it doesn't matter anyway 'cause we all know those birds are gonna die. There ain't no two ways about that.

Once she's finished, there's a pile of 'em lying down there in the dust and Lizzie puts her hands on her hips, exhausted by the work of it. When she looks at us, she's got no life left in her eyes; they're all stony old and gray and she swallows hard. "You want the rooster too, ma'am? He's a tough old bird, but he might as well go now too. He won't be happy without his lady friends." She's breathing hard as she turns around, looking everywhere for him. "Now, where's he got to? Anyone seen that big old boy about here?"

Mrs. Allen says, "I think you should let the rooster be, Lizzie."

"Right you are, missus, though that seems cruel to me, 'cause he'll be mighty lonely."

Lizzie drops those chickens into the basket one by one, then walks across and holds it out to Mrs. Allen. "Here you are, ma'am. Just what you asked for. You want me to walk 'em over to Winnie for you now?"

The missus keeps her cool, I'll give her that. "Thank you, Lizzie, but you can leave 'em for Sicely to bring with her when she comes back to the house."

Everyone felt for Lizzie, but nobody says a thing till the missus has gone.

"I won't eat 'em," declares Levi, and Mary says, "Me neither."

We all agree on that till Lizzie turns on us. "Don't you be so stupid! If I got to kill 'em, the least you can do is eat 'em!"

She takes herself back to the cabin, slamming the door behind her, and the rest of us slink away into the night.

At the table by our hearth, Hubbard takes the polished lamp and turns the wick higher. I ask him how it was the missus could do that, how come she didn't know what it meant to Lizzie. Hubbard had watched the whole thing and hadn't said a word, so I thought he wouldn't answer me now, but he did, and I took it as a measure of how far the two of us had come, 'cause he tells me that if we don't own our own bodies, then we can't have property of our own. Everything we have belongs to our masters. Those are the rules. That's how it is. And thinking it through, I can see the logic of the argument, but that still don't make it right. I tell him so too. Rules or no rules, it made no difference, 'cause we all knew they were Lizzie's chickens.

—

Later that night, there's heavy rain and the chill of a winter wind blows through the holes in the cabin walls. It's enough to wake us, and we push the rags more firmly into the gaps and we stoke up the fire, listening to the rain on the slats of our roof. In the morning when we wake, it's still raining and my feet are cold and numb at the toes. I get up from my mattress on the floor, rekindle the fire, and sit with my feet up close to the grate.

Hubbard has his boots on in bed, so he's right and warm enough. Once he gets up, he fetches me rags to bind my feet, though he says it won't do no good till the rains stop. Still, it is Christmas Eve, the first of our days off, and I'm happy enough to sit indoors by the fire and not have to work.

Hubbard don't get a proper day off since he has to drive Mrs. Allen and Gerald into town to meet the train. He returns with the news that Mr. Allen weren't on it as planned, and there's no word of his whereabouts, nor is there another train for five more days, so it seems we will have to do without him for Christmas.

"I bet Gerald must have been upset."

Hubbard agrees with me. "Both of them were unhappy, but you know how they are—they'll make the best of a bad deal."

Hubbard don't bother to take his wet things off since he's taking advantage of having a bona fide pass to see his wife and child. "I'll be back for the roast tomorrow evening," he tells me as he goes back out.

I go over to see Lizzie, running through puddles in the mud, my feet slip-sliding and cold till I hammer on her door to let me in out of the rain.

"You heard the news?" I ask her, once I'm settled by her fire.

"Sure, I heard it."

"And do you know why he hasn't come home?"

Lizzie adjusts a cup that's positioned on the floor to catch a drip that falls from the roof. "I expect he got delayed. War ain't no convenient thing."

We pray for Mr. Allen at our evening prayers, all of us gathered together in Hubbard's cabin to keep out of the rain, and it's a sober affair, despite the nip of brandy that Mrs. Allen gives us. After she has gone, I read the final part of *A Christmas Carol* and we learn how Scrooge woke up on Christmas morning, how he bought the biggest turkey in the shop and had it sent over to Bob Cratchit and Tiny Tim so they could have the best Christmas feast they ever tasted.

I like the idea that even a man as mean as Scrooge could learn the error of his ways and meet with God's forgiveness, though to be honest, I don't think the other slaves believe it could happen here, and my reading fails to lift the gloom that has arrived with the rain and Mr. Allen's absence.

That night, being on my own, I drag my mattress to the fireplace and sleep there, hoping to benefit from the heat before it dies in the night. In the morning, I wake up to a tapping on the door and hear Gerald's voice. "Friday! Come to the door. Friday!"

That boy has the loudest whisper I ever heard. I jump up to let him in. "What do you want?"

Straight away he gives me a hug. "Merry Christmas!" He sure is excited. He's wearing his Confederate tunic with a wide leather belt and a sword that I can tell must be new. "Get your clothes on and come with me."

"Where we going?"

"We got to get to the yard before everyone wakes up. Come on and hurry up." He grabs my arm, pretty much pulling me out of the cabin and onto the path. He holds me up as I slide on the mud. "We're gonna make a Christmas sleigh just like the one Santa uses."

So that's his big idea. His daddy had always slung a sack of presents over his shoulder and played at being Santa Claus, so now that he ain't gonna be here, Gerald's decided to go one better.

We pull the cart out from the barn and into the yard. We load it with well-seasoned logs for the cabin fires and with new blankets and with cloth that will make our winter clothes. We also bring two sacks from the house, one filled with nuts and fruit and a second filled with gifts, each of 'em wrapped in paper and string, the way I'd been told it always happened.

"They ain't as good as usual," Gerald tells me. "But everyone'll still have something to open for a Christmas gift." We cut sprigs of fir from a tree and twist 'em around the cart for decoration. "Go and get the mule," Gerald orders me.

"I'm not getting that thing," I tell him. "I ain't going anywhere near a mule. Not on Christmas Day."

"You're absolutely right. You sit right there." He runs back to the barn and returns with the mule, which he straps into the harness, and we find two sticks, which we tie on to the mule's ears so they look like antlers.

"What do you think?" Gerald stands back to admire his work.

"I think that mule's mean enough without you giving him horns."

But we ain't finished there. Next we go along to the gin barn and scrape the biggest clumps of cotton from the walls and tie 'em over our ears so it hangs down like a beard, 'cept that mine falls off 'cause I'm laughing so much and I have to do it over again.

Sicely comes out of the cookhouse to see what all the fuss is about.

"Merry Christmas!" we shout across to her.

"What have you done to that mule?" She comes in closer for a better look. "Oh, my word!" she shrieks, and takes herself back inside, shaking her head and laughing out loud for Winnie to come and see.

Gerald puts an arm around my shoulders. "You haven't asked me for a Christmas gift yet. What do you want, Friday? You oughta have first choice."

"Oh, I don't know . . . There's nothing I can think of."

"Course there is. Tell me what you want. If you do it now, I can give it to you before someone else gets it. I wrapped all these myself, so I know what's there."

"I suppose I'd like some shoes. Now that it's getting cold and wet, it'd be nice to walk around in comfort, same as Hubbard does."

But Gerald shakes his head. "I'm sorry, Friday, but we ain't got shoes. I don't have nothing like that."

"That's all right. I only said it 'cause you asked." I close my eyes, reach inside the sack, and take out a package. When I unwrap it, I find a tin soldier just like the one I never got to buy at the Middle Creek shop. "It's just what I wanted!" I hold it up for Gerald to see. "Which side do you think he's on?"

"He's a redcoat. I took him from my own set. I'm glad it was you who got him."

We set off to the cabins, me riding on the back of the cart while Gerald leads the mule. He's ringing a brass bell to wake everyone up and get 'em to come outside. "Christmas gifts!" we shout out. "Christmas gifts for everyone!"

Mrs. Allen comes down from the house and she's smiling again, looking all angelic and kind. She brings butter for our ashcakes and they never tasted better than that morning, washed down with coffee that has half a spoon of sugar from a jar that Sicely said the missus had put aside especially. It had been the last one in the shop, purchased over two months ago, and they hadn't seen the like of one since.

Some of us get bright shiny buttons and some of us get ribbons of silk, either yellow or red, and if you didn't get what you wanted, then Lizzie said you had to swap with someone else or save it till you could take it to the market in town to barter. I get a blanket that's thicker than the one I have already and I'm glad of that. I also get a palmful of tobacco to sell or smoke myself, though I don't have a pipe and ain't never tried it before.

In the evening we gather at the house for our meal.

Sicely and I bring all the tables together into one room, and when we're all sat down and ready, Winnie brings the chickens in, each of 'em on their own plate, ready to be carved and served with vegetables. We can smell their juices as Hubbard stands nervously and says prayers, thanking the good Lord for our daily bread and hoping for the swift return of Mr. Allen from the war.

When he's finished, Mrs. Allen stands and says a few words, thanking us for a fruitful year of hard work and telling us that she has saved a chicken for the master's return, so we can finish the food on the table without fearing we should be too polite.

Winnie and Hubbard carve the chickens, putting the meat on plates that they set before us, though none of us moves to eat till we see Lizzie take the first bite.

Oh, but she is ever so gracious!

She behaves just like a lady. She takes a decent chunk of meat onto her fork, chews it through, and swallows it down before she turns to the rest of us and says she wonders why she left it so long, those birds are that tasty on the tongue. The missus smiles to hear it—we all do—and then we tuck right in.

After the meal, we return to the cabins and build up the fire till the sparks fly high in the air above our heads. A few fellows come by with a fiddle and drum, happy to play a bit of music for their supper, and we dance and clap our hands and sing songs. There are some that I don't recognize and some that I have known before but forgotten—songs I had heard my mother sing to me when I was young. Those melodies come back to me now. I remember the smell of her and the gentle rise of her chest from when she sang to me softly. Thinking 'bout her always makes me think of Joshua and I ache for him too, wondering what sort of Christmas he might be having, all cloistered up with the rest of those boys and stern ol' Father Mosely.

At the end of the evening, there are prizes given for the best dancers. The winners are chosen by Mrs. Allen and Sicely, who does not dance herself and so is better able to judge with fairness. Harriet is thought to be the best of the girls and she receives a bonnet, while Levi wins a flask of brandy that is stopped with a cork. Little Gil wins himself a bat and ball for being the best of all the kids, and Gerald gives the prizes himself, handing 'em out from the back of the Christmas cart, looking happier than he's ever been. I can see the man in him more than ever, see the life and soul of him, battling to become a person his father will be proud of, and I thank the Lord for that. In fact, when I say my prayers, all curled up on my mattress and ready to go to sleep, I don't list the good things that I did today. All I do is thank the good Lord for making this a special day, just like it should be.

"May the Lord look after Lizzie and bless her with new chickens. May He keep Hubbard safe and Gerald too. He won't be happy till his daddy comes home, and I pray for Mr. Allen, although I've never met him. I pray for Mrs. Allen too. Just like Scrooge, she ain't always easy to get along with, but it ain't easy for her, I can see that too, and I thank the Lord that, today of all days, we felt like a family."

Now Christmas is done, we fear the new year.

Lizzie told me this is when the books must be balanced and our owners think to buy or sell their slaves. Many hearts have been broken on the auction block on New Year's Day, she says, and everyone's nervous, hoping it's the master, newly home from the war, who'll get to do the sums that will decide our fate.

But Mr. Allen don't make the next train home either, and we're back at work by New Year, up to our knees in mud, as we haul logs inside the barn to be stacked and seasoned for the winter after this one.

Mrs. Allen says she don't want no fuss and she gets Henry to drive the wagon into town. In the back sits his wife, Nancy, and their children, Charles, Benjamin, Lily, and Mary. The missus sells 'em to a man who grows sugar, but at least they are bought as a family and will stay together, so that is a blessing of sorts, we think.

She returns to collect Kofi, our blacksmith, and Robert, the fittest of our men. They are taken into town and hired out for the period of a year, the two of 'em commanding the highest fees from among us, on account of their particular attributes. At evening prayer, Mrs. Allen says these two transactions will balance the books for the coming year, though only if we are vigilant and prepared to work harder in the fields. She also tells us she'll be working alongside us from now on, getting her hands dirty with the rest of us. "There ain't no point in running a house I can't pay for." Those are her exact words.

In the days that follow, I take to spending time with Gil, since Benjamin had been his closest friend and he feels the loss of him more than most. I fill in as best I can and the two of us are playing hopscotch in the yard when Sicely beckons us to the back door of the kitchen. "Have you heard the news 'bout Mr. Allen?"

I shake my head. I haven't heard a whisper.

She steps closer and lowers her voice, since we are in earshot of the house. "He's gone and got smallpox. That's official. They've put him in a pest house. The missus received a letter when we were in town this morning. It were waiting for her at the store and I was there when she opened it. You shoulda seen the look on her face. She couldn't shut her mouth for a full five minutes. I tell you, she couldn't."

I guess we all must've looked shocked, since there weren't one of us who didn't have a story 'bout that dreaded disease. Even Gil knew of it, though he weren't certain of the name. "Is that the one that makes you scratch till you're raw?" he asks us.

"That's the one," says Sicely, placing a hand upon his head to comfort him in case he thought to start scratching immediately. "George had it. You'd be too young to remember, Gil, but he did. I saw him covered with blisters. He had so many, they joined up with each other and I seen him lie on the floor like some big ol' sack of pus with staring eyes and he weren't good to do anything for a month."

I could remember something similar: Mannie Western at the orphanage, put in a heated room of his own and told to vomit into bowls. Father Mosely made us all wear cloth across our faces for a week, and when they came to take Mannie away, he had so many blisters up inside his mouth that he couldn't have said good-bye if he'd wanted to, or at least that's what we were told. We never saw him back again and, though I am relieved at the thought that Gerald won't be making me read to the master after all, I wouldn't have wished that disease upon a living soul.

CHAPTER 15

We slaughter our pigs late in the season.

I bring 'em into the yard one at a time so Hubbard can slit their throats with the biggest knife I ever set my eyes on. He takes their heads off with a handsaw and we bleed 'em into buckets so Winnie can save the blood for sausages. I cut the whiskers from their snouts and tie 'em together with string, for the missus to sell in town to a man who makes brushes.

Hubbard opens up the carcasses and we hang 'em by their hind legs, stringing 'em up in a line along the fence and leaving 'em to drain into the gully that we've dug in the soil beneath 'em. We carry the offal to the cookhouse, keeping some for the missus while we put the rest aside for the butcher, since he knows who likes to buy a bit of kidney or a heart for their supper on a Sunday.

We let the rain wash down the yard.

Come the morning, we scald the carcasses and scrub 'em spotless. Hubbard butchers the meat and we settle the cuts into salt, turn 'em, then lay 'em up to rest in barrels marked with chalk, which we store for the coming year in the shed behind the cookhouse.

Those pigs take three days' work. By the final evening, I'm so stiff I can't move and Hubbard joshes me, says a young thing like me should be able to do twice as much work as that and still have legs left to dance. He's in a good mood now that it's done, and I lie on the floor by the fire and see him take out the pass I wrote him from his box on the shelf. He puts it in the pocket of his shirt and picks up the bag with his flask of water and a blanket for his shoulders. He puts on his hat.

"You going to the Hope plantation?"

Hubbard nods and tells me he'll be back by morning. But when I wake, he ain't nowhere to be seen. That ain't happened before, and when he don't show up, I got a feeling something's wrong. The horn's still hanging over by the door and I wonder 'bout blowing it myself. I get up and take it off the wall, giving it a go softly, to see if I can get a sound from it, but some things are harder than they look.

I take it with me to Lizzie's, knock at her door, and hold it up, but she can already see the color of the sky and she knows it's later than it ought to be. "Where's Hubbard?" she demands.

I shrug. "He went to see his wife last night and I don't think he's come back."

We cover for him as much as we can. I go knocking on the doors of the cabins to get everyone up and we start work by ourselves, each of us already knowing what's expected of us. Mrs. Allen comes into the field later that morning and she asks me where Hubbard is. I say I don't know. There don't seem no point in lying for him.

I'm up at the house when they bring Hubbard in, his hands strapped to a saddle in the same manner I was marched through town by Gloucester on the day he sold me at auction.

The men have got dogs, three of 'em, running on ahead with their tails wagging, all excited and pleased. It's the noise of 'em that draws me out the house and I see the posse of men coming up the drive, two of 'em on horseback and three walking along to one side. Even from a distance, there ain't no mistaking the size of Hubbard. Those men come slowly up the driveway to the house. They ain't in no hurry like their dogs.

Winnie comes bustling into the yard and she says for me to go fetch the missus and I find her bent over in a field with a hoe in her hands. I tell her the patrol has caught Hubbard and she better come quickly, so she comes to the house directly, the rest of us following on behind, knowing in our bones there'll be no good that comes from this.

We fan out around the yard to get a view of what's happening, though we don't want to get close enough to become a part of it. Hubbard's at the center of us all, still tied to the saddle, a pile of fresh manure on the ground between himself and the hind legs of the beast he has followed. He still manages to look proud, standing tall with his chin held high, though he is bleeding and badly bruised around his left eye. A single line of blood tracks its way across his cheekbone and disappears into his short clipped beard, though it shocks me more to see his trousers torn and filthy, because I've never seen Hubbard looking anything less than smart when he ain't in the field. I notice he wears no hat and figure it must have been lost when they got hold of him.

There's a pull on my sleeve and Gerald is there beside me. "What's happened?" he whispers. "Where'd they find him?"

"I don't know."

The posse of men is led by Peighton. Chepstow's there too, dressed in his black shirt and priest's collar, but I don't recognize the others. They might be soldiers. Two of 'em have got tunics and another wears braided trousers, though there ain't a Confederate cap to be seen among 'em.

They're relaxed, though, standing by the steps to the house, drinking glasses of water, their dogs laid out at their feet with their tongues hanging out. It's obvious to everyone that Peighton's in charge and he watches us, his mouth just aching to break out into a smile as he waits for Mrs. Allen to come to him. "Good day, Mrs. Allen," he calls out eventually. "This here's one of yours, ain't he? I thought I recognized him as your driver. Am I right? I am, aren't I?"

"We don't use a driver here, Mr. Peighton. But, yes, he is my foreman."

Peighton offers his hand to the missus and she shakes it, but then he turns his hand over and inspects the dirt she's left there. "I shake the hand of a lady and get a palmful of dirt? Oh, my Lord. Is that what this war has done to us?" He rubs his fingers together briskly. "It's a shameful day when women such as yourself are forced to work the fields, Mrs. Allen."

Mrs. Allen takes a look at her own palms. "Ain't nothing wrong in getting your hands dirty, Mr. Peighton. God didn't mean for the earth to be unpleasant. You can find water in the kitchen if you wish to wash."

Peighton tips his glass of water over his fingers and quickly rubs 'em together. "Why, that's all right. I don't want to be no trouble." He wipes his hands against his thighs, then looks over at Hubbard. Mrs. Allen looks at him too. She walks across to him, circling the front of the horse to which he's tied, all the time trying to catch his eye, though Hubbard won't look at her and stares at the side of the barn as though it's the most interesting thing he's ever seen.

The missus turns back to Peighton. "Where'd you find him?"

"Over by the Paradise plantation. They grow mostly tobacco out that way and it's hard work so we get a lot of niggers taking leave of the place. There's a wood to the south of it that's a favorite spot for runaways, though I don't believe your man was running away. He's got family abroad, that's what I heard, a wife and a girl who live over on the Hope. That's the next one along from Paradise."

"I'm aware of that, Mr. Peighton."

Sicely opens up the back door and walks steadily down the kitchen steps, carrying a large enamel bowl filled with water for the dogs. Mr. Chepstow scolds her as she sets it down. "I asked you for a pitcher so we can refill our glasses." Sicely bows her head and apologizes. "Sorry, sir. I was just getting it. I won't be a moment." She hurries back up the steps and Mrs. Allen calls after. "Sicely! Be kind enough to bring another glass, would you?"

Chepstow says, "I remembered you had forbidden any leave to your Negroes, Mrs. Allen, so I knew Hubbard's pass must be a fake." He takes a folded piece of paper from the pocket of his left breast and walks across the yard, opening out the pass I'd written for Hubbard and handing it to the missus.

I panic, every nerve in my body getting ready to run, 'cause I'm sure she'll know straight away that it was me who wrote it. But she looks at it a long time, probably concentrating on my sad attempt at her signature. Chepstow pats the head of the horse to which Hubbard is tied. "One wonders how they get hold of these things when none of 'em can write."

The missus looks across at me and she must see me jump out of my skin as I begin to pray to the Lord, muttering away under my breath for Him to help me, telling Him I'll do whatever He wants if only I ain't caught. I did a bad thing when I wrote that note, and I knew it too. It don't do to lie and cheat, even if it's in a good cause, but if God'll forgive me, if He'll only get me out of this, I'm sure I can make things better and I'll make amends for all that I've done wrong.

Mrs. Allen comes up close to Hubbard. She holds the pass in front of his face. "Who gave you this?"

He won't say.

She brings it right up close to his chin. "I forbade anyone to leave this plantation and that included you, Hubbard. You knew that. Now you tell me where you got this."

Hubbard ain't the kind of man who finds it easy to lie, and he says as much. "I won't lie to you," and the missus says, "I hope not," and then Hubbard says, "So I can't tell you, ma'am. I'm sorry."

I let out the breath I been holding in, and it's loud enough that Gerald hears and he looks at me.

Peighton comes across to Mrs. Allen. "We brought him back for you, Mrs. Allen, but we ain't punished him. You should know that. We thought it only proper for you to decide yourself what should be done with him." He steps closer to Hubbard and looks up into his face. "If you'd like, we can whip him till he talks. We can surely do that for you, if that's really what you want?" He looks back over to his men. "I wouldn't let Cormack do it. Last nigger he whipped never lived to see the next morning, and that would be a shame, seeing as how the man belongs to you 'n' all." He inspects a fingernail, then smiles. "I wouldn't want you to lose your investment."

Sicely comes back out through the kitchen door, carrying a wooden tray set with a pitcher full of water and a single glass. She puts the tray down nervously on the steps and takes the pitcher around to the men, filling their empty glasses.

Peighton comes across and has her fill his glass too. He lifts the clear water up and takes a look at it. "No. I would have to do it myself, Mrs. Allen. You can be reassured on that. It'll take but half an hour, then we can be on our way and you can all get back to work." He tips back his head, empties his glass, and puts it back on the tray. Then he returns to the horse to which Hubbard is tied. It has a whip on the saddle and Peighton takes it and flicks the length of leather out upon the ground.

Mrs. Allen holds her own glass of water up to the light. "How long has my foreman been without a drink?"

Peighton chuckles and puts a hand to his chin while he considers the question. "Well, we found him last evening. Kept him in my own barn overnight and brought him out here this morning. I don't recall him drinking anything during that time." He calls back to the men. "Any of you boys let the nigger drink?"

Mrs. Allen puts the glass up to Hubbard's lips. "Drink the water," she tells him.

Hubbard drinks from the glass as the missus tips it up and the water goes half in his mouth and half down his chin, moistening the hairs in his beard and dripping down into the dust at his feet. He swallows hard. "Thank you, ma'am," he says, and looks at her properly for the first time since they brought him in.

Mrs. Allen pulls at the rope tying Hubbard's hands together. "I can look after my own slaves, thank you, Mr. Peighton." The rope comes loose, dropping to the ground, and Hubbard rubs at his wrists under the sleeves of his green shirt.

But Peighton still has the whip in his hand. "You ain't gonna go soft on him, are you, Mrs. Allen? These niggers only need the slightest indication of leniency and before you know it . . ."

Mrs. Allen looks over at me again; she fixes her eyes on me and it sends a shudder through me, 'cause there ain't no mistaking it this time. She definitely knows it was me who wrote that pass, and I oughta make a run for it. I oughta run like the wind 'cause the good Lord has abandoned me, I know He has. I can't feel Him anywhere around here. Not right now. He ain't nowhere around.

Mrs. Allen turns back to Hubbard. "Take off your shirt."

Hubbard hesitates. He looks down at her with those big brown eyes of his, then undoes the two buttons down from his collar, pulls the shirt up over his head, and lets it fall at his feet. I have a sudden urge to pick it up and fold it for him as he stands before us, half-naked and waiting without protest, his bare chest all gooseflesh from the cold midwinter air, and I swear I've seen smaller muscles on a horse.

Suddenly, Mrs. Allen turns and walks over to me and I might have died right then and there, 'cept I'm wrong again.

"Gerald, come out here."

He doesn't move from my side, so she says it again. "Come out here, Gerald." It's clear to us all that she ain't asking him, she's telling him, and then I realize she hadn't been looking at me at all. No. She was looking at Gerald, who is stood right next to me. She must assume it is him that faked the pass for Hubbard, since she believes there ain't no one else here can read and write, 'cept

Gerald and herself. And now he looks like a six-year-old who's been caught stealing cookies from the jar. He must know it was me who wrote the note. He must've worked it out and he's bound to give me up. Ain't he?

He steps out into the circle and I'm expecting him to point the finger at me, to tell Mrs. Allen it was me all along, and I pray a little harder, asking the good Lord to somehow get me out of this.

"Mr. Chepstow?" Mrs. Allen turns back to the preacher. "Would you be so kind as to instruct my stepson on flogging his slave? I would appreciate it, seeing as I lack the knowledge to do it myself."

The preacher puts aside his drink. "I'd be happy to, ma'am." He steps forward, taking the whip from Peighton, who picks the rope up from the ground, saying, "I'll string him up for you, Reverend. Make it easier."

The whip they got is made from two different leathers, one dark, one light, braided together to make a pattern along its length, like the skin of a snake. The preacher puts the whip into Gerald's hand and he rolls up the sleeves of his shirt, first one arm, then the other. "This here's a bullwhip, son."

I'm looking at Gerald, thinking he won't do it, thinking that he can't do it, not with all the things he says he believes. But he swallows hard and lets the length of the whip fall out across the yard. He's got his back to Hubbard as he looks up into the preacher's face.

Peighton and the man he called Cormack lead Hubbard over to the barn door. They tie a length of rope to each wrist and they string him up, stretch the rope over the top of the door so he's up on his toes, his arms out to either side, his bare back spread wide, just about as big as the flank of a buffalo waiting to be skinned. They tie the ropes off tight and step aside.

Chepstow has an arm around Gerald's shoulder as he walks him to the barn. "A bullwhip has got a reach of about nine feet, son, so you want to be standing about here. Do you see?"

Gerald's hand looks too small for the whip, but he holds it tight, looking so scared you'd think he was the one about to be whipped. He keeps pushing the hair from out of his eyes. Chepstow grips Gerald's arm and lifts it in the air so it's in a position to strike. He turns back to Peighton. "What's the punishment for getting caught without a pass?"

"Hundred lashes?" offers Peighton. "Could be more but it wouldn't be less."

Someone tuts.

Chepstow has kept his arm around Gerald's shoulders and his voice is kind and reasonable, like a teacher in a school or a father with his son. "You want to connect at the end of the lash, so the tip of the whip strikes the target." The priest lets go of Gerald's arm and takes a step back. "You'll have seen your daddy do it, I'm sure. Go on. Try it out and see how you do."

The whip trembles in his hand, but Gerald doesn't move; he just stands there with his arm up and I think he's going to say something, he's going to stop it—but he don't do that either. He looks across at Mrs. Allen and then back at Hubbard strung up over the barn door. Maybe he's thinking 'bout what his daddy would do—only he don't seem to know. We're all waiting in a circle, watching him, needing to see whether he'll whip Hubbard or not, this boy who owns the lot of us and says he's our friend more than our master, who's promised he'll set us free.

Gerald cracks the whip. He brings his arm down quick, but the lash falls short, the tip of it scraping at Hubbard's waistline on its way to the ground.

The men all laugh at him. "Why don't you get in closer? He ain't gonna hurt you."

Gerald bites his lip. He's got the same look on his face that I saw when he bid for me at the auction. He steps forward and tries again, but this time he brings his arm up high so that the whip loops up in the air and falls in a weak arc, hitting Hubbard's shoulder on the way down but without any force. He tries again quickly and misses completely.

The men wind him up. "Now you're too close. That's no good at all. Take a step back, then step forward on the swing."

"Chepstow!" Peighton complains loudly. "This ain't no good. Take a shot yourself and show him how it's done."

So the priest takes the whip from Gerald's hand, steps back, and lashes so there's a sting in the tail of it, a fierce crack that draws blood across the blade of Hubbard's left shoulder.

"That's the first one," shouts Peighton. "Those others didn't count."

Chepstow takes another shot, putting his full weight behind the blow, though that ain't so much, on account of him being a thin and spindly sort of man. He hands the whip back to Gerald, who tries again. This time he hits Hubbard, though he still struggles to get the whip high enough and it leaves a mark at the bottom of Hubbard's spine.

Peighton circles the two of 'em like a prizefighter. "This ain't fair. He's only a little fella. I'm gonna get him a chair." He calls across to Mrs. Allen. "Is that all right, ma'am, if we borrow one of your chairs?" He turns on Sicely, "Hey, girl, go get me a chair and bring it out here quick."

Gerald lashes out again and the bullwhip comes down across Hubbard's back and leaves a mark upon his skin.

"That's better," says Chepstow.

Well, Hubbard doesn't flinch. To look at him, you'd think he hasn't even noticed, and that's only going to make things worse, as far as I can tell.

Peighton steps alongside the barn door so he can see into Hubbard's face. "That ain't hard enough, son. It's got to be harder. Look at this man. He's a beast. Ain't no way he's gonna respect you till you make it hurt. Do you understand me?"

Gerald tries again quickly, putting so much effort into it that he misses completely and lashes the wood of the door close to Peighton's head. That makes the men laugh louder. "You're gonna need to sell this man soon as you cut him down, Master Gerald. Ain't no way he's gonna do a stroke of work for you from now on."

Sicely hurries down the steps of the kitchen, carrying a wooden chair, and Peighton takes hold of it, walks across and places it next to Gerald. "Try that for size, boy. That should make it easier."

"I don't need it," Gerald shouts out, and I can see he's close to tears, but Peighton reaches out, picks him up, and stands him up on the seat. The men all hoot with laughter, but Mrs. Allen has had enough and she explodes, like a great dark cloud that's been waiting to burst, like a river that's come up over the banks and is ready to wash away anything in its path. She strides over to the chair and snatches the whip from Gerald's hand. "Get down from there!" She pulls him by the arm so he stumbles from the chair and falls into the dust at her feet. I think she might be about to whip her own son, she looks that angry, only Gerald scuttles away on his knees and runs off to the house in tears and I don't know what is worse than this, seeing the people I care for getting hurt and upset.

Peighton offers to take the whip from her. "I'm sorry, ma'am. We've gone too far. Let me finish this for you and we'll be gone."

Mrs. Allen composes herself, then walks right past Peighton and she don't say a word as she lashes Hubbard hard, like she hates the very soul of him, and she does it again and again, whipping him as though he were Abe Lincoln himself, and she don't stop to look around her. No. She don't hesitate to hear what might be said. She whips that man who is twice her size, whips him till his back is more red than black, till his muscles look more like ribbon than flesh, but even then, Hubbard don't move or make a noise and you would think it was a fly had landed on him for all the emotion he shows, and I reckon that makes her madder still, so she keeps whipping him. She don't stop. She looks calm while she's doing it, but you can see the fury and the strength of her, like she ain't got full control of herself, and I don't think anyone is counting how many lashes he's had, 'cause it goes on and on until I have to shout out, "How many is that? Who's counting how many he's had?" Only no one answers me.

Well, it says something 'bout the pride of the man that Hubbard's legs give up before his head goes down. I see him buckle at the knees and hang there by his wrists and I'm asking God to make her stop, but she carries on, gives him about ten more lashes, and with each one I'm whispering, "Bow your head, Hubbard. Bow your head. If you bow your head, she'll have to stop."

Only he holds his head high. That man won't bow his head even though he can't still stand on his own two feet.

Finally, Chepstow steps forward and puts a hand on Mrs. Allen's shoulder. "I reckon you'd be wise to stop, ma'am, unless you want to risk permanent damage to your property. I make that a hundred and fifty. Give or take. He's had enough."

Mrs. Allen hesitates. She is breathing heavily and she straightens her dress. She hands the whip back to Chepstow. "Thank you for your help in returning my foreman."

Peighton takes his hat off to her. "We'll be on our way, then, Mrs. Allen."

His men rouse their dogs from the water bowl and they mount up and take leave of us as Mrs. Allen takes herself back inside the house.

It's Levi who cuts Hubbard down from the barn. He finds an old door and we lay the big man down upon it. Winnie appears with a bucket of salt water, which she pours over Hubbard's back, and we watch him shake as though convulsed and then be still. He closes his eyes. It takes four of us to carry him back to the cabin and we lay him down upon the floor and leave him there, going back to our work, weaving baskets for the new season and checking on the plows, making sure they are oiled and in good working order.

Later, when I return to the cabin, Hubbard hasn't moved. Not as far as I can tell. I can hear him breathing, and though he doesn't speak, I'm sure he's conscious. I build up a decent fire and cook a broth by boiling water with a little pork and rice. I make sure there's fresh water in the bucket.

Mrs. Allen knocks on our cabin door. "How is he?" she asks, and I stand aside so she can see for herself. She walks past me, kneels by his side, and puts a hand to his head. "He ain't hot. That's a good sign. Bring me over my bag, will you?"

I bring the leather bag from where she's left it at the door and she opens it and brings out a brown glass bottle and a cloth. "I made a flaxseed poultice." She holds the bottle up to show me. "It should help to soothe the pain."

I don't know nothing about that, and I would have told her, if she'd asked me, that she wouldn't have a need of it if she hadn't flogged him half to death. Only I don't. I stand watching her dab at his red raw back and Hubbard don't move nor make a sound. He lies still as can be, his eyes closed like he's dead, though we can hear him breathing, and Mrs. Allen hovers over him, all sweet as an angel, the very same vision I saw that first time we met, and to look at her, you would have thought butter wouldn't melt in her mouth.

She stays sitting with him till the sun is almost set. She sure is gentle, I give her that, and that affects me in a way that's strange and I feel uncomfortable and don't know where to look. I find myself something to do with the pots and pans, but it ain't no good. I can't take my eyes from the missus and I find myself edging closer and closer till I'm kneeling beside the two of 'em. And suddenly I'm crying. I'm blubbering like a little child as I wipe an arm across my eyes.

Mrs. Allen puts a hand to my head and pulls me down upon her lap, where I lie hopeless, sobbing like a little child, watching her soothe the last of the ointment into the wounds on Hubbard's back.

"Do you understand why I had to whip him?" she whispers as she runs her fingers through my hair.

"I think so, ma'am."

"Ain't no one born who don't make mistakes, Friday. Only we can't learn from those mistakes till we accept the punishment we deserve."

I breathe in deeply, drawing the snot back up my nose, knowing it should have been me that took the punishment if it was going to be anybody. "He ain't never been whipped, ma'am. He told me once as a matter of pride."

"Did he tell you that? Well, pride can be a wicked thing, Friday. I've seen you listen to the preacher, so I know you understand. You're a good boy, Friday."

"Yes, ma'am," I tell her. "I do try to be."

But I ain't a good boy, and the good Lord knows it. I'm a bad, bad boy who lies to her and steals her books and I ain't even got the decency to tell her. Not if I don't have to.

When she's finished with her soothing, Hubbard's back is a wide stretch of milky white and there ain't no red or black left visible upon it. Mrs. Allen shoos me from her lap and then packs her bag so she's ready to leave. "Shall I have Lizzie come and stay with you tonight?"

Hubbard's lying half-dead upon the floor, but I tell her I can manage.

"You come and fetch me if he takes a turn for the worse. Do you hear me?"

"I will, ma'am. Don't you worry. I'll come up to the house straight away."

"Thank you, Friday." She smiles uncertainly. "You're a sweet and gentle child and this place is better off for having you here."

"I'll pray for him, missus."

"You do that. And let's hope we have no more need of this type of nonsense. Goodness knows there's enough misery in the world without us making any more for ourselves."

Mrs. Allen leaves the bottle and the cloth on our table. She tells me to apply another poultice in the morning and then she goes outside and gathers us together at the fire.

Tonight she don't read to us from the Bible, reciting to us instead the Lord's Prayer, as she is sometimes wont to do.

CHAPTER 16

First time I see Gerald after the whipping, we dig a grave for his father.

Mr. Allen might have died the same night Hubbard lay on our cabin floor—I don't know—but the news of his death arrives the very day Hubbard is able to pull on a shirt and return to work. The missus had gone into town intending to buy flour but returned instead with two bags of black dye and a letter that said her husband was dead.

Sicely brings us the news from the house. She tells us Mr. Allen had dictated the letter to a nurse as he lay on his deathbed and in it he had promised Mrs. Allen they would meet again in heaven. Sicely thought that was the most beautiful thing she'd ever heard. To Gerald, Mr. Allen asked that he love and obey his stepmother in everything, that he protect his baby sister, and that when he came into his inheritance he run the plantation on the sound principles that his father had already established, in the hope that it would one day thrive and provide a good life for everyone who lived there, just as he had once dreamed it would.

Gerald offers me a choice of shovels and pushes the hair back from his eyes. "You ever dug a grave before?"

"Never," I tell him.

"Well, we better get to it," he says, a look of grim determination in his bright blue eyes.

I take the biggest of the spades and Gerald leads me to an old elm tree, which is situated in the woods on a rise that overlooks the house. This is where he will bury his father, and we choose a spot fifteen feet from the foot of the trunk to start our digging. "Daddy made me promise I'd bury him here if he died."

"It's a nice spot," I tell him as we look down upon the view. We can see the road making a straight brown line through the fields. We can see the shining river as it curves its way around to the sea. In the yard directly below us, Sicely has set up a pot to boil Mrs. Allen's clothes till the dye turns 'em black, and a row of somber dresses already hangs dripping from the corner of the cookhouse, right on over to the barn.

"I'm sorry 'bout your father." It don't seem like much to say in the circumstances, but I want to say something. "I prayed for him like you asked. We all did."

Gerald nods as though he understands. I don't think he wants to talk about it. He only wants to focus on the job at hand. "It shouldn't be so difficult," he says, measuring it out with his feet. "Six feet long and six feet down." He stamps his shovel into the soil and turns it over. Then he digs again.

I choose my own spot about three feet from Gerald and tread my spade down the same way he did. We don't talk for a long time and Gerald digs two spades of dirt to every one of mine, but eventually he says to me, "You never did get to read to my daddy like I hoped you would. That's a shame. Shame you never met him too, 'cause you'd have liked him. He'd have liked you too, I guess."

Now, I don't know about that. I dig the dirt out and we lay it up in piles at the foot of the elm tree. I get a blister on the heel of my hand, feel it rise up sore till it's 'bout ready to burst. Maybe that's what makes me angry, I don't know, but digging that grave for Gerald's father makes me want to strike out and hurt someone. We're digging down through fibrous roots, lumping out wet clods of earth, and I can feel myself getting more and more angry. We've gone about a foot down when I blurt out, "It weren't fair for your daddy to die."

I say it like I blame him, like Gerald has made this happen on purpose, and he stops his digging. "Fairness don't come into it, Friday. It's just bad luck. Mother reckons you got a one-in-four chance if the smallpox gets you. That's why we had to pray for him. He just weren't lucky. That's all."

I bite my lip, but it don't help. It only makes the feeling stronger.

When the blade of my shovel hits a stone, I dig around its edge, teasing it out. "He should never have gone to war. He shouldn't have left you like he did. It's a stupid war anyway. He should have been here looking after us."

Gerald takes offense at that. "Now, hold on there a minute," he says. "My daddy's a hero. There ain't no two ways about it."

We stop our digging and glare at each other, but that don't stop my mouth rattling away like it has a life of its own. "Maybe if he'd been where he was meant to be, then Lizzie would still have Milly.

Maybe Connie'd still be around and Hubbard wouldn't have got whipped. Would your daddy have whipped Hubbard? I don't think he would. You told me he never whipped a man himself. It was you who said that. I remember you did."

"So that's what this is about."

"Why'd you do it, Gerald? Why didn't you stop it?"

Gerald stamps down, lifts another spade of earth up out of the grave, and throws it farther than he needs to. "Hubbard deserved what he got. He was caught fair and square and we didn't have no choice but to whip him. My daddy would have done the same thing. I'm sure he would. Maybe he wouldn't have done it himself, but he would have made sure someone did it."

"You could have refused!"

"They'd have done it anyway!" He stops his digging and stares at me, exasperated. "There are folks who think that darkies ain't good enough to be free. Now, I ain't one of 'em, but that's who you got to convince—and you can't do that when they've brought in a runaway and everyone's howling for blood."

"But it was *you* who did it—at least you would have if you'd been any good with a whip." That stings him and I'm glad of it. "You could have tried to stop it! I mean, I thought you owned all of us. Or don't that mean nothing? Just like freeing us when you come into your inheritance. Is that just one big ol' bag of shit as well?"

Now, I don't know where my foul mouth comes from. It's like the Devil has ahold of my tongue and I'm possessed of his anger so much that all I can feel is his fingers around my throat, trying to throttle all the goodness out of me.

Gerald looks like he might be about to cry, but I ain't even sorry for him. In fact, it makes me glad.

"Well, is it? Is it all just talk? After all, your daddy seemed to say a lot about freedom, but he still went to war to fight against Lincoln. So was that just bull? 'Cause I would sorely like to know and so would everyone else."

Gerald drops his head. "That ain't fair, Friday," he says quietly.

"It's true enough and both of us know it."

"Oh, is that so? Well, what about your daddy? Where's your daddy now, Friday? He ain't here for you either, is he? I bet you don't even know where he is, do you? He probably went off whoring and—"

I hit him hard as I can, swinging wildly so my knuckle slaps bang against his ear, and then I jump him, sending the two of us down onto the soft fresh earth of his own father's grave. I grab a handful of hair and push his head down into the dirt, but he puts a hand up quick and claws at my cheek with his nails. It's bad enough to draw blood, and both of us are wriggling and squealing like frightened pigs on slaughter day. Then a sudden blow lands on the back of my head, hard enough it shakes all the strength from my knees. Gerald must've hit me with a rock. He must have, but no, suddenly I'm lifted into the air, a hand on the back of my shirt dragging me up out of the grave as another blow spins me around in the air to face Hubbard.

He lets go of me, hitting me again on the back of my head as he does it, and I cower at his knees. "What do you think you're doing?" he barks at me, and taking a handful of my shirt again, he begins to drag me down the path that leads toward the house, and all the time I'm shouting that I'm sorry and that I didn't know what I was doing.

"Hubbard, let him go!" There are footsteps behind us as Gerald shouts out desperately, "I said for you to let him go. Now, you do as I say!"

Hubbard stops walking. He takes his hand from my shirt. "He can't ever raise a hand to you! The missus ought to know about this." He scowls at both of us. "She's gotta decide what should be done."

"Please don't tell her, Hubbard." Gerald wipes the dirt from underneath his eye. "It was my fault. I started it."

I begin to protest. "No, that ain't right . . ."

But Hubbard's still glaring at me. "It don't matter who started it."

"*I* started it, Hubbard." Gerald cuts us short. "I started it, and it wouldn't be right for Friday to be punished twice." Gerald straightens my shirt out across my shoulders. "My daddy always said I had a bit of the bully in me, and I'd be letting him down if I let it get the better of me." He offers me his hand to shake right there and then. "I'm sorry, Friday. I won't let it happen again."

I shake his hand, my fingers all limp with the shame of what I've done. "I'm sorry too. I really am."

Hubbard looks angry with the both of us. "You boys are too old for this. You shouldn't be playing together. Do you hear me? You're too old, and the missus doesn't like it. You should be working at behaving like responsible young men. Now, I don't want to see you two together again. Do you hear me?"

We tell him that we do, and he sends us both packing in different directions before finishing the grave himself.

I apologize to Hubbard soon as he comes in through the door of our cabin. "Don't you ever let it happen again," he tells me directly. "I mean it. People get killed for less than that. Do you hear me?"

I tell him that I understand and spend the evening inside, thinking of all the things I might do that will balance out the bad I'd done today.

It ain't long till we find out we don't have need of the grave. A second letter says that Mr. Allen's body has been disposed of in the hospital grounds as a precaution against the spread of disease and he will have to lie where he died, like every other unfortunate man who lost his life in this war and will never return home.

We hold a ceremony for him anyway, and we use the grave at the elm tree as though he is right there in it. Hubbard fashions a cross out of oak, carves Mr. Allen's name upon it, and hammers it into the ground under the tree.

On the day itself, Gerald brings his daddy's favorite suit from the house and lays it out in the open soil, putting a pair of shined-up shoes on top of the jacket, together with a parcel of letters that were written by Mrs. Allen, back when the two of 'em were courting. We all gather around the grave, and Chepstow leads us in a short service as we look down upon Mr. Allen's clothes. Gerald says a few words 'bout how his father was a good man and how he intends to live up to the same standards himself, and then we sing a hymn: "How Blest the Righteous When He Dies."

Gerald's wearing a Confederate tunic that was bought in town, and Mrs. Allen lets him shoulder one of the muskets that she keeps inside the house. When the speaking's all done, he discharges a single shot into the air before we each take up a spade, me and him, and cover his daddy's clothes with earth till it looks proper and decent to all of us that stand there in a circle and pray for that man's soul.

—

Now that the shadow of death has crossed over us, it looks like it'll never leave.

Mrs. Allen takes to the house in mourning for her husband. She has Sicely tidy away the jewelry into drawers, since it ain't done to see something sparkle with light when your world's so full of darkness, and she covers up the mirrors herself, using the shawls that have been dyed black. On one occasion, I see her uncover a corner of the glass to fasten her veil with a pin.

"I don't see how I'm supposed to look right if I can't use a mirror," she complains when she catches me looking, and she slides her thin white fingers into the black lace gloves that are the only items of mourning she has allowed to be bought new from the store in town.

It ain't usual for me to be in the house now. Mrs. Allen has moved most of us out into the fields and a hush has come over the place, which I find unnerving. It seeps out into the yard, which has begun to look uncared for, and even down the track and into the cabins so that it seems like every day is winter.

I don't remember the last time I saw sunshine. I don't remember any light at all. Not that it is particularly cold, but it is miserable, everything wet and gray and heavy, like water that never has a chance to flow. There ain't no life left in anything we do anymore, there ain't no joy at all, and we all could be half-asleep if only we were so lucky.

The Confederates are surely losing the war—everybody knows that by now—but we don't feel either joy or despair at the news, not any of us. It's simply a fact of life that means more trouble is probably on its way and the only light in the darkness is knowing that there's people here still eager to read.

I haven't spoken to Gerald much since we dug his father's grave 'cause we done as Hubbard told us and kept our distance from each other. Anyway, neither of us has the time to meet now we're working all the hours God sends. I see him a lot out in the fields, though. I thought he might be mourning with his mother, but he ain't. It's as if he's got more energy than anyone else here and has taken it upon himself to make the plantation stand on its own two feet. I think he sees it as a testament to the memory of his daddy.

One thing he did was to make a list of all the jobs that need doing on the plantation and who should be doing 'em. It goes from the cookhouse to the woods, to the farming and the fields—a list of every task and all the people who could do 'em. When it's finished, he reads it out to Winnie, who tells him, "I knew that already. You think this place been just running itself?"

He has taken to coming into the fields and directing the work himself, often taking advice from Hubbard as to what needs to be done and when is the right time to do it. Hubbard don't appear to mind the imposition of it. After the humiliation of being whipped, he has returned as foreman, but his heart ain't in it, we all can tell, and once Gerald starts taking over, Hubbard seems content to let him.

I've seen the change in Hubbard more than most. At the very beginning, when he put his green shirt back on and walked outside, he was surly and given to fits of temper. He wouldn't meet my eye, kept to himself, and only said something if it was really necessary.

I got scared of him all over again. I didn't dare speak in case I put a foot wrong, and sometimes when I did, he'd snap at me and I'd leave the cabin and go out by the fire pit to give him space. I reckoned his spirit was broken, but gradually he became more gentle and I saw this wasn't so. Over time, the loss of his pride seems more like a relief to him, like he's thrown some heavy load from his back and is glad to see it gone.

He's become friendlier with Lizzie and also with the rest of the slaves. I think he sees he ain't resented and so he's become more confident and he speaks to people more than he ever did before he was whipped. It feels like he has become the same as everyone else here, although the truth of it is that aside from a large cabin, a good pair of boots, and a shiny bright lamp, he always was.

One night in the cabin, he takes his mother's book from the box on the shelf and stands holding it, not doing anything but look at it. I'm sat at the table near him and I don't know what he's thinking. Eventually, he holds the book out to me. "Would you teach me to read this?"

I open it up and read a few lines to myself. "Sure. I can teach you to read, but you can't start with this. It's too difficult. You gotta start with the easy books first. That's the only way to learn."

"You mean I gotta go in with the kids?"

"Do you want to come to class?" I don't know what I think

about that. All of us have spent so long hiding from him that it don't feel right to invite him along without everyone's say-so. Hubbard nods. He says he'd like to, and I give it some more thought. "Most of the kids are on more advanced reading now, but Levi ain't a kid and he's only recently begun. Sicely too. I could teach you with them."

"Is Sicely coming to class now?" Hubbard sounds surprised. "I didn't think she would."

I smile at that. "She's learned the error of her ways." That's all I say.

Hubbard stands there like some big ol' lump of wood, not knowing what to do with himself, realizing he'll be just about the last person on the plantation to learn how to read, 'cept maybe Winnie, who still says she's far too old for stuff and nonsense like that. "If you prefer, I could teach you here. We could do half an hour last thing at night. It wouldn't be no bother."

But Hubbard shakes his head. "No. Thank you for the offer, but I'll come to class."

He is as good as his word.

When I bring him into Lizzie's cabin and sit him down in the group, the room is quieter than usual. I can see everyone sneaking a look at him while they get on with their work. I give him the primer, then sit down with him as he tries to read. He makes the same mistakes as all of us do who've never read a word before.

The dog ran.

Hubbard has to start at the same place we all did and he smiles like a child the first time he gets it right. When little Gil begins to giggle, Lizzie clips his ear and we all think she done right.

After the lesson, when we return to our cabin, Hubbard is quiet and he looks tired to me. "I thought you done good," I tell him. When he doesn't answer, I tell him, "There's no shame in not knowing something. The only time you should feel ashamed is if you never let yourself learn new things."

That was something that Miss Priestly used to say, back at the orphanage, and I am proud I've remembered it.

"I know that already," he snaps back at me. "You might know how to read, Friday, but that don't make you God's gift. Do you understand? I seen a lot of things and I know stuff, so let me tell you this—you need to live a lot longer than you have before you start preaching to me in my own home."

Now, Hubbard is a man of very few words, and if I have provoked him to say as long a sentence as this, then I know that he's annoyed.

"I apologize."

He looks all sheepish. "Well, that's all right."

"And I'm sorry for being a smart aleck."

"Just so long as you don't do it again."

"Absolutely. Sometimes, I'm just too clever for my own good."

He could see the smile behind my eyes and he softened. "If you need to practice being a little dumber, then this is the place to do it."

"Thank you," I tell him. "I am reassured."

CHAPTER 17

April brings us warmer weather and the talk of war.

I follow the plow, pulled by the nag that Hubbard leads across the field. He's the only one of us big enough to drag that old horse in a straight line. Peighton came for our last good horse while we were planting corn. He came right out into the field, unstrapped the beast himself, and apologized to the missus for taking it. Said she'd be among the first to be compensated once the war is done, and we look on that dimly as a new mark of respect.

Right now we're planting cotton. Gil walks in front of me and he bends and sows, bends and sows, planting seed in the shallow gullies, which the rest of us cover, using hoes.

"Hey, Friday! You missed a bit a back here."

I turn to see the missus, standing like a scarecrow in her black dress, a hoe in her hand and baby Virginia riding on her hip.

I hurry back along the furrowed line. "Sorry 'bout that."

"Don't wanna leave it for the birds," she tells me.

"I know, miss. I was going too fast. I should slow down a bit."

"Whatever you do, don't do that, Friday." Mrs. Allen moves a strand of hair from the front of her face. "You're the only one around here still willing to work hard."

I shrug weakly. Ahead of us, Hubbard pulls the horse to a halt and the whole caravan comes to a stop, making Mrs. Allen's face pinch up in agitation. "For goodness' sake, what's wrong now? And where's Gerald and the others? They should have had the wagon here by now."

"I don't know, ma'am. Do you want me to take a look?"

She hands the baby to me. "You may as well. Take Virginia back to the house and give her to Sicely, would you?"

We walk in opposite directions across the half-plowed field and I take the track that leads back up to the house and come across our wagon lying crippled by the roadside, with Levi, George, and Lizzie all standing and looking at it.

"What happened?"

"Wheel come off," said George, but I can see that for myself. "Pin broke." He has the bits in his hand and he shows me. I have the feeling that it weren't an accident, 'cause it seems to me that almost every day, something goes wrong that takes an eternity to put right.

"There's spares back at the barn," I tell him.

"Sure. Could be."

So we all stand there looking at the wagon.

"I'll bring one back with me." I leave 'em to it and go on up the track, holding Virginia's hand while she tries to walk for herself. A hundred yards on and Gerald hurries toward me from the direction of the house. "Why's the wagon not in the field? They came for it an hour ago."

"The wheel's come off."

He shakes his head and is about to hurry on, but then says, "Friday? Will you meet me at the river?"

I know we won't be swimming. Everything's changed between us these last few months, but I agree to go.

I return with the pin just as George and Levi are lifting the wagon from the ground, their backs wedged beneath it and their legs bent and straining.

"If we hadn't rented Kofi out, we'd still have a blacksmith," Lizzie reminds Gerald as he edges the wheel into place on the axle.

"We can manage," he says.

I give him the pin and a hammer from the barn and then step back.

"See what we can do if we all work together?" Gerald announces once the wheel is on, and we all take hold of the wagon and start back up to the field.

——

Gerald's waiting by the riverbank when I get there. He looks different from the last time we were here. He's taken to slicking his hair back with grease, and although I already knew that, seeing him here makes it more obvious, and I take a moment to look at him properly. He seems taller than he used to be and I tell him so. "When did you get to be so tall?" I reckon he must have had that growth spurt while I weren't looking.

"I been getting taller for ages. You just haven't noticed."

"Maybe." I look around us. "It's been a while since we came here."

"I'm sorry that I stopped your lessons, Friday."

"That's all right."

"No, it isn't. I've let you down and I apologize." He hesitates. "It was you who wrote Hubbard's note, wasn't it? I've thought about it often and I don't reckon it could've been anyone else."

"Is that why you stopped teaching me?"

"I don't know. Maybe. I didn't think you'd use it to cheat on us."

"It weren't like that. His wife was ill."

Gerald nods. "I thought it'd be something like that. Mother reckoned it must have been me who wrote it. She knows I've always had a soft spot for Hubbard."

"So you didn't tell her it was me?" Gerald shakes his head. "Did she punish you?" Gerald shrugs. "And is that why you wanted to meet me?"

"No. It ain't that at all. I was just saying." I wait for him to tell me why we're here and he puts his hands behind his back before he begins. I guess it makes him feel more comfortable. "I want to know why the others won't work for me. You're the only one who wants to work, Friday. You, and perhaps Hubbard. I feel like I'm pushing a wagon up a hill all by myself. If we keep going the way we are, I doubt we'll have a harvest to sell in the fall."

"We can't sell it anyway."

"You don't know that. The war won't last forever."

"That's true. But if the Yankees get here, we'll see some changes."

"They won't get here." Gerald hardens his jaw. "They can't. The Feds'll stop 'em. I know they will."

He sounds so desperate that I feel sorry for him. "Everyone says you can't win the war, Gerald. That's what we all been hearing. Once the Yankee lines come past us, it'll be Lincoln in charge and Yankee laws." I hesitate to say it, but I do. "We'll all be free, Gerald. That's why they won't work for you. They can already smell their freedom."

That's too much for him to hear. "I won't let the Yankees anywhere near this place! Do you hear me? I won't."

We stare at each other and we button our lips, scared of what we might say next. I don't see how we can talk of this, and I look out along the slow brown river, wondering how it would be to just float away to freedom. I pick up a stone and toss it in the water. "They got boats on their way up here, Gerald. They got boats with guns all over 'em, all covered in shining armor so they can't be sunk. They'll be here soon."

"Is that true?" Gerald suddenly don't seem so grown up at all. "I mean about the armor?"

"I reckon it is."

"Then that'd mean my daddy died for nothing."

I stare at my feet, feeling there's a mile between us, but then he reaches out and touches the top of my arm so tenderly that I remember how we were friends. "How come *you* still want to work hard for me, Friday? Why don't you follow everyone else?"

"I don't know."

"You've never been like the others. They might be up to no good, but you've always been special. That's why I taught you to read. I always knew you'd be able to do it."

Soon as he says it, I feel the weight of all those lies and it's just too much. I can't do it anymore. I can't keep lying to him. "You didn't teach me to read, Gerald. I already knew how. I've known how to read since I was a little boy."

Gerald looks at me like he doesn't understand what I've said to him. "But why . . . ?" His mouth is open, waiting for his brain to catch up and feed him something to say. "Why would you pretend you couldn't read?"

"Because I needed you to bring me the books. I've been teaching the others to read and write. I've been teaching all of 'em. It ain't just me who can read, Gerald. It's all of us. Every slave you own except for Winnie. Do you understand?"

"So you been lying to me all along?"

I hang my head in shame. When he puts it like that, it makes it sound much worse than it seemed at the time. I try to put it another way, try to make him understand that I did it for a reason. "I did what your daddy would have wanted, Gerald. I did it and it worked. You don't own a single slave who can't say his alphabet and there ain't no one on this plantation that couldn't sign his name to a contract of work if you gave him one. I did what I had to do, Gerald. God told me to do it and I did. I did what was right."

I expect him to be angry, expect him to shout at me, even hit me in the face.

"All that time you were lying to me," he says quietly.

And then he walks away.

━━━

When I return to the cabins, Mrs. Allen is standing knocking at our door, and Peighton is waiting over by the fire pit with two of his men, both of 'em holding chains with shackles that hang open like the mouths of thirsty dogs. He shouts over to the missus. "Mrs. Allen, do you mind if my men take a look around?"

The missus nods and the men drop their chains on the ground and go toward the doors of the other cabins. Hubbard opens our door, and Lizzie comes outside and watches what's going on.

I step up onto our porch. Mrs. Allen has rolled the sleeves of her black cotton dress up to her elbows and she folds her arms and stands there looking at Hubbard. "Mr. Peighton has brought me news of your wife and child."

"What news is that?" Hubbard looks alarmed and searches her face for clues. "Are they both OK?"

"They've fled the Hope plantation. Been gone two days now and no one's seen 'em or can say where they are." She watches him closely. "Hubbard, can you tell me where they are?"

Hubbard shakes his head. "I don't know, ma'am." He wipes the back of his hand across his brow. "I hope they're all right, though. Where do you think they might have gone?"

Peighton steps up onto our porch and leans against a post. "We thought they might have come here."

"Why would they come here?" Hubbard shakes his head again. "They ain't stupid, Mr. Peighton. It's the first place you'd look for 'em. I expect they've gone as far away from here as they could."

Peighton comes in closer, leaning against the frame of the door so he's next to Hubbard. "Tell me what you know about it. Either you know where they are or you don't."

Hubbard ignores him. He only speaks to the missus. "This is the first I heard, ma'am. The very first."

He's twisting the fingers of his hands together and I can see he's anxious.

I try to interrupt. "He'd have told me if he knew, ma'am. But he ain't said nothing to me."

But Mrs. Allen don't pay me no heed. She says, "You wouldn't tell me if you knew, would you, Hubbard? That's the problem I have. Do you see? I don't think I can trust you to tell me what you know."

"How could I know, ma'am? We ain't allowed to leave the plantation and we don't get to speak to anyone. We've been in the dark about things for a good while now."

Mrs. Allen walks to stand by Peighton. "Mr. Peighton believes you ain't the kind of man who lets his wife and child go off alone, and I'm inclined to agree with him."

"He'll be gone, Mrs. Allen." Peighton smiles with satisfaction. "You take my word for it. With the Yankee lines this close, he'll make a run for it soon as he gets the chance." He walks off the porch, calling back to the missus over his shoulder. "Soon as you turn your back, this one here'll be gone." He lifts the fetters out of the dirt. "I'd sooner chain him now than let him leave you in the lurch like that."

Mrs. Allen sucks at her bottom lip like she still ain't sure. "Will they slow his work?"

Peighton shrugs and ambles back toward the porch. "They'll restrict him for sure, but he can still work. The length of the chain will let him walk OK, but he couldn't run."

Lizzie comes up close to the porch so she's near the shoulder of the missus. "We ain't never had no one chained here, ma'am," she tells her quietly. "It ain't the kind of thing the master would allow."

Mrs. Allen nods. "I know that, Lizzie, but it seems I'm damned either way."

"Do you really want to take the risk?" Peighton holds up the length of chain and I feel the panic rise from my stomach to my throat as he reaches the porch steps. "It's a short-term measure, Mrs.

Allen. It won't be forever. And it'll protect your investment till we find his wife."

Seeing those chains up close makes the dread slither through my stomach like a snake, but Hubbard don't look alarmed and I find that strange.

"Sit on the step," Mrs. Allen tells him.

Hubbard comes to the top step slowly, but he sits himself down without protest.

"Take off your boots."

Hubbard places his big ol' boots, heels together, on the step beside him and lets his feet rest in the dirt. Peighton drops the chains at the side of the porch, then kneels and opens up a gate on the set of leg irons.

"Let me do it." Mrs. Allen crouches beside Peighton, who stands back to give her room. "Put your foot up here so I can see what I'm doing." Mrs. Allen reaches down and takes hold of Hubbard's heel, then lifts his foot so it rests in her lap. She takes the shackle and eases it around the back of his ankle, taking care to check that his skin won't get caught before she closes the gate. "It's pretty tight." She checks with Peighton. "Is that all right?"

"Please, miss," I say. "I'm sure it ain't necessary. I'll keep an eye on him if you want me to. You can trust me, miss. I'll even vouch for him myself."

Peighton takes a padlock from the pocket of his trousers and hands it over. "They don't make 'em to size, but he'll get used to it."

Mrs. Allen puts the padlock in place and locks the gate, putting the key in the pocket of her dress, then she takes Hubbard's other leg and does the same again. "Stand up," she tells him when she has finished. "Take a walk to the fire and back, so I can see."

Hubbard stands and steps away from the porch. He walks over to the fire, and the chains sweep the dirt between his feet, making his stride half its usual length, so it looks like he stutters when he walks. He seems like a smaller man. We all can see it.

Peighton lifts the second set of chains so they dangle at his side. "You want me to do his hands as well?"

But Mrs. Allen shakes her head. "I don't think that will be necessary."

"It's up to you. I'll leave them up at the house so you can use them if you need to."

Peighton's men have finished with the other cabins and they come past Hubbard and go up into ours. I can hear 'em walk the length of it, though they could see straight away that no one is there. When they come back onto the porch, they shake their heads at Peighton, letting him know that it's empty. "Well, that's just as I expected," he announces. "But you all should know that we'll be back."

Mrs. Allen extends her hand to Peighton. "I'm hoping you'll catch up with his family soon. Please let me know if you have any news."

"I'll come straight over myself, Mrs. Allen."

The missus takes one last look at Hubbard. "I hope this won't have to be for long."

"I hope so too, ma'am. Please be sure to tell me if there's any news of my wife and daughter."

Mrs. Allen nods, then accompanies the patrol back up to the house, and we all gather around Hubbard as he sits down on the step and feels around the edge of the irons with his finger. I go and fetch his pipe, and Levi fills it for him with his own tobacco, though Hubbard could have done it himself; he ain't helpless.

Lizzie's got a face like thunder. "This place is turning to the bad. I've seen it coming," she warns us. "I told you all."

Hubbard seems calmer than the rest of us. I don't understand how he can just sit on our porch and let the smoke roll out of his mouth. When he's finished his pipe, he stands up and takes himself inside the cabin. I follow him in and close the door. I wait for him to speak, but he don't. He keeps his back to me, making like he's busy with the hearth.

"You can't let them do this to you."

"She can do as she likes. That's the way it is."

"Hubbard, this ain't right." He pokes at the ashes instead of answering me. I go and kneel next to him so I can see his face. "You ain't even upset about it! What's the matter with you? Why ain't you fighting it? Why ain't you standing up for yourself?"

Hubbard stands up and walks away toward the door, his chains dragging across the floor as he goes. "Don't go on about it," he tells me bluntly.

I think of when he slapped me and how I said I hadn't ever been so disappointed in a man. I won't say it again, but I'm thinking it again and he knows it too.

Later that night, when I pray to the Lord, I try to list everything I've done that's good today, but I can't do it. I can't work out what's good or bad anymore. It's like I don't know my right from my wrong and I can't think what to do to make it all work out for the best.

I decide to trust in the Lord. That's what I'll do. I'll put my faith in His kindness and the mercy of His ways, to keep all of us safe, Mrs. Allen included, 'cause if she only knew the error of her ways, she could make everything OK again. I know she could if she wanted to.

CHAPTER 18

The next day is a Sunday and Gerald knocks on our door just as soon as it is decent to do so. "Do you mind if I come inside?" he asks when I answer.

I let him in and he goes straight across to Hubbard, who's sat on a chair up close to the hearth. He takes a moment to look at the shackles, then he kneels at Hubbard's feet, feels the weight of the chains, and runs a finger across the locks. "I'll talk to Mother," he tells Hubbard. "I'm sorry this has happened."

It ain't done, for a master to apologize to a slave, and Hubbard's embarrassed by it. He empties out his pipe and begins packing it again with new tobacco. "You don't need to do that, Gerald. This won't be for long. Your mother said so herself."

"It's Peighton's fault," I tell 'em both. "Every time he comes here, there's trouble, and now that him and the missus are getting along fine . . ." I don't bother finishing whatever point it is I think I'm making.

Gerald stands and looks at me squarely. "Tell me where you learned to read, Friday."

Hubbard and I exchange a worried glance, but I tell the truth this time 'cause it's all too late for anything else. "I've been reading as long as I can remember. I was taught at an orphanage along with a class of boys, all of us black."

"An orphanage?"

"Yes, sir. You see, I ain't really a slave. I was stolen away and sold by a trader who threatened to harm my brother. I should have told you long ago that I got a brother. It was that trader who named me Friday, named me after the day of the week, just like in *Robinson Crusoe*. But that ain't me. Not the real me. Friday's just someone that I had to be."

Gerald turns on Hubbard. "Did you know this?"

"No. I mean, not at first—not at the auction. Samuel told me later."

I could kiss him for remembering my name.

"And you didn't think to tell me?"

"I don't see how we could have," Hubbard says steadily. "What were we gonna do about it?"

It takes a moment, but Gerald comes up good, that big ol' heart getting the better of his hurt feelings. "No," he says. "No, I don't suppose you could." He puts a hand to his forehead as though it hurts. "Could I have a glass of water?"

I hurry across, take a tin mug from the table, and fetch it back, full to the brim. Gerald takes a good swig of it. "Can I ask you both a question? What would happen if you were all free? Right now, if you had the choice. Would you stay and work for a wage?"

Hubbard and I stare at each other, unsure what we should say, but then I shrug. "Where would everyone go? They'll still need a job and they'll need a home, same as they always have. They've got those things here."

"You don't think they'd go and join the Yankees?"

Hubbard shakes his head. "I can't see that happening. Those that wanted to fight have already gone."

And suddenly, I can see what Gerald's thinking, that freedom is on its way and there's no stopping it, so if he frees us now, he can make the best of it. We all can.

"They'll stay," I tell him. "I'm sure of it. And if they're getting a wage, then they'll work harder, 'cause it's for themselves as much as it is for you. It'll be all of us working together, just like you wanted. We'd be like a family. Your daddy always thought it would work out, didn't he?"

"Yes, he did." Gerald's eyes are gleaming with the possibility of doing what his daddy always talked about.

But Hubbard stops us right there and then. "You boys need to hold on. You're forgetting 'bout the missus. It ain't you who decides about that sort of thing, Gerald. It's your mother."

And of course I knew that all along. I'd got carried away—we both had—'cause there's more chance of the Confederates winning the war than there is of Mrs. Allen setting her slaves free.

But Gerald don't appear to think the way that I do. "Hubbard, listen to me. The truth is that Mother thinks Negroes are inferior. She said as much herself. So we got to change her mind." He looks at me. "That's why I want you to read to her, Friday. Remember when I asked you to read to my father? Well, I want you to do it tonight for my mother. She's got to see for herself what a Negro can do when he gets the same chances a white boy gets. Once she does, she won't be able to believe the things she does. I'm certain we can convince her. I'm sure we can."

And suddenly, I see it, clear as daylight, as if God were there in my head answering all my prayers Himself. "We've all got to read to her, Gerald. Not just me but every single one of us. If she's gonna set us free, then we've got to show her what we all can do."

—

I draw a line in chalk along the floorboards in Lizzie's cabin.

Every slave on the plantation is there and they stare at the white line. "Tomorrow we could all be free," I tell 'em.

"How's that gonna happen, Friday? Do you know something we don't?"

"I know we're all gonna read to Mrs. Allen and we're going to do it tonight at evening prayers. We're gonna convince her to give us our papers. I won't have her think it's just me who can read. She needs to know it's all of us. She needs to know there's not a slave in this country who can't be educated if they're given the chance to learn."

"I ain't reading." Levi points a shaking finger at me. "You can count me out. She'll have me whipped soon as look at me. What are you even thinking about?"

Everyone starts shouting at once and arguing among themselves. It's so loud I can't make sense of what's being said. I tell everyone to be quiet, but it makes no difference. No one can hear me anyway. So I take a pan and spoon from the hearth and bang them hard like the place is on fire. I make a real racket and it works. Suddenly everyone's silent and they're looking at me.

I point the wooden spoon at Levi. "Are we a bunch of no-good Negroes?" I wave the pan above my head. "Is that what we are? Just an ugly bunch of niggers who ain't good for nothing except breaking our backs? Because I know I ain't. I'm better than that, and you are too."

Lizzie looks at me, all shamefaced and scared. "You've been free all that time, Friday. You don't know what might happen. You don't know what it's like."

"That's true," I agree with her. "That's very true. But it's the same the other way around. You all don't know what it's like to be free. You ain't never owned your own body. You don't dare think your own thoughts. You don't even know what's it like to be you. But if you never stand up for who you are, then no one else will." I look down at Gil, 'cause he makes me think of Joshua. "We got to be brave. All of us have got to stick together and show some trust in one another." I point my spoon in the direction of the house. "Mrs. Allen has no idea what we're capable of. That's the truth of it and she couldn't treat us the way she does if she knew. You told me that, Lizzie. That's the only reason they won't let us read. It's 'cause they're scared of what we can do."

"But *I'm* scared of what *they* can do," says George.

"Well, I can't force any of you." I point to the line of chalk that separates them from me. "But this is our one chance to stand up for ourselves, it's our chance to convince Mrs. Allen to do the right thing, and if we ain't willing to do it, then who else should?" I look around the room, taking in each of their faces. "So who'll come and stand with me?"

Hubbard's the first one to step across the line.

———

When Mrs. Allen comes to read to us, the sun has set and rolls of thunder come in from the north on the warm night air. We are gathered by the fire pit and the flames light up our faces as we watch her oil lamp on its way past the trees, the missus carrying Virginia, and Gerald walking beside her with the lamp held high.

In one hand I have a grease lamp and in the other I hold a copy of the Bible, hidden from view behind my back with a bookmark ready at the right page. When Mrs. Allen arrives, she don't notice anything different from any other evening. She calls for us to come in closer to the fire, then takes her usual place, with the flames crackling and spitting between us. She gives Virginia to Gerald and he stands her on the ground and takes hold of her hand as Mrs. Allen lifts her prayer book and clears her throat to speak.

"Excuse me?" I step forward. "Mrs. Allen?"

She lowers her book and lifts her head. "Yes, Friday. What is it?"

"Tonight, ma'am, I would like for *us* to read to *you*."

The missus puts a hand to her forehead and squints to get a better view of me. "What do you mean?"

I open up my Bible. "It's a passage from the Psalms." I clear my throat and begin before she can say another word. "'The Lord is my shepherd; I shall not want. He maketh me to lie down in green pastures; he leadeth me beside still waters. He restoreth my soul.'"

I hand the book to little Gil, who stands ready to my right, and he brings the grease lamp closer to the page so he can see it properly. "Go on now," I whisper. "Read it like we said."

Gil doesn't let me down. He lifts his chin, and his voice is sweet and clear. "'He leadeth me in the paths of righteousness for his name's sake.'"

Across the fire from us, Mrs. Allen looks like she's seen the ghost of Jacob Marley. "What is this?" she asks me. "What do you think you're doing?"

Gerald puts a hand on her arm. "They're reading, Mother. They've been learning how to read."

Gil passes the book to George, who speaks up loudly. "'Yea, though I walk through the valley of the shadow of death, I will fear no evil.'" George passes it to Harriet. "'For thou art with me; thy rod and thy staff, they c . . . c . . .'" I lean across and give her the word she struggles for. "'They comfort me,'" she repeats after me.

Mrs. Allen has shaken Gerald's hand from her arm and she walks quickly around the fire, never taking her eyes from our faces. "But they're not reading," she says uncertainly, shaking her head and smiling, thinking she has the truth of it. "You're reciting from memory. Everyone knows this Psalm. I can see you've been listening to Mr. Chepstow, and well done—yes, well done to all of you. But that's enough now." She holds out her hand for the book. "I want you to stop."

"Listen to 'em, Mother," Gerald calls to her across the fire. "They ain't reciting. They're reading. They can all do it, some better than others, but even so, they're all gonna learn. Just listen, Mother. Hear how good they are."

Sicely has ahold of the book, and though she can't look the

missus in the eye, she still says her line. "'Thou preparest a table for me in the presence of mine enemies.'"

Mrs. Allen keeps her arm outstretched and steps toward her. "Give me that book!"

I ain't never seen Sicely disobey the missus, but she steps away and passes it on to Hubbard, who stands there in his chains and reads perfectly. He really does. "'Surely goodness and mercy shall follow me all the days of my life,'" he recites in his deep voice, sounding something like the thunder overhead. "'And I will dwell in the house of the Lord forever.'"

Mrs. Allen snatches the book from his hands.

She comes straight for me, letting the Bible fall open at a random page, which she presents to me. I notice it is Leviticus, chapter 3, verse 2. "Read it," she tells me, and I do. I read it in a loud, clear voice with no mistakes and I keep reading, till I see her black-laced hand take hold of the top of the book and snap it shut.

She fixes me with her stare. "That'll be enough. Thank you."

Gerald brings Virginia around to our side. "It's like how Daddy said, isn't it? If you give a man a chance, who knows what he can do. We got to give 'em their chance, Mother. We've got no choice. We got to give 'em their freedom and we've got to do it before the Yankees get here."

Mrs. Allen blanches and I see her swallow. She turns to Sicely. "You will collect up any books belonging to me and bring them back to the house immediately." A single finger picks out me and then Gerald. "You two come with me."

Mrs. Allen takes the lamp from Gerald's hand, scoops up Virginia, and starts away to the house without another word as we both follow her, walking three steps behind, though the missus goes so fast we almost have to run to keep up.

When we get past the trees, baby Virginia bursts into tears 'cause she wants to walk and not be carried. Gerald skips forward. "Mother, let me take her for you."

"You've done enough damage for one day." Mrs. Allen marches on through the yard and into the house. She opens the door to the library. "Come in here, you two. Virginia, sit on that chair there and be still."

"Bed!" says little Virginia.

"You can't go to bed. You must wait for a moment." Mrs. Allen turns up the wick on the oil lamp as Virginia starts to wail again and I sneak a quick peek at Gerald to see how brave he looks, but as far as I can see, he's about as scared as I am.

Mrs. Allen addresses neither of us in particular. "Would you like to tell me exactly what's been going on?"

"It was me, ma'am." I speak up first. "I've been giving lessons to the others, teaching 'em how to read and write. We wanted to show you what we could do, ma'am. We thought it might convince you to give us our papers."

"Why would it make a difference?"

"Well, you see, ma'am . . ."

Sicely appears at the open door with an armful of books.

"Put them on the table by the door, Sicely. And take Virginia up to bed, would you?"

"Yes, ma'am." Sicely curtsies, takes Virginia by the hand, and leaves the room, looking ever so anxious.

Mrs. Allen goes to the table. She runs a finger up the spines of the books before she turns on me. "Have you been stealing my books?"

"No, Mother," Gerald confesses quickly. "It was me. I've been taking them for Friday. I've given him everything he needs."

Mrs. Allen nods like she had already guessed. "Then come and put them back on the shelves for me, would you?"

Gerald goes across to the table and his mother slaps him hard across the face when he gets there. "Is that what you think of me?" she demands of him. "You have brought the ideas of our enemies into this house . . ."

Gerald has a hand to his face. "It's what my daddy wanted!"

Mrs. Allen points out the window. "Your daddy is up on that hill. He's still warm in his grave and yet you can't even remember what he died for."

Gerald glares at her. "He believed in paying a living wage to a man for his work. He believed a man was worth at least that, regardless of his color."

Mrs. Allen shakes her head as though she is tired of it all. "Your daddy would never have done the things he liked to talk about, Gerald. He was interested in the ideas. That's all. It was all just words. He was never gonna do it."

"We've got to free the slaves, Mother, and we've got to do it now."

"Do you intend us all to starve?"

"Of course not, but—"

"Your father died fighting the same people who want to rob us of our property. They want the riches that God bestowed upon us for themselves. Are you saying you'd simply lie down and give everything to 'em? Why, he'd be as ashamed of you as I am!"

"Daddy knew what was right!"

"Yes, he did." Mrs. Allen walks to the door. "I've had enough of this. Now please go to your room."

"Mother, you can't just send me to—"

"Go to your room now, or so help me God, I'll fetch your father's belt."

"Mrs. Allen," I interrupt, "the Yankees'll be here soon. Everyone says so. And once they're here, there won't be no slavery. Not anymore. So you've got nothing to lose. By letting us go, you might just be able to keep us."

Gerald pauses in the doorway as Mrs. Allen looks at me with a kind of horror. "Friday's right," he says. "If we do the right thing now, they might stay. I'm sure they will, Mother. They'll stay and work for us."

"I told you to go to your room." She points her finger toward the stairs. "Don't think you're too old," she warns him.

Gerald slinks out the door, accepting that it's useless to argue any longer, and I can hear his shoes upon the staircase as he goes upstairs.

Mrs. Allen turns back to deal with me and I fear the worst. All the confidence I had is gone, and suddenly, I ain't a soldier of the Lord at all; I'm a little boy who's been caught out and I wonder where it is that God has got to, 'cause He seemed so close when we were down by the fire, He seemed like He was right there with me, but now He's gone.

"I'm disappointed in you."

I wait, not knowing whether she means to hit me too, but she stands aside from the door and indicates that I should leave. Then, as I walk past her, she says, "Ask Hubbard to have the wagon ready for me in the morning. I need to visit the auction house. I imagine Mr. Wickham will have the clearest idea how best to be rid of you."

CHAPTER 19

Mrs. Allen left for town the next morning, just as she had promised, and though she was back at the house by the afternoon, we heard no news of what had occurred with Mr. Wickham. In the evening she comes down to the cabins as usual, reciting the Lord's Prayer, then giving us a speech about faithfulness and loyalty. She does not mention the previous evening and we do not bring it up ourselves.

"I don't like it," mutters Lizzie as we watch her go back up to the house. "I don't like it at all."

Sicely pulls on my arm, taking me to one side so we have some privacy. "I got a message from Master Gerald. He says Peighton has agreed to take you to Alabama and sell you at auction. He's gonna leave in a week's time and take his own slaves with him." She grips my arms as though I might be about to fall. "Oh, Friday, I'm so scared. What are you going to do?"

She's got tears at the edges of her eyes, and I feel called upon to comfort her instead of worrying for myself. "It'll be all right, Sicely," I tell her. "I ain't going nowhere. I'll talk to Gerald. I belong to him by rights and he won't let her sell me."

But Sicely shakes her head. "You can't do that. Master Gerald's been confined to the house till you've gone. You won't get to see him, and anyway, he can't do anything about it. He told me so himself, said she's got the right to manage you as she pleases. He said for

you to run away. That was his advice. He told me to say good-bye."
She hugs me so hard I can't barely breathe. "What are you gonna do,
Friday? I been so worried thinking 'bout it."

I manage to stay calm. "I'll think on it, Sicely. I've still got some
time to think it through."

Sicely goes back to the house, and once she's gone, I tell Hubbard
the whole thing. We're standing out on the porch and the sound of
distant thunder comes in across the fields as it did the night before.
"I got to get away, Hubbard. I can't go to Alabama with Peighton—I
just can't."

"Don't worry," the big man tells me. "You won't be going to
Alabama." Another boom from the skies makes me look up, expecting rain. "That ain't thunder," says Hubbard. "Those are cannon
and mortar. Least I think so. I heard there are boats on the river,
shelling a town only ten miles away. There's rumors of an army
too, a whole load of Yankees walking through to meet 'em from
the east."

I cock my head and listen again to the distant rumble. "You
mean that's actually the Yankees? They're really that close?" I'm
amazed that Connie's promises are coming true, just as he said they
would.

Hubbard nods. "It won't be long now." He walks back to the
door, dragging his chains with him across the porch. "Why don't
you come on in and we can talk some more?"

As we go inside, I notice Hubbard is limping. He walks across to
the hearth and sits down.

"Let me take a look at those for you." I take the lamp from the
table, light it, and kneel before his feet. Taking hold of the shackles,

I ease the edge away from his skin and his legs look like the trees that we girdle out in the wood, with a circle of blood around the top of the irons. "We should put some rags around the top of those," I tell him. "It might stop 'em chafing."

"There's no room." Hubbard winces and takes his leg away. "It's not for long. I'll be all right."

"Then you should have ointment on it. I'll go and see the missus tomorrow, first thing. I'll tell her you need it."

Hubbard pours us both a cup of water from the bucket. "Now, you listen to me. You can't go running off by yourself. Do you hear me? It ain't safe."

"I'll be all right," I lie.

"Just hold on, Samuel. You got to slow down and think it through. Sicely told you Peighton would be leaving in a week. Is that right?"

It makes me smile to hear him use my name again, but I ain't giving in. "I've got to go while I still can. What if Peighton brings a set of chains for me tomorrow? What if he leaves for Alabama early? I'd rather go now, Hubbard. I'll be on my own so I got a good chance of not being seen if I'm careful."

"Whoa! Hold on there." Hubbard shakes his head as though it's out of the question. "You're not going anywhere without me. Do you hear?"

"You mean you're leaving too? Where are you going, Hubbard? Do you have a plan?" He looks embarrassed and turns to the hearth to prod at the embers, his shackles scraping on the wooden floor. "Are you going after your family? Is that what you're trying to tell me? You are, aren't you? You know where she is!"

Hubbard smiles. I don't think he means to, but he can't help it. It's only a little smile that itches at the corner of his lips, but then it breaks out across his face.

"See! You do know! Are they safe already? They must be or you wouldn't be smiling like that. Hubbard! Stop laughing at me. This ain't funny."

A woman's voice takes me by surprise. "I never thought freedom would be anything like this." It comes from somewhere behind me and I spin around in my chair, expecting her to be standing right there, but the space is still completely empty.

Hubbard thinks that's hilarious. And I can hear another laugh too—I'm sure I can—the giggle of a little girl.

Hubbard turns to face the back wall. "Don't just laugh at the poor boy! Why don't you say hello, Celia?"

Another giggle. And then the woman speaks again. "Hello, Samuel," she says. "I'm glad we've finally been properly introduced."

She sounds far away and yet very close, and I walk out into the middle of the cabin, looking for their hiding place, but there's nothing there, there's nowhere to hide, and I stand bewildered.

The little girl giggles again and Hubbard shakes his head. "They're playing games with you." He gets up and walks to the back wall of the cabin. "Come here, Samuel. Come and meet my daughter." He beckons and I go to him, still unsure of what is going on.

A girl says, "Hello." Her voice came from the wall—I'm sure it did—and I put my ear against the wood.

"Her name is Sarah," Hubbard tells me.

I say, "Hello, Sarah," and a finger appears from a notch in the wood, just under my chin, a little girl's finger with a twisted braid of grass for a ring. It reminds me of Joshua when he said good-bye to me in the privy, and I take hold and shake it politely. "It's nice to meet you, Sarah." Then suddenly, I laugh out loud. "All this time I've been thinking you was a mouse!"

She laughs so loud that Hubbard has to quiet us down. "Shhh, you two. We still got to be careful, remember. We ain't there yet."

I ain't never seen Hubbard as happy as he is right now. He looks like a little kid at Christmas and I have a hundred questions for him—about how he got 'em in there, how long it's been and how they got food and where they slept—but he won't answer any of 'em. He puts a hand on my shoulder and walks me back into the middle of the room. "We've got a few days till Peighton leaves. That gives us enough time to plan our escape, and the closer those Yankees get to us, the less dangerous it'll be when we leave." He nods at my mattress. "I think we all ought to get some sleep and see how things look in the morning. That goes for you two as well," he says to the wall.

I lay my mattress out and sneak in under the blanket, wondering whether they're watching me from behind the wall. Hubbard turns out the lamp and finds the way to his mattress in the dark, the chains all clinking together as he arranges his legs to be comfortable as he sleeps. I lie there listening for sounds from the back wall, wondering how much room they have and whether they have food or blankets and what they do if they need to visit the latrine. But I don't hear another sound from 'em.

That night I ask the Lord to deliver us to freedom and keep us all safe in the face of such misfortune. Yes. I say amen to that.

———

I stand at the fire pit with Lizzie. It's dawn and we're still rubbing the sleep from our eyes when a Yankee soldier rides through the plantation on a black horse. We see him soon as he trots past the trees from the direction of the house, all calm as you like, as though he's out for a morning stroll.

"Do you see that?" I ask Lizzie.

"I do."

She takes hold of my hand. "At least he looks like he's on his own."

The soldier comes down to the fire and stops his horse to take a look at us. We look back at him. He don't appear much different from the rebel soldiers I've seen in town, and all of 'em would look better for a plate of food and a shave. We don't have a word to say to each other, not him to us or us to him, but once he's got the measure of us, he kicks the flanks of his horse and rides away in the direction of the river.

"The Yankees are here!" Sicely comes running down from the house, hollering her alarm. "The Yankees are coming!"

Lizzie takes her daughter by the arm. "We saw him, Sicely. Now you calm down and tell us what happened at the house."

Sicely is all out of breath. "There was one of 'em on a horse. He rode up the driveway and through the yard. The missus reckons he's looking for things to steal, but where there's one of 'em, there'll be more. She said you can be sure of that. She already took Gerald with her in the wagon. They're going into town to get help. She says Peighton ought to know that we're here alone and in peril."

Hubbard has gone out to the field already and I go to find him, shouting to him as soon as I see him there on the back of the wagon. "Hubbard!" I run to him. "There's a Yankee soldier!"

"I saw him too. He just came by. Probably a scout, I reckon."

"Ain't you worried?"

Hubbard looks out along the river. "It's good news, ain't it? If the Yankees are this close, maybe we don't need to run after all. Maybe they've already come to us."

"Sicely said the missus has gone into town. What do you think we should do?"

Hubbard thinks about it. "We don't do anything just yet. We'll keep our eyes and ears open but be ready to go if we need to."

I look at the chains on his ankles. "How you gonna go like that?"

"Don't you worry about these." Hubbard climbs down from the wagon. "There's tools in the shed that'll take these off in an instant."

The two of us come back to the cabins and join the others at the fire pit. "What should we do?" Levi asks of Hubbard. "Should we be working or not?"

"I don't know. I suppose so. We should do everything the same as we usually do."

We go down to the field and gather up our tools, but then we stand around, unable to put our minds to it. We send George to look down the river and tell us what he sees, but he comes back looking blank—says everything looks the same as it ever did.

An hour or so later, the distant boom of the mortar and cannon starts up again. Out of all of us, Lizzie looks the most nervous.

"What'll you do when the Yankees arrive?" I ask her. "Will you go and find Milly?"

She shakes her head. "I'll stay put right here. That way she knows where to find me."

Later, when Mrs. Allen returns from town, she gathers us together in the field to tell us that the northern hordes are at our doorstep and we should pray to the Lord for our deliverance and for the safety of the brave boys who are laying down their lives in an effort to defend us.

"Will the town send soldiers to protect us?" asks Lizzie.

"There's no one there to help us." The missus rolls the sleeves of her black dress up to her elbows. "Mr. Wickham said we'd have to take our chances." She puts her hands on her hips and looks over the plantation. "We got to hide anything that can be stolen. Hubbard, you should go to the woods and find a place to bury the food. Levi and George, you two go with him. Be sure to take the barrels of pork from the barn. The rest of us will take care of the fields and the house."

I spend the morning with Lizzie and Gil, hauling wood into the fields and bringing kindling from the barn so we can set a fire to destroy the crops if we need to. We choose a dozen or so plants that are upwind, then we lay the wood in pyramids around the roots and stems. The missus orders a small fire to be lit on the bordering path and some torches to be made, so it's ready and waiting. She chooses me to sit and feed the fire. "Look out for Yankees coming into the plantation from along the river," she tells me. "Can I trust you to do that? I'll be nearby, so if you see anything, you only got to holler."

I walk around the field and sit in a place where I can see the path that comes into the plantation from that side, but nothing moves 'cept red butterflies that flit their way across the sheet of white cotton. I hear the plop of fish catching flies out in the river. I don't know if I'd be glad to see soldiers on the path or not. It's that peaceful here in the field, I find it difficult to believe there's even a war on, and if it weren't for the distant guns, I'd think that none of this were true.

When the Yankees come into view, there's about eight or ten of 'em, walking casually along the path with packs on their backs and rifles slung over their shoulders. I watch 'em till they turn from the river and choose the path that cuts along the far side of the field, the dark blue of their uniforms standing out against the white cotton, so there's no mistaking 'em, and I duck down out of sight. I look back toward the cabins, wondering whether I should be hollering, and that's when I spot Peighton with four of his men. They're crouching down behind a clump of trees, waiting to ambush the Yankees.

I don't want to go anywhere near 'em. If the missus wants to set a fire, she better do it herself, 'cause I'm getting out of here.

I run crouching into the field, flitting between the roots of bushes till I reach the middle of the cotton where the cover is thick, and I lie flat on the ground, panting, hoping I can stay out of sight till the gunfight's over.

The first shot makes me jump like a rabbit and it scatters the Yankees into the field. I hear voices shouting orders and then there's a silence, followed by three or four more shots, all in quick succession. I stay where I am, trying to gauge what might be happening, but nothing moves or makes a sound for a long time, almost long enough for me to think it might be over.

A second round of shooting comes from the left of me and some more from the right. Quiet again. Above me the cotton waves like little white flags in a bright blue sky that is silent and still. I raise myself slowly to my knees, bending back the top of the bushes with a nervous hand to see what's happening. Peighton has moved along the line of the trees and is firing into the cotton field to the left of me.

I duck back down into the bushes and crawl the opposite way. If I can reach the edge of the field, then there's a path that will lead me safely to the cabins, so I keep my head down and run crouching till another volley of shots forces me to the ground. A movement behind me makes me turn and I spot someone coming through the bushes. It's a man, crawling toward me on his knees. "Samuel?" Hubbard whispers loudly. "Samuel, is that you?"

"Hubbard!" I hiss at him. "Hubbard, I'm over here."

That big man comes crawling to me and I see straight away that he has no chains. "Peighton arrived at the house to fetch you." His big brown eyes are alive with urgency. "He's gonna take you to Alabama if we don't get you away."

"But he's over there, Hubbard. I just seen him firing on the Yankee soldiers."

"I saw him too. That's lucky for us if he's caught in a fight, but we got to go now. Come on."

He makes to crawl away, but another volley of shots rings out and it's close enough for us to hear the buckshot flicking through the cotton.

I hold on to his wrist. "What about the Yankees? What about Celia and Sarah?"

Hubbard has droplets of sweat sitting gently on his beard and he runs a hand across his chin. "Don't worry about the Yankees. They ain't after us. Celia and Sarah are safe. It was you I was worried for. Come on and follow me. We got to go."

Hubbard hears them the same time I do, 'cause his eyes flick quickly to the right of me and we catch a glimpse of the soldiers coming through the bushes. A line of 'em about fifteen feet from us, all crouched low with their rifles held out in front of 'em. I see their blue tunics and I think we must be caught. Perhaps Hubbard does too, 'cause he puts his hands up above his head and calls out, "Don't shoot! We just a couple of slaves caught out in the field. Please, sir. We don't want no trouble."

He stands up slowly, raising his head above the cotton so they can see who he is, and I rise on one knee, intending to do the same. Three quick shots ring out from across the field and Hubbard falls hard against me, knocking me to the ground and I land underneath him. He's pinning me down with his full weight on my chest so that I have to turn my head to the side. "Hubbard!" I kick my feet, scrabbling to get a hold so I can get out from under him. "Hubbard?"

The Yankee footsteps are coming through the cotton, so I stay very still, thinking they might shoot me if they see me alive. Hubbard's so heavy it's all I can do to take a breath. "Hubbard?" I whisper his name, whisper it barely loud enough to hear it myself.

I freeze as the boots come past me and I hug the big man close, hoping he'll cover me while the Yankees pass. Above me the sky is bright blue. A butterfly lands on a boll above our heads and there's a drop of blood, bright red upon the white flower. The last one of 'em looks down at me. He can see I'm alive and watching him and he puts a finger to his lips, meaning for me to stay quiet, then he kneels up on one knee and fires his rifle. The smell of burnt powder and smoke wafts over me as he crouches back down and moves off into the field.

Once they're gone, I manage to free one of my hands. I take hold of Hubbard's arm and roll him off me. He's facedown in the dirt and I pull him around onto his back. He's bleeding from a wound up near his shoulder, but he's still alive. He looks scared, though, like the rabbit we found in the trap, and just like then, I don't know what to do. I watch the blood pooling on his shirt and I'm taking short, quick breaths just the same as his. "What do I do, Hubbard?" His eyelids begin to close and I shake his shoulder, trying to wake him up, all the time rocking on my heels and whining. "How do I make it stop, Hubbard? Tell me how to make it stop!"

I don't think he can speak. I hold his head in my hands to keep it off the ground. I should drag him from the field, that's what I think, so I put his head down gently, then, taking hold of his arms, I pull 'em till his shirt lifts halfway up his chest and the buttons come out of their holes, but I can't get him to move hardly an inch.

"Get out of here," he mutters to me softly, opening his eyes to look at me. "Go on and get."

"Hubbard . . ." I take hold of his head again as I say his name. I'm watching his lips. I can see he's hurting and it hurts me too, sharp, stabbing pains in my chest and head.

I want to shout for help but I daren't. I daren't do anything at all. But I got to do something. I remember that the missus has some medicine in the house. Hubbard's head feels heavy when I lay it down and I lean back across his chest to whisper in his ear, "Hold on, Hubbard. You hold on here while I get some help."

I break cover and run for the path, not minding that I might be seen and shot, running fast between the bushes, making for the edge of the field, looking for the way back to the house. But I stop dead when the missus shouts my name.

"Friday!"

I turn around and she's coming for me, walking quickly through the cotton with Virginia held in one arm and a burning torch in her free hand, the smoke rising up from the fires behind her.

"Don't you move now, Friday!" she shouts at me. "You come to me right now!"

I'm rooted to the spot, not knowing what I should do. Peighton and his men are running around the path from the far side of the field, hoping to meet us at the river, and I know they'll take me if they can; they'll put me in their wagon and be gone from here without a second thought. A volley of shots forces 'em down again, making 'em take cover in the field.

"Don't you run now, Friday," Mrs. Allen warns me, and she's only a few steps away, almost within reach of me.

I duck back into the cotton. "Friday!" she shouts as I run again, keeping my head down. I charge along the line of bushes, and when I come to the path, I straighten up and go full pelt without looking back. Everyone's at the fire pit. They're looking scared at the sound of gunfire and they shout to me as I run toward 'em. "What's happening, Friday?" Lizzie calls out. "We heard shooting."

I run past 'em. "Hubbard's in the field—he's been shot. I'm going to the house for medicine."

Sicely comes tearing up the path after me. "I know where she keeps it," she shouts out. "Wait for me, Friday. I know where it is."

We run together into the yard, where Peighton's wagon and horses stand tethered and waiting. As we start up the stairs to the back door, Gerald shouts at us from the open window of the drawing room. He's wearing a Confederate cap and has a musket in his hand. "Samuel! Get in here, quick."

Sicely and I run through into the hall. "Go get the medicine," I tell her as I dash to the drawing room door. I have to tell Gerald that I'm leaving and I want to say good-bye.

He leans against the wall to the side of the window, a musket standing upright in his hand, with the butt on the floor and the barrel stopping close to his chin. "Get in here," he tells me urgently. "You got to run away, Samuel. Mother's made plans for you to go to Alabama with Peighton. You've got to get out of here."

He takes a cartridge from the pouch on his belt and rips the blue paper open with his teeth.

"What are you doing with that? Put the gun down and come away from the window."

He rams the bullet home with his rod, then pulls back the hammer, fits a percussion cap, and props the gun against the wall. "There's Yankees in the fields, but I won't let 'em in the house."

"They shot Hubbard," I tell him. "I came to get some medicine."

Sicely bursts in through the door. She's holding two glass bottles that are stopped with cork and there's bandages spilling from the pocket of her pinafore. "I got some things might help."

"You go on," I tell her. "Get Lizzie to go with you and I'll be there in a minute."

Sicely runs away down the hall and I glimpse her chasing out across the yard as I turn back to Gerald. He's sitting on the floor, taking off his shoes. "You should run to the woods, Samuel. You'll be all right there. They won't come after you." He holds them out to me. "Here, take these. You're gonna need 'em more than I do."

"I can't take your shoes."

"Go on." He puts 'em in my hands. "Try 'em on. I always wanted to give you a pair of shoes and I think they'll fit. Hurry up and put 'em on. You haven't got much time."

I sit on the floor and loosen the laces. "I wouldn't go unless I had to, but I'll try to come back with my brother once this is all over."

"I'll give you both a job. You know that."

I have my feet in his shoes and Gerald stands back and admires them as loud voices arrive in the yard outside. He runs to the window, then ducks down below the sill. "There's Yankees in the yard!"

He seizes his musket from the wall, laying it out across his knee, and I'm trying to tie the laces of his shoes, when he suddenly stands up, steps back from the window, and fires. There's a loud crack as the musket kicks up out of his hands, throwing him backward as it clatters to the floor.

"Gerald!" I scramble across to him as he gets to his feet. "What're you doing?"

Soldiers shout instructions to one another as they scatter, and I count three voices, maybe more. Through the window, I can see a body on the steps of the house, a crumpled leg and a foot that hangs down into the yard. "Oh, sweet Jesus," I whisper.

Quick footsteps make me turn and I glimpse the flash of a blue tunic as a Yankee darts around the back of the house. Gerald is already priming his gun for a second shot and I scramble across to him as he rams in the bullet and lifts the hammer back. "Stop it, Gerald." I take hold of his arm. "You'll get us both killed. You've got to stop it."

A windowpane smashes behind us and a burning torch is thrown inside. It crackles on the floorboards, sending black smoke to the ceiling, and I run across, pick it up, and throw it back out through the broken glass. When I turn back to Gerald, he's standing in the middle of the room with his musket raised and there's a soldier in the yard, taking aim at our window. I throw myself to the floor. "Gerald, get down."

There are three shots that come almost at once. Two hit him in the head and the chest, lifting him from his feet, while the third hits a mirror on the wall behind and he falls back hard on shattered glass.

I run the few steps to him, scattering shards with my leather soles, and when I reach him, there ain't no life left in his eyes at all.

"Gerald?" His head is limp in my hands. "Gerald?" I shake him hard, but it don't get rid of the look in his eyes. "Gerald?"

He won't stop staring at me. I let go of his head and it rolls to one side—but at least he ain't looking at me the way he was.

My lungs ain't working and I can't breathe, but when I hear

footsteps from beyond the window, I suddenly find my voice. "Don't shoot us! Don't shoot me, please!"

I scramble across to Gerald's gun and throw it out the window as a sign of surrender. Gerald ain't moved at all, but now that I'm here at the window, he's staring at me all over again. He's got a hole in his head where the blood comes out and it drips onto the floorboard. I curl up into a ball, curl myself up on the floor with my hands around my head and my legs tucked up into my gut, 'cause if I don't see him, if I don't see Gerald staring, then maybe he might move. Maybe he's just playing at being dead. Maybe he don't like me watching him while he's hurt.

Mrs. Allen is somewhere outside in the yard. She's shouting at the Yankees, telling 'em to get off her property, telling 'em she has a son inside that house. Another torch hits the floorboards behind me, but I don't move to put it out 'cause Gerald's over there, still crumpled on the floor, staring at me. I force myself to look at him and he looks ever so lonely. I shouldn't be scared of him. I shouldn't leave him on his own.

I unfold myself, edging across to him on my hands and knees, the scattered glass pinpricking me. When I bring him onto my lap, I got blood on my hands, but I hold his head to comfort him, and his Confederate cap is on the floor beside us, so I reach across, pick it up, and put it on his head.

"Gerald?" Mrs. Allen shouts his name. There are men shouting too. Everyone's arguing with one another. Mrs. Allen shouts out, "Let me be! My son is in that house, sir." She calls his name again. "Gerald! You come out here at once! Do you hear me?"

He ought to be with her. Gerald ought to be outside with his mother, but he can't go by himself and I'm too scared to take him. I'll get the blame for this. I know I will. They'll hang me on the fence and butcher me. They'll have my guts for garters and sell my hair to the man who makes brushes. I wipe the sleeve of my shirt across my eyes 'cause they're hurting from the smoke. I wipe my nose so I can breathe. But now I got him all over my face. I got his blood up in my nose, the smell of him, and all over my cheeks, same as it's in his golden hair.

I don't want to go outside. I don't want to do it. But I can't stay here, not with the hellfires burning all around.

"Gerald?" she shouts again.

"I got him, Mrs. Allen!"

I put a hand under his knees and a hand under his head and I pick him up slowly, my fingers gripping his clothes so tight it would hurt him if only he were alive. "I'm coming out! I'm coming out with Gerald!"

I grip his shoulders, moving from my knees up onto my feet, and he seems so light, light as a feather, like he never grew up. I walk with him to the door. "Don't shoot me! Please God, don't shoot me too, 'cause I'm coming outside."

I go through the hallway and out through the back door, waiting for the shot that will kill me—but it don't come. I step over the dead Yankee, and suddenly, Gerald's heavier, he's making me stagger down the last two steps into the yard 'cause he's a dead weight in my arms, dragging me down, pulling me toward Mrs. Allen. She's standing fifteen feet away, holding baby Virginia. Beside her is an officer of the Union army and he points a pistol at my head as we approach.

Soldiers are edging out cautiously from where they'd taken cover, their guns trained upon me, but I walk straight to Mrs. Allen and lay Gerald at her feet, 'cause I can't hold him a moment longer.

Now I'm covered in blood, same as he is, the both of us looking like we been up to no good, and I'm bound to get the blame for this, I know I am.

"If he hadn't shot at 'em, he'd have been all right," I tell her. "I'm sure he would've been all right if he hadn't shot at 'em."

But Mrs. Allen ain't even looking at us. She's watching the soldiers torch the house, an empty look on her face as the pretty yellow shutters catch fire and flames flick out across the walls like snakes.

"Look at Gerald, Mrs. Allen." I reach across and tug at the sleeve of her dress. "You got to look after him. You gotta see what happened to his head."

She shakes me off, flicking me away like an unwanted bug on her dress, and when she does look down, she don't move to touch Gerald at all. "I suppose you couldn't wait to steal his shoes."

That's a strange thing to say. But then I see his bare feet. And I step away from her. I edge away, taking slow, sure steps, more scared of Mrs. Allen than I've ever been.

The Yankee officer looks down at the shoes I'm wearing. He says, "Now hold on there, that's not right," and he tries to grab me by the arm, but I turn and run. I run down behind the gin barn and on through the woods, too scared to call the names of Hubbard's wife and daughter, too scared to stop and think of anything at all, a picture in my head of Gerald lying dead on the ground, all alone and bleeding at his mother's feet.

And I run through the trees till I'm out in the open. Ahead of me the fields are ripe with fire and behind me the air is thick with smoke, a big black cloud of it, rising up above the plantation house.

But I keep running, the stiff black leather of Gerald's shoes slapping hard and quick upon the ground.

And I make for the river and the distant guns.

And everything is burning.

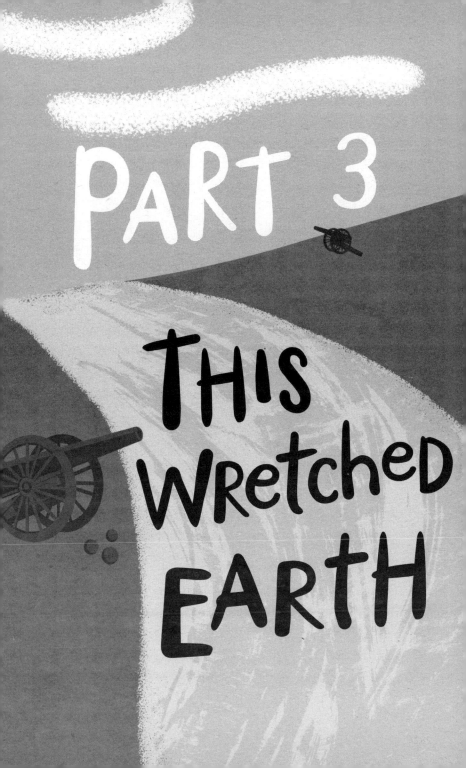

PART 3

THIS WRETCHED EARTH

CHAPTER 20

Mostly I keep to the riverbank. I creep through corn. Hide from men on horseback. I don't know who they are, and though they ain't following me—I'm sure of that now—they have stretched my nerves till they're tight as the wire on a snare.

I follow the noise of guns, and it ain't right for that to feel safer than the silence. Every time one booms, I think of Gerald. Sometimes, I think of Hubbard. Soon I'll be dead in a field, dripping blood from open wounds.

When the bark of dogs brings me down to the water, I walk in past my waist. The cold numbs my skin. It takes away the hurt. I lie back, my arms and legs stretched wide on either side of me, and let the river take me.

I don't know where we're going but neither does the river.

When the branch of a tree passes, I take hold, and it carries me along like we're old friends. I expect it's dead too. We drift downstream together, each of us in the other's arms, two bits of deadwood cut from a tree the Lord don't want, being drawn toward the war like water to a plughole.

—

I'm colder now the sun's gone. My chest is cramped up tight as a fist.

The gunboats surprise me, coming from behind and bearing

down on me, already too close. I find my feet and kick for the river-bank as the first boat passes only twenty feet away, its engine making so much noise I can't believe I didn't hear it. The ship lies low in the water, like a turtle in its shell. It has four open hatches, and a cannon points from every one. The eyes of a sailor look out from a view hole as his ship makes waves that I swallow if I try to breathe.

I let go of the branch and thrash at the water, my head twisting from side to side. I swallow air and then water, air and then water, as the river tries to throttle me. I turn over on my back, kicking hard with my legs, getting one good mouth of air and then a second before a boom rocks the river and a streak of fire leaps out across the sky, exploding the bank above my head and sending mud into the water like a patter of rain.

The force of the explosion hits my stomach like a punch and I roll back again to my front, gasping as the night rips itself into shreds of red and yellow. I swim like a dog, panting toward the land. Ahead of me, a burning tree leaps up into the air, then disappears into the river with a hiss. I change direction, my arms slapping at the water all around my head, and when my foot touches a rock, I kick one last time and stumble forward onto wet mud. I got the ground beneath my feet and I crouch there, breathing hard, my wet clothes clinging to me like they're more scared than I am. Another explosion makes my ears sting before they go dull and I can hear my own heartbeat as the smoke drifts across me like a mist.

A bugle cries out once. There are muffled shouts and the crackle of muskets.

I take a deep breath and then another, forcing myself to stand and then run, my shoes slip-sliding and stumbling against rocks. But figures appear up ahead of me, black shadows caught out against the moonlight on the water, some waist high in the river while others leap from small flatboats toward the shore. I can't go there, so I turn and run back the way I came, crouching low, hoping there's somewhere else for me to go. But the river's full of fire and guns. As I crouch and rest again, one of the ironclads gets hit so hard it rings like a bell.

I try a different direction, turning in toward the steep bank and using the roots of trees to climb, one hand over the other, one shoe cutting into the moist soil and then another, till my hand touches the top and I pull myself up onto a lip of grass and mud. I lie flat on my stomach, breathing hard, the whiff of a fox in my nostrils. Now that I'm not moving, the cold bites on my bones. It makes my teeth ache in their sockets.

I edge forward on my knees, a hand stretched out ahead of me, feeling my way. And then the ground disappears, leaving me patting nothing but the night air, and I stop sharp, bring my hand back toward me till I feel the edge of earth, which descends straight down past the length of my arm.

In front of me is a dark hole and I hesitate, not knowing how deep it is, thinking it might swallow me whole. But then I hope it does. I don't care if it takes me forever, for I am forsaken of the Lord and I disgust him. I know I do.

And I let myself fall.

I drop about eight feet, slipping down the wet mud bank till I come to rest on my stomach in damp earth. There's the click of a gun being cocked before I can even see where I am. "You better put your hands in the air pretty quick, boy."

I got no life left in me and I can't move.

"Did you hear what I said?"

I put a hand up somewhere near my face.

The barrel of a gun kisses the back of my head, just behind my ear, but then a second voice says, "Let him up," and a hand brushes the gun away. A mortar explodes above us, lighting the sky with falling fire and showing me the edge of boots stood close to my cheek. Two hands take hold of me under each arm, gripping my shirt and pulling me up till I'm propped against the cold mud wall.

Four men are in the pit with me.

"It's a slave boy!" says one of 'em.

"What's he doing here?" says a man with hollow eyes, and he brings his rifle to my forehead. "He might have a gun! Look in his pockets. Check if he's got a knife."

"He ain't got a gun," says another, and I see it's a rebel soldier sat opposite me, a prisoner with a gun held to his head just the same as me. "We don't let 'em carry guns," he says.

"Let's kill him," says the man holding the rifle to the rebel's head. "Let's kill 'em both."

"We're not killing anybody," says the soldier who helped me up out the mud. "That's not what we're gonna do."

I'm shivering so much I can't keep still, and my jaw don't work properly either; it just chatters of its own accord, rattling the teeth all together in my mouth.

They can shoot me if they want to. It'd be a blessing.

The man puts his hand on my shoulder to keep me from falling on my face. "You ain't armed, are you?" I stare blankly and he says, "I thought not," and takes a piece of hardtack from the pocket of his tunic. He breaks off half the biscuit and puts it in my mouth. "Eat that. It might help."

"What you doing?" The man with the rifle leans across and breaks the edge of it away before I have it past my lips. "You shouldn't give it to him."

"Don't I get any?" asks the rebel, and all three of 'em turn on him, saying, "No."

He shakes his head with a wry smile. "First time I've ever been lower than a nigger boy. Is that what you Yankees are fighting for? You wanna see a good American like myself laid lower than a nigger?"

I chew on the biscuit I have saved between my teeth and it sticks up between my gums.

A shell explodes close enough to shake the pit we're squatting in. And then there's another and another and the sky becomes bright white and filled with screaming metal. Each blast seems louder than the first and I close my eyes tight and curl up in the mud with my hands around my head and my knees up in my chest as the world splits itself apart. This must be how it all ends.

But it don't.

The barrage suddenly stops and there's an eerie silence that makes me wonder whether there's anything left beyond this hole.

I'm still shaking from the cold. I begin to blubber. I can't help it. I begin to cry like a baby.

The rebel laughs at me. "I ain't never seen a kid so scared. Look at him. He's almost turned white." He laughs again and when he stops, there's just the silence. Nothing but the silence. The soldier sitting closest to me adjusts his feet with a squelch of mud and looks up at the edge of the pit.

The rebel laughs again, more nervous than he was before. "If the boy's scared now, he better not hear Whistling Dick. Any of you boys ever heard that gun?" He grits his teeth and whistles till he's out of breath. "You can hear him coming for ya. You know what I mean? The louder that whistle gets, the closer you are to death. I'm telling y'all, you ever hear old Whistling Dick, you better make your peace with God."

All of us cock our heads to the sky, listening out for Whistling Dick. But the night is so very quiet. When the crack of a rifle shot finally comes to us through the darkness, we all breathe easier, knowing we ain't the only ones left alive on this earth.

The soldier that gave me the biscuit suddenly stands and steps toward the rebel. "Give the boy your clothes."

"I ain't giving him my clothes."

The soldier takes his pistol from its holster and cocks it. "I'm the only person here keeping you alive, but I'll kill you myself if I have to."

That changes the rebel's mind. He unbuttons his shirt, takes out his arms, then throws it at me. He begins to unbutton his trousers too.

I look at the butternut shirt in my lap.

"Go on, then," says the soldier kindly. "You don't want to catch your death."

The rebel's shirt is covered with mud, but it ain't drenched wet like my own and so I peel the shirt from my back and put his on instead, my fingers fumbling at the buttons till I get some help. I feel the warmth from it too. I put on his trousers, then throw my linsey-woolseys back at him, though he won't wear 'em. Says he'd rather die of cold than put 'em on, and he crouches naked in the pit, telling me that if the two of us should ever meet again, he'll kill me. I believe him too.

We sit and wait, each of us keeping our eyes on the other, wondering what might happen before a new day dawns. But nothing happens. Come sunrise, we're half-dead from cold and scared somewhere near to madness.

A Yankee officer comes upon us in the pit and stands at the edge to look down on us. He's wearing a smart tunic with buttons that gleam in the morning sun and I realize we must look like monsters to him, dragged out from the cloying mud.

"You boys all right?" he asks, and points to the rebel squatting naked in the dirt. "Is this man a prisoner?"

"Yes, sir."

"Get him some clothes."

"What'll we do with this one?" The man with the hollow eyes flicks his rifle in my direction. "Should we give him back to the rebels?"

The officer looks me up and down. "Do you want to go back to the rebels?"

"I never been with the rebels."

"You got somewhere to go? You got someone can look after you?"

If I ever had anyone, it was Hubbard. But I got Joshua. He's the only soul alive that knows me and I know him too. Suddenly, I miss him so much it hurts.

"Do you know Middle Creek?" I ask the officer once he's helped me climb out of the pit.

He shakes his head but points downriver. "There's a camp a few miles that way. Someone there might know."

——

At the camp, the white folks call us contraband since they regard us as the spoils of war. We live in the same camp they do. Only thing that divides us is a path where we stand in the mornings, hoping to be chosen to work on laying railroads or digging new trenches.

They don't make us do it. We're free to starve if we choose to, but I work for three weeks, trying to buy the fare back to Middle Creek, and I never make more in a day than it costs to feed me and put a roof above my head.

So on the first day of the fourth week, I start walking.

CHAPTER 21

The wasps at the crossroads have all gone wrong. I don't know why. I watch 'em buzz around in circles, bumping into each other like they've lost their minds. It must be something like that, to make 'em behave that way. A few of 'em stagger over Gerald's shoes and I kick 'em off into the wet mud, then stand and watch 'em wriggle.

It starts to rain again.

A wagon comes along the road. It's driven by a soldier. When he reaches the crossroads, he panics and swipes at the wasps. He thinks they're after him but they ain't. They've just gone wrong like everything else.

"Going into town?" I shout out, but he ignores me like I knew he would. He knows I want a lift and it ain't allowed for soldiers to give lifts to people like me. I didn't expect he would. Raindrops tap on my shoulders. They hit the top of my head. I didn't expect sunshine either. No sunshine or shelter. I don't expect a thing.

My legs are cold. The bottoms of my trousers are rolled above my knees, and my shins have mud for skin. Father Mosely once told me that the road to heaven ain't paved with gold. I don't know if that's true, but I know about the road to hell. It's made from mud. Has to be. There ain't a road been built that could be any worse than this one—but it's a slow road back to Joshua.

I start walking in the same direction the wagon went and the rain runs down into my eyes. I try not to put my feet into the puddles. Gerald's shoes are a deep, wet brown and they don't keep out the cold as much as they would if they were boots. I could have got boots. Back in the last camp I was at, I could've stole 'em but I didn't. Just 'cause the world's gone to killing and stealing, doesn't mean I have to do it too.

A tree offers shelter from the rain, and when I reach it, I settle myself against its trunk. This rain makes the world so miserable. Everything is dull and gray and hopeless. I wipe my face with my hand. If I stay here too long, I'll get even colder. I can't remember the last time I was really warm, and I hug myself, waiting for the rain to ease.

Another wagon comes into view. It's moving slowly down the road. A couple of men are hunched up in the front. One of 'em has a hat and the other one doesn't. When they reach me, I see a white gentleman in a coat and bowler who's well wrapped up against the rain. He's got a beard. He's got a pair of spectacles on his nose. He's being driven by a Negro who ain't so well dressed, though it's still an improvement on the clothes I got on.

I watch 'em pass me by, but I don't shout out. About twenty yards up the road, they come to a stop and turn to look back at me. I can see 'em talking. The black man jumps down onto the road and his big boots make a splash in every puddle between us as he runs to my tree and comes in under the shelter of its leaves.

"Get in the wagon," he tells me.

I know I shouldn't. I look back up the road to where the wagon waits in the rain, but the man steps in front of my face to block my view. "Don't you want work?"

"You got some food?"

"I told him you wouldn't be no good." He reaches down, takes hold of my arm, and lifts me to my feet. "The doctor's got a position needs filling. So get in the wagon." I don't think he can smile.

Now that I'm standing, the idea don't seem so bad. Not if they got food. I could do the job for a day or two. Do it long enough to get a meal and a lift in the wagon.

I walk out into the rain with the man by my side and we splash through the puddled mud till we're alongside the wagon. The man in the bowler hat has a good long look at me, then takes a bag of boiled sweets from his coat pocket and offers 'em. "You free to work?" His accent has the ring of money, all clipped and neat around the edges. I don't know where he's from.

Sweet sugar brings my mouth to life so that all I can think about is food. "How much you gonna pay?"

"A dollar a day. You get to live in, though, free of charge. You get food as well, and if you work hard, I'll give you decent clothes." He takes off his spectacles and wipes the lenses with a grubby handker-chief. "Do you want to work?"

I nod my head. The money ain't bad. More than I got in the camp and he says I get my meals on top. I don't like to wait, but I can't get to Middle Creek if I'm too weak to walk.

The doctor flicks his eyes to the rear of the wagon and I go around the back. A coffin takes up most of the space, its lid already screwed in place, and I stand and stare. "Get in, then!" he calls out. I climb aboard, squeezing in beside the coffin as the driver whips his horse and we ride on through the rain. Another mile down the road, we pull to a stop outside a shack of a shop that stands on its own at the roadside. A man is stretched out asleep in the bay window.

He has his hands across his chest and it's a long time since I seen anyone look that peaceful.

A Negro boy walks out from behind the shop to meet us. He's a few years older than me, but I see straight away he's been bullied sometime in his life, 'cause he's a whole ball of uncertainty and resentment. It's obvious from the way he walks. He takes hold of the handle and slides the coffin along till it hangs off the back of the wagon by a couple of feet. "Don't just stand there," he mumbles at me. "Get ahold of it and help."

I grip the other end and we lift the coffin off the wagon. It's heavy. Takes both my hands and a shoulder to get it around the back of the shop, where there's a barn. When we go inside, the place is dark and full of coffins and we rest ours on a stack near the door as the doctor hurries in after us. He pushes past, tying a label to the handle and, without thinking, I take hold of it to read the name. COLONEL BARNABY JONES, 1ST DELAWARE INFANTRY. That's what it says.

"So you can read, can you?" The doctor watches me closely. "Can you write too?"

I don't see why I should lie anymore and I ain't got much to be proud of. "I can do the both as good as anyone else I've met."

"See, Jermaine?" The doctor turns to the boy. "He's already more useful than you. How do you like that?"

Jermaine looks like he hates me.

The doctor takes hold of my shoulder. "What's your name, boy?"

"Samuel."

He bristles very slightly. "No 'sir' when you speak to me? Well, never mind. No 'please' or 'thank you' either, I bet, but that's OK; that's just as it should be. You're a free man, Samuel. You can bestow your honors as you choose. But congratulations are due." He shakes my shoulder, smiling. "You've just been promoted. Not bad on your first day, eh? There's no more money in it, mind, but it might mean your work is a little less arduous than it was only a moment ago."

"Can I have some food?"

The doctor offers his bag of sweets again and I take one. He don't offer one to Jermaine, putting 'em back in his pocket as the driver comes in out of the rain. The doctor rubs his hands together, chuckling. "I picked out a scholar. Do you see, Drudge? The boy can read." He wags a finger in the man's face. "I still have an instinct for good character, Drudge, whatever you might think of me."

He turns back to me, shaking me by the hand. "Welcome, welcome! I'm Dr. Klinghopper. You've already met Jermaine. This is Drudge. You won't find either of 'em have much in the way of conversation, but they're survivors—oh, I'll give 'em that—and it's not a bad gift to have at this particular moment in American history. Wouldn't you agree, Samuel?"

I don't know about that. I still don't know what it is he wants me to do. I look back in the direction of the shop and move the sweet to the side of my mouth before I ask, "Who's the man asleep in the window? Does he work here too?"

The doctor laughs at that. "We don't actually know who he is, Samuel, but that shouldn't stop you from making his acquaintance. Come along. Come with us and say hello."

He leads the way outside, all of us in a line as we walk around to the front of the shack and go in through the shop door. The room is cold and smells of turpentine. We line up along the window, and the doctor spreads his hands wide, taking in the man asleep on the sill.

"Behold, Samuel—the unknown soldier. Miraculously preserved and restored to us in the form of a working companion." He bows and brings his lips closer to my ear. "We call him Lucky because he brings in the customers—those that have had the foresight to plan for their likely demise."

Drudge sneers and Jermaine snickers like a dog with a cold.

The doctor walks across to a side table, picks up a decanter, and pours himself a drink. He holds the glass in the air like he's going to make a toast. "Don't be alarmed, Samuel. We shan't wake him with our loud talk, will we, Drudge? Do you want to tell our new friend why we won't wake Lucky up?"

"He's dead," says Drudge.

I look again, but the sleeping soldier appears to be in better health than all of us. He's got good color in his skin and his cheeks are fresh and plump. But he ain't breathing. Now that I look properly, I can see he ain't breathing.

"Go closer," the doctor prompts me with a hand in my back, and I step closer to the corpse. "You could almost kiss him, couldn't you?" The doctor puts an arm around my shoulder. He's close enough I can smell the whiskey in his glass. "That's the beauty of your new position, Samuel. We're in the business of bringing the dead back to life. And very rewarding it is too."

I swallow the last of the sweet. "Like Lazarus?"

"Exactly. We're raising the dead. Just like Lazarus." He takes his arm away, produces a card from his top pocket, and hands it to me. "Go on and read it out loud. Impress me some more, why don't you?"

I clear my throat. "It says, 'Dr. Klinghopper, Medical Practitioner and Embalmer.'"

"Yes, yes. Oh, you're really very good. Quite exceptional." He takes back the card, nodding enthusiastically. "What's your handwriting like? Are you neat?" He waves the other two away. "Drudge, Jermaine, haven't you got something to be getting along with? Food perhaps? Samuel looks hungry to me. Why don't you make us all some food?"

They disappear out the door, and the doctor pulls aside a curtain at the back of the shop and shows me in behind. A naked man is spread across the top of a long wooden table and this one's dead for sure, all pale and shrunken on the bone. His uniform lies across the back of a chair. I spot a wound in his arm and another in his chest, and although they've been stitched, they look bad enough to have done him in.

The doctor puts down his glass, unties the label from the man's toe, and hands it to me. "Sit down at the desk and take hold of the pen." He settles me down, gives me ink and paper, then takes a letter from the desk drawer. "I want you to transcribe this letter but change the name and address to this man's details. Do you think you can do that?"

I begin to copy it word for word and it says this:

Dear Sir or Madam,

It is with regret that I must confirm the death of your son.

I have managed to reclaim his body from the battlefield, at much risk to myself, and by using the latest techniques in embalming have preserved him as you will have known and loved him before these troubled times. He surely is a handsome young man.

It is entirely possible for him to be shipped home and be with you in less than a week. You will find him delivered in a fit condition to allow for an open coffin, should you wish him to lie in state prior to his funeral. I believe you will find the results of my embalming procedure truly miraculous and fit for the hero your son most surely is.

Please could you reply in haste, providing for the sum of $100 so that I may release his body and make the necessary arrangements for his return.

Yours in sincerity,

Dr. Martin Klinghopper, Medical Practitioner and Embalmer

As I write out the letter, I see that the doctor has inserted a needle and tube into the armpit of the naked man and is pumping a liquid into him from a tub placed on the floor beneath the table. After a short while, he puts the pump down and comes across to check on my work. "You have a neat hand, Samuel. A very neat hand." He points to the bottom of the page. "But raise that figure to two hundred dollars, would you? Believe it or not, this boy had already risen to the rank of brigadier before his untimely demise. I imagine his family will be very keen for his return."

———

There's no table or chair in the barn. There's no furniture at all except the coffins, some of 'em empty, some of 'em not. They're stacked up against the walls or left on the floor so we can sit on 'em. I reckon I'll have to sleep in one tonight.

The doctor lives alone in the shop and he has oil lamps to see by, but Jermaine, Drudge, and I have only a single grease lamp and we eat our supper off our knees without being properly able to see our food, though I ain't complaining, 'cause it's hot food—rice and pork—and I can feel the good it does me as I chew upon the gristle.

When we're done with eating, Jermaine settles himself down into a coffin on the floor. Jermaine and Drudge don't like me. They think I'm too clever by half and they're only interested in making me look small.

"You seen the battlefields yet?" Drudge asks me, sneering. I don't know if it's worse when he speaks to me or when he don't, and I shake my head. "No," he says. "I didn't think so."

"I been in a battle," I tell him quickly. "I floated down a river on a log and got caught in the crossfire."

"You seen dead men?"

I nod.

Drudge puts his face up next to mine. "Bet you've never been up close, though. Have you?" I think of Gerald and Hubbard. I couldn't have been any closer. But I won't tell him that. I don't want to.

Drudge smiles, satisfied that I'm only half the man he is, even if I can read and write.

Outside the barn, the rain starts up again, tapping impatiently at the wooden slats above our heads.

"Ever seen a white man turn black?" Now he's teasing me. "You'll see it tomorrow. You'll see plenty, 'cause there's boys out there been dead for weeks." He shows me his full set of teeth like there ain't a thing could make him happier. "Their skin'll be the same color as ours."

"You don't know how some of 'em look," Jermaine shouts out excitedly from the darkness near my feet. "You'll see it for yourself tomorrow. I saw one yesterday had a mouthful of maggots. Can you believe that?"

I've already seen things I wouldn't have believed, and none of 'em were good. Neither is Drudge or Jermaine. I try to impress 'em by bragging. "When I was at the river, I heard Whistling Dick."

Jermaine lifts himself up in the coffin, enough that I get a glimpse of his face in the dim light. "You reckon you heard that gun?"

I nod.

"Nah. You're lying. If you'd heard Whistling Dick, you'd be dead. Everybody says so."

"And you ain't dead, are you?" Drudge says, looking at me like I'm nothing.

"No," I say quietly, feeling like I want to be. "I ain't dead."

——

In the morning, we take the wagon up to the camp. Drudge is driving, sat next to the doctor, and I'm in the back with Jermaine. We've been told to smile as we go through the camp and we do. Sometimes we wave at the soldiers, and the doctor lifts his hat and shouts out, "Good day to you, sir," to anyone who meets his eye. He says it's all part of the service.

The first tents we come to are full of contraband. Women are cleaning pots and pans or cooking outside makeshift shelters, and their kids walk alongside our wagon with empty buckets, on their way to fetch water. We pass a line of men standing and waiting for work, though it's too late in the day for 'em to get anything that'll pay well.

Ahead of us, a hillside of white tents stands out of range of the guns and we take the wagon through the middle till we're out the other side and closer to the front. We set up a table and chair for the doctor where he'll spend the day canvassing for trade by handing his cards out to soldiers who'll pin 'em to the front of their jackets so that whoever finds their bodies will return 'em directly to us.

It ain't raining like it was yesterday. There's even a bit of sun now and then to cheer the place up. "Take the litter, Samuel," the doctor tells me. "Take it and go with Drudge and Jermaine. Watch them work and see what they do. They are highly skilled operatives in the field, so take good notice of them and they will teach you well."

Drudge thrusts two long poles at my chest. "Carry this." I take one end and Jermaine takes the other. Drudge leads us through the camp, keeping out the way of horses or wagons that come by us. Between the straight white lines of tents, I glimpse soldiers doing drills, and elsewhere they're sitting on stools, sometimes cleaning rifles or washing their faces from small tin bowls. No one seems to be doing much fighting, though every now and then, there's still an explosion, a crack and boom that shakes the air, then comes back to us off the hillside before rumbling away into the distance. The first one makes me flinch, but then I know better than to show it.

Past the last tent, the ground opens out into a wash of mud that rises more steeply to the ridge. We pass a picket line of horses. At the first outpost, Drudge nods to a sentry as we walk through a defense that's been made by piling cotton bales two deep and two high, then driving stakes down into the ground behind 'em. The next line of defense has a row of mortar dug into a bank, and the guns look like little black pigs with their heads in a trough.

We move out into open ground and I know we've reached the battlefield when we quicken our pace across the wet mud. "Hurry," orders Drudge, and Jermaine thrusts the poles forward. I got to skip along to keep up. There ain't no trees here, and the only cover comes from rocks too big to move. I see the first dead soldier after we've gone a hundred yards, but then a cloud moves aside and the sunlight picks 'em out for me, a whole field of scattered bodies, each one a patch of blue against the black-brown earth.

Drudge takes in all of 'em with a quick eye as he leads us forward, moving lightly over the broken ground. Sometimes he changes direction and we follow him, turning the litter sharply to the right or left, getting close enough to see whether a man's uniform has stripes and so is worth our while.

"This one could be all right." We stop at a fella lying facedown and Drudge turns him over with a foot. It gives me the shivers, thinking it might be Hubbard or Gerald, and that's stupid, but it's what I think.

Drudge kneels quickly. He undoes a button on the man's tunic, puts his hand inside, and pulls out a pencil sketch of a girl—a sweetheart. He turns it over and I see her name, Louise Caburn, and a date, 1860. Drudge thrusts it under my nose. "Is that an address?" I shake my head. "Thought not," he says, then drops the letter and pushes past me.

Another fifty yards on and the bodies are more frequent. Drudge thinks we could cover more ground by splitting up and he directs me away to his left. "Take that side over there. Look for officers. Check for an address; otherwise they ain't no good to us. Pick the clean ones too. Understand? They can't have no damage to their face unless it looks heroic."

I leave the litter with Jermaine and start out on my own, making for three corpses that lie close to one another, until I see they ain't right. There's not enough of 'em left. I can tell before I get too close. So I change direction, watching where I tread as I try and pick my way through the blood and bones of battle. I look back across my shoulder, unsure how far I should wander away from the others. Jermaine drags the litter over the stretch of wet earth between the two of us. He's turning clods of mud with his foot, looking bored while he waits for one of us to find a customer.

And then I see another possibility. This one's lying spread across a low flat stone with open arms, like he's inviting me over. I go closer. His clean-shaved chin looks promising and he's still got his rifle. It's right there by his side, and I reckon that's a good sign too, so I hurry across to him. He's got a young face, but I can't see a wound on it. He's just perfect. I step slowly toward him, coming close enough that I could reach out and touch the glinting buttons on his tunic. He's got a cutlass too, still hanging from his belt, with a twist of gold braid falling across it like a pony's tail.

I edge closer, too scared to touch him, hoping a letter will just drop at my feet from the pocket of his tunic.

Jermaine shouts out, "You got one?" and I turn and shout back, "I don't know. Maybe."

I step up onto the rock, putting my boot near the man's shoulder. There's no need to be afraid of him. There's no way that he can hurt me. But I don't like looking him in the face and I turn my head aside as I reach out a hand and slip it inside his breast pocket. I feel a wallet and remove it, stepping quickly back off the rock and turning my back on the man before I open it up. First thing I see is a five-dollar bill. I fold it quickly, twice over, and kneel to put it down the inside of my shoe. Now, that's stealing, I know it is, and it don't matter if the fella's dead, it's still not right—but if I don't do it, someone else will. Probably Drudge or Jermaine. The doctor for sure. And five dollars is a lot of money.

I make the sign of the cross, whispering, "Forgive me, Lord, for I have sinned," then look around to see if anyone saw me do it. Jermaine ain't even watching me. He's looking the other way, out toward the enemy line.

I open the wallet back up, searching for a letter, and I find one, not in an envelope like Drudge said, but that don't matter because there's an address across the top. I read the start of it, "To my darling mother, if you are reading this, then I fear the worst . . ."

I don't want to read more, but I'm suddenly excited. "I got one, Jermaine." I wave at him across the battlefield. "Over here. I think I got a good one."

All the fear I had is gone as I walk back to the soldier, stepping up onto the rock as though we've just become friends. It's then I hear a faint, faraway wheeze. It's so quiet I can barely hear it, but it turns my blood cold. I got a strange sense he's whistling at me. I look at his lips as my own mouth turns dry. And the whistling gets louder. I step back off the rock, stumbling down onto a knee as I turn, 'cause he's alive for sure—I know he is. He's alive and whistling at me. He's whistling like a steam train and I turn in terror to Jermaine, but Jermaine ain't where he was; he's lying flat on the ground with his hands over his head. He's screaming, "It's Whistling Dick! It's Whistling Dick!"

And then the breath of God blows through me to my bones.

CHAPTER 22

I am not alone.

They touch me.

They pick me up and put me down.

They put their hands upon my head.

—

The Devil took me for himself. He must have. Found me right there, under the sole of his boot, and dug me up again.

Now he's in my head with needles and he's stabbing at the good bits so it hurts like hell.

Sometimes the Devil smells of grass, but mostly he smells of whiskey.

—

Hell is full of people. Talking. I don't know why.

I don't know what they're saying.

You wouldn't believe how many there are here. All the people— screaming.

—

I remember a cabin in the woods. The scratch of squirrels in the branches. The hoot of an owl overheard at dusk.

There are frogs close by. Croaking. They're all up inside my head, smelling of whiskey. All stretched out in a window, sleeping.

Though mostly I'm alone.

───

A man belts out "Home, Sweet Home." He's singing out of tune. Croaking. When he finishes, he starts the same song over again.

Sometimes he sings, *"Hold on, Abraham, I'm going down to Dixie."*

One time I heard the church bell ringing. Four chimes. And all of 'em for me.

───

I seen a pond that's frozen over.

Men come and cut the ice with big knives.

Some of 'em got saws.

They're up inside my head, all of 'em, with their big knives, cutting the ice into blocks to take it away on wagons.

And they have their hands upon my face.

───

There's a man I hear more often than the others, but mostly I'm alone.

───

He says, "Come in. Thank you for coming."

There's another man. A voice I don't remember. He says, "I can't stay long. Prop him up and let's take a look."

They take hold of me. Turn me right side up. Touch my shoulders. Touch my legs. He puts his hands on my head.

"The danger is the other eye."

"Yes, you told me."

"Deprived of the loss of one, the other will often react in sympathy and swell. It can become diseased. Be a shame to lose 'em both."

The men unwind my head and dazzle me with a light that puts out my eye.

I don't want to look, but they make me. They pull the lid apart and I see a man with a telescope. He's staring right at me. He puts his finger in my cheek till it comes through the other side and it's only when I'm screaming that he takes it out and winds my head back around the right way.

He says I'll live.

———

"'This is what you shall do: Love the earth and sun and the animals. Despise riches. Give alms to everyone that asks. Stand up for the stupid and crazy. Devote your income and labor to others. Hate tyrants. Argue not concerning God. Have patience and indulgence toward the people. Take off your hat to nothing known or unknown or to any man or number of men. Go freely with powerful uneducated persons and with the young and with the mothers of families. Read these leaves in the open air every season of every year of your life. Reexamine all you have been told at school or church or in any book. Dismiss whatever insults your own soul, and your very flesh shall be a great poem and have the richest fluency not only in its words but in the silent lines of its lips and face and between the lashes of your eyes and in every motion and joint of your body.'"

—

When I open my eye, there's a man.

A white man. A soldier.

He's sitting on a chair a few feet from my head, reading out loud from a book. We're in a white room.

That's why I opened my eye.

To look at him.

Now that I seen him, I shut it tight again.

—

When I look another time, he sees me. I know he does. He puts his book aside on the table by his chair and walks across to me, his heels and toes tip-tapping on the floorboards.

I got my eye tight shut before he gets to me.

He touches the part of my face that ain't bandaged. Asks me, "How are you feeling?"

But I can't speak.

I don't want to, and even if I did, I couldn't do it.

"Does it still hurt?" He has a kindly voice. Or so it seems. "We couldn't spare the morphine for more than a few days, so I've been giving you whiskey to help with the pain." He laughs gently. "I think you've got a taste for it, but I intend to stop. The doctor tells me I should let you get used to managing the pain on your own, and I suppose he's right. Anyway, it's pretty difficult to ignore a man who charges his prices."

I open my eye. See his face and the ceiling to the side of his head, all turned upside down. The man looks older than his voice. He's got some sort of a wild animal for a mustache and his hair rears up to one side, like I imagine how a wave might break onto a beach.

He says he don't need me to talk. He tells me it's too soon.

—

My eye is watering. If I blink, it'll trickle down the side of my cheek like a river.

I'm just one great big eyeball—it's like there ain't nothing else of me at all—though if I concentrate, I can feel the other parts of me. I touch my hip—put a finger on it, just to make sure I'm still all here. When I put a finger to my face, it hurts like hell. And it don't feel right.

—

When I turn my head, I see the bed at the other end of the room where the soldier sleeps. I hear him breathing in the night just like Hubbard used to, the proper deep breath of a big man. He's got a desk with books and papers. He's got clothes hung up on pegs and a trunk on the floor and there's people who wait on him, day or night, if that's what he needs. They come and go and tidy his things. They bring him clean shirts that are folded or they bring water for his washbowl and they call him Major.

—

My body punishes me every day, insisting I take notice, and nagging at me in aches and pains that I don't have the energy to resist. My bladder and bowels humiliate me. When I call for a bedpan, a man arrives. A Negro. I don't know his name. He sees to my needs in silence and is rough with me when the soldier's not here. Sometimes he changes my sheets.

There's a girl comes too. Another Negro. She brings a bowl full of broth with bits chopped up so small I won't have to chew, and she spoons it into my mouth faster than I can eat. She won't look at me and I don't like to look at her either 'cause she makes me think of Sicely or Lizzie—all those I've lost who might look after me.

Sometimes, I choke and then she lets the spoon rattle back into the bowl, frightened, and she hurries out.

—

Mostly, I am here on my own. Often I get lonely.

Sometimes, if the Major returns in the evening, he sits and reads his books out loud, and when he breathes, the leather on his braces creaks like I imagine the ropes of a ship might do if I were at sea. They let me drift away.

He tells me who wrote the books he reads—says whether it's Emerson, Thoreau, Walt Whitman. I don't know any of 'em and I ain't never heard their like before. They leave their words inside my head.

One evening he brings his chair close. "I'd like to know your name. Do you mind me asking?"

I don't know if I do. I don't know what to think of this man.

"My name's Solomon Winchester," he tells me. "It was me who brought you here." He waits for me like we have all the time in the world.

"Samuel," I tell him eventually.

"Well, Samuel, the bad news is you missed Christmas completely and pretty much slept through the New Year." He walks away to the door. "You'll have to wait till next year."

———

Samuel. My name is Samuel.

I got a brother by the name of Joshua. I got a brother.

I was going to meet him when . . . I was out upon the road . . . walking.

I was getting there slowly.

———

Often, there is singing from the porch outside my room. Always the same old songs—always out of tune.

Today, I put my feet upon the floor. First one and then the other, taking small, slow steps toward the window as the pain shoots up my legs. I can't straighten my back. I take one step and then a second, like an old man, hobbling toward a wheelchair, putting one foot in front of the other at the end of his days.

When I reach the glass, I grasp the sill and hold on tight to steady myself 'cause I'm all out of breath. Outside my room, the weather is fair. There are rows of huts and beyond that there are tents. To the left of me, three buildings built of brick are set around a courtyard, and there are Union soldiers everywhere. There's horses and wagons full of supplies and they're coming and going and it seems like no one's still for longer than a moment, 'cept an old man who sits on the porch beneath our window and sings his heart and soul out. His dark skin is stretched tight around his neck and cheeks, like he ain't never been indoors, just lived outside under rocks and trees, like he's a lizard or a tortoise.

"That's Old George." I didn't hear the Major come in through the door. "Must be ninety years old, I reckon, though he doesn't even know, himself." He looks out over my shoulder. "He'll be singing till his dying day, I swear he will. That boy won't ever stop." The Major fetches his chair from across the room and brings it over to the window. "You're shaking, Samuel. You should sit and rest."

My legs are weak and I'm thankful for the chair. I sit down heavily.

"I'm glad you're walking," he says to me proudly. "I wasn't sure I'd see this day."

"What happened to me?"

The Major hesitates, searching for the right words. "You took an awful big whack to the head, Samuel. I guess you already knew that. You lost a lot of tissue and bone, right there around the socket of your right eye. I found you a good doctor, but he had to operate and remove the globe in order to save the vision in your remaining eye. I'd say he saved your sight."

Every piece of me knows this must be true, but I concentrate on my face, try to sense if my eye is there or not and I move my good eye, hoping for some movement in the other. I don't feel it move but I can't be sure.

"I want to look." I touch the bandage on my face. My fingers search the back of my head for the pin that holds it in place. "Do you have a looking glass?"

"I don't think so. I can maybe—"

"I want to see."

"Hold on." The Major hurries for the door. "Hold on and let me see if I can find one. I expect someone here will have . . . Just hold on a moment." He leaves the room in a hurry and I hear him shout again from somewhere down the hall.

I wait for him with a hand on the back of my neck and another on my cheek, holding my head as though it's about to break apart. Outside the window, Old George is singing a mournful song 'bout a man and his horse going off to war.

The Major comes back with a looking glass, but offers it to me reluctantly. "Are you sure you want to?"

I take hold of it. "Would you help me with this pin?"

He comes to stand behind my head. "You're going to be pretty raw under there, Samuel. Do you understand? It ain't a pretty sight right now, but it will heal if you give it time. You got to remember that, because it's bound to come as a shock. It's bound to."

I hold the mirror up to my face and it shows me the side I know, my mouth and eye and an ear that has always stuck out a little too much for my liking. That's me for sure, good as I'll ever get.

The Major unclasps the pin and loosens the white bandage from around my head until the end falls limp across my shoulder and I see myself revealed in the glass, a face I'd mapped out in bruises and the parts I couldn't touch for hurting.

Only this ain't me. Not anymore. This face I see ain't mine.

My nose is flattened and points out at a strange angle. The right nostril stays flared, allowing me to breathe, but the socket of my eye has dropped an inch below the place where it should be, like it has slipped onto my cheek. And it's empty as a crater.

I touch it ever so gentle, run a fingertip around the smooth bowl where my eyelid has been laid across and stitched up tight to close the wound.

If I turn the mirror to the left, my good eye stares back at me, all fierce and bright, but when I turn it back and take in my face fully from the front, it's an awful portrait, as though someone has sketched me in charcoal, then smudged me with the heel of their hand or used their thumb to rub me half away.

Above the eye and below it, my face is a mess—red and scabbed and stitched with thread. The Major is right—that will heal in time—but I still won't look right, not in the eyes of God, because my face has lost all symmetry and I am a horror to behold. I have become unnatural—all the bad in me exposed.

I put the mirror to my lap, unable to look at my reflection anymore. "Why'd you do it?" I ask the Major. "Why'd you have to save me?"

"I don't know," he says quietly. "I suppose I reckoned on being kind."

———

I have folded the bandage and left it to one side. I won't wear it again, since it serves no purpose now, except to hide me from the gaze of others. I asked to keep the looking glass and have used it often, trying to become accustomed to my face as it heals.

Now when the Major reads to me, I sit up and listen. He assumes I can't read it for myself and I don't tell him any different.

On the days that I'm happy with the Major, I'll sit with my best side toward him, but when I hate him, I present myself to him as an open wound, weeping.

He lets me stay a month with him. He lets me stay another.

I think he must want me for a servant or some such, but he never asks anything of me, and when I offer to work, he tells me I'm not strong enough and that I need to rest. I sense he doesn't want me to leave, but I don't know why.

I ask again why he saved me. This time he gives it more thought, then leans forward in his chair. "I believe in this war, Samuel. It's about justice and freedom, and those things are worth fighting for. But the struggle itself—and by that I mean the actual fighting—well, that ain't something to be proud of. You have to do things that make it hard to believe you're any better than a savage." He pauses, sucking at his bottom lip, perhaps wondering about me being a Negro.

"I have seen such things, Samuel . . . I have done . . . things. And when I think of them, it's hard to see how this war is good in any way and I lose sight of what I believe in. So when I found you there in the mud, when I knew you were still alive, I decided to save you—I had to at least try—and I picked you up and carried you back through the lines. I made sure you had the best care possible. And now, every day that I see you here, always improving, I can tell myself I've done something good in this war. Whatever else happens, whatever else I gotta do, I'll know I've at least done one good thing before I die."

One night the Major asks me about myself, and I tell him about growing up with Father Mosely at the orphanage and how I was sold at the auction and became a slave on the Allen plantation, only to run away when the war reached us and the Allen place was burned. I tell him about Gerald and Hubbard dying.

"I thought I was doing God's work by becoming a slave. I thought because He'd brought me there, He'd keep us all safe. But He didn't."

"Why would God want you to be a slave, Samuel?"

"To teach 'em how to read. And I didn't mind—not once I understood."

"You're telling me you can read?"

"Yes, sir. I can read just about as good as anybody. I should've told you sooner."

The Major takes the book he has been reading, opens it, and hands it to me. "Would you read to me now?"

So I do. I read to him as he has read to me for so many months now, and when I finish he shakes his head and smiles at me, like the proudest of fathers might smile at his son. "The world is a strange and beautiful place, Samuel—and it never ceases to surprise me."

———

When I ask for my clothes, the Major brings me a pile of new things, red trousers and a navy blue jacket, all laundered and folded up neat. They're well made and the jacket is warm. On the top of 'em is a pair of black leather boots.

"Did you save my shoes?"

The Major shakes his head and lifts the boots from the pile. "These are better. They'll keep your feet dry when you walk. Here, try 'em on." He kneels to put 'em on my feet and they're a good fit.

They'll keep my feet warm and dry, like he said, and Gerald wouldn't mind if he knew. He'd be pleased I have my own boots.

I get dressed slowly, feeling like my arms and legs have forgotten how to do it. I get my foot stuck in the leg of my trousers and I can't lift my arm above my head without a sharp pain shooting up my neck. I have to sit in the chair to put my boots back on and the whole thing must take me half an hour or more and I have to rest again before I go outside.

But I do go outside. I take a first step, then another, and the air tastes fresher than I ever knew it could. I make it as far as the bottom of the porch before I start the long trip back.

—

On my next trip, I go farther. I reckon on people staring, but the soldiers that I see don't look at me any longer than they have to. Perhaps they know that come tomorrow, it might be them instead of me, and most of 'em avert their eyes, taking a sudden interest in their feet as I pass 'em by.

I go farther the next day too. I stay out longer. Within a week, I've got some strength back in my legs and I wander through the camp, finding new paths.

Today, I reach a clearing in the tents, a circle of ground maybe twenty feet across. Opposite me is a tent with one side opened out to create a canopy that's held taut by guy ropes and pegs. Inside it is an altar. It has a table with a stiff white cloth, and paper flowers in a pewter vase—bright yellow, red, and blue. No one's here, so I walk closer to look. There's a wooden crucifix about a foot high, and next to it a framed picture of a blue-eyed Christ, a crown of thorns around His head, staring up into a blue sky. It looks just like the pictures that Father Mosely had in the orphanage, the same Christ, so beautiful and peaceful, that I talked to every day, knowing He was listening to me.

Why won't He talk to me now? I step closer. *Why won't You say something? Ain't You got anything to say to me at all?* But He won't even look at me. He's staring away into heaven. He's looking at nothing at all, 'cept a piece of blue sky. And suddenly I'm shouting at him. "You ain't being fair! You can't ignore me!"

I yank the cloth off the table, putting a hand underneath and turning the whole thing over so the flowers fall in the wet mud and the picture's at my feet. Then I stamp my heel into His face, breaking the frame, 'cause I can't stand to look at it.

I run away, dodging between the tents, just like I ran from Mrs. Allen, just like I've been running ever since.

I can't go far before I have to crouch down and rest, taking huge gulps of air like I just been chased. And suddenly I'm scared for Joshua, scared like I've been blown up all over again and everything hurts.

'Cause if God don't love me no more, I don't suppose He loves him either.

———

Three days go by that I don't see the Major, and when he finally returns to the room, he is brisk with me and ill at ease. He don't want to talk to me any more than he has to. "I have some news for you, Samuel. We're moving on. I have orders to take the town and there's going to be a big push. It'll happen soon, perhaps the day after next, and it means you and I must part company." He puts a hand up to my head, bridging the gap between us, and he's softer when he says, "There's a soldier I'm fond of. He's a nice young man who'll be more use to me if he accompanies you to Middle Creek. I assume that's where you want to go, isn't it?"

My heart leaps into my mouth at the thought of seeing Joshua and the urgency leaves me breathless. I nod like an anxious dog, but the Major is already walking to the door. "It's only a two-day ride from here. My man will come and collect you after breakfast."

He returns to the room much later, once I've gone to bed. He smells of whiskey as he walks through the door and I hear him clatter and bump as he gets into bed. After a moment, he speaks to me across the room. "When I found you, I was hiding. I was scared to death, Samuel, and I was hiding instead of leading my men. I was trying not to get shot."

"There ain't nothing wrong with being scared," I tell him.

He thinks about that for a moment. And then he says, "I won't be scared this time. I wanted you to know."

CHAPTER 23

Middle Creek is only two days' ride away. That's what the Major told me. He gave me a good horse and a traveling companion with a letter in his pocket to ensure our safe passage through the ranks of Union soldiers. But Harry Maguire can't bring himself to talk to me and he won't look at my face. He's sulking 'cause the Major won't let him go into battle, and I know he blames me. We're only a few miles from the camp when the big guns start to boom and he stands his horse and stares back down the road, sniffing the air like a dog that senses something good.

He takes a while to catch up with me and then rides alongside, all sullen and slumped in his saddle. "Looks like the Major saved you too," I tell him. "You should be grateful."

"I ain't scared. There's no point joining up if you don't wanna fight. If it weren't for people like me, you'd still be in chains."

I nudge my horse forward on the open road. "I guess that's true."

But I soon begin to see what the Major likes about my companion. Harry Maguire is a good-looking boy of nineteen or so with a naturally cheerful disposition, and if he wanted to stay mad at me, then he wasn't very good at it. Before long he's telling me interesting things about the countryside we ride through or the people that live close by. I don't know how he knows 'em but he does, and he's a good talker too, with a way of describing things that lets you see 'em like a painting.

Later, when we make our camp around a small fire, I cook up some hominy grits and cured meat that the cook gave Harry before we left. He's got some coffee too—the real stuff, not chicory and dirt—and there's enough for a cup each. He divides both the food and drink equally, which I appreciate.

I lift my steaming cup into the air. "To the Major!"

Harry's too generous to hold a grudge and he raises his cup with mine. "To that son of a bitch." He grins. "Till I get back and give him a piece of my mind."

That coffee sure warms my soul.

"Say, have you ever been to New York?" Harry asks me.

"Who, me? I've never been anywhere much. Is that where you're from?"

"Best place to live in America."

Harry's eyes start to sparkle as he tells me about New York, and by the time he's done, I almost believe I've seen the great big buildings and the busy streets for myself. I hadn't ever dreamed there could be a place with so many people in it.

He asks where I come from and I tell him it's Middle Creek, the town where we're headed, then I tell him my story, the same as I had told the Major. Harry listens patiently and doesn't interrupt till I'm done.

"What you going to do with the preacher when you get there?" he asks me.

"I don't know. Why?"

Harry shrugs. "He must have known what was going on."

I haven't thought about that for a long time. Even if it was God's plan for me to go to the plantation, it was Father Mosely who was selling us boys into slavery, and I wasn't the only one. All the things he'd said about us boys—how we should never be second best to anyone, how we ought to take pride in ourselves and what we might achieve—and all that time he was selling us off on the quiet. Perhaps it wasn't even Joshua who laid the turd on the altar of God. Perhaps it was Father Mosely himself.

The thought unnerves me. What'll I say to him? And how will he react to seeing me? It sends a shiver right through me just to think of it and I hug my blanket closer, trying to think of Joshua instead, trying to fill my head with his face, till there's no room in there for anyone else.

I can't imagine how my brother might have changed to look at, 'cause it's been two long years since I saw him. He always had a line of straight white teeth and he's got dimples that appear out of nowhere when he smiles. Yes, I remember that. I guess he'll be taller than he used to be.

I wonder how he'll see me too—wonder whether he'll mind having a brother with a face like mine.

———

In the morning, we eat some bread and a thin slice of cheese, which Harry unwraps from a bit of brown paper.

Once we're packed and ready to go, he produces two pistols from his saddlebag and hands one of 'em to me. "The Major said for you to have this. Do you know how to use it?"

I turn the gun in my hand, feeling the weight of it. "I ain't sure I want a gun."

Harry shrugs. "You can always sell it."

He decides I need to practice and stands a row of stones along the top of a boulder, then shows me how to load the gun, and we take turns at shooting, though I miss every time. "Don't go picking any arguments with a shot like that," Harry warns me. "And hide that gun in your saddlebag. Folks don't like to see a black boy carrying arms, even if we are at war."

It's getting late in the day by the time we reach Middle Creek. "Is this it?" Harry looks disappointed. "It ain't a lot, is it?"

That makes me smile 'cause the place has changed so much I can hardly believe my eyes. I catch sight of a large camp of tents spreading out from the south side of High Street, and as we ride into town, it's busier than I've ever seen it or could imagine it might be, full of the kinds of people I've never seen here before, like soldiers and young women in pretty dresses and traders who've set up stalls at the side of the road to sell food to the people from the camp. The muffled sound of a piano comes from a bar that we pass as a group of men spill out onto the street, holding bottles in their hands, all whooping and hollering. I laugh at Harry for thinking this is quiet. "You should have seen it before," I tell him. "There ain't never been anything exciting happen in Middle Creek till the war got here."

The orphanage is another half a mile out the other side of town and we turn into the side street that leads toward it and quicken our pace. Harry lets me go ahead. "You better lead the way if you know where you're going."

We ride past the Bakers' house and go on toward the orphanage. At Turner's Woods, we come out of a bend and I can see the old schoolhouse. It looks just the same as it always did, but then, as we get closer, I notice soldiers at the gates and it's obvious this isn't an orphanage any longer.

I get a spooked feeling as we get off our horses. Looking through the gate, I see that soldiers are billeted here and the boys must all be gone. That means Joshua too and I think 'bout how I ain't been praying or doing the good things I did to keep him safe.

"Come on," says Harry once the guard lets us through the gate. A soldier takes us to Father Mosely's old office. He knocks on the door, as I have done so many times before, and we wait. The commanding officer doesn't even stand when we enter and he looks me up and down with disdain once he's read the Major's letter. "So you're looking for your brother? It's hardly a military matter, is it?"

"His name's Joshua, sir. We used to live in this house, about fifteen of us boys, together with the Father and Sister Miriam. I don't suppose you know where they went?"

The officer scratches his chin. "The priest who ran the orphanage has a mission in town. Far as I know, he still keeps some boys. He holds a service most evenings in a tent out back of the hospital block. That'd be your best place to start." He looks at Harry. "This letter says you're to stay here under my command, so I'll have someone show you where to report."

"But, sir, I understood I'd be reporting back to the Major. They're making a push for the town and I ought to be there."

The officer hands the letter to Harry so he can see for himself. "The Major a relative of yours, is he?"

"No, sir. He's not."

The officer shrugs. "Well, he seems to like you. You're stuck here now, and I suspect you won't find much to do other than make sure the drunks get home safely. I don't like it any more than you do, but there's nothing either of us can do about it."

"I could curse that old man for this," Harry says once we're back at the gate.

I shake his hand. "Good luck," I tell him. "Give my regards to New York when you get home."

He wishes me luck too and then stands at the gate, watching as I walk back into town.

———

By the time I get back to Middle Creek, it's already night, and there are campfires glowing in the dark. I slip away from the road, passing through the first line of white tents where a group of soldiers are playing cards around a makeshift table, each with a pile of coins stacked at his right hand. Someone, somewhere, plays a sad song on a harmonica. Ahead of me, a man sits alone at the doorway of his tent. "I'm looking for the mission," I tell him. "I'm after a priest by the name of Father Mosely."

He looks me up and down. "You got a need to confess?"

"I suppose so . . . Who don't?"

He laughs at me—I don't know why—but he leans forward and points away to the left. "The tent's that way, 'bout another couple a hundred yards or so. You'll hear 'em before you see 'em. That's normally how it is."

I walk quickly through the lines of tents, listening for the sound of singing, and then I hear it hanging in the air, mingled in with the noise of the busy camp. I listen closely, turning my head to find the direction and recognize the words to "Am I a Soldier of the Cross?" a song I know from my time at the orphanage. I hurry in its direction and when I stop again, it's loud enough that I can hear a tambourine keeping the beat and I spot the tent, another fifty yards away, but taller than the others and brightly lit inside by lamps. There are silhouettes of standing men flung up against the canvas, all of 'em clapping their hands like we used to in class.

> *Sure I must fight if I would reign.*
> *Increase my courage, Lord.*
> *I'll bear the toil, endure the pain.*

I hurry toward it, excited at the thought that Joshua might be inside. I arrive at the back of the tent as the singing stops, but there ain't no way to get in. Then suddenly, Father Mosely speaks. His voice is only a few feet on the other side of the canvas, asking 'em all to be seated. "I want to talk to you about sacrifice," he tells 'em. "I want to talk to you about the reason for loss, and the sacrifice you make to give us a better life for those we love."

His voice puts the fear of God in me. It takes the breath from my lungs, dropping me to my knees like a young boy about to get a hiding, and I crouch on the ground, breathing fast, unable to even think straight. There's nothing I can do but wait till my heart climbs back inside my chest where it's supposed to be.

Father Mosely begins with his sermonizing and I hear him shout and I hear him whisper gently. He can only be a few feet from me, but it's not the distance that matters. He could be on the other side of the world and I'd still hear him, 'cause I got his voice inside my head, teaching me right from wrong and tormenting me like he always did.

One moment he's being as kind as a father and the next he's angry, full of the wrath of God, hurling fire from the skies onto some poor soul inside that tent, the same as he'd done countless times to all us boys—one day telling us we were no good and the next that we were little lambs and blessed of the Lord Himself.

One of the congregation interrupts him. The man says, "Listen to me, Father, for I am a lucky soul! I tell you I am. I know you all must be looking at me, wondering what reason I got to call myself so fortunate. But it's true. I'm the luckiest man alive."

"Tell us why, my friend," Father Mosely says softly. "Tell us why that is."

I struggle back to my feet. It doesn't matter if I'm scared or not. I got to see if Joshua's inside the tent. So I edge around the outside, ducking under guy ropes and hoping to find a place where I can see inside.

The man who interrupted is still talking in a loud voice. "The shell that did this to me killed six other men who were standing either side of me. But the Lord smiled on me that day, I'm telling you all, because if those pieces of shell had gone six inches to the left or right of me, I'd have met my maker. Sure as hell I would, Father. I'd be a dead man now."

I reach the entrance and put a hand to the canvas flap, pulling it aside and putting my head inside. Father Mosely's there at the opposite end of the tent. Between us are the congregation and they must be mostly from the hospital, 'cause all of 'em look bandaged, bruised, or broken.

But I can't see Joshua. I don't see any of the boys at all.

"Tell us why He saved you, Frank!" Father Mosely shouts out, pointing at the man the way he once pointed at me. "You were a sinner, Frank, and the good Lord struck you down," he tells him. "But He will lift you up again. I know He will."

The man he speaks to has no arms. I can see the sleeves of his shirt tied up in knots where his elbows should be. "The way I see it, Father, the good Lord's given me another chance to make things right, and I'll make amends for everything I done that was bad. I surely will."

I duck back outside the tent, anxious that I shouldn't be seen. But I got to go inside. Joshua ain't here and Father Mosely is the only way I got to find him. I tell myself I shouldn't be scared of him. After all, he's only a man and I got the better of him once before, when I got up on that desk to save my brother. I weren't afraid of him then.

But that was when God loved me. That was when I thought God was fair, when I thought He'd protect me. Only He didn't. And now I know He's the kind of God who saves a man's life but takes away his arms, and that ain't being fair. Just the same as taking away my eye weren't fair. Just the same as shitting on a table and trying to blame my brother for it. No. That weren't fair either.

"Repent," Father Mosely bellows at the gathered men. "Repent of your sins before the Lord and you will be saved."

I walk inside the tent and march down the center aisle that runs between the chairs, and the men all turn to look at me as I come through the middle of 'em.

Father Mosely stands at the altar, a clean white tablecloth and the golden cross of God upon it. He don't even recognize me at first, and I'm only ten feet from him when he finally knows me—I can see it spread across his face—and I know he must be filled with the same dread I felt when he stopped in front of my brother's desk.

His voice falters to a stop. He coughs, then wipes the palms of both hands upon his robes. And then he walks around the table and, taking hold of my shoulders, turns me around to face his congregation. "This is what makes this awful war worth it," he says softly. "We're fighting for freedom, gentlemen. We're fighting for freedom and the dignity of boys such as this one here."

There's a tear in the corner of his eye, but he bows his head before it falls and every head bows with him. I bow mine too. I don't know why.

"May the love of Christ be with you always, wherever you may go. This is the end of our service, gentlemen. We shall meet again in two days' time."

I'm still staring at my new boots as the men stand up and leave the room. One of the congregation comes across to us. "Father, may I have a quick word?" But Mosely waves him away. "Come and see me in the morning."

He keeps his hand on my shoulder and I don't try to move it. When the tent has emptied, he takes me to one side and offers me a seat. "Come on, Samuel. Come and sit down."

I slump down on the chair, immediately hating myself for doing what he told me.

"You poor child. What on earth has happened to you?"

He tries to touch my face, but I pull away. "Don't you dare feel sorry for me!"

He hesitates. "I was thinking about you only yesterday . . . Gloucester was here . . . Now, Samuel, listen . . ."

"You gotta call me Friday," I tell him. "That's my slave name."

"It was never meant to be you," he says quickly, and the fondness in his voice makes me want to spit in his eye.

I feel a sudden need to move. I'm all tight in my legs and stomach and I can't sit still on this chair—it's making me feel like a schoolboy all over again.

I get to my feet and stand up in front of him, same as Daniel did with the lion, the same as Moses. I'm less afraid of him now. "It was you who shat upon the table of the Lord. I know it was. You did it so you could pretend it was Joshua and sell him into slavery."

I expect him to deny it, but he says, "I did what I had to."

I cannot believe my ears. I wait for an apology or some sort of explanation but get neither. "How did you do it?" I demand.

"What?"

"The turd on the altar. Tell me how you did it. Did you climb up there and squat? Is that how you did it?"

He waves it away with a tired hand. "Oh, it doesn't matter."

"It does! It matters to me! I got a picture in my head of how it happened and it was you who put it there, so I got a right to know."

Father Mosely sits down heavily on the same chair I used, but he won't meet my eye, staring instead at the bottom corner of the tent. "I carried it in a box from the latrine."

"You carried it in a box from the latrine?"

"Yes."

"And is that the way God works?" I fold my arms like I can wait a whole lifetime for his answer. "Is it? Do you think He was proud of you, looking down from heaven and seeing one of His own priests behaving like that? Do you think that's how He expects His priests to behave?"

Father Mosely suddenly looks defiant and for a moment I lose my nerve. He ain't the kind of man to be humble for long, I know that, but I ain't finished with him yet. "How do you think God feels about a man who calls himself an abolitionist and then sells boys into slavery to line his own pocket? You're no better than a thief."

"But you haven't understood, Samuel." Mosely gets to his feet quickly, shaking his head. "I never took a penny for myself. Never. I picked one boy at a time, but only when I needed to, and I always picked the worst of you, the one who was the slowest to read or the one who showed no desire to learn their math. They had to pay the price for the costs of running the school so that boys like you could go on to become the brightest and the very best of men. That's the only way I could afford to run the orphanage, Samuel. But only good came from it. Do you understand?"

I think of how I behaved with Gerald—all the lying and cheating to do God's work.

Mosely leans over me. "Do you know how rare it is for a colored man to read?"

"I been finding out."

"Out of all my boys, Samuel, you were the brightest and the best. You have what it takes to be a leader of men."

"Just like Moses?"

"Exactly! A black man coming down the mountain, bearing tablets of stone. That's what it takes, Samuel. You have to do extraordinary things before they'll question their beliefs."

"I tried it." I swallow hard, trying to be rid of the bitter taste in my mouth. "It doesn't work."

Father Mosely falters, his eyes moving from one side of my face to the other. "You were always so full of hope, Samuel. I don't know what might have happened to you, but . . ."

"I don't believe you're sorry."

He hesitates. Goes and sits back down. "I won't apologize to you, Samuel." He taps the seat of his chair with a fingernail. "If this is the seat of judgment, I'll sit on it with confidence. What I did was for the greater good. The money Gloucester gave me for you kept us open for another six months. Perhaps I might have managed eight if we had no logs for the fires and only ate the vegetables we grew out back."

There's that name again—Gloucester. He was only here yesterday. That's what he said. Was he here in this tent?

Mosely raises an eyebrow. "What was I to do? If the orphanage had closed, you'd have probably *all* ended up in slavery or else dying in a ditch from starvation. The time I bought us by selling you gave the other fifteen boys a chance to make something of themselves. Your sacrifice gave them a future, Samuel."

I've barely heard a word he says, but then he stands and puts a hand on my shoulder, bringing me back to him. "God will only help us if we help ourselves. I think I taught you that."

I shake his hand away, glancing around the tent, searching for some clue of where the boys might be. "Where's Joshua?" I turn back to Mosely as his mouth drops open. "What have you done with my brother?"

I fumble the gun from the belt of my trousers and he's afraid of me as I come for him, putting out a shaking hand to ward me off or perhaps to plead forgiveness. "Gloucester came yesterday to collect an outstanding debt. What was I to do? I still have some boys in my care. I had to think about what would happen to them, same as I always do."

If that trigger was less tight, I swear, I might have killed him right there, 'cause I point the gun at his head with a shaking hand.

"Where is he? Where's my brother?"

Mosely tells me everything he knows—where Gloucester is going and how he's traveling—and he better pray I find Joshua or I'll be back to hold him to account. I tell him that I will.

Chapter 24

I arrive at the back of the saloon bar with a plan to steal a horse. I don't know how that's done, but I can't catch up with Gloucester any other way. A line of 'em stands out front and I look around to see who might be watching. There's no one around. I'm telling myself I got to be more like Joshua. I got to think like him, I got to act like I don't care. Anyway, I can always bring it back when I'm done, so it's not really stealing.

I choose a black horse that looks strong and fast, then saunter across to stand beside him. There's still no one watching, so I rest a hand on his neck to keep him quiet as I untie him. Any moment I'm expecting a hand on my shoulder or a loud voice shouting, "Hey! What d'you think you're doing?" but it never comes and I climb up and kick at his flank and ride away into the night.

Father Mosely had told me Gloucester was headed down south to a town called Darwin. From there he would take Joshua on to Alabama by train. The town was about a two-day walk from the camp, and I hope he'll be using a mule, the same as he had with me. If I am quick and get lucky, I might still catch him.

Well, I ride that horse flat out and we go through the night without pausing to take breath or water. I'm thankful for stealing myself a fast horse and to be riding under the cover of darkness. I even have a sliver of moon that lights my way across the flat earth.

I ain't exactly sure when I pass into Confederate territory, but I keep a lookout for firelight, assuming there'll be patrols searching for runaways or deserters. I know if they catch me, they won't ask questions, but I see only one such fire, a glimmer of flame in the lee of a hill, and I ride around it at a distance where I can't be seen or heard.

I reach Darwin just before dawn and there ain't a part of my body that don't ache. I come to a stop about half a mile short of the town, where the train tracks cross my path. Even in the dim light, I can see the station building on the edge of town. A line of roofs show the main street right behind it. My brother might already be there, locked up in a house or a shed. But I've no way of knowing where.

He might be waiting to board the train with Gloucester. If he does, he'll be lost to me forever. But do I dare to ride into town, bold as brass, and knock on all the doors till I find him? I won't last more than a minute if I do, 'cause there's nothing more suspicious than a black boy on a decent horse. They'll probably sell me straight back into slavery or, worse still, lynch the two of us from a high beam as a lesson to their own slaves who might be thinking about running away to join the Yankees.

I have to think about that. I need to slow down and work it out.

I ride the horse back the way we came till we reach a brook and I let him drink while I work things through. His dark skin glistens with sweat as I pat him down. I got to do something, but I don't know what. The longer I think about it, the less clear it becomes. What should I do? I begin to panic. What should I do? I can't even think straight and my mouth goes dry and my heart beats faster than it should. I find myself looking around, hoping to find some-one who can help me—anyone at all—but there's nobody here, there's nothing but scrubland and the faraway town shimmering in the low light.

I try to be rational about it, but that don't help. I just can't see how I'm going to get him back if he's already in town. The only thing I can do is to make sure I'm at the station when the train arrives and hope to snatch him when I see him. But in my heart of hearts, I don't think it's got any chance of working. I know it won't. I'll be lucky if I even get to see him.

And it's all my fault. If I hadn't cursed God, if I hadn't turned my back on Him, perhaps Joshua would still be safe. And how come it was only yesterday that Gloucester came to take him? God had kept Him safe until then. I remember trampling on the altar at the camp. Was that when God decided He'd had enough of me and my brother? He's punishing me—I know He is—'cause I am unworthy of His goodness, and I have shown Him little faith.

Blessed are those that have not seen Him and yet still believe.

Blessed are the children in the arms of their Father.

I fall to my knees, right there in front of the horse. "Oh, Lord Jesus, forgive me for I have been weak and selfish. I have thought only of myself and nothing of You. But please don't punish Joshua. Give him back to me, Lord. Show me how I can find him. Because I need him. Do you see that, Lord? I need him and he needs me."

I finish my prayer and stay on my knees, waiting. Above my head the horse snorts loudly, but God don't say a word to me and I sit upon the wretched earth, surrounded by the silence. I look to the left and right of me, hoping there might be an answer in the rocks and sand, but there ain't a rock on earth that ever told anyone anything. A beetle scuttles across the dirt toward my knee. Is that a sign? I don't see how it could be.

I scoop a handful of water to my face and wash the dust from the socket of my eye, taking care of where I touch. The Lord has not forgiven me. I would know it if He had. I would feel it. But I don't feel anything 'cept a fear of Joshua all alone with that man.

I stand up and mount my horse. Ahead of me, the sun rises above the ridge. It'll be warm soon. There are foothills in the distance and a scattering of small trees that might offer me some cover. I'll wait there in the hope that Gloucester has made camp somewhere back along the road and I might meet him as he comes into town to take the train. It's not much, but it's the only plan I got.

So I go back the way I came, stopping my horse at the first trees I reach, and I tie his tether to a wizened branch. Yes. This will do. I can still see the town from here, and if the train arrives, I'll have time to ride back and maybe get on board before it leaves.

I sit down on the ground to wait. The morning air is fresh and clear, but there ain't much to see or do 'cept to worry. I start to feel hungry. I've got nothing to eat and I can't see how I'm going to find anything either. Not in this wilderness. In the sky above me, there are ravens and a buzzard. They're gliding in wide circles, floating on currents of air I can't see and I don't know how they do that without so much as a flap of their wings. They're waiting for their breakfast to appear. See! There he goes now, that big ol' buzzard, circling over one spot. He must've seen something.

And that's when I spy the thin line of smoke that rises up into the air from somewhere below him. A fire! There must be someone with a campfire! Over there, in another stand of trees, about a mile farther back along the road.

I rush back to the horse, untether him, and mount up. It may not be Joshua, but someone's there, I know that much, and I approach slowly, trying to keep a line that will shelter me from view. Once I'm closer, I dismount and take the pistol from my waistband. Did Gloucester carry a gun? I hadn't seen one when he took me, but I wouldn't bet against it.

I make for the left of the smoke, running quiet as a rabbit, until I look down on their camp from the top of a bank that sits fifteen feet above it. The scene is exactly as it had been for me. The mule stands on the far side of the camp, and Gloucester is by the fire, crouching over the silver pot, dropping tea leaves into the open lid as he chews his stick of licorice.

I look for Joshua. There's a boy with a sack over his head, sitting at the foot of a small tree to my left, and I'm sure it's Joshua—I know it is. Seeing him all strung up like a chicken nearly breaks the heart of me. But I've found him! I've found him!

Gloucester stands up and stretches. He walks over to Joshua and crouches down real close. "So, boy, you got any idea what day of the week it is today?"

Joshua tells him it's a Wednesday. I recognize his voice.

"That's right—it's a Wednesday." Gloucester stands up. "You better remember that 'cause . . ."

I step out from behind my tree and start to scuff my way down the bank, my boots scraping against old roots and stones as I arrive, my gun already out and trained on Gloucester, as steady as I can keep it.

340

"Well, what the . . . ?" Gloucester sees me coming. He sees my face before he sees the gun. "Oh, my good Lord, look at you. Now what in the Devil's name—"

"Put your hands up!" I tell him. "Go on, do it!"

Gloucester puts his hands in the air. "Now, hold on there . . . I am unarmed."

"Samuel?" Joshua calls out, and his head moves quickly from left to right in the sack as he tries to locate me. "Samuel? Is that really you?"

I keep my eye on Gloucester as I clamber down the last bit of slope. He smiles uncertainly. "Don't I know you from somewhere? I'm sure I do. Why, yes, you're one of Father Mosely's boys. Ain't that right?" He becomes less afraid of me and brings one of his hands down from above his head, stepping toward me like we're long-departed friends and he might shake my hand. He must know I ain't got the nerve to shoot him. He can see it in my face.

"Don't come any closer!" I shake my gun and he hesitates. "I'll shoot! I will! I'll do it if I have to!"

"Now, you don't want to shoot me. Why don't we talk about this? I reckon you already found out what they do to niggers who go around shooting at decent folk." He takes a step closer, nodding at the gun in my hand. "You better put that thing away, boy."

I step back and he steps toward me again, the stick of licorice moving from one side of his mouth to the other.

Behind his back I see Joshua stretch himself out along the ground and start rolling toward us, his wrists still tied behind his back, the rope appearing and disappearing as he turns full circles in the dirt.

Gloucester takes another step, moving slowly into the space between us. He sees me swallow hard. "You ain't gonna shoot me, boy." He puts his hand out for the gun. "You ain't got what it takes."

But Joshua's almost reached us. He's arriving at the back of Gloucester's legs. He's on his way to help me out and he's my only hope. Suddenly, I shoot my mouth off, screaming "BANG!" so loudly that Gloucester steps back, alarmed, and trips over Joshua, who is already there at the back of his heels, kicking out like a blind mule.

I am instantly upon the man, all kneecaps and fists digging down into his shoulders, but he rises up beneath me, too strong for me to hold. I hit him hard, on the back of his head, dropping the gun as I do it.

"Aaargh!" Gloucester falls flat on his stomach.

"I'm sorry." I step away, horrified, as the man's bowler hat rolls away on the ground, that ten-dollar bill still tucked up inside it's rim.

Gloucester puts a hand up to his head as a spot of blood appears and widens across the top of his bald patch. He snarls and rises on one knee. Joshua kicks him again and Gloucester turns on my brother, grabbing at the sack on his head. "Why you little . . ." He slaps him hard. First once and then again, and I stand and watch him do it, knowing I got to act, hearing the Devil in my head, telling me to pick up the gun and shoot him dead.

There's a rock at my feet, 'bout the size of my head, and I pick that up instead, lift it up to my chin, and run the few steps to Gloucester. He looks up at me as I bring it down on him and the blow sends him crashing into the dirt. The sound it makes, the feel of it, turns my stomach. I stand there shaking, waiting for him to rise, still holding the rock in both hands but praying he won't make me use it again.

Gloucester doesn't move at all. He ain't dead—least I don't think so—but he's dazed and breathing heavy, all the fight in him concussed.

I drop the rock and kneel beside Joshua, picking at the rope around his wrists with quick fingers. "It's all right, Joshua. Just keep still," I tell him. "I'll be quicker if you stay still." I work the knot loose till the rope falls to the ground and Joshua's hands go straight to the cord that holds the sack around his neck. "I can't do it, Samuel," he says. "It's too tight."

Beside us, Gloucester stirs in the dust and moans.

"Hold on, Joshua." I run across and jump on Gloucester's back again, forcing the air from his lungs and keeping my weight on him till I've tied his wrists, using the same rope he used on my brother.

"I got it!" Joshua announces and I turn back as he takes the sack off his head. I still can't quite believe it's real. I can't believe he's actually right here in front of me.

I give him the biggest smile.

Joshua screams and scuttles away from me, looking like an insect exposed to the light, his eyes all wide in his face.

"Samuel?"

"Joshua?" I creep over to him, my hand outstretched, the same way I'd approach a nervous dog. "It's me. It's Samuel. It really is."

His face crumples in disbelief. "What happened to your face?"

I turn my head so he only sees my good side. "Whistling Dick came for me, Joshua. He came right for me and I forgot to duck, but I'm all right. I am, Joshua. I just don't look too good."

He crawls to me on all fours, then reaches out to touch me. I don't mind. I let him take his time and he holds my chin, turning my head to the left and the right till he's searched every inch of my face. "It makes you look disappointed," he says finally.

That makes me smile. "I ain't disappointed, Joshua. Not now that I found you."

He lets me hug him. After a moment, he even hugs me back.

"Does it hurt?"

"Yeah, it hurts—though not as much as it used to."

"Hey!" We turn around to find Gloucester has pulled himself up into a sitting position. The cut on the top of his head has puckered up like a pair of lips, and a streak of blood runs around his neck like a noose. "You better untie me if you know what's good for you. You keep me here like this and I'll hang you myself when they catch you. I won't even mind about losing the money."

"What are we going to do about him?" Joshua asks me.

"I don't know." I put a hand on my brother's shoulder once we've stood up. He's grown a lot since I saw him last. "We better get out of here as quick as we can. We need to get back behind the Union lines. We should be safe then. I stole a good horse and I reckon it's strong enough to take us both and still go quick."

"You stole a horse?" Joshua laughs at me. "I don't believe it!"

"Why not?"

"Samuel, you ain't never done a thing wrong your entire whole life."

"I didn't know what else to do. I'm gonna take it back."

"Thieves as well," says Gloucester, shaking his head. "I knew you two were no good. I knew it as soon as I saw you."

Joshua bends down, takes the ten-dollar bill that is tucked into the rim of Gloucester's bowler hat, and puts it in his pocket. He looks at me sheepishly. "Well, I might as well, mightn't I? If that's what he thinks."

"HELP!" Gloucester suddenly starts shouting out at the top of his voice. "Help me, someone! Thieves!"

"Shut up!" I snap.

"Or what? If you had the guts to shoot me, you'd have done it already." He turns around to face the road. "Help!" he shouts out again and he struggles to his feet.

A shot rings out and a bullet bites the ground, just an inch from Gloucester's boot. Joshua has picked my gun up and he's not scared to use it. "I ain't as nice as my brother," he tells Gloucester. "Everybody says so. So you better do as he says or I'll shoot you for real and be done with it."

He points the gun at Gloucester's chest as though the man has a heart. "Go get that horse, Samuel," he tells me with a grim face. "We better get out of here."

I do as he says, and when I return, Joshua has put the sack over Gloucester's head and tied his hands to the back of his mule, same as he did to us.

I take a moment to apologize. "I'm sorry 'bout my brother, Mr. Gloucester, but he's been naughty since the day he was born, I swear he has. I've tried to teach him right from wrong, but I can't do nothing with him."

But I don't set Gloucester free. I leave him where he is 'cause what you sow is what you reap. I've learned the lesson in that, and we leave him and his mule to wander blindly in among the trees as my brother and I ride away into the new day.

—

Joshua holds to me tightly, his arms around my waist as we make for the border. After a long while, he tugs at my shirt and puts his mouth to my ear. "I need to take a leak." I pull the horse to a stop in the lee of a large boulder and he wanders away to relieve himself.

"You got a drink?" he asks when he comes back to the horse. I take Gloucester's flask from the saddle and watch him swig it down. This Joshua is older than the brother I left behind, like he's grown into himself without any help from me. And I don't know how he did that. I always thought he needed me for everything.

"Bet you're surprised to see me, aren't you?" I ask him when he's drunk enough. "I told you I'd come back for you. Didn't I tell you? Bet you didn't believe me, did you?"

"You took your time."

"I know and I'm sorry. It took a whole lot longer than I thought it would."

I tell him my story as best I can in a short time and he listens to me, then says, "I thought it must be something like that had happened."

I thought he'd be more impressed. "Didn't you believe I'd been taken by the Devil?"

"I don't know. Maybe I did a bit, but I always had my doubts. We all did."

"And did you believe it was me that laid the turd?"

Joshua just shrugs.

"Father Mosely was going to blame you. You know that, don't you?"

Joshua nods like it's nothing. "We found out the truth when he came for Abel Whitley. We kept watch and saw what happened."

"How come Gloucester didn't take you? You should've been the next one to go."

"I don't know."

"But if you knew what was happening, why'd you stay? Why didn't you tell someone?"

Joshua shrugs. "There weren't no one interested. Anyway, I reckoned if I got took, I might end up in the same place as you and that wouldn't be so bad. Not if we were there together. I wasn't going to find you any other way that I could think of."

It warms me up to know that Joshua had been waiting all this time to find me, just like I'd been waiting for him. I take hold of his hand and kneel. "I think we should pray to the Lord and thank him for everything He's done."

"What for?"

"'Cause God just saved you, Joshua. He's saved us both."

But Joshua pulls his hand away. "You believe what you want, Samuel."

He walks away from me, but I get up and go after him. "What if I told you that I prayed for you every day that I was away? I asked the

Lord to keep you safe. I made a deal, to do good works in exchange for all the bad things I knew you'd be doing."

But Joshua won't look at me. "You didn't need to." That's all he says.

———

We head north, and by nightfall I'm sure that we must've crossed the border into Union territory. That gives me some comfort, and we stop to make camp. I have nothing to light a fire, and anyway, I wouldn't want to risk it, so I tie the horse securely and lie down with Joshua at the back of a large boulder, hugging each other for warmth as the darkness comes upon us.

"Do you know a place we can go?" Joshua asks me just when I think he's fallen asleep.

"I'm going to take us to the Major. I've been thinking it through. He'll help us, I'm sure he will, and even if he can't look after us himself, he'll know what we can do. He's a good and righteous man, Joshua, and I'd like you to meet him."

In the morning, Joshua convinces me that we shouldn't return to Middle Creek with a stolen horse. "They won't let you explain that you're bringing it back, and it won't matter anyway, 'cause you still stole it in the first place."

I know he's right.

We search out the road I traveled with Harry only a couple of days before and ride till we come to the outskirts of the camp where I spent so much time recovering from my injuries. I stop the horse to look upon it. "There it is, Joshua. Now all we got to do is find the Major."

Joshua slides down from the horse. "Come on and get off the horse," he tells me. "If people see us riding it, they'll ask all sorts of questions."

I don't know when he decided it was OK to boss me around, but I step out of the saddle, and Joshua takes hold of the reins as we walk on down the road. The first army wagon we see, he calls out to the driver. "Hey, mister, we found one of your horses wandering on its own and bought it back for you."

The soldier stops his wagon and looks at us suspiciously. He can see it's a good horse and he knows it ain't ours. "Where'd you find him?" he asks.

"About three miles back down the road." Joshua points the way and smiles at him sweetly, his little cheeks breaking out in dimples. "You can take him in if you like. Say it was you who found it. All we want is a lift into camp so we don't have to walk."

The soldier thinks about it, then comes around the rear of the wagon, ties our horse to it, and lets us ride into camp on top of the boxes he's got stacked in the back. Joshua plays the cute little kid by sitting up straight and saluting every soldier that we pass. Once we're inside the camp, he thanks the driver, then says to me, "Where'd you say this Major lives?"

I lead him through the tents toward the redbrick buildings, knowing that the Major's barracks are out back of 'em, and I hear Old George singing before I even see him. "Here we are now," I tell Joshua, all excited 'cause it feels like I'm coming home. "That's Old George, that is. He sits outside the Major's hut and sings. I don't know why, but he does."

"Perhaps he likes it," says Joshua, eyeing Old George suspiciously.

"Hi there, George." I wave to him like an old friend as we step up on the porch. "This here's my brother, Joshua. We've come to see the Major." Old George looks up at me, but he don't say nothing. He just keeps on singing.

We go inside the barracks but find the Major's room locked. "What'll we do now?" asks Joshua.

I recognize the servant who had attended to my bedpan. "Do you know when the Major will be back?" I ask him, feeling bad at not knowing his name.

The man acts like he scarcely knows me. "He ain't been seen. Not since the day before yesterday. They reckon he's either dead or taken prisoner. Most likely he's dead."

The news makes my heart stop as the servant walks away.

Suddenly this place feels cold and unfriendly as we stand outside the locked door. "What are we going to do now?" Joshua asks me.

"I don't know."

"Ain't there anyone else you know?"

I shake my head.

The servant comes back along the corridor, carrying fresh bed linen to another room. "You can't be standing around here," he tells us and he lifts his nose in the air as he pushes past. "The officers'll be back soon." He shoos us back out onto the porch. "Go on and get away now."

"You got no right . . ." I begin to tell him, but Joshua takes hold of my arm. "C'mon." He pulls me away. "We oughta find some food before it gets dark."

So we walk back into the camp. We go from tent to tent asking for food, but no one gives us a thing till we offer to pay. By then I'm glad of the money Joshua stole from Gloucester's hat. It costs us fifty cents for a plate of pork and rice and that ain't cheap. We eat our meal at the side of the path, and when I try to say grace, Joshua makes a point of telling me that it ain't the Lord who has provided for us, it's him. "We need to be fending for ourselves," he tells me, and I take offense at that.

"What do you think I've been doing all this time?"

"I don't know. I'm just saying, that's all."

It begins to rain as the darkness draws in and that don't improve our tempers. The only shelter we find is a row of wagons parked up close to each other, near to where they keep the horses in a pen. Joshua spots a guard hunched under a tree, but we come around his blind side so he don't see us crawling in beneath the big wheels, all dripping wet and silent. Sleeping under wagons ain't exactly a bed of roses, but it's the best we can do till morning.

Joshua leans against me like a rock, all hard and grumpy. It feels a long time ago since we were thrilled at finding each other. You'd think that sort of happiness would last a little while, but it seems it don't, not if you're cold and uncomfortable.

Still, I feel bad about letting him down. "It ain't much, is it?" I whisper.

After a moment he says, "Could be worse."

I take off my jacket and put it around his shoulders. "If you put this on properly, it'll keep you warm."

"What about you?"

"I'll be all right."

Joshua slips his arms inside the jacket and he feels a lot softer when he leans back against me. "I did try to be good when you were gone," he tells me.

"How do you mean?"

"I did my math. I tried harder with some of the other subjects too."

"I'm glad." Perhaps that's what saved him the other times that Gloucester came to call. Perhaps it weren't me at all. "Tomorrow we got to figure out what to do. There's a place where you line up if you want to work. You got to be there first thing in the morning if you want to get chosen."

"OK."

I don't offer up a prayer for my brother as we go to sleep with the rain hitting the wagon just above our heads and dripping down through the gaps in the boards.

But I pray for the Major, hoping he's still alive. Perhaps he's been luckier than the servant said. Perhaps he's been rescued by someone who'll be as kind to him as he was to me. I sure hope so. And if not, may the good Lord take pity on his soul.

Chapter 25

In the morning, we walk out along the path that divides the contrabands from the white folks in the camp and we join the men out looking for work.

After a while, an officer arrives wanting men to lay a new section of rail track and he walks along the line, choosing those he wants to work for him. He touches the arm of a man three down from us, then chooses the man right next to me, but he doesn't even glance at me or Joshua. I ain't disheartened, though. I figure it's pretty hard work and he won't want boys for it. Even though I'm strong enough, it ain't the same for Joshua, and I can understand that. So I don't mind too much when the next fella does the same thing. Nor the one after that.

But then a cook arrives from the canteen and announces he's after a couple of kids to run errands and do light chores. He's paying a dollar a day plus food from the kitchen and we lean out of the line, hoping to catch his eye and make a good impression. I put my arm around Joshua's shoulder, hoping he'll be chosen with me, and we both give the cook a big smile as he arrives at us. "We got experience in a kitchen, sir. We can tell carrots from potatoes and we'll chop 'em any way you like."

The man moves quickly on to another boy farther up the line and taps his arm. That boy don't seem to have anything special about him, not that I can see, but he gets the job all the same and we watch the two of 'em walk away toward the barracks.

"Is it always this difficult?" Joshua asks me.

"It'll be all right. We'll get something."

But we wait another hour and still have no luck. "Is that it, then?" I ask the old fella standing next to us.

"I expect it is. There might be something if you don't mind standing around half the day, but the work won't be worth much. Better to try again tomorrow."

I know the truth in that and we watch most of the men drift back to their tents, leaving only those of us who are too old, too young, or too ugly to be given work. Eventually, Joshua takes me to one side. "It might be better if I do this on my own tomorrow."

"Don't be stupid."

"But you're putting people off. That cook woulda give me the work if it wasn't for your face. You know he would."

"That ain't true."

"Yes, it is. I don't mean to be hurtful, Samuel."

"Then don't be."

"It's better to be honest."

"Well, to be honest, you're starting to get on my nerves. I would've got a laboring job if you weren't so small. I used to get 'em all the time."

Joshua glares at me. "Have it your own way."

"Come on." I take hold of his sleeve and walk him away, making for the edge of the camp where there are army stores and blacksmiths shoeing horses. Perhaps we can find some work there instead. On the path, we pass two ladies who are struggling to get through the mud with the buckets of water they've fetched from the well.

"Let me help you with those," offers Joshua. All of a sudden, he's being helpful and sweet. One of the women—the one with her hair tied up in red cloth—she gives her bucket to my brother and she's all smiles as she pats him on the head. "That's very kind of you, young man."

Her friend looks me up and down doubtfully. "You gonna offer too, or what?"

I take her bucket grudgingly and we follow them to their tent.

"How come you ladies are doing such hard work?" asks Joshua, trying to keep up with the heavy bucket. "Don't you have boys of your own to do this?"

"Ooh . . . he is smooth." They laugh together, speaking as though we can't hear 'em. "Such a smooth tongue and still not old enough to have all his teeth. What do you think he wants?"

"I can't imagine," says the other. "But I'm sure we're gonna find out."

Joshua smiles sweetly at 'em. "I ain't after much, ladies, 'cept a bed for the night for me and my brother here." He's holding the bucket away from his legs as he walks, trying not to spill a drop, and I do the same thing, hoping they won't notice my wet trousers.

"Don't you have any parents looking out for you?"

"No, ma'am, we don't. We mostly look out for ourselves."

The ladies smile at him, then look back at me with unease. "Your brother don't say much. Has he got a tongue?"

"Sure, he can talk," Joshua answers for me. "There ain't nothing wrong with him 'cept for the way he looks, but I'm the clever one, so he keeps his mouth shut when I'm around." They laugh at that as well. Oh, yes, they think it's real funny. "He's a hero, though," Joshua tells 'em. "He was out fighting against the rebels and they tried to blow him to pieces. That's how he came by his face, so I hope you won't be holding it against him, 'cause we all of us owe him a lot. I know I do. If it wasn't for people like my brother, then none of us would be free."

The ladies manage a smile in my direction, and when we reach their tent, they say, "Well, here we are. Home, sweet home."

It ain't much of a place, but it's better than having nowhere to stay. We put their buckets down just inside the flap, and Joshua nods at the floor. "We could just tuck in there and you wouldn't notice us. We wouldn't make no noise, and we'd fetch your water every morning and evening."

"It'd be nice to have some help around the place," says one, but the other says, "I don't know. We ain't got much space."

"What if we paid you?" Joshua spreads his hands wide as though it's more than fair—the best offer they'd get for sure. "We could manage ten cents a day." He already has a coin in his fingers and he holds it up for 'em to see. "First day in advance."

So he bags us a place on their floor, just inside the door of their tent, and I'm glad of it when the rain begins again.

——

The next morning, Joshua keeps his promise. "Don't you follow me," he says, putting ten men or more between us, and I don't know where to look when he gets chosen for a job in the officers' mess. I'm still standing in line an hour later, with all the work already gone.

I don't give up, though. I spend the whole day asking for work, going from one place to another, but it seems that if your face don't fit, people won't even trust you to dig dirt. I don't go back to the ladies' tent until I have to, and it's already dark when I come inside the flap. The three of 'em all have empty plates on their laps.

"Where you been?" Joshua asks me.

"Around."

One of the ladies hands me a plate with corn and rice. "We saved you something to eat. It might be cold." I take a mouthful and it is. "You been looking for work?" she asks, and I nod. "You get anything?" I shake my head.

"My brother's made for better things than laboring," Joshua tells 'em. "He always has been. Did I tell you he could read and write? He's a teacher too. A good one."

Those ladies look impressed. "Maybe you could charge a few cents from the parents roundabout? There's plenty of folks want their kids to read. Maybe you could set up a little school or something."

"I don't do that anymore."

"Why not?"

"I ain't got no books or boards, and anyway, I don't like the thought of taking money from people when they should be learning by rights. It ain't fair."

Those ladies look a bit put out. "Seems a shame to waste a gift the good Lord gave you, particularly if you're going to be a burden on the rest of us."

It doesn't do to pick fights with people who are putting a roof over your head and I ain't so sour that I've lost all my common sense.

"I know that, ma'am," I say. "I'll find a means to pay my way, you can be sure of that."

In the coming days, we find the women to be decent folks, if not overly generous. They are both heading eastward, searching for their sons, who had been sold away some years before, and they let us know that they won't be staying at the camp any longer than they have to and we can't go with 'em.

I'm the first in line every morning, but it's useless. I go to the barracks. I go to the stores. I even go from one tent to the next, but I don't find work and I don't think I ever will. Once the women leave, I'll be a burden to my brother. I know I will, 'cause nobody wants a Negro with a face like mine. Perhaps Joshua won't want me either. Perhaps he can't wait to get rid of me.

One afternoon, I'm sitting at the side of a path when a coin drops in my lap. I call out to the officer who must have dropped it, holding it up for him to see. "Sir? You just . . ." The officer looks back and nods, but he keeps on walking and I realize that he didn't drop it at all. He assumed I was begging. I hold the dime up to my face, the first money I made since we arrived at the camp. I put it away in my pocket quickly.

That evening, I put the coin on the upturned crate that the women use for a table when we eat. "It's not much, I know."

"Where'd you get it?" the ladies ask suspiciously.

"A soldier got me doing his chores. Says he might want me to do 'em again."

The next day, I take myself around the soldiers' tents, begging for money. I say, "Please, sir. Some money for supper," making sure they see my face, knowing it makes 'em feel bad. I make a couple of dimes before I stop. I find a tin that I can put 'em in so tomorrow I can rattle it and then I won't have to talk.

———

One morning, I'm waiting at the well when a girl walks past, holding her mother's hand. She takes a good long look at my face and that's rude, but I forgive her. I even give her a smile, though I know it don't look too good.

Well, that girl can't take her eyes off me and she pulls at her mother's arm. "Look, Mama!" she says. "Look!"

Her mother turns to look at me and her mouth falls open. She takes a couple of steps toward me, then stops, hardly daring to come any closer. "Samuel?" she asks me finally. "Is that you?"

Now, I know I have never seen these people before—I'm sure of it—so I have no idea how they know my name, but the mother knows me for sure. I can see it in her eyes as she takes me by the arm. "What happened to you, Samuel? Oh, dear God, what happened to your face?"

She can see I don't recognize her. "It's Celia," she says immediately. "Hubbard's wife. And this here is our daughter, Sarah."

The girl holds her finger up to my face and there's her ring of braided grass, the same one she offered me through the wall of Hubbard's cabin. I put down my bucket, astonished that I know 'em both, even though I've never seen their faces. "You're Celia? And Sarah? It's really you?" The little girl beams up at me when I touch the top of her head. "I'm so relieved you're all right . . ." I stammer to a halt, ashamed at having left 'em to wait in the woods when Hubbard lay dying in the cotton field. "I'm sorry I didn't come to find you, I'm sorry I left you there not knowing 'bout Hubbard, but once I started running, I couldn't stop . . ."

Celia puts a hand to my mouth as though none of that matters. "I'm so glad we found you. Hubbard will be so pleased to see you. I know he will."

It takes me a second to hear the truth of what she just said. "You mean he ain't dead?"

"He weren't five minutes ago." She laughs.

I can hear the words but I can't believe my own ears. "But I was with him in the field. I saw how he was . . ."

And for a moment, I'm back there again, watching the light disappear from his eyes, the blood spreading quickly across his green shirt. There was so much blood . . . Could it be that he really is alive? That all the time I thought I was alone, Hubbard was alive and that he's here, right now, in the same place I am?

"Come on." Celia takes me by the hand. "Let's go and find him."

They lead me through the tents in a state of shock. If it weren't for holding her hand, I wouldn't believe she's real. But she is. The woman leading me along the pathway says she's Celia and I can't find a reason to think she might be lying. Except that Hubbard's dead. I've been thinking he was dead for so long, I can't believe he's actually not dead at all and that I'm gonna see him any moment. We walk back along the path and I look at the faces of everyone we pass, expecting 'em to be Hubbard, though none of 'em are. Then, just for a moment, I lose my nerve. Perhaps he won't want to see me. Perhaps when he sees my face like this, he'll wish we'd never met. I'll be a burden on him. I'm sure he'll think that, same as the women at the tent.

But then little Sarah takes hold of my other hand and she's skipping along like she just got the best toy in a grab bag. And she looks a lot like Hubbard. I can see him in her face and she's got a smile like the sun itself and it warms me through, giving me courage when I'm losing it.

They bring me to one of the larger tents on the far edge of the site, a makeshift structure of coppiced wood and tarpaulin, all held together with rope and string. Beside it stands the old nag and a wagon from the Allen plantation, the same one I sat in when I first met Gerald.

"Hubbard?" Celia calls out at the entrance. "Hubbard? You come out here right now. I got someone to show you."

They stand back, leaving me exposed, as a pair of thick black fingers grip the edge of the canvas and pulls it aside. And suddenly, Hubbard's in front of me, having to stoop as he comes out, then straightening up till he's standing as tall as he ever was and looking down at me, his eyes adjusting to the daylight.

I'm hugging him before he's even sure who it is and I'm feeling like a little boy again. I could be Joshua. I could be any of the lost kids at the orphanage, hoping one day they'll be hugged by someone who loves 'em.

"Samuel? Is that really you?"

If Hubbard's scared at seeing the state of me, he don't show it. He hugs me so hard I can scarcely breathe, and Sarah laughs out loud, seeing me struggling for air, 'cause she must know just how it feels, being hugged like that by her daddy. She looks 'bout as happy as I feel.

When he lets me go, Hubbard holds me by the shoulders to get a good look at me. "I didn't ever expect to see you again."

"I thought you were dead," I tell him, and then I go and burst into tears and that makes me ashamed, wiping a hand around my face and smearing myself all in snot. "I was sure of it. I was sure you must've died."

"Oh, I ain't even close," he tells me, smiling. "Matter of fact, I'm feeling better than I have for a very long time."

"Don't make the boy stand there, Hubbard." Celia takes us both by the arm and pushes us gently back to the door. "Bring him inside. We got a lot to talk about."

They sit me down on some stuffed sacks that they got for chairs and I arrange myself with my best face forward as Celia brings us all some sliced apples on a plate with a spoonful of jam. She lights Hubbard's oil lamp—that very same big oil lamp—and hangs it from a pole so we can see each other clearly.

"I thought you were dead," I tell him again, unable to think of anything else to say.

Hubbard raises an eyebrow. "For a week or so, I thought so too."

"But you know how stubborn he is," Celia interrupts. "I don't think he'll let the Lord take him till he's good and ready. Anyway, Sicely turned out to be a good nurse and she knew a thing or two about Mrs. Allen's medicine cabinet."

I can picture Sicely immediately, the same as she was when I last saw her, with bottles of ointment and her pockets full of bandages. But I don't like to dwell on that moment 'cause Gerald's there in the same room. I can still see him standing over by the window and I don't want to think about how he was only moments later, spread out bleeding on the broken glass.

"What's happened to Sicely?"

"She's safe," Hubbard reassures me. "Least I think so. Lizzie wanted to stay on at the cabins. Far as I know, that's where they'll be."

"She would've been waiting for Milly."

"That's right. That's what she wanted. You know the Allen house burned down? Well, there weren't much of the plantation worth saving by the time the Yankees left, and Mrs. Allen had no interest in it. She returned to live with her family just as soon as we buried Gerald."

My heart breaks right there as the little piece of hope I had turns cold. I have to swallow hard before I can speak. "Did you bury him up at the old elm?"

"Yes, we did," replies Hubbard quietly. "It's where he would have wanted to be set to rest, right next to his daddy."

I know the truth of that and I nod enthusiastically. "He'll be happiest there."

We each take a moment for ourselves.

"Tell us what happened to you," says Celia, and she leans across and takes hold of my hand. "You look lucky to be alive."

"I suppose I am." I take a deep breath and begin from the point where I ran from the field. I tell 'em about the river and the embalmer, how I got to be blown up by old Whistling Dick and how the Major saved me. I get a lump in my throat knowing he's probably still missing. "I ain't as certain about things as I used to be," I tell 'em once I'm done. "The world's a lot more complicated than I thought it was. I suppose if I've learned anything, it's that."

Celia smiles at me and says, "You're still only young."

Hubbard brings out his pipe from the pocket of his shirt and opens the tin where he keeps his tobacco.

"So how come you're here at the camp?" I ask him. "How come you didn't stay on at the plantation?"

"We're on our way to the Sea Islands. They're off the coast of Carolina. So we ain't here for long. Just till we make some cash."

"Oh. I see." I weren't prepared for that, but I should've been, 'cause that's the way it always goes. All the good men always leave.

"There's a place called Port Royal," Hubbard continues. "It fell to the Yankees in the first few months of the war and they're letting the slaves work it for themselves. I heard they'll give you forty acres and a mule if you look like you can handle it."

"That can't be true, can it?"

"I think it is." Hubbard sits up straighter on his sack. "Lincoln wants to see what happens when us Negroes get our own land. It's sort of an experiment. To see if we can make it work. People say that when the war's over, they might do the same for all of us."

"We want to be a part of that," says Celia. "We want to show 'em we can survive on our own when we have the opportunity."

"Of course," I say quietly, thinking how I could never get me and Joshua there, not when it took me such a long time to get us where we are now.

Hubbard has his pipe in his fingers, all ready to be lit, and he leans toward me as he puts a flame to it. "Did you ever find out what happened to your brother?"

"Sure," I say. "I found him. He's out working at the minute, but he'll be back. Him and me always stick together, for better or for worse."

"Good!" says Celia, smiling. "Then we won't have to go and find him before you come along with us."

Celia's nice. I don't think I ever met a woman who's so full of sweet thoughts as she is.

When I bring Joshua to meet her, he comes ready to impress, tells her he already has a job that pays a dollar a day, with a selection of fresh vegetables to bring home if there's any left over. She tells him that'll be ever so helpful.

When Sarah takes Joshua outside to show him the horse, I let Celia know that he ain't as grown up as he likes to think. "He can be naughty too, but you don't need to worry 'cause I can keep him in line."

"He seemed sweet as pie to me, but that's good to hear."

"I've been looking after him since the day he was born, so there's no way he can pull the wool over my eyes. I'll be onto him soon as he begins to misbehave."

"Thank you, Samuel," she says again. "I am reassured."

———

When Hubbard takes me out to the work line, he stands right next to me. The first officer that comes along wants men to dig trenches, and he passes me over but touches Hubbard's arm.

"I ain't stepping out without my son," says Hubbard. "The two of us come together as a team."

The man looks back at me doubtfully. "The boy's too young."

"No, he ain't. He'll do the work of a fully grown man and I'll do the work of two. That's three days' work for the price of two. Take it or leave it."

The officer takes another look at the size of Hubbard, then he touches my arm and we both step out together.

After three weeks of work, Celia says we've got enough put by to move on, and she reckons, if we're thrifty, we might make it all the way to Carolina without needing to stop again. Hubbard agrees. "We'll get to the Sea Islands," he tells me. "It won't be long now, and if they give us land, we can build a house. There's a lot you can do with a few acres and a mule."

I say amen to that.

For my Father is a shepherd and He leads me to lie by still waters.

Surely goodness and mercy will follow me always and I shall dwell in His house forever.

———

There's a long way ahead of us and the horse we have is worn out. She was worn out when Mrs. Allen owned her and she's worn out now, so she only takes small steps along the road. I don't mind. I just hope her big ol' heart don't give out along the way.

Above us the sky holds dark clouds and sunshine, the sort of day that can't decide which way it wants to go. It ain't raining but it ain't warm either. A patch of sunlight pools on the distant road and the hill we have to climb. It'd be nice to get there before it's gone.

In the back of the wagon, Joshua and Sarah are squabbling like little kids. I'm riding up front with Celia and she says to 'em, "Why don't you two jump out and run alongside for a bit? It'll do you good to stretch your legs."

"Don't want to," says Sarah.

"Me neither," says Joshua.

He's been getting younger by the day, but I reckon that's a good thing, 'cause it don't do to grow up too soon, not if you don't have to. Sarah made him a ring out of braided grass and he won't take it off his finger 'cause he says they're married now. They might be too, for the two of 'em ain't stopped arguing ever since. Those kids always make me laugh.

Hubbard's walking out in front. He's leading the old nag so she goes in a straight line. These days his boots have got holes in the toes where they never did before, but he don't mind—at least I don't think so.

A broken-down shack comes into view and there's an old fella standing out front, hoeing at the dirt as he watches us arrive. Sometimes these poor folks give us trouble when we come their way. They ain't never had much to call their own and they don't like to see a family of black folks with a wagon and a horse. Used to be they could at least say they weren't slaves. Now they can't even say that. Not this side of the battle lines.

I jump down from the seat and run ahead to be with Hubbard. That way there'll be two of us if there's a problem, but it's OK; the old man don't hardly give us a second look, just keeps scraping at the earth as we walk on by.

"You want me to take a turn with the horse?"

"Sure," says Hubbard. "Be nice to sit up with Celia for a while."

I take hold of the bridle and lead us on along the road. It ain't hard work 'cause the nag don't have the strength to pull against me. Our horse sure has got the kindest eyes I've ever seen, and she nickers when I rub my hand along the length of her nose. Perhaps she likes being free just the same as we do. "When we get there," I tell her, "we won't ever make you work again. We're gonna build you a lovely little shed all your own and you can stand in it and eat hay all day."

When we reach a trough that has water, I let her drink till she's ready to move on. She sure takes a long time, but that don't matter. We're going so slowly, another few minutes at the trough won't make any difference.

Sometimes, I think we'll never get there, but then I look back the way we've come and that shack we passed is nearly out of view, so I guess we've traveled farther than I thought.

The horse lifts her head from the trough, the water still dribbling from her chin, and she looks at me like she's the one been waiting. I lead her back out on the road.

Up ahead of us, that pool of sunshine is still there on the hillside. I don't think I ever seen grass look so green as it does up there. And we make our way toward it, putting one foot in front of the other, taking each slow step at a time, knowing one day that we'll get there.

Sometime soon, I'll stand in sunshine.

AUTHOR'S NOTE

It's a common belief that authors have a very clear plan before they sit down to write something. That might be the case for some, but it wasn't for me—at least not with this book.

This book began as a writing exercise in an Arvon Foundation class—a moment of panic when I had ten minutes to get something down on paper. It had to be a scene that used a sense other than sight, and I wrote about a boy, alone in darkness, thinking he'd been taken by God.

That boy turned out to be Samuel—a child from the American South, who believed completely in a personal, interventionist God. At this point I had no idea where or when he lived and I tried to keep those decisions open as I completed the first scene and then the backstory to it.

So I didn't set out to write a historical novel. In fact, the idea of writing a historical novel made me wary. It felt like a burden and I think this was because I had an idea that history has an accepted canon of opinion that you shouldn't mess with. I didn't like the constraints this suggested, imagining myself having to chisel away at stone rather than type.

But that's not how history works. The story of slavery has changed over time, with each generation of historians interpreting and unearthing source material according to their own values and the politics of the period in which they write. Everyone wants to put their own story into history, and I came to realize that the America of the Civil War era held a multiplicity of truths, exactly as we do today.

Far from being a burden on my story, history became its inspiration. It didn't confine me. It held me. It suggested scenes and plotlines. It mapped out themes that intersected with the unformed ideas already in my head. And my task as a novelist was the same as it would be had I set my story in the present or the future. I had to use detail to portray a narrative that was believable and then make choices about how best to illuminate the truths contained within the story.

One of my first choices concerned the use of accent and dialect, and I chose to use only a few words that gave the reader a suggestion of the time and place. I thought to do otherwise would be too intrusive. This decision was particularly acute in the use of the word *nigger*, which would have been used more commonly in the period by both black and white, but which I chose to use infrequently and—with a single exception—only from the mouths of whites who were invested in slavery. This seemed to me the right balance—to bear witness to the past and still keep sight of the present.

There are several historical accounts that I have referred to or used within the book, mostly because I couldn't improve on them. The lame man at auction is taken from a famous eyewitness account of a slave auction published in the *New-York Daily Tribune* in 1859.

Reading Harriet Jacobs's *Incidents in the Life of a Slave Girl* had a huge influence on my understanding of the "peculiar institution" of slavery. I was particularly moved by her story of a female slaveholder who relieved her slave of her life savings, promising to pay the poor woman back when she could. This seemed to me as cruel as any beating and it inspired the scene with Lizzie's chickens. Her book also gave me the hiding place for Hubbard's wife and child.

The chapter with the Major contains many references to the works of Walt Whitman, Emerson, and Thoreau. These are fragmented and scattered throughout the text as the Major reads to Samuel while he is semiconscious. The passage from Walt Whitman's *Leaves of Grass* is pretty much verbatim and I thank him for it. It feels to me like the heart of the story.

Finally, to those who might read the book hoping to plot a precise time line of the Civil War—you are bound to be frustrated! Some of the place names are invented and the time scale is obscure. Those who know their history might recognize Whistling Dick as a particular gun made famous in the Siege of Vicksburg. They will also know that the cotton embargo occurred in the first year of the war. But if they use these as clues to when and where the scenes occurred, the clues are likely to reveal themselves as red herrings and force the reader to declare that the whole story is impossible and it couldn't have happened exactly as I said it did, because history and geography and all the textbooks in the world tell us otherwise.

But this is fiction, even if it is historical, and the truth is that it didn't happen at all. At least it might not have done. And probably not exactly as I have described.

The Economics of American Slavery

I thought it could be helpful to give an indication of the economics involved in buying and owning slaves at the time the book is set.

It became illegal to import slaves into America from 1808 and this produced a steady increase in the value of the slaves that were already owned. Although the average prices at auction rose or fell due to factors such as the price of cotton, this increase continued right up until the Civil War.

> *Estimates say there were 4 million slaves in America by 1860, with an average worth of $800 a piece.*[1]

The worth of a slave would vary according to many factors, such as whether they were male or female, young or old. It also varied according to the skills a slave might have, such as carpentry or cookery.

Although it is impossible to reach an exact figure, a single slave would represent an investment of between $30,000 and $91,000 in today's money.

I use the word *investment* because that's exactly how it was seen. A slave owner would calculate the cost of keeping a slave over their lifetime and the likely returns in productivity. Though this would mostly be through cotton profits, there was also a market in hiring out slave labor. The high price that Milly commands at the auction

---

1   *Measuring Slavery in 2011 Dollars* by Samuel H. Williamson & Louis Cain, at http://www.measuringworth.com/slavery.php

is not only due to her sexual desirability and her experience in serving at the house. As a young woman entering childbearing age, she would be expected to produce children, who would then become the property of her owner to sell or keep as he wished.

Although most of the slave trade existed to serve the cotton and tobacco industries, it was not uncommon for townsfolk to own slaves as well. About 25 percent of households owned a slave, many of them inherited through wills, and they were regarded as both status symbols and additional sources of income.

Even the outbreak of the war did not immediately undermine the price of slaves, and auctions continued to be held in Confederate states that were not occupied. As the war drew on, the market for slaves did become increasingly haphazard, as this piece from *The New York Times* from 1863 illustrates.

Slaves command a higher price in Kentucky, taking gold as the standard of value, than in any other of the Southern States. In Missouri they are sold at from forty dollars to four hundred, according to age, quality, and especially according to place. In Tennessee they cannot be said to be sold at all. In Maryland the negroes upon an estate were lately sold, and fetched an average price of $18 a head. In the farther States of the Southern Confederacy we frequently see reports of negro sales, and we occasionally see boasts from rebel newspapers as to the high prices the slaves bring, notwithstanding the war and the collapse of Southern industry. We notice in the Savannah Republican of the 5th, a report of a negro sale in that city, at which, we are told, high prices prevailed, and at which two girls of 18 years of age were sold for about $2,500 apiece, two matured boys for about the same price, a man of 45 for $1,850, and a woman of 23, with her child of 5, for $3,950. Twenty-five hundred dollars, then, may be taken as the standard price of first-class slaves in the Confederacy; but when it is remembered that this is in Confederate money, which is worth less than one-twelfth its face in gold, it will be seen that the real price, by this standard, is only about $200. In Kentucky, on the other hand, though there is but little buying or selling of slave stock going on, we understand that negroes are still held at from seven to twelve hundred dollars apiece.

Acknowledgments

Thanks to everyone at DFB—Simon Mason, Phil Earle, Anthony Hinton, and Charlie Rashid—for taking such good care of me in my first year as an author.

In particular, thanks to my editors, Bella Pearson and David Fickling, who listened while I told you things about the book you already knew before showing me the things I didn't know myself.

Thanks to Linda Sargent for your astute observations and invaluable suggestions, and to Rosie Fickling for not putting the book down and then letting me run away with your notes, and to Bronwen Bennie for your work on the foreign rights.

Thanks to Emellia Zamani and Elizabeth Krych at Scholastic for all your care with this American edition. Thanks to Joy Simpkins for the copy edit and to Ellen Duda for your lovely cover.

Thank you to Sallyanne Sweeney for all your early work on the text and for believing we should take the time needed to make this book as good as it could be.

Thanks as always to the Lovely Tuesdays for reading and telling me your thoughts—Catherine Smith, Philip Harrison, Same De Alwis, Roz De-Ath, Stuart Condie, Yvonne Hennessey, and Judith Bruce.

Thanks to Tracey Fuller and Ali Bishop for your insight and generosity.

Thank you to all my family and friends, for your love and enthusiasm.

And of course, to Tanya, for just being you.

Read on for a sneak peek at
another thrilling, stirring
story from Jon Walter

CLOSE
TO THE
WIND

The boy and the old man arrived at the port at night.

There had been clouds in the sky but now the moon shone brightly and they stood in the shadow cast by a row of terraced cottages that lined a cobbled street, polished through the years by wheels and feet and the hooves of horses.

The boy held the old man's hand.

The air smelled of motor oil and charred timber. At the far end of the street, the quayside was lit by a bright white lamp that glared upon the skeleton of a single black crane, its hook hanging solemn above the cottage roofs, and above the crane loomed the tall ship, a string of yellow bulbs along the rails of its upper decks as though it might be Christmas and not a warm autumn night.

The boy sneezed loudly.

"Shhh, Malik," hissed his grandfather.

Malik let go of his grandfather's hand and pinched his nose through the white cotton handkerchief that covered his face—his grandfather had tied it across his nose and mouth to protect him from smoke. Malik could have removed the cloth, since they were a long way from the fires, but he kept it, believing it made him look older. He held his breath so that he wouldn't sneeze again. When he was certain, he took his hand away. "Sorry, Papa."

Papa settled a hand on Malik's shoulder. "No. I'm sorry. I didn't mean to bite." He glanced back down the road behind them. "I'm still nervous. I'm sure there's no one here, but we ought to be careful."

"Careful as a cat," said Malik.

"Fearful like a fox," said Papa, and he adjusted the rucksack that he carried slung from a single shoulder.

Malik nodded. He felt sorry for the foxes—nobody ever had a good word to say about them. He saw Papa's eyes flick to either end of the street and his stomach tensed as though he were about to be punched. These moments of uncertainty were the worst. He put a hand to the front of his trousers and held himself.

Papa looked down at him. "Do you need the toilet?" Malik shook his head. "Then don't do that, eh? You're too old for that."

Malik put his hand in his trouser pocket. He shuffled on his feet, stepping from one side to the other so that the tops of his green rain boots flapped against his trousers. Papa's eyes went up and down the row of cottages; he was checking for something.

Malik stopped shuffling and lifted himself on tiptoes so as to be closer to Papa's ear. "Is that our ship?"

Papa pulled the collar of his thick winter coat away from the back of his neck. His brow was damp with sweat. "I expect it is," he said quietly. "I can't see the name, but it's the only ship here."

Malik looked again and he agreed. There were no other ships.

Papa put a hand to his short white beard and tugged at the hair, something he did when he was thinking. "We're too early. We can't go there yet. I think we must wait till the morning."

The muscles in Malik's stomach twisted—Papa would need to find them a place to stay again. Last night they had slept in the basement cellar of a burnt-out office block and there had been a dying dog. He followed Papa's eyes to the row of cottages, silhouetted in the bright light from the quay, the chimneys standing proud of the gray slate roofs. If they couldn't go to the ship, then perhaps they could spend the night in one of these. Malik hoped so. He imagined a chair to sit in. A basin for washing. His own bed.

"Will the ship leave tomorrow?"

Papa ignored the question and Malik felt guilty for having asked it, but he had other questions, all sorts of questions, and he couldn't help himself.

"Is this where we're staying?" he asked. "Is this where Mama will meet us?"

Papa raised his voice. "So many questions. I've told you about that. How many questions is that you've asked today?"

Malik dropped his head. "I don't know."

"You don't know? Well, I don't know either. There's been so many I've lost count. But we agreed on ten, didn't we? We had an agreement and we shook hands on it. Only ten questions each day." Papa took a deep breath and lowered his voice. "I reckon you've got just one left and that's being generous. You should be careful—think about what you say before you open your mouth."

Malik tightened his jaw. Papa never liked too many questions: He had learned that in the last two days. He stepped again from one foot to the other, thinking of what he could get away with saying next. A question mark hung over everything. "How do you . . . I mean . . . what should I . . . ?" He reached for Papa's hand, gripped his index finger. "It's impossible."

"No. It's not impossible. It's difficult, I'll grant you that." Papa squeezed Malik's fingers, then knelt beside him and pointed. "See that cottage there? The one with the dark red door?"

Malik was disappointed. "The one with the broken window?"

"Yes. That's the one. I want you to count the houses from this end of the street till you get to the one with the broken window. Tell me how many houses there are before you reach the one we want."

This was one of Papa's games. Malik knew them now, the little things Papa gave him to do to keep his mind occupied. It was what Mama used to do when he was young, but Malik didn't mind Papa doing it now. It was better than having too much time to think.

He began to count under his breath, nodding his head at each house. "Thirteen," he said.

"Are you sure?" Papa narrowed his eyes. "I made it twelve. Let's do it together."

They began to count and Papa pointed at each cottage in turn. Malik took hold of his hand to stop him after seven. "No, Papa. Look. That one's different. That's two houses. There's another front door. See? A shared porch with two front doors."

Papa's eyes flicked to the walls on either side of the porch. He checked the windows. "Yes, I see. You're right. One porch but with two front doors. Two eyes are better than one, eh?" He touched the top of Malik's head. "We make a good team."

Malik's mouth whipped up into a smile. "Who lives there? How do we know them? Are they friends of ours?"

Papa didn't seem to mind the questions. He checked the street again to make sure they were safe. "I hope no one lives there. They should have left when the trouble started. I don't think anyone still lives in these streets."

A cloud moved across the moon and the cobbles on the street turned black. An engine started up from somewhere in the distance, probably from the quayside.

Papa took hold of Malik's hand. "I think we should go."

"Is it soldiers?"

"I don't think so. But we've been here too long. We should be out of sight. Come on."

Papa stepped out across the street and Malik ran to keep up, his head ducked low to avoid the rucksack, which bounced from side to side on Papa's back. They hurried to the opposite pavement, rounded the final cottage, and slipped into the alley that divided the back of the houses in this street from the next.

Papa stopped running and drew Malik close to him by the hand. "It's very dark, isn't it? Now the moon has gone, I can't see my own feet."

Malik looked for his own feet and saw nothing but black. He held a hand up to his face, moved it toward his nose, and away again.

"We'll go slowly," Papa whispered. "Count the houses for me, will you? We want number thirteen."

"I can't see the houses, Papa. It's too dark."

Papa put an arm around Malik's shoulder. "You're right. It's too dark to see the houses." He lifted Malik's hand and his fingers brushed against brickwork. "Feel that, Malik? That's the back wall to the yard of the first house. We can count the gates till we reach thirteen."

They walked into the darkness, holding hands. "It's too dark," Malik complained. "I don't like the dark."

"No," agreed Papa. "Nobody likes the dark. But you should remember that there's no one here and the dark can't hurt us."

Malik knew that Papa couldn't really know that

for certain—you can never know for sure if there's anything in the dark. "Can we use the flashlight?"

"No. We don't need the flashlight."

"I do."

"No, you don't. Feel with your fingers."

"It would be better with the flashlight."

"Malik! We can't use the flashlight. They could see the flashlight." Papa caught his breath and stopped walking.

Malik came up close against him. He tried to see Papa's face. "You said there were no soldiers. You told me it was only us. If there's no one here then no one can see the light."

"Yes." Papa sighed. "I suppose you're right." He took the rucksack from his back and placed it on the floor. "You're using logic and I can't argue with that. I suppose we don't need to whisper either."

"The flashlight is in the top pocket, Papa. The one on top of the flap that goes over."

"Yes. Thank you. I remember." Papa slid back the zip and took out the thin metal flashlight, twisting the bulb casing till the light came on and turned the edges of his fingers pink.

"Can I hold it?"

Papa put the flashlight into Malik's hand and directed it down to the floor. "Keep it pointed at the ground. Just down near your feet." The thin beam picked out the green rubber of Malik's rain boots. "Your feet must be hot in those boots. You'll be able to take them off soon."

"I don't mind." Malik nudged the flashlight beam ahead of his feet, and the shaft of light showed a little yellow flower, sprouting up between the broken stones that paved the alley. "Look. I nearly trod on a flower."

"It's a weed, Malik. A dandelion."

Malik stooped and broke the stem of the yellow flower. "It's for Mama," he said. "I'm going to save it for her."

They went on through the darkness, but quicker now they had some light. They counted the gates as they passed. The flashlight picked out one that was painted red and another that was green. At the thirteenth gate, an upturned metal bin lay on the ground with rubbish spilling from the open top. Something smelled rotten. The flashlight showed them an open can lying on its side, used tea bags, and half a cauliflower that was almost black. Malik stepped on a soiled newspaper. Above him the clouds thinned

enough to give them a little light. This was the thirteenth house.

"Is this it?" Malik's breath moved the handkerchief on his face. He flicked the flashlight up to Papa's
face and saw him turn and scowl.

"Yes, this is it. Put the flashlight out now, will
you? The moon will give us enough light."

Malik turned off the flashlight and they paused.
Papa put his hand into the pocket of his coat, and
Malik knew that in Papa's pocket there were two
red apples and the knife with the blade that folded
back into the curved wooden handle. He had seen
Papa reach into his pocket and touch it before, always
when he needed courage. Malik wanted a knife just
like that.

Papa took two steps to the gate, twisted the metal
latch, and opened it. The moonlight showed them
the back of the cottage through the open gate. Malik
could see a back door with pretty glass squares, and to
the right of it a window. It looked like a nice house.
Small, but comfortable.

Papa tugged at his beard. "You better stay here."

"Why? I don't want to."

"It's better for you to wait while I check to see
that it's all right."

"To see if there's a dead dog?"

"No. Not to see if there's a dead dog. There won't be another dead dog, Malik."

"How do you know?"

Papa put a hand to his head and closed his eyes. "No. No, that's too many questions. You're doing it again." He held out his hand and sliced the air into sections as he spoke. "I don't know for certain. Of course I don't. But it's unlikely. It's very unlikely. It would be unfortunate to find another dead dog."

Malik gripped the little yellow flower in his hand and remembered the dead dog on the cellar floor, down by the metal grille. It hadn't been dead at first, but it was now. It was probably still on its own, lying where they had left it.

"Please, Papa. I don't want to wait here on my own." Malik tried not to whine, and hoped Papa wouldn't be angry.

Papa nodded. "OK." He took hold of Malik's hand. "Let's go together."

They stepped across the yard and found the back door locked. Papa went to the window, put his face against the glass, then came back to Malik. "I need the handkerchief from your face." He reached around, undid the knot at the back of Malik's head, then wrapped his hand in the cloth and punched through one of the small panes, just above the doorknob. The sound of breaking glass shattered the silence. Malik held his breath, half expecting a shout or a rush of feet, but nothing happened.

Papa unwound the handkerchief from his fingers. He had a single small cut on the middle knuckle and he put it to his mouth, sucked away the blood, then reached inside and turned the key that was in the lock. The hinges of the door creaked as he opened it and stepped inside. He looked back at Malik. "You'd better turn the flashlight on."

Malik twisted the top of the flashlight and followed Papa. The beam picked out wallpaper the color of cornflowers, and that looked very pretty, but it was only the top half of the wall. The bottom half had bare plaster with corrugated ridges of brown glue where the kitchen units had been pulled away. Two pipes ran along the baseboard and had been capped off with a simple tap where there had once been a sink. On the floor, below the tap, stood a yellow plastic bucket full of discarded drink cans. Malik trod on screws and broken bits of masonry as he turned the flashlight around the empty room. He should have known it would be like this.

"It might be better through here." Papa stepped onto the bare floorboards of the dark hall. "Come on, hand me the flashlight."

They crept along the passage till the beam picked out a door. Papa pushed it open and stepped inside the hollow room. There was no furniture and no carpet. A ragged hole in the brickwork of the opposite wall showed where the fireplace had once been, and no curtain hung across the broken glass of the window. There was no comfort to be found here. None at all.

"There's nothing here, Papa."

"No, Malik. I can see. People have been here. They've stripped the house bare. Everything that was worth anything has gone. You can be certain of that."

Malik walked over to the window and looked out across the empty street. This was only just better than the cellar. Mama wouldn't like this house at all, and she wouldn't want to come here.

Malik stood with Papa at the foot of the staircase. He should have known, the moment they'd sneaked in through the back, that this house would be no good.

There had been a time when Malik used only front doors. He would ring the bells or give two raps on the knocker and his friends would come outside or they would invite him in. Everyone he knew had nice houses, not all of them as large as his, but always pleasant in one way or another, and there would be food and drink and games to play.

He stared at the front door of the cottage. It had two panels of frosted glass that were dark with the night. A single brown envelope hung from the inside of the mail slot, halfway up the door, sticking part in, part out. Papa reached out and pulled it free. He put the flashlight close to the paper, read the name on the envelope, and then opened it. Malik saw writing in red ink.

"Final notice from six weeks ago," said Papa. "They must have left the house before it arrived."

They climbed the stairs, Papa out in front and Malik following behind, his rain boots squeaking on the wooden staircase. At the top of the stairs was a bathroom that had the fittings removed. The outline of the bath and sink could be traced from the tiles that finished halfway up the wall, and the toilet was nothing but a sluice pipe that sat up ten centimeters from the floor.

They pushed another door and found a bedroom. This room at least had furniture. A white painted wardrobe was at the other end to the door and there was a single wooden chair and a bare mattress on the floor. The window had a thick blue curtain drawn back to one side. Balanced on the windowsill was an ashtray brimming with the crushed tips of thin cigarettes that had been rolled by hand.

Papa looked inside the wardrobe. He let the rucksack drop to the floor beside the mattress and shone the flashlight back to the doorway where Malik stood. "We have a mattress. At least it's something. It's better than last night."

Malik shrugged.

Papa said, "Who's going to have it? You or me?"

"Mama should have it." Malik hesitated, but he asked the question anyway. "When will she be here?"

The questions about Mama always annoyed Papa the most, but Papa answered him gently. "Not tonight, Malik. I said she would meet us when the ship sailed, and that's not till tomorrow. We'll see her at the dock when we go there tomorrow. I'm sure we will."

Malik's head dropped. He saw the dandelion in his fist and he held it up. "What shall I do with this?"

Papa took the dandelion from his hand. "Let's go and see whether we have any water."

ABOUT THE AUTHOR

Jon Walter is a former photojournalist with a special interest in social welfare issues. His debut middle grade novel, *Close to the Wind*, was chosen as a *Sunday Times* Children's Book of the Week in the United Kingdom. *My Name Is Not Friday* is his debut young adult novel. He lives in East Sussex, England, with his family.